Cities in Chains

An Apocalyptic LitRPG
Book 4 of the System Apocalypse

By

Tao Wong

Copyright

This is a work of fiction. Names, characters, businesses, places, events and incidents are either the products of the author's imagination or used in a fictitious manner. Any resemblance to actual persons, living or dead, or actual events is purely coincidental.

Cities in Chains
Copyright © 2018 Tao Wong. All rights reserved.
Copyright © 2018 Sarah Anderson Cover Designer

A Starlit Publishing Book
Published by Starlit Publishing
69 Teslin Rd
Whitehorse, YT
Y1A 3M5
Canada

www.starlitpublishing.com

Ebook ISBN: 9781775380917
Paperback ISBN: 9781775380900
Hardcover ISBN: 9781989458495

Books in The System Apocalypse series

Main Storyline

Life in the North

Redeemer of the Dead

The Cost of Survival

Cities in Chains

Coast on Fire

World Unbound

Stars Awoken

Rebel Star

Stars Asunder

Anthologies

System Apocalypse Short Story Anthology Volume 1

Comic Series

The System Apocalypse (On-going)

Contents

What Has Gone Before

More than thirteen months ago, the System came to Earth, bringing with it monsters, aliens and glowing blue boxes of notifications that detailed their lives in this new Galactic System. Humanity was forced to evolve, their lives dictated by statistic screens, Classes and Skills that gave them strength and abilities beyond the norm, providing them a fighting chance to survive. Still, the apocalypse saw the death of nearly 90% of humanity, the malfunctioning of everything electronic and a new, blood-filled existence.

John Lee was camping in the Yukon when the change occurred. Gifted with perks beyond the normal, he journeyed to Whitehorse and aided in the establishment of the city under the rule of the alien Truinnar, Lord Graxan Roxley. With the help of other survivors, the Village of Whitehorse was quickly established to provide a stable environment for growth, battling rampant dungeons, monster hordes and crazed humans in equal measure.

As Earth's Mana levels and the System stabilized, new alien threats appeared that sought to takeover the city. After a heated battle and political maneuverings, John is able to push back against the Truinnar Duchess's Envoy and her Weapon Master, only to be betrayed by Lord Roxley.

With Whitehorse now firmly under the aegis of the Duchess, John has left the stable, if alien owned, Village with his team mates and journey's south to lend what aid he may to the surviving members of humanity.

Chapter 1

The world has changed. Over a year ago, a series of blue boxes popped into existence, notifying humanity that we'd joined the Galactic Council. Along with that, we inherited the System—a reality-bending setup that appeared to us as a blaze of blue boxes—and it gave us strength, endurance, Skills, and healing beyond human norms. The new System was more akin to a video game, with magical spells and Skills, but dying was still very real.

The world has changed. I get that.

But that still doesn't explain the evolved tiger trying to eat my face.

"This is a tiger, right? And we're what? A good hundred kilometers south of the Yukon?" I say, holding the monster around its neck with one hand as it attempts to escape and claw me. The occasional scratch is painful and annoying but not at all life-threatening.

"Just hold him still a little longer," Lana says, laying a slab of steak a short distance from me. The buxom redhead is clad in Adventurer chic—a skin-tight armored jumpsuit with a weapon vest, along with the requisite weapons, and straps criss-crossing her toned frame. "And yes, it's a tiger."

"What? My Status information not good enough for you?" Ali, my three-foot Spirit companion says as he floats cross-legged next to me. He might look Middle Eastern, but Ali's got as much relation to them as I do an amoeba. Since there's no real threat right now, Ali's choosing to be visible.

I glance again at the status information hovering over the tiger.

Evolved Tiger (Level 27)
HP: 358/478
MP: 275/349
Condition: Enraged

Of course, the tiger isn't willing to just be held in the air without a struggle. With a flick of his tail, the tiger glows, calling forth its Skill—Sharp Claws—again. Okay, Sharp Claws is what I've named it since it's not as if I have access to the tiger's Skill menu. Twisting around, its legs scrabbling against the ground, it tears into me. Wounds that have been clawed open and healed are widened under its newly empowered attacks. Dealing with the damn cat just because Lana demanded we herd it here once Ali picked it up is annoying.

"Owww! You ready yet, Lana?"

"Done. Don't hurt it!" Lana calls.

I roll my eyes and toss the kitty cat toward Lana. The animal twists and lands with grace, bunching its legs and snarling at me. Before it can lunge, Lana's pets ring it while the redhead shifts to put herself directly in front of the animal. Considering the pair of pony-sized huskies are nearly the same size as the evolved tiger, it's not as unfair a fight as you'd think. And of course, a single look from the tiger is enough to make Anna erupt with flames, fire dancing along her lean, foxy body. Elsa, Lana's turtle, is no longer with us, having been gifted to a child as a pet due to its inability to physically keep up with us. Says something about the world we live in that a fire-breathing pet turtle is considered an appropriate gift by a tear-filled mom.

"Now there, boy, calm down. We've got food for you…" Lana says to the tiger, holding out the piece of meat. Her voice is low, soft, soothing, and almost seductive.

I turn away from Lana and her weird taming session, asking the question that has been on my mind. "So how does a tiger end up so far north? I mean, sure, if it was a monster, it could have spawned here. But a tiger?"

"Someone's illegal pet?" Ingrid says. The dark-haired First Nation woman is seated on the roof of the truck that she's pulled over to the side of the road, taking in the sun while she waits for Lana to finish. Who would have known that the woman is a sun-worshipper, being the Assassin/Thief/something sneaky Class that she is?

"A zoo?" Mikito says. The tiny Japanese lady dangles her feet off the edge of the mecha she rides. Mikito's personal assault vehicle is somewhat different than Sabre, being both lighter and more agile with significantly less armor. Also cheaper. I'm just glad that the System-bought language pack Mikito got for English gave her a slight Japanese accent, rather than something like Australian or Irish. It's very, very strange to look at a giant, green, tusked alien and listen to him talk in a strong Australian accent.

"Makes sense." I glance at where Lana is wrestling with the tiger. I never saw her tame Anna, so I have no clue if fighting is supposed to be part of the entire taming process. "You think this is going to take long?"

I receive shrugs in return, so I pull out a bar of chocolate to snack on. A few moments later, I'm handing out bars to the ladies. One nice thing about the System, there's no more concern about weight loss. In fact, most of the time, we work hard to eat enough calories to handle the stress we put our bodies through. Admittedly, a significant portion of our energy needs are supplied by Mana, that weird all-encompassing thing that makes our spells and Skills work, but we still need to eat. Somewhere out there, I bet there's some Personal Trainer Class who has worked out the exact calorie and Mana requirements to make the most efficient use of our Level-ups and everyday skills. I just know it.

"Is she going to be okay?" Sam asks from the driver seat of his truck. He's one of our more recent additions to the retinue since we left Whitehorse.

Behind him, on the flatbed, a group of hunters are carefully watching the surroundings, taking care to not just look around but up as well. In the distance, another hunter is on his way back on Ingrid's borrowed hover bike.

I could tell them not to bother—Ali's ability as my Spirit Companion allows him to scan data from the System directly, and my own Skill – Greater Detection -is picking up no major threats currently. But I don't tell them that for a few reasons. Firstly, constant alertness is a good trait to train. Secondly, what Ali and I consider a significant threat is rather different than these guys. And thirdly, we won't always be with them.

"Oh, she'll be fine," Ingrid says, yawning slightly. "Lana's got a base heal spell she can toss on if things get hairy."

"Which she's using on the tiger," Sam says incredulously, stepping out of the truck. His salt-and-pepper hair and beard suit the man, as does the worn leather coat and easy air of command. Helps when you top six feet. Maybe I'm still a little jealous of people that tall, even if I'm no shortie anymore, not since the System. Whatever he was before the System, Sam was certainly in a post of authority.

My eyes sweep over the convoy of refugees we've picked up, most of them whispering furtively as they watch Lana put on her one-woman taming show. The convoy's a weird mixture of vehicles, most from the early part of the twentieth century since they don't need the electronics that were inherent in newer vehicles. There are a few exceptions—a Lamborghini that's been designated as a "personal vehicle" via a Skill, and the minivan that its Mechanic owner modified stand out. Most modern vehicles don't work well with their electronics fried by the Mana that surrounds us all.

"Probably trying to mollify it," I say, answering Sam's unspoken question. "We might be here for a while. Might as well tell them to get out, stretch their legs and have lunch."

Sam's the de facto leader of the refugees, being one of the few willing to actually talk to us. I admit, walking in covered in the blood and guts of the monsters that had been laying siege to their town might have something to do with their wariness. I kind of get the feeling the refugees consider us as much a group of monsters as the ones made by the System. Still, they're with us because staying in their various small towns was a death sentence.

"You…" Sam starts to say but stops as Mikito chuckles softly. After a moment, Sam decides to do what I say, calling out orders to the group.

The hunters drop out of the flatbed and step out of the other vehicles, spreading out to cover both sides of the road while we wait.

"Nice day for a picnic," Ingrid says, her eyes closed. "Want me to pull some more monsters for them?"

"Sam asked us to stop doing that." I walk to the edge of the road and dump out some camping supplies, including a camping table I appropriated recently. Even as I begin getting lunch going, I can hear the snarls, growls, and occasional yips of pain coming from Lana's scuffle. "Something about scaring the kids."

"Wimps," Ingrid drawls.

Mikito joins me, helping with prep and getting more than a few envious glances. Since my Skill Altered Space basically gives me an extra dimensional space I can store anything I want in, I have a lot more leeway than most people in what I can drag around. Everyone else has to contend with good old-fashioned luggage or the System inventory option, and the System inventory only works for System-registered items. Which, for the refugees who have never visited a Shop, is nothing.

"Think we'll make it to Fort Nelson soon?" Mikito asks Ali.

"We're about a hundred kilometers out," Ali says. "An hour's drive if the roads were good. About three with the state they're in now—if you guys stop babying the children. And if we don't find anyone else holed up."

"They need the experience," Mikito points out, retreading the old argument. "We'll be leaving them in Fort Nelson after this anyway."

"If it's still in one piece," I add, grimacing at that thought.

We know, thanks to Ali, that Fort Nelson has a Shop, so the chances of there being no survivors is low. Any location with a Shop has a distinct advantage. The ability to purchase System-registered weapons, Skills, and trade loot in for Credits makes a huge difference. The fact that the Shop connection is still present after the grace period of a year means that someone has spent sufficient Credits for the link to be kept up. Not all the locations that had a Shop managed to keep theirs after the first year ended. Based on all this, the town and some of its inhabitants should still be there.

Theoretically. It is an apocalypse after all.

"Hey, watch the meat!" Ingrid calls out.

I quickly flip the steak, realizing I'd begun to overcook it, lost in my thoughts as I was. Right. Time to focus on the important things. Like lunch.

***

"What was this again?" Lana says, holding up the strip of green steak on her fork before dabbing it in the gravy. The tiger lies curled up next to her possessively, gnawing on a three-foot-long haunch of the same creature.

"Mer... M'r... the green worm mantis thing," Ingrid says, snagging another piece from the pile we've cooked. There's enough food on the table to feed a hockey team after a game, which is just about enough for all of us.

Lana brightens up as she chews and swallows. "Oh, right! Think we'll run into any more of them?"

"Hopefully. That was the last of what I had stored," I say. "I'll ask Ali to keep an eye out."

I think toward Ali. Since my Level-ups, our connection has extended quite a distance, allowing the little Spirit to do a lot more scouting for us. Since the

Spirit can't actually eat, I sent him out on a scouting trip. While none of us really expect to find survivors in the middle of nowhere, hope burns eternal. That, and it's not exactly as if I have to cover the ground. *"Hey, Lana wants you to keep an eye out for the green worm mantis things. Maybe drag them back if you see them."*

"You know, boy-o, I think you guys have been getting a little too lax," Ali thinks back. *"The M'rimul Worms are Level 41 monsters and fight in swarms of ten. They're not snack food!"*

"Might as well be. Anyway, we could use the experience if you can find them. We've barely shifted the meter since we left the Yukon."

I hear his mental grunt of acknowledgement. You'd think that with the monsters being generally of a lower Level, there'd be a higher survival rate, but it doesn't really work that way. Doesn't matter if it's a Level 10 or a Level 50 monster; when you're Level 1, you're just as dead.

"So…" Sam says as he walks up to our group, his voice punctuated by the crack of rifles and the sizzle of beam weaponry going off toward the tail-end of the column. "People are wondering how long we're going to be here. We've attracted some attention…"

The group looks at me, and I take a moment to check the little monster radar in the corner of my eyes. With Ali away from the group, he can't share the information with everyone else. There's nothing too major out there though—just a bunch of Level 20s, from the look of it.

I look at Sam and shrug. "We're about two, maybe three hours out from the city. This is a decently Leveled area. The hunters should be able to rack up some experience while picking up some loot. If they strap some of the corpses to the cars, they should be able to bring in some of them too."

"But the women…" Sam falls silent as the three women seated around me just dare him to finish that sentence. Sam coughs and changes his tune. "The non-combatants, they're a bit nervous."

Diplomatic as he might be, we know he's talking about the small group of women who have been making our lives miserable. Somehow, they've missed the memo about the earth-shattering change in the social order and seem intent on ignoring certain realities—like violence and the need for Leveling.

"Tough cookies. They're safe," I state flatly. "It's the last chance for their hunters to gain some Levels and Credits safely, so they can sit and stew for all I care." At the pained look on Sam's face, I sigh and offer him a little salvation. "We have to leave in an hour if we want to get to the town by daylight."

"An hour. I can work with that," Sam says, bobbing his head. He casts a hungry look at the food on our table, and Lana sends him off with an impromptu steak sandwich literally dripping with gravy and monster bacon.

"You're too nice to him," Ingrid says.

"Not his fault," I say.

"Well, he should tell those idiots to come tell it to your face."

"Eh… I'd rather not." I grimace, recalling the first few days.

Dealing with that group, especially Ms. Starling, had been painful. I'd actually tried to listen to them bitch about the lack of proper accommodation until I nearly lost my temper. Thankfully, Sam stepped in before things got too far, but I had seriously considered hitting them till they shut up. Which, when you think about it, isn't exactly the most civilized or smart behavior. Look, I said I thought about it—I didn't actually do it.

Clearing her throat slightly, Lana redirects our conversation. "What's the plan for Fort Nelson anyway?"

"Ummm… plan?"

"Yes, plans. They're not just for clearing dungeons," drawls Ingrid.

I glare at the First Nation woman. Just because I don't really talk about my plans doesn't mean I don't have one. "What's there to plan? We go in, we drop them off, and we see what's up. After that, well, we move on."

"Oh, John…" Lana sighs. "What if the local government doesn't want refugees? What if they stop us from going in? What if they need help? Do we want to stay and help? Clear a few dungeons for them or something?"

"Uhh…"

"And what are we doing out here anyway?" Mikito says, pointing a pair of chopsticks at me. "You haven't actually told us."

"Didn't exactly ask you guys to come along," I protest. I get a pair of snorts and an eye roll, making me rub the back of my neck. "I didn't… well, I do have some plans. But mostly, I'm looking to check out how the rest of the world is doing. Maybe help out a bit here and there…"

Truth be told, I have a goal. A few actually. But they're so nebulous, so far away that I dare not breathe them out loud. Never mind the fact that anything I say can and will be registered by the System and be potentially sellable to someone else; my plans just aren't pertinent to the discussion. Not yet at least.

"Great. We're the A-Team," Lana says.

"Dibs on Face," Ingrid says.

"Well, I guess I'm Hannibal then," Lana says while Mikito looks puzzled.

"And John's BA, of course," Ingrid says, which makes Lana frown in thought.

"I don't know. He's more Murdock than Mikito," Lana points out.

I open my mouth to protest then decide against it. When faced with two arguing women, one of which you occasionally bed, I pity the fool who gets involved. Instead, I explain to Mikito what they're talking about.

Chapter 2

"Ahoy the gate," I called out, hours later, when we finally arrived at Fort Nelson. Or technically, the outer gates of the city.

There must be something instinctive in our desire for walls, even if they are somewhat useless. These walls aren't normal brick—and their slight silvery sheen hints at them being System-assisted at least—but I could probably punch through them given enough time. Or heck, jump over the twenty-foot walls.

Then again, that's not exactly fair. I'm comparing my Advanced Class Level 37 strength of 97 against their wall while the surrounding zone is only around level 15+. The most dangerous thing we've found close to them is a Level 35 dungeon, and that's a good two-hour hike east. So perhaps the wall isn't entirely irrational.

"Who are you people?" a voice calls down, the owner hidden behind a gun.

I absently note that a beam rifle is pointed at me—a rather nice one too. A moment later, Ali flashes the guard's status above his head.

Ian Crew (Level 24 Hunter)

HP: 280/280

MP: 180/180

Condition: Scared

"Hunter? That seems really generic," I send to Ali.

"The idiot took a Basic class and traded his perk for a Soulbound beam rifle. At least he got an upgradeable toy," Ali says. He's not actually here with me, instead floating deeper in town. He's scanning the System for information about the place and feeds back to me.

"Visitors from up north. We've brought some refugees from the communities above," I shout back. "We have women and children here. Along with some trained fighters and a whole bunch of loot."

I watch the guard glance at the convoy behind me, then at our hover bikes. Interestingly enough, while he's noted Lana's pets, he doesn't seem as concerned about them, even if his eyes keep straying to the redhead herself. The menagerie of animals is rather awe-inspiring to most.

"Sorry! I can't let you in. I need to tell Arik and get his okay," Ian says. "Do you mind waiting?"

I nod agreeably and settle in to wait, letting my eyes run over the other guards, who have relaxed after seeing that I'm happy to wait. As I said, I could force my way in, but what's the point? A few minutes of waiting won't hurt us.

"You came from up north?" Ian calls down once he's sent off one of the guards with his message. His eyes roam over our gear again, stopping to linger on Lana before he stares at me. I know what he sees—armored jumpsuit, high-end beam pistol, expensive hover bike—and can see him doing the math in his head. "Things must be going pretty good up there."

"You could say that," I call back. Memories flash through my mind—the fights and the losses we saw in Whitehorse. Richard, Ulric, Miranda. Roxley and his betrayal. My hands clench and I push aside the hurt.

Tired of shouting, I get off the bike and flex my feet, jumping up onto the wall and landing next to the startled guard. I see more than one gun swing toward me, the guards' eyes wide, but no one takes a shot. Very good discipline. I'm impressed.

"What—"

"Sorry. Got tired of shouting." I lean back against the wall, purposely crossing my feet and putting myself in a disadvantageous position. After that is done, I hold out my hand. "Chocolate?"

"You..." He stares at me then down at the wall then back at me. "What Level are you?"

"That's a bit rude, don't you think?" I smile at him absently as I take the time to read the notification that's popped up since I crossed the boundary of the town. "At least take me out for dinner first."

You have entered a Safe Zone (The Village of Fort Nelson)

Mana flows in this area have been forcefully stabilized. No monster spawning will occur within boundaries.

This Safe Zone includes:

- *Village of Fort Nelson City Center*
- *The Shop*
- *Quest Hall*
- *More...*

Chastised, Ian quiets down. I can see him mentally consider and discard asking me to move. Funnily, I actually would, if he asked, since my point has been made. This should dissuade them from doing anything stupid, but considering they've been hesitating to help out a bunch of refugees, I'm not exactly enthused with the welcome we've received so far.

"We sent people north, but they said... well, it gets harder," Ian says to fill the silence.

"It does. Gets pretty high up in the Yukon." Out of the corner of my eyes, I watch him twitch, and I pop the chocolate into my mouth since he hasn't taken it.

Behind me, I hear the hushed conversations of my friends as they wait, the refugees trying to convince each other that they'll be let in. The guards are still tense, shooting me worried looks.

"You're from the Yukon? Watson Lake or…?"

"Whitehorse," I answer.

From a building, another guard pops out and runs up to Ian, who walks over to listen.

"*Arik is coming. They're to stay outside till they take the Oath,*" I lipread the guard saying to Ian.

Ian nods and walks back to me, smiling slightly, nervousness quite well hidden. "Arik, the ummm… owner of the town is coming to greet you himself. If you can just wait…"

"*Ali, get back here. And see if you can figure out what they mean by an Oath,*" I send to the Spirit before looking at Ian and smiling languidly. "Sure. Mind if I let the others know that we'll be waiting a bit?"

"Of course, but he won't be long," Ian says.

"We're getting greeted by the owner himself. So we've got to wait," I call to the group below.

I kind of wish I had set up some kind of signal for potential trouble, but well, I didn't think about it. Naïve, I guess. Or maybe, as Ali says, overconfident. Still, my friends have been living on the razor's edge for over a year now and their instincts are as good as mine. Perhaps better. I can see the subtle shifts in their demeanor as they get ready for potential trouble.

While we wait, I engage Ian in some small talk. Trading information about the System, learning a little about their experiences. Fort Nelson was hit badly in the initial few days, the city spread out as it is. Luckily, a group of survivors found the Shop and managed to rally others, eventually becoming able to purchase a few safe zones in the city center. After that, it was just a matter of time before they established the Village. Lucky for them, no external party was that interested in picking up the Settlement Key here, so they could purchase it themselves.

"And now the entire Yukon/Alaska region is under control of this Duchess," I say as I finish a summarised version of our year.

"Who is a dark elf. But not…?" Ian says, his voice rising a little at the term dark elf.

I don't blame him. The concept of dark elves isn't something that popular consciousness knows much about. It's more a geek thing. Heck, I mostly know of them from a book series my ex used to rave about and I never got around to reading.

"Truinnar. Just think of them as Truinnar. Black-skinned, very pretty elf-looking creatures with a highly sophisticated, back-stabbing society," I say.

"That's insane," Ian says then turns his head as figures walk down the street.

I watch the group come, a larger blond gymrat in the lead, followed by a middle-aged lady and a teenager at the back. The blond gymrat is obviously a bodyguard, the way he watches everything, though from the way they move…

"The kid in the back is Arik, isn't he?"

"Got it, boy-o. Don't forget, he could have gotten a gene treatment," Ali sends back, reminding me that age is much more difficult to pinpoint these days. So he could either be a really smart teenager, like Jason, who's taken over the town or just someone who has had their physical body reset to a younger age by the System.

Within minutes, the group is up on the wall and making greetings. Or at least, some greetings.

"I'm Arik Dorf," Arik says, offering me his hand and a smile. "This is Piotr and Min."

Level 31 Justiciar, Level 29 Bodyguard, and Level 31 Administrator respectively. Ali floats, invisible to everyone else, behind the group, staring at Arik with a fierce expression. My entreaties for information have been ignored in favor of making faces, which annoys me since I really want to know what type of Class a Justiciar is.

"John Lee," I say. "So what's the holdup? Sun's setting, and while it doesn't necessarily get much more dangerous after dark, it certainly gets more uncomfortable."

"Straight to the point, aren't you?" Arik says, smiling agreeably. Seeing that I'm not biting, he continues. "Well, Mr. Lee, the problem is that you have a large number of fighters. Many of whom, I understand, are nearly as strong as my guards."

"You're worried about them taking over?" I say, slightly incredulously.

Arik raises an eyebrow. "You really have an untrusting nature, don't you? No. I'm worried about them causing trouble in the city and us being unable to do much about it. We've had incidents with survivors who have… accepted… the violent nature of our present lives."

"Oh…" I consider what he's not saying. Right. Idiots with power, especially young idiots with power, throwing their strength around. I recall Amelia, the ex-RCMP, complaining about that more than once. "So what do you want us to do?"

"It's actually quite simple. I have a Skill that allows me to take an Oath from others. Those who break the Oath are penalized significantly, which will make handling them easier," Arik says.

"That's really interesting. I've heard of Skills like that before—Lords, Kings, and the like often have them—but this is the first time I've seen a Justiciar," Ali comments to me.

"Sounds a lot like a Contract to me," I send back while speaking to Arik. "And what is this Oath?"

"I swear to do no harm to the citizens within the Village of Fort Nelson, to abide by the orders of duly-appointed guardians of the peace within the Village, and to leave the Village if so requested," Arik says. "And to clarify, all the guardians wear these pins." Arik taps a small oblong pin with a castle on it that shifts like it's a holographic projection. "They're also linked to each individual, so if they get removed forcefully or aren't in contact with the designated individual, they lose their luster and break down."

"Seems mostly reasonable." I'll admit, I can see the potential for abuse, including the stratification of those in power and those not but... "You'll have to ask Sam and his people about this yourself. As for me, I don't intend to stay long. Amend the Oath to add a timer and a designation that it's only for the town and we're good to go."

Arik's eyes narrow while gymrat bristles at my tone. The Administrator leans in and whispers into Arik's ear.

He nods, smiling at me. "Of course. We'll designate that the Oath only takes effect in the city."

"For a period of two weeks," I said, smiling. "I'll be gone by then."

"For a month."

"Done," I say.

After that, I take the Oath easily and send Ali down to relay the information to the team. Arik takes his leave too, to stand at the gates to greet and administer the Oath to the refugees. I absently note that no one gives him trouble, except for Sam. He balks until Lana pulls him aside. A short while later, he's back, helping the Administrator manage the refugees. I have to admit, the village is efficient at sorting and housing our little convoy, sending the groups to various empty houses or, for the eager, the Shop.

"So, Ali, what're the consequences of breaking this Oath anyway?" I ask the Spirit while waiting.

"They vary, but mostly depend on the level of the Skill. With only a few points, you'd probably take a hit to your own Levels temporarily," Ali sends back to me as he stares into space, reading whatever information he can see in the backend of the System. *"Won't make a huge difference to you, but I'd be careful about taking an Oath with a real King."*

When Lana and the group get in, I hop down from the wall, after waving goodbye to Ian, and command Sabre to follow. I hear a few muted gasps as the PAV moves by itself, quickly muted.

"So, Shop?" I grin at the group and get confirming nods.

A couple of weeks of fighting and not having access to the Shop means that our inventory is filled to the brim. We'd even taken to dumping some of the less valuable items with the refugees, just so that we didn't waste them. And of course, in my Altered Space, I have a few corpses that desperately need a good Butcher or Harvester.

"Shop!" Mikito says happily, gunning her PAV.

We all follow the young Japanese woman till we come across the central pedestal with its silver-steel sphere. Each person who touches it disappears, transported to a Shop location—an extra-dimensional retailer. Of course, which Shop you enter is dependent on a number of factors—personal invitations, your reputation, the amount of Credits you have spent, all of that.

The Shop I'm transported to is green. Lots and lots of green, from the simple reception desks to the waiting couches to the personal shopping rooms. A few seconds after I appear, the anthromorphic Fox who seems to be my personal shopper comes hurrying out of a room, all kinds of toothy smiles.

"Redeemer!" Fox greets me. Clad in a vest and blousy pants combo, his dark brown eyes glint with avarice as he ushers me into a quiet room. "It has been too long."

Ali darts off to speak with his own friend in the Shop and take care of the selling of our loot.

"No Shop access," I explain. "I've not got much to buy today. Just need a refill of some of my consumables."

"Ah…" The Fox deflates a bit before he perks up like the consummate professional he is. I probably wouldn't even have noticed the first if it wasn't for my high Perception. "Perhaps I can interest you in a portable link?"

Portable Shop Link (Single Connection)

The portable shop link transports a single individual to the connected Shop. May only be used outside of dungeons and on the designated world (Earth).

Uses: 3

Cost: 20,000 Credits

"That seems cheap," I say after I finish reading over the information and staring at the small chip that makes up the link device. Over in the corner, I see the Fox finishing up my order for the various bullets, missiles, and grenades that make up my refill.

"The link is subsidized by the establishment," Fox says. "And is, of course, only for our most valuable customers."

"Gotcha. Probably too expensive for me though. Oh, I finished up the last few books, so I'll need the next five on the System Quest," I say.

Fox nods, tapping in the information as he pulls out the next few books on my never-ending list. Not surprisingly, someone had put together a list of books to read that would generate experience points for completing small milestones in the System Quest. Of course, while each book might give minor revelations about what and how the System works, they still don't answer the real question—what is it? In many ways, I feel very much like I'm a blind man feeling an elephant with books.

So far, what I've gathered is that the System is something that precedes all publicly available records of the Galactic Council. In addition, the System has administrative points—control areas in each zone. Take control of enough of these and you can make minor adjustments to the System within the world of that zone, much like how we can adjust our villages and towns. The Galactic Council then is just the governments and individuals who control a significant number of these administrative points, getting together to decide the rules of the System overall. Outside of the rules imposed by the Galactic Council, the System itself controls and adjusts everything in our worlds, upgrading, Leveling, and developing both material and organic objects without care to "normal" scientific laws.

Most of this is done by using the Mana that flows throughout System-registered worlds. In fact, Mana seems to be the main controlling force for the System—the electricity, if you will, of the System.

One of the major arguments in the books I've read is whether the System is sentient or not. Numerous tests have shown that the amount of Mana input into the System—from Spells, teleportations, Skills, and the like—is always higher than the output. In fact, there's a "loss" of about 5%, give or take a few decimals here and there. It's a weirdly specific number, which many on the "System is a software" side point to. Of course, others have noted that just because it's a software doesn't mean it can't be sentient. A lot of fluctuations in the overall amount of Mana that flows into and out of the System lend credence to the argument that there's something more than just an out-of-control software program at work.

"Redeemer? Redeemer?" Fox calls, and I blink, staring at the retailer who has been trying to get my attention for a bit. Interrupting a customer's thoughts might not be a good sales tactic, but Fox and I have known each other long enough now that he doesn't worry about it. "Do you have anything else for me?"

I grimace, hating that name. That title, even if most of the aliens seem to think it's something I should be proud of having. System-generated titles are a big thing, marking a significant achievement by the individual. How big seems to vary depending on the culture of course, but it's a still mark of respect—similar to tattoos in older cultures or prisons.

"Sorry. Go ahead. I'll browse some Skills while I wait for Ali."

"Of course. Do call for me if you need anything else." Fox bobs his head then exits the room, leaving me alone.

I consider pulling out one of my new books and dismiss that thought, instead taking the moment to refresh my memory about my Status and what I might need to buy.

Status Screen			
Name	John Lee	Class	Erethran Honor Guard
Race	Human (Male)	Level	37
Titles			
Monster's Bane, Redeemer of the Dead			
Health	1700	Stamina	1700

| Mana | 1310 | Mana Regeneration | 98 / minute |

Attributes			
Strength	94	Agility	161
Constitution	170	Perception	58
Intelligence	131	Willpower	133
Charisma	16	Luck	30
Class Skills			
Mana Imbue	2	Blade Strike	2
Thousand Steps	1	Altered Space	2
Two are One	1	The Body's Resolve	3
Greater Detection	1	A Thousand blades	1
Soul Shield	2	Blink Step	2
Tech Link*	2	Instantaneous Inventory*	1
Cleave*	2	Frenzy*	1
Elemental Strike*	1 (Ice)		
Combat Spells			
Improved Minor Healing (II)		Greater Regeneration	
Greater Healing		Mana Drip	
Improved Mana Dart (IV)		Enhanced Lightning Strike	

Fireball	Polar Zone
Freezing Blade	

My build, as a friend would say, is weird. I'm part tank, part damage dealer, part Mage. While I once chided Jason for thinking of this world like one of his games, he did have one point that I've been considering for a bit.

If you're working in a team, specialization might be the way to go. That way, if you compare yourself to someone of the same level who generalized, you'll generally be more powerful. Of course, you want a pretty stable base first—running around with a 100 Health is just asking to die—but at a certain point, specializing makes sense. Especially since I can't seem to shake off my friends.

The truth about Jason's words is something I've noted while sparring with Mikito or Ingrid, the way they're significantly better than I am in their areas of specialization. I can keep up in a fight, but if I stick to playing fair, I'm normally hard-pressed to win. Mikito's got a bunch of speed abilities, along with Class Skills, that make her a dangerous melee fighter, while Ingrid is more the glass cannon type—able to hit with a ridiculously high amount of damage, but squishy.

In fact, one of the problems with bouncing upward to an Advanced Class the moment the System arrived was that the Erethran Honor Guard Skill tree is mostly about supporting others. The individual combat Skills are mostly in the Basic Erethran Guard or Erethran Soldier Class. That's also why I've been poking around a bunch of Basic Skill trees, searching for things I can purchase from the Shop to give me more oomph. Problem is, Skills are nice, but they all come with a cost. Credits to purchase them, then an on-going Mana and Stamina cost when you use them. I'll admit though, a lot of my desire for more strength has to do with the fact that I got my ass kicked before we left Whitehorse.

All that said, I still have no clue what my specialization would be. I can do a little of everything, but none of the roles attract me. I like being able to switch between the front-line and back depending on the situation. It's saved my ass quite a few times, being entirely self-reliant. But now I've got a party…

I stare at my Status screen one last time before turning back to the Shop's inventory. Time to stop mulling over things and get back to it. I haven't made a decision in weeks, so why should I be able to make one now? Better to focus on what I can do right now. Maybe I can find something to augment my ranged attacks…

***

I'm the first one back, though I've probably spent more time in the Shop due to the better time dilation in my Shop. Knowing that the others will be a while, I get moving on arranging our accommodations for the evening and leave Ali to guide the group to the abandoned house I locate. By the time they all arrive, I've already gotten a few plates on the table illuminated by some System-bought lamps. We're all kind of used to it by now, so the lack of electricity isn't a big problem. The lack of hot water on the other hand…

"Couldn't you find a place with hot water? I was looking forward to a bath," Ingrid grumbles with nods from the other women.

"Use a spell," I say. "They don't even have enough upgraded places for their own people. What makes you think they're going to let a bunch of tourists into an upgraded house?"

"We could pay," Ingrid says.

"Sure. You going to knock on the doors?" I wave at the exit.

Ingrid just stuffs her face rather than chat. As sarcastic and occasionally rude as she is to us, I've realized Ingrid is actually a tad shy among strangers.

Lana, who has taken over cooking the rest of the meal, walks by, dropping another platter of food. "Ali tells me there's a dungeon close by. One that's pretty close to over-running itself."

"You want us to clear it?" I ask while Mikito perks up slightly.

"It'd take a day at most," Lana says. "And the first clear bonus is always nice."

I consider her words. The first clear bonus is a significant chunk of experience, for sure. In fact, it's about the only thing that has given us any real experience since we left the Yukon. The rest has been dribs and drabs from beating up under-Leveled monsters. "All right. I'm in."

"Yes," Mikito says.

"Fine. I'm in too," Ingrid says.

Lana flashes all of us a smile of gratitude before plunking a case of bottles on the table. We all stare with disbelief at the familiar brand of Apocalypse Ale. As one of the Yukon's most popular exports since the System, we all know how expensive the beer is.

"How...?" Mikito asks, and Lana laughs softly.

"What? There are some advantages of part-owning the brewery through the foundation we set up," Lana says then fixes me with a look. "If someone actually looked into it, he might be surprised what he could get."

"Huh..." I say, snagging a bottle and popping off the screw-top. "With this kind of incentive, I just might..."

Lana grins and snags a bottle before we all settle in for dinner and rest in an actual bed. Now that we've decided on actually testing out the dungeon, we drag Ali over and probe him for more information. Not that he has much, but we often find that anything is better than nothing.

Chapter 3

"Doesn't look like much of a dungeon," I mutter, staring at the notification floating in front of my face the moment I step into the gloomy, shadowed forest. It's subtle, but the change in the ecology is there. One side of the barrier is less lush and more shadowed than the other.

"It is only Level 35," Lana says, stretching slightly and pulling her skintight jumpsuit tight in all the right places.

When she catches me looking, the redhead flashes me a grin and a wink, making me blush slightly. Living and traveling with a group, we've not had a lot of private time lately, which has been a bit annoying. That, and we want to verify her birth control options are still working. Ever since we figured out that the System has a bad tendency of degrading purchased birth control options, we've all gotten a little paranoid about double-checking things like that.

"True," Mikito says, her naginata resting on her shoulder as she straddles her bike. The polearm dwarfs the tiny Asian lady, who's clad much like Lana, albeit with slightly more armor plating. Like me, she hasn't yet bothered to transform her PAV. "We doing this on foot?"

"Probably for the best. It's only a few kilometers in radius. Figure the boss is in the center," I say, eyeing the fuzzy readouts that my minimap is giving me. Damn dungeons and their weird rules.

"Ingrid and the puppies are on scouting duty. Pull anything you find back to us..." I look around before sighing, realizing that the woman has already disappeared. "As for Tigger..."

"No. Just no," Lana says, glaring at me.

"But..." I snap it shut as Lana continues to glare at me. "Fine. What is he called?"

"Roland," Lana says, scratching the tiger, pushing his head into her waist.

"Roland staying with us or…?" Thus far, beyond being big, I've yet to see anything particularly special about the tiger, but I wasn't exactly paying attention either. Without knowing its specialty, I'm leery of giving suggestions.

"He'll stay for now with Anna," Lana says, the red fox content to trot alongside the redhead.

All that done, I nod and wave her and Mikito on, letting my eyes dart over their information one last time before I play rearguard.

Mikito Sato (Middle Samurai Level 3)
HP: 770/770
MP: 430/430
Conditions: None

Lana Pearson (Beast Tamer Level 49)
HP: 380/380
MP: 600/600
Conditions: Bestial Senses, Linked x 4

It takes about ten minutes before a body drops in front of us, all dark blue hair, muscles, and blood. Mikito bisects the body before it even hits the ground, while Lana has a gun trained on it in seconds. That's before we realize it's a corpse. A moment later, I hear giggling beside us, Ingrid having shifted positions immediately.

"Ingrid…" Lana sighs then prods the corpse with her feet.

Now that we're no longer worried about our lives, we spend some time actually looking at the monster corpse. It's similar to a chimpanzee in size but with blue fur, an extra pair of secondary arms, and a tail that looks as though it should belong on a scorpion. After assessing the monster, we get moving.

We barely take ten steps before Lana stiffens, swiveling to the left. Her lips tighten and she drops to a knee, her gun raised. Roland lets out a low growl and pads to her left, his entire body shimmering. Within seconds, it's hard to see the creature, his body camouflaged against the background terrain. Anna shifts to a safe distance away from Lana, flames bursting from her body and licking against her fur.

"Howard's on his way back with company," Lana says as she settles in.

Mikito makes a noise of assent but doesn't move, continuing to watch her side of the forest. I grunt, consider my options, and pull a beam rifle from storage. Mana Darts, my favorite spell, is just a little too low Level for these guys, and everything else I have is a bit too destructive. A Fireball in a forest is a bad idea, especially since the undergrowth here doesn't seem to have had a good forest fire in a bit. Hmmm… something else to consider. Who would have thought that bringing death and destruction actually had so many different facets?

Tension mounts as we wait, but we don't have to wait long. The sounds of branches breaking and the padding of a pony-sized husky reaches us within seconds, then the large hound is here. Close behind him are a dozen of the ape-creatures, swinging through the trees and loping on the ground in a weird knuckle, knuckle, feet gait. The transition from peace to violence is sudden as Roland claws apart the first to cross the threshold, then he launches himself against a second. Lana opens fire with her rifle, and Anna lays down a low wall of flame to ward off the majority while Howard spins around to fight.

I add to the carnage and manage to catch sight of Ingrid coming out of the shadows to do her thing. The fight is fast and furious, but we out-Level the apes by a significant margin. By unspoken agreement, we let Lana and her pets do most of the work, the Beast Tamer having the least number of hours in the field and thus the lowest Level.

A short couple of minutes later, I'm looting the bodies and storing them in my Altered Space while Lana heals her pets.

"Think we should get lunch ready while Lana takes care of the dungeon?" Ingrid says from behind me.

I sigh, refusing to jump even if her sudden appearance is a bit startling. I finish putting the corpse in my Altered Space before I turn around. "Might not be a bad idea."

"You guys…" Lana says, sounding exasperated. "I'm not that far behind all of you. And the boss might be a little tough for me and the boys. And Anna."

"A little tough is good," Mikito says. "Good training."

"Sounds like we're decided. I'll lend you Ali," I say while setting up the picnic table. "Ingrid, your turn."

"Hey!" Lana says, growling at us.

"Fine. Stew and bannock?" Ingrid says.

"Sounds delicious."

"Rice too, please," Mikito says.

"Hey!" Lana says again.

"You still here?" I look at Lana, humor dancing in my eyes as she stands there, hands on her hips while we ignore her protests.

She glares at me, mouths, "You'll pay for this," then stomps off, followed by her pets. Within minutes, her passage fades and I stretch.

"Going for a stroll?" Ingrid says, her voice full of mirth while Mikito snorts.

I shrug, refusing to answer. Ingrid waves the ladle at me and I nod before following Lana quietly. I might not have Ingrid's Class Skills, but I've got some skills.

Look, we might be idiots, but we aren't exactly going to let our friend solo a dungeon without some backup.

***

The next couple of hours are rather boring. Between her Bestial Senses ability and the pets, I have to give her a significant amount of space just so that she doesn't know I'm here. Add in the fact that I need to be far enough away that the System doesn't hurt her experience gain too much and I end up having a really uneventful stroll through the woods. Even so, the occasional extra-large explosion, tree breaking, or scream carries back to me. Thankfully, with Ali floating alongside Lana, I get running commentary to keep me entertained.

"Ooooh, that's an amazing suplex, John, just makes those legs really defined…

"What a move, sticking her gun in its mouth…

"That kind of language from a woman! Who would have thought…

"Two dozen. We might be in trouble here, sports fans. Wait! Is that…? Yes! It's the Pearsons' signature move—the Chaos Grenade. It lobs, it flies, it explodes with pink confetti! This might be troublesome for our young hero!

"… by the skin of her teeth. Well, Roland's teeth, but there you have it. The latest member of the Pearson Prowlers is showing his value already. Much faster than a tall Asian, I'll say.

"And that's the Boss. Whoa, he's big. No worries though, boy-o, she can take him. Well, not her, herself but together, I'm sure…

"And that's the second summons. Wynn is off to tangle with those other dozen little bastards. Lana's tossing those grenades like there's no tomorrow, even with her arm broken. But the smokescreen's letting our young heroine move to a new location while Roland and Anna double-team the Boss and Howard does mop-up.

"It's down! Down. The Boss is down and its minions are fleeing."

***

When Ali finally gives the all-clear, I find myself sagging against a nearby tree. The Spirit is good at giving a rundown, even if he makes it a little more dramatic than it needs to be. While Lana mops up, I head back to our temporary rest stop. It might seem strange to let her go by herself and then wander along behind her, but I know Lana's been feeling a little out of place, out-leveled and underpowered. Mikito has years of martial arts training to back her up, Ingrid is a frigging Assassin, and well, I'm me. Lana, until a few months ago, spent most of her time running the foundation and a bunch of businesses in Whitehorse. Even if I think she's a lot tougher than she believes, especially with her pets in play, she needs to know it. Letting her take out the Boss by herself is a good way for us to reinforce her self-esteem.

Even if it is a bit hard on my heart.

Chapter 4

You would think that clearing a dungeon the Village would make them happy. But if I've learned one thing about humans, it's that they're never happy. Acting as if we should have asked them for their permission to kill monsters is ridiculous, especially when they haven't been able to clear it. Still, the entire incident soured us on Fort Nelson, and we decided to leave the very next day. Which is why we're surprised to see Sam waiting in his truck as we head out of our borrowed accommodations.

"What are you doing here?" I ask Sam, admiring the much younger looking gentleman. I mentally approve—gene therapy is probably one of the best deals in town. It not only shaved a quarter century off Sam's visage, it also probably boosted quite a few of his physical stats. That Sam decided to keep the silver-grey hair actually makes him look more distinguished, I think.

"This isn't the place for me," Sam says, looking around the Village, eyes lingering on the few inhabitants who are up at the crack of dawn. "I'm not a fan of swearing binding Oaths to people I don't know."

"Sam…" I consider my objection. While I do so, I take the time to review his Status bar.

Samuel K. Turner (Level 29 Technomancer)
HP: 170/170
MP: 540/540
Conditions: None

Very low health, not at all what I'd consider acceptable. On the other hand, his Mana pool is very good, especially for someone at his Level. Add in the fact that he has a rather rare Basic Skill, which lets him manipulate technology—mostly for his own use right now, but supposedly for others eventually—and he could be a pretty decent back-of-the-line supporter.

In the end, I decide to let him come for two reasons. Firstly, Sam's got the willingness to fight—something that, even if one has the Skills, can be lacking—and secondly, it's his life. I'm not here to dictate what he does.

"Fine," I answer and watch Sam relax slightly.

He slides into his truck a moment later, with Ingrid taking rearguard on her bike. Mikito and I lead the way over the bridge that straddles the town. South, down to Prince George, it is. Hopefully our reception there is a lot less chilly.

***

It's eight hundred kilometers on the highway to Prince George. Even with the destruction caused by the change and the lack of maintenance, the highways are still the fastest way to travel. No one from Fort Nelson has successfully made contact with those down south though, since the 97 swings close to the Northern Rocky Mountains Provincial Park. The damn System seems to consider every provincial park and place of beauty the perfect place to put a high Level zone. At the closest point to the provincial park, the highway sits at nearly Level 50. Definitely too high for the people in Fort Nelson, and even a threat for us if we were moving alone.

That's why, by general consensus, we're taking things slow and sending the puppies ahead to herd some monsters for Sam to play with. I've even kindly let him ride Sabre so that he doesn't have to struggle in and out of the truck while killing them. For all the consideration we've given him, you'd think he'd be more grateful.

"Help me!" Sam shouts as he lies on the ground, holding the mutated bear off his face through sheer desperation.

"Oh, come on, it's only a Level 15," I call back.

"Two nights of cooking says he's going to get below 50%," Ingrid offers.

"Bah! Three nights and 30% of his health," Ali counters.

"You guys are insane!" Sam screams. He finally levers a hand free, pushing the beam pistol against the bear's side, and opens fire.

The bear takes the shots, chomping down hard on Sam's shoulder and making his hand spasm open.

"Hey! Stop that," I say as I glare at Ali. "No betting on my behalf. It's not as if you're doing the cooking if you lose. But we'll take that bet."

"John..." Lana says, looking at Ingrid and me. "I don't think she's been a good influence on you."

"You wanted me to lighten up..."

"Exactly. Lighten. Not indulge in dark humor," Lana says, shaking her head.

"I note you aren't doing anything to help either," I say.

Sam screams and I glance at his health, doing some quick math. He can take one more hit before I have to heal him. Of course, if I do, his experience gains drop, since the System will count it as help, which kind of defeats the purpose of all this. As it stands, he's getting reduced experience as it is. Still, I don't want him to die either. I pay a little more attention, pre-casting a portion of the Healing spell and holding it in abeyance.

Mikito is dancing with another bear to the side, using her fists rather than her polearm to strike the monster. She's even got a few light cuts across her face, courtesy of her practicing dodging by the millimeter. We pulled the pair to us a short while ago and Sam learned a major lesson about being a support fighter—don't let the monsters get close.

Sam jerks his head aside enough to dodge the next bite and pulls the trigger of his recovered pistol a few more times. Flesh sizzles and the bear finally has enough, falling and flattening the poor Technomancer. Before we can help, Howard has pulled the body off Sam and settled down to snack. I release my spell the moment I can actually see Sam, watching as he heals all the damage in seconds.

"I didn't say this wasn't necessary," Lana says, rubbing the back of her neck. "Just, you know, a bit rude."

"A lot rude!" Sam snaps, kicking the bear corpse after he loots it.

Howard growls at Sam before returning to eating the bear, and Roland joins him after a second. Surprisingly, Howard doesn't object. Now that Sam's done, Mikito put down her bear too and lets Shadow and Anna take their turn.

"You complain, but you're getting better," I say, looking the man over. "Though seriously, you couldn't have bought an armored suit or something?"

"I didn't expect to be fighting!" Sam snaps, checking the charge on his pistol and swapping out the Mana battery. "I fix cars and weapons!"

"And you're wandering around the wilderness. At least buy yourself some decent offensive Spells, will you? Perhaps a few to restrict movement. It'll keep you alive longer," I recommend.

Sam growls at me again, stomping back to Sabre and the beam rifle that was discarded during the fight.

Incidents like that pretty much make up the next few weeks. Of course, once the zone levels started creeping up too high, we stopped playing around. Well, until we hit the Level 50 zone, then we hunkered down and did some real grinding.

I ended up lending Sam Sabre in her transformed form during that period, and I had to admit, I was a bit jealous. With his abilities, Sam could use it just as well as I could with my Skills and Neural Link, interfacing directly with the controls to play ranged damage dealer. He even managed to eke out a higher efficiency rate on the Mana engine and linked his beam rifle directly with the PAV so that he could keep shooting without switching Mana batteries.

We spent over a day and a half just off the highway in the Level 50 zone, drawing monsters to us and killing them. Once we finally ran out of space for storing the loot and Sam Leveled up to 32, we called it a day and got moving.

Our high spirits got shut down fast once we hit the next village. Stuck so close to a high Level zone with no Shop and the nearest settlement too far to walk to, there were no survivors. Nor were there any in the next village. Or the next.

For all the joking and ribbing, this was the reality of our existence—less than ten percent of humanity had survived the transition. Entire communities had been wiped out. Among the survivors, a significant number of the young and elderly were slain. This new world has no space for the weak. Perhaps it might have been different if we had transitioned to a normal System world, but as a Dungeon World, we never had a chance.

We don't stop or search the settlements. There's no need. Not with Ali around. And so we drive past empty homes and abandoned vehicles, leaving the past to the past until we reach Fort St. John, a tiny town nearly the same size as Whitehorse. It has no Shop, too small to be considered worth setting up the teleportation link that anchors a Shop to our world. Yet for all their disadvantages, there are survivors. We find a way.

***

"Ahoy there!" I call.

"Ahoy? Seriously? We going with landlubbers next?" Ali teases, floating beside me as we stare at the fortified apartment complex.

"Perhaps we should have someone less intimidating talk to them?" Sam says.

"You mean Lana."

"I mean Lana."

I sigh, noting that there's still no movement from the apartment complex. If it wasn't for the barred doors and windows and the dots on the minimap, I'd have thought they were all gone. Thankfully, they haven't tried to shoot me yet, unlike some others.

"You're up, Lana," I say, finally conceding.

The redhead laughs, giving my hand a quick squeeze as she saunters up the driveway. A high Charisma, breathtaking beauty, and actual social skills have to count for something. I hope.

"We don't mean you any harm. We're here to offer aid!" Lana calls and waits.

"Can I go in and drag them out yet?" Ingrid's voice crackles over the radio.

To make us look less threatening, we left her and Mikito with the pets, out of sight around the corner of the block. Roland might be a cuddly and foolish kitty to us, but I'm sure that's not what most people see.

"No," Sam snaps.

There're only a dozen survivors, so I'm sure Ingrid could do it easily enough, but then what? We're trying to get their cooperation, not turn them into slaves.

"How are you going to help us?" a voice finally calls. It's young and aggressive, challenging Lana and our stated good intentions. I can sympathize.

"Depends on what you need. We've got some weapons, food, and water we can give you if that's all you'll accept. But we'd rather help you get somewhere safer," Lana calls back. We've done this conversation a few times before, and nearly always, there's that caution.

"Safe?" There's a bitter laugh at that.

Another voice pipes up, this one older. "What do you mean safer?"

"There are safe zones, places where monsters don't spawn randomly," Lana states. "If you get to a Shop, you can buy a residence and it blocks spawning inside that house. Whole cities can become a safe zone if enough property is bought. There's a document, a guide we can share with you."

There's silence at her last words, but I can see the dots converging on my minimap.

A couple of minutes later, the older man calls, "Leave the guide and the supplies on the doorstep and then back off. We'll consider your offer."

Lana sighs and waves me forward. A few seconds later, the printed-out copy of *Thrasher's Guide* and a bunch of supplies is on their doorstep. Increased Perception means that I can hear their gasps as I make the paper and boxes of food appear.

After letting them know where we'll be, we meet up with the rest of the crew and repeat the process at another boarded-up building. We do that for the rest of the day, playing diplomat and good guy. Surprisingly—or not, considering how thin everyone in the group is—one of the groups joins us immediately. All the others are way too wary and paranoid, which seems a little strange. Not that we're expecting everyone to join us, but the ratio is wrong.

Dinner is held in the middle of the highway, the young man and the quartet of teenagers devouring the food we provide and only flinching slightly when the puppies or Roland move near them. Anna, the lazy fox that she is, is curled up and getting strokes from Ingrid while Sam pokes and prods at the force shields we've set up around the impromptu camp. We could have taken a house, but considering that monsters can barge through the walls at any time, this is actually safer. That, and we want to let the human scouts have a clear view of what we are and aren't doing.

Once dinner is done, I drag a truck back at Sam's request and we spend the next few hours fixing it up together. I say we, but I was a website hack, so it's mostly Sam who does the work while I hand him tools and play impromptu jack. I do learn a few things, since Sam is one of those guys who likes to talk while working. Of course, I'm not entirely sure what the point is, since gas-guzzling engines are archaic technology these days.

"Right. Let's try it," Sam says after an hour, scooting out from under the vehicle before I lower it.

We pop the hood and he places his hand on the engine, channeling his Skill.

All Tech I See (III)

This Skill allows the Technomancer an intuitive understanding and connection with technology, allowing him to use the technology at will. This Skill also has the ability to attempt to override security features in the affected technology.

Level I effects: +15% bonus to connections with technology, +10% efficiency and productivity (where appropriate)

Level II effects: this Skill will temporarily designate non-System technology as System-enabled with the appropriate bonuses.

Level III effects: Technomancer may designate 3 pieces of technology to be used remotely. Mana Cost: 20 Mana per minute for active use. Passive use (Level II and III effects) 200 Mana per activation. Duration of 3 hours per activation

I shake my head, staring at the details of Sam's Class Skill. It's one hell of a Skill—even better than the Neural Link Skill I purchased—and I'm slightly surprised he's so willing to share the details. Ever since Sam managed to allocate his third Skill point a few days ago, he's been able to designate a couple of additional vehicles for use. Unlike a Mechanic's rebuilding of the vehicle, this is a lot less permanent but a lot faster.

"Sounds good," I say, listening to the engine. We've mostly just swapped out a bunch of starters, pulled a bunch of clogged lines, and made sure the actual gasoline engine works. After that, Sam used some of his other Skills to fix the electronic chips needed to run the truck. It wouldn't actually work without his Skill, though a real Mechanic with the right tools could probably get it fixed up much easier now. "Next?"

Sam nods, and I walk toward the camp exit, glancing at Mikito as she joins me.

"Something up?" I ask her.

"No. Just too cramped to practice inside," Mikito says, and I nod in understanding.

"You okay with all this?" I wave my hands around, indicating both the survivors we're grabbing as well as the destruction.

"Yes," Mikito answers then pauses, looking at me. "Are you?"

"It's what we do, isn't it?" I say. It's not really something I've thought about—just one of those things we can do to help. I mean, why not? It barely takes any real effort, and even if it did, we're saving lives. How exactly is that a bad thing?

"You seem less angry," Mikito says.

I blink, considering her words. I prod at my emotions, noting the churning sea of anger that still resides in the pit of my stomach. But it's more peaceful? Calmer? No typhoon winds, no tsunamis...

"Maybe?" I say hesitatingly. "I'm still angry at times, but it just is, you know? We're not fighting for our lives as much anymore. And even if things are bad, it's mostly done and over with. At least, I hope so. How are you doing?"

It's not an idle question. Mikito has lost more than most. Her husband, dead. Her family, not only separated by a sea but most likely dead too. For a time, I know she wanted to die, but now...

"I exist," Mikito answers me, offering me a tight smile. "It hurts at times. When I remember. But we do good, and when it is time, perhaps I will meet him again."

I don't really know what to say to that, so I offer her a smile and nod. Mikito breaks off soon afterward, walking toward the park we noticed before. I admit, I watch her leave, uncertain exactly what to feel about the conversation we just had. In the end, I push it aside to focus on the work ahead of me.

***

Late at night, I lie in bed, absently stroking the hair of the sleeping redhead beside me. Lana murmurs softly, nuzzling into my chest before falling back asleep, while I stare at the screen in front of me. Page 273 from *A Mathematical Review of Classes, System Skills, and the System*. Riveting reading. Really. But I've got things to do and people to see.

I quietly extract myself from the tent and make my way to the fire, glancing at the young man seated by it with a makeshift spear on his lap. Young, probably in his early twenties, with that wariness that almost all survivors have. He looks up, his hand clenching slightly on the spear shaft while meeting my eyes with his thousand-yard stare.

"You're up late," I say and take a seat next to him.

"So are you," he replies.

I smile slightly, staring at the kid and wondering when I started calling people half a decade younger than me kids. "Perk of a high Constitution. I don't really need to sleep much." Or at all, if I want to push it. But experimentation has shown that the human brain really does like having a bit of downtime.

"You're strong too," the kid says, glancing toward the vans and trucks I dragged over. We'd briefly considered a bus but figured a single point of failure was a bad idea.

"Thanks. You're not bad yourself," I say, and he twitches, eyes narrowing. "There's no way you'd survive this long if you didn't have some decent Levels and strength scores."

Of course, I don't tell him that I can see his Status bar above his head too.

Kyle Leeburn (Karateka Level 28)

HP: 340/340

MP: 180/180

Conditions: Exhausted (-10 to all Stats and Regeneration Rates)

"Not good enough," the kid says, and I clearly hear the regret and self-recrimination.

I glance back at the tent that we designated for him and his friends—all those who are left. He catches me looking and nods slightly. I'm not even sure what the nod means, but I don't push it.

"Did you read the guide?" I ask to break the silence.

"Yes. Not much new there," Kyle says. "I do want to know what you intend to do with us."

"Exactly what we promised. Bring you guys to a safe zone, preferably a city with a Shop. That way you can sell some of your loot and get sorted," I say. "No ulterior motives."

"Not as if I can do anything about it if you did, is there?" Kyle says bitterly.

"No, not really," I agree bluntly.

Kyle looks at me, his eyes shining. "If you lay a hand on them, I'll kill you. I don't care how, I will kill you. All of you."

"Oh god…" Ali says, floating down from where he's been watching all this. "There's two of you!"

"Funny," I tell Ali before looking at the kid and giving him a nod in acknowledgement. "Now, go to sleep."

"I—"

"You said it yourself. There's nothing you can do if I want you dead. And anyway, if I had bad intentions, I'd want to get all of you survivors together. Right now, you'd be more useful as bait than anything else."

I see Kyle twitch at that, but he finally stands and goes into the tent. I can hear him breathing loudly and irregularly, forcing himself to stay awake just in case I decide to attack, but at least I have some peace and quiet. Sort of.

"You've got a pretty devious mind there, boy-o," Ali says, floating cross-legged in front of me.

"Hmmm…?"

"The entire using the kids as bait bit. Cold."

"Never said I wasn't," I say, smiling grimly.

I wait, the darkness deepening until finally, finally the kid succumbs to sleep. That's when I stand and stretch before walking to the force field and letting myself out. I keep silent, walking through the abandoned, empty streets filled with weeds and unraked leaves till we're far enough away.

"Tell me about the sixth group."

"Not much more to tell," Ali says, floating beside me. "Six fighters in the building, all between Level 30 and 40. Three captives, all mutilated so they can't run. You were right—they're probably the reason why everyone is so paranoid and looking worse for wear. Can't hunt or Level up properly if the non-combatants are easy prey."

"Weapons? Classes? Skills?"

"One Thief, two Bandits, one Guardian, a Shaman, and a Gunslinger. One of the captives is a Healer too," Ali replies. "Two System-registered melee weapons. All their guns are System-registered, but it's mostly human shotguns and rifles as their base."

"Anything else I should know?" I ask, my voice going colder as I walk toward the little glowing dots in the minimap.

"Don't make it fast." Ali's voice is raw and angry at the last.

I don't blame him. He's been stuck watching them the whole day when he's not with us.

***

The group has taken over a bank, their resting place underground, where the safe deposit boxes are located. Safe—or at least safer—than a normal building. One entrance to their main resting place, easy to defend against any incursions. Assuming they don't get really unlucky and a monster spawns in the building itself, they've got it good. Of course, they aren't dumb enough to not have a watch out, but they've gotten lazy. Probably been lording it over the groups around here too much. The big fish in the small pond.

I take my time, ghosting up to him when he's not looking in my direction, crossing through shadows till I'm close enough to make my move. *Haste, Thousand Steps,* and agility in the hundred-plus range means that I cover the last five feet in the blink of an eye. There's nothing wrong with the Bandit's instincts, his head turning toward me, but he's nowhere near fast enough. My blade sinks into his neck easier than I thought, forcing me to catch the body with my free hand while the detached head drops. The muffled, meaty thud resounds through the marbled floor, and I hold my breath, wondering if it was too much.

Nothing. I breathe a sigh of relief and head over to the staircase, my sword disappearing back to whatever dimension it exists in when I don't have it summoned. As I near the stairs, I look down, spot the crude attempt of a trip wire, and step over it.

Downstairs is a single corridor and small rooms, sub-divided to allow privacy, before the main safe deposit storage room. From Ali's descriptions, each of the private rooms is allocated to the leaders, with the remnants forced to stay together. Of course, each of the three leaders keep one of the women to themselves.

I'd considered a few ways of dealing with this, but any fight in close quarters is likely to result in the deaths of the women. That's one of the reasons I've chosen to do this myself. I'll admit, I also want to save the group some of what I expect to see. As much as we've seen and done, as many nightmares as we might have, there's no need to add any more.

Downstairs, I tread to the opposite side of the waiting room and make sure to hide myself as best as I can before signaling Ali that I'm ready for the second part of the plan.

"Trouble!" Ali shouts from above in a simulated voice.

Never having heard the Bandit speak, I have no idea if Ali's doing a good enough job, but the roar of gunfire as Ali triggers his weapon is sufficient to drive home his point.

"What is it?" one of the men shouts even as I hear them scrambling inside the rooms.

"They're attacking us!" Ali calls back.

I have to admit, they're not complete idiots. Most of them head up, but they leave a guard for the women. Of course, since I didn't bother to hide the body too much, I only have a minute at most before they realize they've been tricked. But that's more than enough time.

I launch myself forward, crossing the room at a sprint, and tackle the Thief across his body. I hit him like a freight train, his ribs cracking and snapping, even his breath explodes around my ear. I don't stop moving, bull-rushing him into the nearby wall, concrete shattering around us—I put him mostly through it. As I lean backward, I grip his upper arm, crushing it, and throw him to the floor. For all that, the Thief manages to form a glowing red dagger that plunges into my torso, sinking past the jumpsuit and sending a shard of pain through my mind.

Before he can do it again, I beat aside his hand, looking back at the women and wasting a few precious seconds to cast Soul Shield on all three. The glowing walls of force spring to life around their bodies, protecting them against collateral damage. Of course, the Thief manages to stab me a few more times in the meantime, nearly cutting my throat with one swipe. Painful as it is, it's not lethal.

Noise from the staircase informs me that I'll be getting company soon, so I grip the Thief by the neck. Another second and I cross the floor to the staircase, where the Gunslinger is turning, a pair of pistols in his hand. He unloads, uncaring if he hits the Thief I'm using as an impromptu shield. I twist from the hips and heave, taking a pair of bullets in the lower body before the Thief flies through the air, screaming. The Gunslinger is fast, very fast, bouncing up the staircase and crowding his friends to avoid the newly made corpse.

I snarl, another bullet smashing into my helmet and rocking my head back. A thought and the sword is in my hand, Blade Strike throwing a glowing line of red and blue from the blade while Thousand Blades repeats the action with a pair of duplicate weapons. The attacks fly up the stairs, and this time, there is nowhere for them to go. Unlike their attacks, the Soulbound sword I wield has leveled up with me and is backed by a pair of Skills. The difference in damage is like comparing a BB gun and a 9mm.

Screams, shouts, and swearing as the group struggles upward, unloading their shots into my body. I take them all, my body shuddering slightly under the barrage. But I have over 1700 Health Points and a regeneration rate to match it. It'd be a lie to say I could stand here and take it all day long, but I can for the few seconds that it takes them to reach the top of the stairs and slam the door shut.

Then I use Blink Step, fixing the point of my arrival by using Ali's viewpoint, and appear behind the group. I kill the Shaman first, who's busy readying a series of Spells to slow, poison, and kill me. It only takes a single focused strike to kill him. Stupid magic users with their miniscule health.

The Bandit is next, cutting upward with a real sword that glows green with energy. Cleave or Bash or Power Strike or an equivalent Skill. Putting everything he has into the attack. I twist, catching the cut with the sword I've materialised in my other hand, surprising him. Even so, the strength of the blow throws me backward, my feet leaving the floor for a second.

The Guardian makes his move next, rushing and grappling my arm. A quick twist as he shouts, "Disarm," and then he's got my sword, the blade forced from my hand by the Skill. I skip backward, breaking away before he can attack me, even as the Bandit steps up and the Gunslinger shifts to get a line of sight on me.

They come for me, the Guardian—guarding what, his rancid desires?—leading the way. He swings my borrowed sword, intent on ending me. Too bad for him it's a Soulbound weapon and I dismiss it with a thought, then I let him run into the others I conjure. I don't stop, can't stop, as I dance past him to show the Bandit what happens when you pair Cleave, a Soulbound weapon, and nearly a hundred points of strength together. He takes three hits before he finally flops to the floor, dead. After that, mopping up the Gunslinger is a cinch.

It's only when I'm standing in the middle of the bank, covered in blood and guts, my pulse slowing and the rage that ate away at my reason dissipating, that my brain kicks in and lists all the problems I've got. Starting with how I'm going to explain this to everyone.

"You really shouldn't hog all the fun," Ingrid calls from the doorway she leans against, cleaning her nails with a dagger.

I roll my eyes, knowing she's doing that for effect. Of course, I don't tell her it does look as cool as she thinks it does.

"What are you doing here?" I flick my gaze upward to my minimap and blink, seeing more dots slowly coming in.

"You really need to work on your poker face," Ingrid says, eyes dancing with amusement. "And you're about as subtle as a hammer. We all figured you were keeping something to yourself."

"More like a tank rolling down the street." Lana walks up with the puppies beside her. On a nearby rooftop, Roland is perched, watching over the proceedings. "So what's in there?"

I frown, glancing down and then back at them. Another reason I chose to do this was to save them from the sights and smells below. The memories…

"Three women. Mutilated and kept by them." I gesture at the bodies and watch as the ladies straighten, tension going through their bodies.

"Okay. Ingrid and I will go down. You, clean this up," Lana says brusquely, striding forward, trailed by Ingrid.

"Stuck with clean up. Again," I mutter before casting Clean on myself and trying to figure out what to do.

In the end, I go with the easy option and toss the bodies into storage. I'll find a cliff to discard them from later. The blood is easy enough to mop up, using stolen clothing to push it around. Rather than storing them, I keep the Gunslinger's pistols out, reloaded and cleaned, as well as a guard's shotgun. And then I wait.

It takes them over an hour to return, the women washed and Cleaned, in new clothes and looking much healthier. Each of them is still missing the lower portion of a leg, but with Lana's and Ingrid's help, they're able to ascend the building. Once I make it clear they're for them, the ladies grab the pistols and shotgun I've left out, though Lana stops one of the ladies. She glares at Lana, her lip curling until another lady pulls on her arm. I watch the byplay, frowning slightly, but say nothing as I get a series of cold shoulders.

Stupid. Stupid old John for not putting the pieces together. The last thing they'd want is a male presence right now. Even if it's one that saved them.

When we finally get back to the camp where Mikito has been keeping watch, Kyle is woken by the commotion. His jaw drops slightly when he sees one of the girls, and he rushes over to her. She flinches, moving away from his touch, which makes him pause, a flash of pain and self-recrimination flowing across his face. The kid manages to hide it, hovering around the girls and doing the best he can to help. Soon enough, the women are inside the group's tent, asleep and watched over.

Lana walks over to where I've taken post, watching over the surroundings. I know other groups are out there, waiting and watching, trying to glean our intentions. Hopefully this helps.

"I wish you hadn't done that," Lana says.

"What?"

"The guns," Lana replies then gestures to the tent. "Not a shrink, but pretty sure one of them has Stockholm Syndrome."

Oh... I blink, staring at the tent. I understand the concept—that hostages, forced into close confines with their captors, actually come to side with them.

I'm not exactly sure the reasons for this, beyond the fact that humans are weird, but I'd wager their recent experiences could do that. "She dangerous?"

"To us?" Lana snorts. "Maybe if Mikito lent her her weapon and we promised not to move for a few minutes. But still…"

"Sorry, thought they'd like some semblance of security," I say, explaining my reasoning.

Lana nods, accepting my explanation. "Now, are you going to stop doing that shit?"

"Huh?" I blink, staring at her. "Oh. You mean hiding the group?"

"Exactly. And doing it by yourself. We're not shrinking violets here, you know," Lana says.

"Shrinking violets?"

"It's a saying. We're not demure ladies of the night," Lana says.

I pause, waiting.

"Okay, that wasn't… you know what I mean."

"I do." I sigh. "Sorry. Just after the last time…"

"The mountain man incident?"

"Yeah." I sigh again. "But you're right. I need to learn to talk to you guys. It's just… hard."

Lana shrugs. "Try, John. Try very hard. Because we can't be a team if you don't talk to us. And we're getting pretty damn tired of this."

We turn together to look at Kyle, who is seated at the fire and staring at the tent with the look of a puppy that has been put out. I debate asking for details. Why it happened. When it happened. How it could be let to continue. But in the end, I leave it alone.

The past doesn't matter. Not here. What is, is. We can move on or drown in the pain.

***

It takes us the better part of a week to convince the majority of the survivors to trust us and join our little convoy. To get their trust, we do everything from duels to quests to a night of drinking. We scare more than a few groups by showing up on their doorsteps even when they move, but in the end, some still won't come. As the convoy finally moves out, Lana and Sam in the lead, I find myself staring at the trucks and chuckling.

"Fifty for your thoughts," Ingrid says beside me.

"I thought it was a penny."

Ingrid smiles, pulling out a bill and offering it to me. I stare at the fifty-dollar note, the plastic looking almost pristine even after all this time.

"Penny. Fifty dollars. Hell, I got an envelope of it somewhere," Ingrid says. "You want it?"

"Yeah… no," I say, shaking my head. So strange to think that we chased these pieces of paper – well plastic now - for all our lives and now she can't even give it away. An illusion, shattered by the System. "I was thinking I should get a pipe and play a song."

"The pied piper?" Ingrid sweeps her gaze over the refugees, some of them driving beat-up old trucks whose only advantage is their lack of technology. "Wasn't he the bad guy?"

"Depends on what he did with the children after," I say.

At least in the version I read, they never did say what happened. I stare at the string of vehicles, thinking of the journey ahead.

Chapter 5

I sigh as I trace the map of the highway, scribbled pre-System population numbers along each of the cities. We'd been in Dawson Creek for three days now, our search parties spread out and pulling whatever survivors they could from the scattered small towns back to our temporary base of operations. We set up here because the highway split from this point, giving us the best access to the smaller communities along those arteries of civilization.

To the east is Grand Prairie, with a population of around sixty thousand, and much farther along the highway is the city of Edmonton. To the west and south, we hit Prince George, which had roughly the same population as Grand Prairie, and eventually Kamloops. The problem is, with the way the highways worked and the Rockies in between, I wasn't entirely sure we could get across the Rockies if we went east and entered Alberta. Technically we'd be traversing a portion of the mountain range that made up the Rockies if we went west, but it was significantly flatter. Which probably meant that the zones would be lower. I had a bad feeling that that wasn't the case with the southern Rockies, where Calgary was. Certainly if the System continued its usual routine, Banff and its surroundings would be murderous.

However, on a practical note, the populations of Edmonton and Calgary were significantly higher than what we'd find in the numerous smaller cities that made up British Columbia. That is, until you hit Vancouver, which had more people in its greater metropolitan area than Alberta's two main cities. In the end, of course, the numbers came up roughly the same. Give or take a few hundred thousand. Before the System.

"And you can't get anything else?" I ask Ali for the hundredth time.

"No. I've mined the sources I have access to. Anything more, and we've got to hit a Shop," Ali says, his arms crossed.

I stare at the map again, knowing that the decision of where to go needs to be made soon. "We got to get these people to a Shop soon."

That's step one. But realistically, the difference in distance between Grand Prairie and Prince George is minor. I hate playing the pied piper, dragging people from place to place, keeping them alive while they stare at us and our Classes, Skills, and equipment with obvious envy. Or in some cases, reverence, which is almost worse.

East or west. The choice might seem easy, but either way we go, we'll be leaving people behind, people we're choosing not to help. There's no way to save everyone, but what kind of people would we be if we didn't try?

It's not purely altruistic, of course. The more humans there are, the higher our chances of actually controlling our own destiny. People are weird, strange, and selfish creatures, but in the end, we're stronger together than alone. For all our fantasies about being the Lone Ranger, we forget that even he had a companion. I might be an introvert by nature, but I understand that people are necessary. There's no way I could check out all the various towns by myself, no way to clear all the dungeons—heck, no way to even build the equipment I need. People are what make a society strong.

For all that, sometimes the burden of choice is left to a few. We've talked about it, weighed the pros and cons together, determined the various options available. In the end though, a decision has to be made and someone has to bear the burden. Better for it to be me, alone, than the group.

And if I have to bear the burden, I might as well go where I want to.

***

"Thanks," Sam says from where he works on his truck while I watch the convoy roll down the highway.

Lana and her pets are ranging out front with the scouts and Ali, sweeping monsters clear ahead of the group and mapping potential problems. We actually found a pair of hunters, one with a Scout and another with a Ranger Class, who are pretty useful. Their ability to Map and share this information backward has improved our movement speed. In fact, it shouldn't take more than a day to get to Prince George, if we decide to push it.

"What for?" I say to Sam, watching as a Mechanic swaps out some spark plugs in an attempt to start up the truck.

"Heading west," Sam says.

I recall that Sam has family there and find myself nodding. Not everyone wants, or has the funds, to buy the information on their families. Sometimes, false hope is better than nothing.

"Not needed. It wasn't really part of the consideration," I say.

My words makes Sam look at me, dark eyes tight before he laughs. "You are a strange one. All right then. Why are we going to Vancouver?"

"I want to see the ocean again," I say with a smile.

My words make Sam blink. With a forced laugh, he ducks his head back under the hood to get the truck started. I'd chide him for not getting it ready before now, but he's been working all night getting as many vehicles working as possible.

"You going to just stand there?" Sam grouses.

I chuckle, turning my attention to him fully. This is going to be a long trip.

***

No wall. That's the first thing that comes to mind when we roll up to the city. Instead, across the Fraser River are watchtowers, blockades made of twisted metal and concrete to slow down assaults. In the distance, I note the other bridge is destroyed, its debris lying abandoned in the water while more watchtowers dot the surroundings. Most are automated, with only a few manned. Once again, I'm impressed. These guys are on the ball, the reception party having received us nearly a hundred kilometers out. For all their caution and making us wait and verifying details about the group, they've also been very courteous.

You have entered a Safe Zone (The Town of Prince George)

Mana flows in this area have been stabilized. No monster spawning will occur within boundaries.

This Safe Zone includes:

- *Town of Prince George City Center*
- *The Shop*
- *Armory*
- *More…*

Our escorts guide us through the blockades and the watchtowers without a word, the reception party taking care of the refugees and allocating them empty houses and apartments. The refugees are grateful and happy as a small crowd of humans gathers around to greet and speak with those who arrive. There are even a few embraces and tears as those once thought lost are found again.

As the refugees split up, we get escorted in deeper by our guards. I let my eyes roam over the guards, watching the way they move, fascinated by the green-blue variations of color on their scales and the way the frills on their heads flap and shift as they speak to one another. As I watch them, I can't help but note the guards have a certain edge I've come to associate with those of us who live on the pointy end of the stick.

Much like Whitehorse, Prince George had been purchased by an alien species, a Clan of Khminnie. By the time they purchased it, six months into the System change, the population had shrunk significantly. Now, nearly half of the population is made of the Khminnie, the lizards owning and running all the important shops and services with humans relegated to being second-class citizens.

Still, the humans here are happy for the most part, at least according to Ali. Living as a second-class citizen might not be ideal, but it is living. It's easy to say you'd never give up a little freedom for safety when you're behind a computer, resting in a warm home with a full stomach. It's another when you've spent every day of a year fearing for your life.

Soon enough, we're waved into a house. Inside, a massive eight-foot-tall Khminnie sprawls on the floor, casually eating strips of raw meat while he listens to a young human lady playing the cello. I flick my glance over the two, noting the lady's Musician Class before I lock on the Clan Head.

Vrymina Ollimar (Level 39 Goldtooth Hunter)

Title: Clan Head of the Frost Claws

HP: 3840/3840

MP: 780/780

Conditions: None

Damn. That's a ton of Health Points. I've seen monsters with higher, but never a fighter. Of course, I can't read the stats for some of those I've met, but it's still impressive. That's a Constitution of nearly 384, unless he has a Skill or two that enhances it. No doubt that's no Basic Class but an Advanced one.

"Greetings, Redeemer," Vrymina says, sitting up when we come in. He stares at me for a second before he twists his head in an angular direction, almost as if he's offering me his neck.

Unconsciously, I mimic the motion before his gaze shifts to Lana, Mikito, and Sam. Ingrid's ghosting around town, not willing to trust them yet.

"Greetings, Clan Head," I say, bowing to him. "This is my party."

I quickly introduce everyone, watching as the pleasantries complete. Once again, I'm thankful that the language downloads the System sells include a series of basic courtesies and customs from the language purchased. Thankfully, general Galactic custom is that one must abide by the rules of the world that you currently visit.

Which makes certain worlds less popular. The Wiblox are golem-like creatures who swap minor body parts upon meeting a new individual, each body part imprinted with their own aura. Visitors are expected to lop off their own minor limbs when visiting, which obviously doesn't work well for most races.

"Tell me, is your party open to taking on a small request from us?" the Clan Head says, getting around to why he invited us to visit him. Not that we were going to turn down the Clan Head after adding a few hundred refugees to his population.

"Uhh…" I glance back toward my friends. The plan had been to stop, Shop, and hop. After all, if the Town is settled, it certainly doesn't need us.

"It's a small matter, and one that we can certainly make worth your while," Vrymina says, leaning forward.

"Well, it can't hurt to look," I say, curious now.

Quest Received

Collect 150 Lumar Hide Pieces

Reward: 20,000 Credits, improved relations with Frost Claws

Accept Quest (Y/N)

"I'm guessing those are System-registered skins?" I send to Ali when I see the notification.

"Got it in one, boy-o. 'Course we could get the bodies skinned too," Ali says, and I nod.

With a little prodding, I get a full description of the target beast, including their average Level of 48. The Lumar are quadpedal creatures with wide mouths, serrated teeth, and tiny ears, with antenna instead of noses and a high resistance to damage due to their scales. Since we get between four to seven pieces of hide from each monster and they work in herds, it's not an impossible task.

"I recall seeing many strong warriors in the Frost Claw clan on our way here…" I say leadingly, curious as to why he'd offer us this quest.

"They are. However, we have great need for many things. In a month, my clan will be taking part in a large gathering and we must bring many gifts. These hides were rare, found only in one other world before your world's introduction to the System. After being transported here though, these beasts have flourished and are now more populous than in the areas we have access to on their original world. Bringing these hides to my people will bring us great prestige," Vrymina explains unabashedly.

While the hides might initially be in great demand, once they start flooding the market, the price is likely going to drop too. Still, that was a problem for someone else. We've got a decent quest.

"May I have a word with my friends?" I ask and, after getting an easy agreement, pull the group aside. It doesn't take long before I come back with our answer. "We accept. If you'll excuse us, Clan Head..."

"You will not stay to feast?"

"No. Perhaps once we are done," I answer, bowing slightly to the lazing reptile-man.

Outside, Mikito turns to me and informs me of the decision the group has come to without my input. "Two groups. Lana, Sam, and Ingrid. Me and you."

"Not three?"

"No. Sam needs more levels and experience first," Mikito says with a shrug. "And I don't have the carrying capacity."

"Right." I nod slowly. With Lana's pets, they can cover a lot more ground and even carry some of the carcasses on the puppies if desired. "Ali, which way?"

"North and west. We'll be heading into the forest around there," Ali replies, flicking his hand to send a map. Within it is a quick display of monsters that we had come across, as well other information about recent Lumar sightings. Most of it was second-hand information, of course, but it was enough for us.

***

In bike mode, Mikito's PAV looked similar to mine. Sleek, modern lines, inflatable tires which could—and usually did—convert to anti-gravity plates. She had even gone with the austere black paint job. In power-armored mode though, the differences were significant. Sleeker and less armored, hers was also surprisingly more responsive than Sabre. She'd sacrificed armor and strength for greater levels of agility, allowing the mecha to supplement her combat style. Mikito had also sacrificed most of her long-range weapon options, instead using mobile, surface-level shields for added protection. On top of that, an ephemeral outline of ghostly armor shrouds the mecha, her Class Skill activated.

I marvel at the way the woman moves, dancing through the herd of Lumar with her naginata, the blade slicing and dicing. Each movement opens a new cut along a creature's hide, her petite figure moving so fast the Lumar never manage to catch up with her. We'd lucked out and found a herd of eleven, nearly double the normal size, grazing at a waterhole. The moment we spotted them, Mikito rushed into the group to take them on, leaving me to deal with the ugly brown-assed monster in front of me.

Lumar Alpha (Level 64)

HP: 1973/2080

MP: 430/430

Condition: Annoyed

I've just unloaded the Inlin's full load of projectiles into its body and watched them bounce off, doing little but bruise it. I don't need Ali to know that the Alpha probably has a physical damage resistance Skill of some sort. As the Inlin reloads, I trigger the sonic pulser, curious to see if it will have any effect.

Enraging your opponent is an effect, right?

Dancing out of the way, I snarl and cut at the monster, watching my blade slice into its hide. It spins quickly on its four feet, grey hide flaring and gaining a purple sheen. I don't have time to pay attention though, as a trio of Lumar break away from the group that have been attempting to attack Mikito and rush me, drawn by the Alpha's call.

I jump, triggering the anti-gravity plates for a second to aid my gravity-defying leap, and launch some of my mini-missiles at them. They fly down, sticky insta-cement stored inside the missiles spraying out and solidifying around the monsters, hampering their movement as it sets. While moving backward, I trigger my other Skills, sending multiple blade slashes at the trapped group. Blood sprays, flesh parts, and bone shows under the onslaught of Blade Strikes, the blue crescents of force damaging the trio.

Then gravity asserts itself. I never make it all the way down; the Alpha having estimated where I would land charged my falling form. It slams into me, sending me spinning through the air. Sabre's shield flares, its integrity beleagured as I spin through the air and tear apart a couple of trees.

When I finally get back on my feet, the Alpha is halfway to me. I raise the Inlin, unloading the weapon once more even as I run to the right. The Alpha snarls, eyes narrowing as it realizes I'm not targeting it but its trapped comrades. Unlike the Alpha, the rest of the Lumar aren't that tough and the projectiles punch into their mangled flesh. A part of me notes that we're not likely going to get any additional hide pieces from those mangled bodies.

After that, it's a matter of kiting the Alpha, using Blade Strikes whenever I get far enough away, and dodging otherwise. Tough and powerful as it is, without the help of its friends, it can't box me in. It only surprises me twice more—the first being the stored kinetic attack it uses to rip apart Sabre's and my Soul Shield, and the second when it temporarily summons the spirits of its fallen comrades. Luckily, it pulled that trick when it was close to death and its friends disappeared when we focused our attacks on the Alpha.

"That... was interesting," I said, gesturing to where the spirits were.

"Yes." Mikito tugs her naginata out of the skull of the Alpha, glowering at the figure and staring at her mangled arm armor. "You don't mind I jumped in, do you?"

"Har. No, you do more damage than I do," I say frankly. "There's a new armor-piercing attack, isn't there?"

"Yes." Mikito pauses before continuing. "You've been slacking off in the fighting recently."

"Eh. You guys need the experience and well…" At Mikito's prompting, I continue. "I've been thinking about the nature of experience. Ever wonder about what experience actually is?"

"No."

I stare at the young lady and sigh. Of course she didn't. Mikito seems quite happy to take the world as it is, beating up monsters and Leveling rather than probing into the details of the System. Truth be told, she's probably had more important things to deal with. Most people are like her, especially since the Fool's Quest is something only idiots like me feel the need to pursue. "Don't worry about it then."

"No, tell me."

"Okay. So what is experience? We get it by killing monsters, completing quests, and in some cases, fulfilling our Class pre-requisites. But what is it?" I say, then pause. "There're a few leading theories in the books I'm reading.

"Firstly, the stress theory. 'Experience' could be shorthand for the changes our bodies undergo when we're stressed—so the higher the stress level, the higher the chance our body has to accept changes created by the System. There are numerous theories about why—nanomachines that need to burrow deeper or intrinsic Mana alterations by the System are just a couple—but it helps explain why in a disparate Level group, the lower Level individuals receive more experience than the higher Level ones. But in the same encounter, without the higher-Level individual, the lower Levels would get even more experience. More stress, right?"

Mikito nods, frowning. "And quests?"

"That's where it breaks down a bit. After all, we've completed the quest, why would we get experience? Some people say it's actually our experience already, just stored up during the process of completing the quest and given out at once. Others say it might actually be the quest giver's experience—the nanobots or Mana or whatever, accumulated by the individual but stored offsite to be distributed later. It'd explain why quests really only come from higher-level individuals or via quest boards," I say. "The second theory that I personally like is the Mana siphon theory."

Mikito nods, having looted the bodies and started walking out of the clearing, forcing me to follow as we hunt for more monsters.

"Well, experience in this theory is just the System rewarding us for being good Mana siphons. The more Mana we use—say, in a fight—the more experience we get. The more likely we'll use Mana—and survive to do it—the more experience we get, which gets us Levels to use it more. Of course, it also encourages us to not fight stupidly hard monsters and die or pick on creatures we can beat by flicking our fingers," I say. "This theory relies on the System wanting us to use Mana, but…"

"You like it," Mikito states. "But why sit back?"

"Sam and Lana need more levels—so whether it's more stress or more Mana use, me helping doesn't add to their experience. I've also got Ali tracking my experience gains recently while I don't fight and just practice my Spells and Skills. I wanted to see which, if any, made sense and how different it was compared to the books I've been reading. Did you know that you gain Mana on a regular basis even if you aren't fighting? Not a lot, but it's a non-zero amount."

"No. But why are you doing all this?"

"Well, most of the experiments were run on stable, non-Dungeon planets. I figured if I can get a series of baselines, we could run the numbers backward using some of the formulas presented and debunk them or potentially improve on a few." When Mikito just continues to give me a blank stare, I add, "If I can do that, I can publish a paper in the System with my findings. I might even make a few Credits."

Mikito stares at me for a long moment before she turns her mecha away, walking off without a word. I can almost hear the word "Baka," even if she doesn't say it. Okay, fine. My hobbies might be a little weird, but I'm trying to find something a little more productive than being a combat junkie.

Chapter 6

Finishing the quest took a few days of hunting, more of the time spent actually locating the damn monsters than fighting. What was that saying? Hours of waiting and a few minutes of heart-pounding terror? Either way, the Clan Head was suitably thankful and approved the quest completion immediately once we got back. He even waived the charges on the butchering, which boosted our Credits a bit.

Since I had no current needs in the Shop, I decided to save my Credits, though Sam took the opportunity to go shopping. He refused to show us what he bought though, muttering about it "not being ready." The most I could get was that instead of buying completed pieces, he elected to put together his equipment himself.

Other than a few grateful refugees who slowed us down when we left, leaving the alien-owned town was pretty simple. Not surprisingly, there's a significant drop in the number of people who follow us. Most of those who come have family or friends they desperately need to meet.

The drive down to Kamloops was long and boring. Since most of the settlements near Prince George had been cleared of survivors, we had no reason to stop and instead journeyed south directly. It wasn't until we hit 100 Mile House that we found signs of any living being, and in this case, it was a small and entirely unfriendly group of humans. Deciding that we'd prefer not to damage our equipment, we left the gun-happy group to their own devices and swung around the survivors to head to Kamloops.

Late spring was in bloom all around us as we drove to the city, flowers waving gently and alternately perfuming and poisoning the air. As we traveled, we noted the shifting zone levels, some dipping as low as the twenties while other times spiking up to the fifties. Forested mountains surrounded us while hungry bears and other hibernating animals prowled the roadways, occasionally attempting a human-sized snack.

The evolution into a Dungeon World had brought some significant changes to our world. The purple-and-pink forested mountain, the field of poisonous flowers, and the dryad that danced through the trees, tempting us, were just the biggest outliers. Pine and oak now combined with silverkennel and unnzwek trees while squirrels battled imps for nuts and survival.

Sadly, outside of those lone survivors at 100 Mile House, we found no others. Of course, considering it was technically only a few hours' drive between 100 Mile House and Kamloops, it could be that they'd made their way in. It was something I think we all preferred to believe.

Hopefully, that's what happened and not something more sinister. Unfortunately, sinister might just be the case, especially with the group sitting on what looks like a tank at the Thompson River crossing, waiting for us.

"Good day," I greet the group as we roll in slowly.

"Who are you?" one of the group calls. He's got four arms, two on either side, and an orange, ruddy face, his body covered in a silver bodysuit-armor combo.

"Adventurers from the north," I call back, smiling widely. I could say visitors or travelers, but Adventurers has a nice ring to it and carries specific connotations in this new world.

"Registered?" Four Arms says.

Crap. Bluff called.

"No," I call back, smiling widely. "No guild."

"No problem, we're always looking for Adventurers," Four Arms says and waves us forward. "We'll just need to escort you in. Also, you know about our entrance fee?"

"No. What is it?"

"Just five thousand Credits per person."

I cough, staring at the man. Five thousand Credits is insane! *"That is insane, right?"*

"Yup. That's called a shakedown, boy-o."

"John?" Lana asks, glancing dismissively at the group.

Ever since Ali upgraded the last time, he's been able to share the Status information with the party, allowing Lana and group to see their info if he wants to. It still takes a bit of an effort, so he only does that when he expects a fight, like now.

"Chill. We're here to play nice," I mutter softly.

That gets a snort from Ingrid.

"It's okay if you don't have it. We've got some very reasonable loan agreements," Four Arms continues, smiling widely. "Why don't we escort you in?"

"Sure," I agree immediately.

These guys all have Levels in the thirties and forties at the Basic Level, which makes them not much more difficult than the monsters we killed. Admittedly, they're augmented by technology, but I still can't see them being a major problem.

Dropping my voice, I ask the group, "How come they're so confident? We out-Level them by a lot."

"That'd be me," Ingrid says, her voice cackling over the radio. "Upgraded one of my Skills and I can now push false information out instead of just hiding it. Since we're grouped, I dropped all our levels by a bit. Well, everyone but yours, John."

I grunt, nodding. Fair enough. My System level looks weird anyway at 37. Since there's no Basic Class attached to it and my Class is rare enough that most wouldn't know of it—at least not out here at a glance—I basically read as significantly weaker than I am.

The group surrounds us the moment we cross the bridge, "escorting" us to town with the tank at the back of the procession. On our left, the Thompson River feeds into Kamloops Lake, running alongside us all the way in. Abandoned resorts, warehouses, and residences dot the land we drive by. As we pass the golf course, I tilt my head to the side, staring toward where the glowing dot of an established dungeon flashes on my map. The group around us says nothing, so I follow suit, tagging and sending the information to the party. Something to look into when we have time.

On the drive in, I cudgel my brain for information on the town. I've driven by a few times, mostly on the way to a provincial park for weekend hiking. Kamloops was mostly a mining and forestry town, from what I recall, with a decent trade in tourists during the summer. There was a major rail line and an airport, with the 5, 97, and the Trans-Canada highways all connecting in it. Oh, and it had a university too.

As we finally approach the city after swinging away from the lake for a bit, I recall a few other facts. Most importantly, Kamloops is a split city—nearly two-thirds of the city lies across the river in the northwest, connected by a bridge. The northeast, which is also split by the meeting of another river, doesn't really have much. The city center itself is on this side though, which makes me wonder if they consolidated at all.

You have entered a Safe Zone (The Town of Kamloops)

Mana flows in this area have been forcefully stabilized. No monster spawning will occur within boundaries.

This Safe Zone includes:

- *Town of Kamloops City Center*
- *The Shop*
- *11 Farming Centers*
- *More…*

Finally, we're officially in the town boundaries. A quick review of the map information shows that the "town" is actually only everything on this side, the other portion of the town abandoned. It makes sense to do this; after all, it makes hitting the land requirements to create a town easier.

"Looks like they paid to specify the town boundaries," Ali sends to me, staring at the information. His fingers waggle and he stares at more information before grunting. *"That's why. These guys do have the money. They're part of the Thirteen Moon Sect. Cartel? Gang? You get my meaning, right, boy-o?"*

"You're saying that the owners of Kamloops—the Thirteen Moon Sect— are rich and ruthless?" I reply to Ali out loud, letting the party into our conversation over the radios.

"Got it in one. Nasty little group, known more for their criminal activities than their governance—but they are a government. Damn it…" Ali falls silent. Since he doesn't have a radio, he can only talk to me or out loud.

I understand his annoyance. Now that they know we don't have a Guild backing us, we're in an exposed position. Guilds in the Galactic Council are the equivalent of companies in our old world, if you'd accept the use of a loose metaphor. Big enough Guilds are like multinational corporations, often powerful enough to bully smaller countries or groups. In this case, the Sect is probably the equivalent of a small country. Due to a law passed a few thousand years ago, Guilds aren't allowed to own towns and villages, a necessary step to ensure they don't get too powerful.

"Boss, Henri's got a bad, bad feeling about this place," Sam's voice cackles over the radio.

It takes me only a moment to recall who Henri is—Henrietta Poskart, a Seer with Class Skills that dealt with "seeing" things, whether in the present or future.

"No shit," Lana says. "On the left, one hundred twenty meters."

I glance over and spot the group of humans walking along the road, carrying the carcass of a furred and barbed creature on their shoulders. They are dirty, disheveled, and malnourished—which is saying something in a world with a Clean spell and Mana nourishment. Behind them, a Dwarf walks with a whip, cracking it across a back when he thinks they're slowing down. Over the radio, I hear the hiss of exhaled breath.

"*Serfs.*"

"Serfs," I say, repeating Ali as he provides further information. "They've been bought by the Dwarf under an indentured contract for two hundred years."

"Two hundred years!" Lana splutters.

"Don't forget, gene therapy and the System have increased our lifespan a lot," Ingrid says. "How long, we're still not certain, but a few hundred sounds just about right."

"Sounds like slavery to me," Sam says angrily.

"Ali says to keep calm. We can't afford to take them on. They might be smaller as a group than the Duchess, but they're still a government. They're spread out across multiple worlds," I say, doing my best to keep my voice calm and soothing. I stare at the map, quickly resorting the data as I look for information about the Sect in the city.

One mid-Level Advanced Class and three others in the low teens Advanced Classes make up the major punching power of the Sect in the city. Two of the low-Level Advanced Classes are near the mid-Level. The third is at what I'm assuming is the butchering yard or mess hall, from the way the dots congregate and move around in that area. After that, we have another dozen in the Level 30s and a few in the 40s of the Basic Class with nearly a score in the 20s. Quite a few, though at a glance, only two-thirds of them are combat Classers.

It takes me a moment to figure out why. Most of the humans have Levels in the twenties and thirties, and the vast majority aren't combat Classes. The highest non-party human is a Level 37 Marksman, from what I can see, though there might be a few more out of the city right now. With that kind of Level disparity, they'd only need the top group to keep everyone else in check. In the end, the numbers present in Kamloops don't matter. It's their overall strength that is a concern.

"We just going to sit here and let them do this?" Sam growls as we drive through the deserted streets. Whatever you have to say about them, the Sect has done well at clearing the streets of broken down automobiles and other refuse of pre-System technology.

"What do you want us to do? Kill them all? Then what? We might be able to leave and escape their revenge, but what about everyone else?" Ingrid says bitingly. "Ali's right. Stay out of it. Anything we do is going to make it worse."

"This doesn't sit right with me," Sam says.

"Nor for us. But we'll hold back for now," Lana says softly, something unreadable in her voice.

"*Will you look at that, you humans can learn,*" Ali says wryly. Still, I hear the tinge of bitterness in his voice. After all, Ali's presence as my Companion is due to a similar contract, as I understand it. He won't explain it in detail though, even when I've pushed him.

"Button up, people, we're here," I say as we finally come to a stop.

Unlike Roxley's ostentatious silver skyscraper, Kamloops's city center building is a grey, cinder block government building situated near the center of the new Town. Ugly and boring, without a trace of soul.

***

Mikito and I stride through the corridors to meet the titular owner of the city—or is it administrator?—escorted by a trio of guards including Four Arms. The rest of the party is outside, keeping watch over the vehicles and the survivors, the pets spread out around the group and chewing on a snack. The crunch and crack of thigh-sized bones ripple through the coms, a not-so-subtle warning about what the pets could do if released.

Seated behind an oak desk, a slim, nearly cadaverous humanoid-avian creature bobs its head as we enter. No lips, just a beak that chirps loudly, translated a second later through speakers set across its throat. Behind him are his bodyguards, the pair of low-Level Advanced Classes, their arms crossed as they glower at me. One's a black-skinned orc, a Hakarta derivative of some form. The other looks similar to Four Arms behind us, except he's bigger and sports six arms.

"Greetings, Adventurers. I understand you are lacking in funds for the entry fee?" the avian says when my gaze finally comes back to rest on him.

"It's a little steep," I say, coming to a rest position in front of the avian. I'd sit, but there's no chair on this side of the desk. I take a moment and scan his status bar.

Bimmox (Level 36 Sect Sub-Chief)

HP: 1080/1080

MP: 2430/2430

Conditions: None

"*That's not a combat class, is it?*" I send to Ali and get a confirmation immediately.

Advanced Class, but non-combat. On the other hand, that doesn't mean he doesn't have his own tricks up his sleeve. After all, there's no reason why he couldn't have bought combat Class Skills in the Shop. In fact, I'd almost guarantee he has. It does mean, however, that there are only two specialized combat Classers in town and both are right across from us.

"Surely a group as well-equipped as you can afford it," Bimmox screeches before the robotic voice translates a moment later.

"Not for all our people," I say, curious to see where he's going with this.

"Ah, those are not chattel for sale?" Bimmox says.

"And if they were?"

"We could negotiate. Though their Classes are common and their Levels low. We could not offer more than a few thousand Credits per person. The cost of upgrading them to a useful Level, well, you understand," Bimmox says.

"I see." I exhale, staring at the monster. I push down the flash of revulsion, forcing peace and tranquility into my mind by sheer willpower. "We won't be selling them. We'll just keep moving on."

"Well, there's a problem with that, you see. You've already entered my Town and have yet to pay us," Bimmox says.

Behind me, I sense the trio of guards spreading out.

"John, we've got more people surrounding the vehicles," Lana's voice comes over the radio.

I mentally adjust the radio settings, letting them hear my side of the conversation as well as Bimmox's. "Well, Bimmox, what exactly are you saying?"

"That we will get our entry fee, one way or the other," Bimmox says.

"We've got thirteen survivors and my group, so that's ninety thousand Credits in total? How do we do this?" I say, my voice calm. I hear a slight gasp over the radio, too soft for me to make out who it is. I understand though— it's a hell of a lot of Credits.

"Ssss…" Bimmox hisses and stares at me. "Unfortunate, but each entrant must pay for their own entry fee. Unless they are Serfs of another."

"I see," I continue to say calmly. "And if they were?"

"I'd ask to see the contracts of course. Though I should add that falsifying such documentation is a crime." Bimmox blinks, eyelids closing from the front to back in a thoroughly alien manner.

"I think if I brought out such documentation, I'd find that there's another law I'd have to deal with, no?"

"What can I say? Laws are laws," Bimmox hisses after that, its body moving forward and backward. After a moment, I realize it's the monster's equivalent of laughter.

"Perhaps you can send these laws to me. My Companion can check them over to ensure we comply with them all."

"Ah… that is impossible. Only the Administrators may see such information," Bimmox says again, rocking back and forth.

"Sounds like he's taking you for a ride," Lana says over the comms. "We can pay it on our side, but the survivors…"

"Why don't we cut the bullshit?" I say to Bimmox, my smile widening, the walls of peace and calm that surround my mind cracking. "Give me your bottom line."

76

"Bottom line?" Bimmox looks puzzled for a second before clarity returns. "Ah, a colloquialism. We just want everyone to comply with the laws. If the individuals behind you are unable to do so, we can offer a loan of the five thousand Credits with appropriate interest rates."

"I'm assuming we won't be allowed to leave once we take the loan," I say and get a nod from Bimmox. "You're not giving us a lot of choice here."

"The law is the law," Bimmox replies.

"Don't do this."

"Are you threatening us? Just because your party managed to clear a few dungeons and receive some Credits to purchase equipment means little. You're still weak," Four Arms says behind me.

I turn my head slightly and glance at Mikito, who has her helmet down. The black-and-silver reflection from her helmet's visor stares back at me impassively, offering nothing.

"Well, human, are you paying the fee?" Bimmox says, continuing to rock back and forth, obviously amused and reveling in his power.

I grin at him, my eyes going cold as the anger I've been pushing aside rushes in. I tried. I really did.

"*Oh hell, here we go again,*" Ali says.

***

The fireball ripples around their shield, spiking the temperature by hundreds of degrees in seconds. I see the shield flickering even as the aliens behind me shout in anger. Mikito shifts, her naginata spinning and lashing out at those behind us even as her ghost armor flickers into existence, taking a portion of the blast damage. My own exposed skin dries out, scorching and cracking, my body cooking.

Bimmox hisses and cackles, his translator not translating whatever he said. Probably good tactics since its likely orders. Long, clawed fingers dance across empty air, sending out an alert. His bodyguards have a gun and a crossbow leveled at me but do not shoot, waiting for the shield to fall. I've already shouted my warning to the rest of the party, trusting that the group can handle themselves. Sabre's on automated defense mode, transformed and attacking, while Sam's taken control of Mikito's PAV.

My sword and the conjoined blades stab into the shield, punching a hole with ease, but the shield refuses to fall. I channel a Blade Strike, twisting with my hips to cut downward even as the attack feeds directly into the shield. The shield flickers as my Mana drops with the Skill, finally freeing my blades. Another twist and Cleave, the blades shattering the shield when they finally connect. A red dot behind me disappears as Mikito continues taking on all three Basic combat Classers at the same time.

The moment the shield falls, Bimmox hits me with a spell, the red beam throwing me through the door and down the corridor. Pain, as it cuts into my torso, halves my health in seconds. The bodyguards open fire, both of their shots missing my fast retreating body. The crossbow bolt tears into the side of one their friends who accidentally sidestepped into its path.

"Is that all?" Bimmox screeches, the automated translation carrying some of the mocking tone in his voice. "You people are too—"

"Weak?" I ask, standing.

I toss up a Soul Shield and Greater Regeneration, stalking forward. The bodyguards have already shifted to target Mikito, Six Arms dropping his crossbow to wade in with short swords while the other waits for an opening. Realizing I'm still up and moving, the other bodyguard swings his weapon to target me.

"How? You should be dead!" Bimmox says.

"We cheat," I reply.

Bimmox jabs his hand forward again, the spell blasting. I twist out of the way but he's already shifting the beam to track me, falling for my feint. The Shield flares as the bodyguard's and Bimmox's attack caresses its edges.

I Blink Step behind Bimmox, twisting at the hips and knees to let me build up momentum for the cut that enters his waist. He might have a few powerful spells and a decent amount of hit points, but my sword is boosted with Mana Imbue and Cleave as I attack. The first blade cuts into his waist and exits just above the middle of his chest, tearing flesh and cracking ribs. Then the follow-up blades land.

Bimmox screams, his body butchered as his reflexive dodge puts new parts of his body into line with the floating blades that follow my attack. Fingers twist and jerk, clawed tips flashing outward to catch his balance, then Bimmox disappears, leaving my follow-up stab to strike air. His bodyguard elbows me in the face, throwing me backward before bringing his rifle to bear, triggering a series of shots I deal with by cutting his rifle apart.

"Ali!" I shout, knowing we can't let Bimmox heal. That attack of his would have killed most of my friends.

"I'm on it!" Ali spins in a circle, searching.

The remains of his rifle discarded, the bodyguard charges me with a pair of punch knives in his hands. We clash, spinning and cutting, blood flying and my shield failing. A lunge cuts across my face, tearing my cheek open even as I impale the Hakarta. I leave the sword inside him while calling another to hand and finish lopping off his arm, leaving me staggering back as the bodyguard kicks me away. Mikito appears behind him. Her naginata tears through the air and he drops, neck separated by a surgical cut. As suddenly as that, the fight in the office is over.

"Lana," I order Mikito, and she dashes out, her Hasted body blurring.

."Behind you. He's in the city core room," Ali instructs me.

I spin around, staring at the wall behind me, then cut into it. I trigger Cleave again and again, ignoring the Mana cost as I race to get in as fast as possible. If Kamloops is anything like Whitehorse, the city has some automated defenses that are controlled from the city core. I need to turn them off. In the background, I hear shouts and gasped words as my friends fight outside.

A fist-sized hole finally appears and I look inside, triggering Blink Step the moment I can see within the simple cream-colored room. The Skill carries me within and above the waiting Bimmox, my sword swinging as I release a Blade Strike. The attack catches Bimmox across his shoulders, ripping loose his already injured shoulder and bathing the room in too-bright red blood. The avian falls, gasping in pain as its lungs no longer work. Even the regeneration potion it's drunk is unable to keep up with the damage I lay on it as I land, stabbing again and again into the body.

With the alien dead, I grasp the floating city core, the diamond-shaped core fitting easily into my hand. Nothing happens at first, the core taking a moment to check its requirements before it flashes a notification.

Would you like to take control of the Town of Kamloops?
_(Y/N)_

"Yes," I snap, mentally willing acknowledgement.

I snarl as the damn core makes me wait again, a small counter appearing in the corner of my eye. Two minutes. I have to sit and wait for two minutes while the damn System lets everyone who is anyone know that I'm trying to take the city.

Congratulations! You are now the owner of the Town of Kamloops

Current Population: 8,785

City Treasury: 11.7 Million Credits

City Mana: 2,309 Mana Points

Taxes: 20% Sales Tax on Shop

Facilities: Shop, City Center, Educational Institution (1), Retail Outlets (15), Butchering Yard (1), Farms (7)

Defenses: Tier IV Defense Shield, Automated Tier IV Defense Turrets (17), 6 Automated Internal Sentries

First Settlement Acquired!

Bonus +10,000 Experience

A moment and the six changed to five automated sentries. It only takes me a moment to realize why. I snarl, raising my hand as I desperately try to figure out how to turn them off.

"Defense targets change. Target all individuals marked as Thirteen Moons," Ali chants as he floats up to me, fingers waggling in mid-air, then he shoots me a bemused look. "What are you waiting for, boy-o? I got this. Go help the ladies."

I pause, conflicted. If someone gets in here…

"Go," Ali snaps.

I nod, trusting the little olive-skinned Spirit, and run out. Even as I run, I see the dots in my minimap flickering as friends, foes, and neutrals die. Time to finish this.

Chapter 7

The rest of the fight was simple enough. The other Advanced Class Sect member disappeared, never engaging us. The other combat Classers never got their balance long enough to attack us as a group, which meant that my team tore through them without stop. It didn't help them that Ingrid kept assassinating anyone who showed any real leadership qualities. Afterward, it was just a matter of calming the population down. Thankfully, I could leave that to Lana as I walked back into the City Center.

"Hey, the Serfs are going to be fine, right? No death spells or soul chains or anything that will kill them when the Sect is kicked out? Or if it's commanded?" I ask Ali as I walk in, the thought striking me only now. A cold sweat breaks out on my skin as I wonder if I've just condemned a bunch of people to death.

"Not that I can see. It's possible but rare and expensive. And not effective in the long-term. Kind of like the sterility shots," Ali says.

I blink as the System quest updates when Ali mentions that. Well, learning that the System wants us alive, or at least not dead immediately, is interesting but not important at this second.

"How deep in the hole are we?" I say to the Spirit, dismissing the System notification.

"Yes, how badly did we step in it?" Ingrid's voice floats from the corner where shadows gather. Her Skill drops and reveals the young First Nation woman leaning against the wall. She's attempting to look blasé, but I know her well enough to read the tension.

"Ingrid." I nod to her and watch the Assassin pull out a nail file to clean her nails of the accumulated blood. For a moment, I wonder why she doesn't use a Clean spell, but she's probably doing it on purpose.

"Depends. The Sect isn't going to take this lying down, and the fact that you missed a few means they'll probably know sooner rather than later. On the other hand, they don't have a portal or a communication array set up, so they're probably not meant to report in that often. My guess is courier check-ins and arranged meetings via the Shop," Ali says.

I nod, knowing that some Shops even set up specific inter-dimensional meeting rooms to facilitate such transactions. Guilds, for example, all run their own Shop.

"If the survivors really have left, we've probably got a few hours before the Earthbound Sect learns of your attack. For the main Sect? Figure a few weeks to a month at most before they know something went wrong," Ali says.

"And then…?" I extract a piece of chocolate while I wait for the other shoe to drop.

"Then they'll likely try to take it back. They're not the talking type, so they'll come for you. Probably start local first. Kelowna probably, because it's closer, unless they feel they need more heavy hitters," Ali says. "If that fails, they'll pull from Vancouver and Seattle, where they've got their real big boys. If all that fails, I wouldn't be surprised if they pulled from their Galactic forces."

"Master Classes?" I say, rubbing my chin. I got my ass kicked the last time I fought a high-level Advanced Combat class. I can't even imagine what a Master Class is like.

"Unlikely," Ali says. "It's a steep pyramid and the Sect isn't exactly, well, that tight knit. It's not like the Duchess, who can just order her people around. Most of them are relatively independent. Master Classes are a power onto themselves. They'll likely send some mid-to-Advanced tier Combat classes to deal with you. It's easier to dig up a few of those than a single Master. I'd be surprised if they even sent a single Master Class to Earth."

I nod slowly, understanding Ali's point. My Advanced Class is already over-powered compared to a Basic Class, so a Master Class would be an entirely different existence. While Earth has a few Master Class-worthy locations—a certain dragon comes to mind—I've yet to come across many locations that would be worthwhile for them to visit. As I understand it, it'll take a while for the ambient Mana pools to deepen sufficiently. The fact that my experience gain has slowed down also drives home how hard it is to advance after a certain point. And I've got the advantage that I didn't have to go through all the Basic Class levels.

"Great. Just a couple of Advanced Classes." Ingrid snorts, shaking her head.

I glance at her, still seeing the bunch of question marks hanging over her head on her Status bar, before smiling slightly. I understand her point though. Mikito is only in the beginning stages of the Advanced Classes, and the rest of the team hasn't even reached that point yet. If we were to tangle with a bunch of mid-tier Advanced Classes right now, we'd be in real trouble. We only stood a chance today because everyone around here is so low-Leveled that the Sect didn't bother to send high-Level enforcers.

"Repercussions for the population?" I say, glancing outward. If we leave now, we could probably run. I don't like it, but if leaving means the people here aren't killed…

"Varies. Those who fought on your side or helped out? Probably some torture, extended services," Ali says. "The rest will likely be left alone. Higher overall taxes, maybe some beatings and more pressure applied to drive the point home."

"Not horrible," I say, grimacing. "You said they've got Kelowna and Vancouver though?"

"Pretty much all of BC. However, they're focusing their attention on Seattle right now. From the information I've garnered, it's been more troublesome than they expected."

"Interesting," I say.

We could go, take everyone up to Prince George, but I'm not entirely sure bringing a ton of people, especially some indentured individuals, would work out as well as we'd like. If the city didn't take them in, we'd have to drag them over to Edmonton. Hell, I don't think we have a way to transport this many even if we want to.

"We planning on leaving?" Ingrid says, looking at me.

"No. Maybe. I'm exploring options," I say, grimacing.

"We're not leaving," Ingrid says, her tone flat. "We started this, we're finishing it. We can't just go."

"But…" I want to point out the amount of time we'd waste. How big an opponent we're facing. And I shut up, because I realize it doesn't matter. Not to Ingrid. Or me. She's right. We started this. "Fine. Get the girls to clean up and start looking for help. We're likely going to have a bunch of visitors in the next few days and we're going to need all the help we can get."

"Of course," Ingrid says, bowing slightly then fading from view.

"You know, you just called Sam a girl," Ali teases me. When I just stare at the Spirit, he drops the act and gets serious. "What do you want me to do?"

"They lost because they underestimated us and let us in past their defenses. We can't let them do that to us. Let's see what we can do about upgrading the city's defenses," I say. With bad guys on the way, defense is the number one priority.

A moment later, Ali pulls information from the city core, sending it directly to me to review.

Tier IV Defense Shield

HP: 15000/15000

HP Regeneration Rate: 250/minute

Automated Tier IV Defense Turrets (17)

Base Damage: 75

Charges: 20/20

4 Automated Internal Sentries (2 damaged)

Core: Tier II Numax Mana Engine

Battery Duration: 6 Hours Standby, 30 Minutes Active

Weapons: Musashi Grisin Mark III Beam Rifle

Interesting. One thing I've learned is that while beam rifles are ubiquitous, they're also generally considered the lowest form of weaponry. Not because they can't do much damage, but because the amount of damage they can do is limited to their initial construction. Mass manufactured weaponry can do damage, but it isn't as effective as something individually crafted by a support Class. In contrast, projectile weaponry generally varies in damage, especially if you're willing and able to pay for the hand-crafted—and Skill-generated—ammunition.

With a flick of my hand, I call up the map of Kamloops again and pull the map out a bit. The town is settled at a crossing of two rivers. The Thompson River runs west to east and is joined by the North Thompson River, dividing the city into three parts. The northwest section is the most expansive and holds a large number of residential houses, the MacArthur Island Park, and the Kamloops Airport. Northeast, there's little development, mostly industrial and farming locations. Lastly, south of the Thompson River is downtown Kamloops, which the adjusted town boundaries contained.

Another thought and the map flickers, showing the extent of the shield. It covers the entirety of the adjusted town boundaries and reaches almost to the edge of the highway that runs south of the city proper. The seventeen defense turrets are spread equally around the perimeter of the shield wall. The automated sentries are located in the town center. From the looks of it, we managed to damage two of the six sentries from the earlier fight. Oops.

"Hey, why are the turrets on buildings?" I ask Ali.

"Makes it easier to create the safe zone. Building a turret on an existing building adds it to the System, adjusting the Mana flows and property requirements. Also, where else would they put them? In the middle of the road?" Ali says.

I ignore the challenge, looking instead at the defenses. Assuming they intend to send help from either Vancouver or Kelowna, the chances are they'll be hitting us from the east or west via Highway 1. Of course, once the No. 1 approaches the city from the west, it splits up into smaller feeder roads into the city, which means where they'd actually make an entrance is more difficult to tell. At least in the east, there are fewer feeder roads. On top of all that, they could just ignore the roads entirely, entering the city by walking through buildings or the fields that surround the city.

"How are we going to do this?" I mutter to myself, staring at the information.

The shield limits attackers from just strolling in, but since it's a single shield, attackers could split and attack across multiple areas, weakening the shield overall before breaching it. Do it well enough and we'd have to split our troops to deal with each attack. If they were smart, they could trick us in splitting our forces and then make an end run to the city center.

"Are we able to split the shield?" I ask.

"What do you mean?" Ali says, looking at me.

"Maybe have the shield powered in different sections? So that if one side fails, the other still stays up?"

"Sure. A few ways of doing that. We can buy multiple shields and set them to generate side-by-side. There are also fragmented shields which basically do the same thing. A lot spaceships use those."

"Show me."

Tier II Defense Shield

HP: 15,000

HP Regeneration Rate: 250/minute

Cost: 10.3 Million Credits

Tier III Multi-segment Defense Shield

HP: 10,000 per segment

HP Regeneration Rate: 200/minute

Cost: 25 Million Base Cost + 10 Million per segment

"Expensive," I exclaim.

"True. But if you're looking at creating multiple segments, it's a better option in the long-term," Ali says.

"Are the shields upgradeable?"

"Yes."

"Good to know." Not that we can afford it, but the concern of having our forces split continues to bother me. "Sensors?"

"They've got the most basic system," Ali replies. "No upgrades at all to it. Figure they've been relying on their people."

"Make sense. We don't have that."

A thought or two later and new information appears, showing the wide variety of options available for sensor upgrades. I tell the System to hide everything that the town can't afford. I'm still given too many options, so I hide everything that costs more than ten percent of our current treasury. Even then, there are over a hundred options.

"Arse. Ali…"

"I got you," Ali says, smirking at my attempts to navigate the town's Shop options by myself. He waves and the list expands, repopulating everything. Next, the information shrinks again suddenly as he inputs new parameters, the total number shrinking to about fifteen options. He hums, the windows flickering between each quickly.

"What are you doing?" I ask.

"Sorting. I filtered by companies by Galactic Reputation points first and then by reviews from trusted sources. Got rid of your percent cost too because you won't find anything worthwhile. Right now, I'm looking for the knock-offs," Ali says.

"Trying to get rid of them?"

"Goblin's arse, no! I'm keeping them. No such thing as your patent laws in the System, so companies copy each other's designs all the time."

"Then why would anyone make anything new?" I say with a frown. Doesn't seem to make much sense.

"A few reasons. For Engineers and other craftsmen, you can't advance and gain as much experience if you stick to copying. Then of course you've got the innovators, the ones who just have to make their own thing. Also, most companies are smart enough to ensure that their schematics require a high-Level individual to make the final product or a portion of it, which limits their competition," Ali explains, the windows finally stopping their flickering. "So what are you looking for?"

"Data about our attackers—visual, audio, and minimap. Preferably far enough out that we can spot them before they arrive, but I'll settle for stopping hidden attackers," I say.

"All right then, boy-o. How about these three?" Ali says.

Tier IV Musami Sensor Array

The Musami Sensor Array is the venerable workhorse of the sensor world. Providing an all-round suite of sensors, the Mumsami sensor array will provide real-time data for towns the Galaxy over.

Range: 10km

Sensitivity Rating: 6

Cost: 7.1 Million Credits

Tier III Kangana Nanite Net

Developed from a nanite factory, the nanite net spreads across its designated scanning area, providing real-time, high-accuracy data on all personnel. Additional add-ons available.

Range: 5km

Sensitivity Rating: 8

Cost: 10.1 Million Credits

Tier IV Sahwano Bionetwork Sensor Grid

A bionetwork sensor grid relies on ambient Mana to power its functioning. While less sensitive than other options, the bionetwork grid is more circumspect and has a lower upkeep cost.

Range: Varies. Initially 3km, with growth up to 40km

Sensitivity Rating: 4

Cost: 3 Million Credits

I frown, staring at the information.

I don't have to wait long before Ali explains. "The first one is your bog-standard tech option. The second is an upgrade of the sensor suite—more expensive obviously and higher Mana cost for set up, but much more likely to punch through Class Skills and other tech-related stealth options. You also have the option of adding additional fun programming to the nanites, including attack options. Lastly, the bionetwork starts close to the city but will grow out the farthest. It'll take time, but because it uses ambient Mana sources and has a natural camouflage ability, it's actually much harder for attackers to know they've been spotted."

"Interesting," I say, staring at the windows once again.

I have to admit, the low cost of the last option is extremely enticing. I run through in my head what I need for the upcoming fight. A way to mark the Sect's approach, preferably good enough to pick out potential feints or distractions. Then a defense or two to stop them from breaking in immediately, which is why splitting the shield helps. It'd be nice to get a secondary shield layered directly behind the first, but that's just as expensive as splitting the shield. On top of that, we actually have to deal with the attackers. Which means we'll want additional firepower if possible. Unfortunately, we just don't have enough funds in the town, and considering all these upgrades are in the millions of Credits, I can't even reach into my own pocket to help.

"Any way to know what they'd send at us? Immediately and in the future?" I ask.

"Even the System can't tell the future," Ali says with a snort. "However, we could pull information on the people the Sect have on Earth and do some guessing."

"How expensive would it be?"

"Expensive," Ali states with a flat tone that says it all.

Buying information from the System is never cheap. Purchasing information that we have no good way of getting always makes it more expensive, and if the Sect is trying to hide that information, it'd be even higher.

"All right, let's get the bionetwork sensor grid up first. That'll give us at least some information," I say, making some quick decisions. Even if it is purchased from the Shop, it'll still take a few hours for the entire sensor grid to spread. Figure it'll take the survivors five to six hours to get to Kelowna, another five to six back, and a few hours of talking, and we'll likely see some company by tomorrow.

"Done."

I watch Ali drop the sensor grid over the city, the map shifting and the town's Credit amount dropping. I bite my lips, thinking of what next to do. What was it again? Know yourself, know your enemy, know the terrain? I've got Lana and the team figuring out our resources. The enemy we don't have time to really dig into—not without costing us too much. That leaves the last…

The Sect knows the terrain probably better than we do. If you don't like the rules, change them. If playing tower defense games ever taught me anything, it's that defenses need depth. Of course, it's not a game and towers built out here are likely to get destroyed, but the idea holds merit. So, disposable and wide-ranging.

"Mines," I say, waving my hands at the map. A few quick adjustments and I've marked out the boundaries, blocking off the area just outside the shield.

Once the area is highlighted, Ali pulls up the cost.

High Explosive Mine Field

A standard, high-explosive mine field that mixes anti-personnel and anti-vehicular mines.

Damage: 100 per mine

Cost (for marked area): 2.5 Million (Tier V) / 4.5 Million (Tier IV)

Tier IV Chaos Mine Field

For the customer who likes a surprise, this mine field consists of a series of buried chaos mines which released stored chaos energy. Effects, as always, vary. Chaos Inc. takes no responsibility for the use of this product.

Damage: Varies

Cost (for marked area): 12 Million

Lumen Standard Enchanted Mine Field

A standard enchanted mine field consists of a mixture of basic elemental and basic technological mines, offering a wide mixture of potential attacks to deal with a wide variety of resistances. Our most popular product by far.

Damage: Varies per mine

Cost (for marked area): 5.5 Million (Tier V) / 8.5 Million (Tier IV)

"Expensive." I grunt, rubbing my temples.

Still, I like the idea of buying something properly the first time, especially when it comes to things that go boom. While this doesn't give us the ability to directly engage the Sect members as they arrive, not only will we know where they're coming from, we can dictate where we'll fight them by limiting their options. Or if they choose to just go through the fields, the condition they'll be in.

With that thought, I confirm the purchase of the Tier IV standard enchanted mine field, though I make a note to look into adding the Chaos field at a later time. I'll admit, I've always found them quite fun.

"You just going to add a mine field and not tell anyone about it?" Ali says after I've made my purchase and the System starts teleporting in the mines.

"Shit…" I blink, waving. I exhale in relief when I realize that no one, luckily, is actually in the creation zone at this moment.

With a thought, I purchase a simple six-foot-high stone wall around the mine field on both sides. My fingers twitch for a second as I consider adding a series of big signs then decide against it. If you're going to hop a six-foot-high wall, you kind of deserve what you get.

"Ladies, Sam, I just created a mine field outside the city and put a wall around it. Let people know, will you?"

"A minefield?" Lana says, her voice rising at the end. Silence comes down the line, along with some very measured breathing, before she speaks, her voice carefully controlled. "Fine. We'll let people know. Let us know if you add anything else."

"Thanks," I say, relaxing a little.

Ali's fingers are moving and, a moment later, a new notification window appears in front of my eyes, a small map attached to it.

City Wide Announcement

A new defensive measure has been added to the Town of Kamloops. There is now a mine field outside of town. To enter and exit the town, please use only designated entrance corridors.

"If you want, I can send that out too to everyone," Ali says. "As the owner, you've got the ability to do so. There're a few other things that you benefit from, including the ability to access and purchase System-generated Shop items without being at the City Core."

"Huh. Like Roxley's tax announcements?" I say, recalling the few times Roxley used that ability. "Do it."

"Done," Ali says. "So considering you just blew the entire town budget in oh, about an hour, can we get to the fun stuff?"

"Fun stuff?" I frown at Ali, and the little Spirit rolls his eyes.

"Yes. The loot!" Ali says and waves, dumping out the corpses of the Sect members we killed.

I blink, slowly recalling that I do get to loot their bodies. Somehow, it seemed so secondary to everything else. Still, the Spirit has a point and this could easily fall under commandment number two—Know Thy Enemy. And well, loot.

"Well, come on then," I mutter and walk over to the first body, which in this case is Bimmox.

Unfortunately, unlike System-generated loot, looting bodies is a more grisly task, requiring me to strip the body. Unfortunately, everything that was in Bimmox's System storage is lost, which means all that's left is what's here physically. Well, that and a portion of its Credits.

Omnitron V Portable Shielding Unit

The Ominitron Portable Shielding Unit is rated for zones 10-20s. This high-level utility shielding unit is an omni-directional shielding unit and suitable for non-Combatants.

HP: 250

Regeneration Rate: 50 per hour

Mana Battery: 100% Charge

Integrity: 87%

"Omni-directional?"

"Marketing speak for you can't shoot through it," Ali explains.

"Junk pile it is," I say, dropping it into my System storage. Frankly, I'm surprised the damn bird had something this cheap and useless on him.

Osmaa Integrated Bio-Armor

Osmaa technologies weaves organic carbon-fiber tubes through their award-winning design, providing a class-breaking level of protection against multiple forms of attack.

Armor Rating: Tier III

Additional Resistances: +20% to Lightning, Thermal, Cold, Dark and Light Spells. +25% Resistance to Mental resistances

Integrity: 07%

"Damn," I swear, running my finger over the bio-armor. Not much left of it unfortunately, and getting it fixed would cost more than buying one. Pity, but that's what happens when you cut your opponent into pieces.

Unfortunately, there's nothing else on Bimmox worth looking at—a wand it pulled out is shattered, never even brought into play. And most of its quick injection potions are broken or used. On the other hand, as I use the System to Loot the avian, I have to smile.

12,385 Credits Gained from **Bimmox**

I stare at the Credit notification. That's actually very, very good. Obviously, most of their fortune has been taken by the System, but even the small portion I've been "gifted" by the System is more than I'd get for killing an equivalent level monster. If I hadn't destroyed most of his gear, I might have made off even better. Almost makes the case for killing sentients rather than monsters. Even the XP bump is slightly higher, though just barely.

A small part of me is pointing out that I should feel something a little more than annoyed after killing a group of sentients. But it's a very small part, and it's mostly doing so in a dispassionate sort of way. Between the fact that I'm mostly emotionally retarded anyway and I've bathed in rivers of blood in the last year, killing, even killing sentient creatures, is just another damn day. In the end, I don't have the emotional energy or the intellectual desire to care. They started it; I finished it.

"Tell me more about the Sect, will you?" I ask Ali as I pull out the discarded crossbow to inspect it. I'll have to return it to Mikito since she killed its user, but no reason I can't take a look.

Rudola Tier III Crossbow

When beam rifles do too little damage and projectile weaponry is too noisy, shop Rudola!
The Rudola series of projectile weaponry is guaranteed to provide pointed satisfaction!
Base Damage: 15 + Ammunition Damage

Not my kind of thing.

I move over to the bodyguard's body, stripping and inspecting each piece of equipment.

Punch Daggers

Created by an unknown artisan, these are personally forged punch daggers.

Base Damage: 75

Durability: 87/107

Special Abilities: +15 Piercing Damage

Nice. I add it to my stockpile of weaponry. Not sure what I'll do with them since none of my friends use that style of fighting. Might make a good gift, especially since they're personally forged. Maybe I could get an Enchanter to work on them later…

"The Thirteen Moon Sect isn't a large organization, as I mentioned. They're on about sixteen planets, spanning just over four solar systems. Within those, they have about seventy-three cities, towns, and settlements under their control, most grouped at the edges of other domains. They're in conflict with at least twelve major, six minor, and a bunch of trivial powers, including two large Guilds," Ali says, his eyes darting from side to side as he reads and summarizes the information he's pulling from the System. "Current strength is just over ten thousand members with a dozen Master and two Legendary Class members. Officially."

BioMarine Potion of Haste

All BioMarine potions are guaranteed mixed and produced to Galactic Standards. Don't buy sewage, buy BioMarine!

Effect: Haste

Level: II

Duration: 5 Minutes

"What do you mean officially?" I say, raising an eyebrow at the piece of gear. Huh. Definitely a keeper.

"I'm pulling those numbers from the Galactic equivalent of their corporate website. So, you know, take everything with a grain of salt," Ali says. "Probably reduce the number of total members and add to the number of higher Level members. No one wants to let everyone know the whole truth after all."

Tam's Boots of Titans

These enchanted boots of titans provide boosts to strength and speed, with additional self-cleaning and stitching enchantments layered. Produced by the Cobbler Tam.

Durability: 76/87

Armor Rating: Tier IV

Special Abilities: +11 Strength, +5 Agility, Self-cleaning

"Fair enough," I say. Pity the boots are constructed for a creature with webbed feet and are about six sizes too wide across my toes. "Anything else?"

"Not much more. They're the Galactic equivalent of official thugs—they deal with legal slaves, loan sharking, gambling, drugs, smuggling, and the like," Ali says. "They take control of settlements next to other, more restrictive groups and set up shop and then rake in the Credits. They're not well-liked, which is why they're in so many conflicts."

"Doesn't seem like their thing to take over a town in a Dungeon World," I say, frowning. Stripped of its gear, the body's last piece of clothing dares me to go ahead.

Tervik Ballistic Underwear

Provides ballistic and minor beam protection. Trust only Tervik for the most important jobs!

Armor rating: Tier III

Durability: 63/63

I twitch my hand, dropping the underwear into my inventory to let Ali sell at our next Shopping trip. I blink, the sharp, angular spiky projection with the bulging purplish egg sacs next to it an education in alien biology that I could have done without. The body disappears into my Altered Space, joining its compatriot. Another note brings a slight smile to my face.

7,389 Credits Gained from Bodyguard No.1

"Edge cases. You guys were—are—slightly ahead of schedule. Killing the Envoy and ending up a Dungeon World put a kibosh on a whole lot of plans. Everyone's scrambling, and the smaller and more nimble groups are the ones coming in first. The big boys… well, they'll move in when they're good and ready. That's the thing about being the ten-ton juggernaut. When you move, nothing stops you," Ali says.

"Then why would anyone move in at all?"

"Because it can be cheaper to buy someone out than fight. Then there are alliances and deals that can be made and hell, you might just get lucky and not get targeted," Ali says and waggles his finger, showing me the next piece of good news.

Level Up!

You have reached Level 38 as an Erethran Honor Guard. Stat Points automatically distributed. You have 6 Free Attributes and 2 Class Skill Points to distribute.

"Okay." I nod, standing and stretching out of habit. Allocating my attributes can wait. A small organization or not, the Thirteen Moon Sect is still larger than my party and me by orders of magnitude. It's only because they're so spread out that we even stand a chance. "Let's find out how the others are doing."

"On it, boy-o," Ali says.

Before we exit the room, Ali spends a few seconds to fix the damaged wall, hiding the center once again. It won't stop anyone who's actually serious about getting in, but half the battle with security is making sure you don't put the fifty-dollar note out for people to take.

Chapter 8

Finding Lana and Sam takes me only a few minutes. Mikito's at the edges of the town, moving with a group of grey dots that denote neutrals. For now, at least. I'm guessing those are potential helpers, hunters, and others who Mikito's running through their paces. Levels are easy to tell; combat experience is another thing entirely. Sure, if you're a fighter Class of some form, most likely your Levels are from combat, but it still doesn't mean you're good at it. Ingrid, of course, is nowhere to be found, a ghost in the System as always.

Next to Lana and Sam is another pair: a tall, thin human with a black beard and hooked nose, and a masculine figure with a series of frills across the top of his head and a long hairstyle. I can't help but think he's a Klingon, though his entire temperament seems far from the famous TV character. Another case of Mana leakage? Or just a coincidence?

"John," Sam greets me when I approach and scan the pair.

Torg Lavar (Farmer Level 37)
HP: 470/470
MP: 250/250
Conditions: Serf

Benjamin Asmundur (Architect Level 28)
HP: 210/210
MP: 470/470
Conditions: None

"Torg here is an import by the Sect and the farm overseer," Lana says, gesturing to the man. He taps the side of his shoulder with two fingers in greeting as Lana speaks. "He's been in charge of assigning tasks to the Farmers,

Herbalists, and Gatherers for the various herbs and other crops they're developing. Mel, who's with Mikito right now, and his team kept an eye out for monsters while they worked. Anything gathered was sent off to the Sect for processing though, so we don't have any high-Level Alchemists or Herbalists in town. The ones we have mostly produced things for internal use.

"Benjamin's one of the few free humans in the settlement—an Architect. He was telling us how he managed that," Lana finishes, gesturing to the human.

He smiles at me, eyes twinkling with good humor while he extends his hand. "Call me Ben." It's a firm, controlled shake, the kind that doesn't try to overwhelm you with strength. "I'm an architect. When the System came, I was still at home with my family. I took the Class too, and well, I had—have—the Skill to devote my Mana to 'purchasing' a building so I can reconstruct it. I did it for my apartment building and just kind of upgraded it."

"You can buy buildings outright without the Shop?" I say, my eyes wide. That's one hell of a gamebreaker in the early part of this year.

"Yes. It requires Mana and I'm still paying off the buildings I bought. Kind of like a loan from the System," Ben says. "Really messes with my regeneration."

"You should see it later, John," Lana says, pointing into the distance with a slight smile. "It's a damn fortress. It takes up a whole block."

"Huh." I rub my nose and kind of wonder why we never had anything like that in Whitehorse. Then again, the non-combatants had a tendency to die fast, so maybe we did and they were just another daisy-pusher. "How'd you keep the monsters out?"

"One of my Class Skills lets me create traps. I turned the first few floors into death traps and funneled them into my entrances. I set it up so that the traps only triggered for enemies, so my people could use the exits easily," Ben explains. "When the assholes came, they figured it was easier to leave me and my people alone than dig us out. Since then, they've been trying to starve us out while levying one tax after another. We're real happy you guys came."

"Your people?" I say.

"His fortress is pretty impressive for a Level 28 Architect. There's just over two hundred people in there, though most are non-combatants. He's reinforced the walls and entrances and even has the occupants devoting a portion of their Mana regeneration to the building Mana pool. You'd have to blast the entire wall apart at one go and move fast, or else the building would fix itself around it."

"Those under my protection," Ben says, shifting to face me and angling his body slightly. I wonder if it's a conscious decision or not, the way he's giving me less of a target. With the amount of violence we've all seen, it's sometimes hard to tell who is a fighter and who isn't. "I gathered as many as I could."

"Fair enough." A nagging thought surfaces—a conversation with an acquaintance in college during one of the few parties I ever went to. Red cups and beer in a smoke-filled kitchen. "Architects have to do some city planning too, right?"

"We do," Ben says, frowning.

"Good," I say and leave it at that. We'll worry about building up the town later, once we've survived the upcoming fight. On that note… "How are the fighters?"

"Pitiful," Sam replies, shaking his head. "Beam weapons or modified gunpowder rifles. No one's above Level 20. Average around the low teens mostly."

I frown. I knew the zones around the city were low, but they've had a whole year to grow. There are higher-Level zones easily within reach, never mind potential Swarms. Though from what Ali has told me, Swarms were more common in Whitehorse due to our high Mana saturation. I guess it's less of an issue here.

"They took the higher-Level hunters away," Torg finally speaks up, ducking his head immediately after. He shifts under my regard, almost as if he's embarrassed to be speaking.

I nod in understanding. No point in making your life more difficult by keeping potential threats around. Still, from the grimace that flashed across Ben's face, it was probably not something that went down well.

"How about the defenses?" Lana asks, cocking an eyebrow at me.

"Not great. There's the city shield, but it's only Tier IV. I've got a mine field out there and a sensor array built out now, so we'll have at least some warning. We could use the sentries, but two of them are damaged." I look at Sam as I say that and he offers a nod in understanding. "We'll probably have to deal with the attackers ourselves."

"I'm assuming we'll expect them soon?" Lana says, rubbing absently at her arm where a beam attack has scorched the material, turning the dark blue black.

"Yes. Most likely from Kelowna to start."

"Think they're that confident?" Lana says, waving her hand around. "We did just kick their ass."

"Definitely," Torg says.

"Indubitably," Ali echoes at the same time. When Lana stares at the little Spirit, he explains. "Ingrid's ability hid your true Levels and no one survived the attack in the office. Considering the Levels you showed, they probably assumed you launched a sneak attack on them. Without their main fighters, the guards you fought were killed off easily—but that's easily explained by the PAVs and other equipment. Add on to the fact that the Sect is just that arrogant…"

Torg nods at that.

"And they'll be sure to strike back immediately," Ali says. "Problem with ruling with strength is that you always have to be seen to be strong, you know?"

Lana nods slowly, looking toward the east for a second. After a moment more, she speaks up. "We going to take Kelowna then?"

"What?" I blurt, staring at her.

"In for a penny…" Lana meets my eyes. "If we're going to free them, we might as well do it right. If they're sending their fighters here, if we beat them, there won't be much left in the other city."

"I…" I pause, natural objections falling silent. The plan… well, there was no plan. I just intended to help where I could. However, conquering a few cities was never part of it. Still, Lana is right. If we're going to do this….

Sam stares at the two of us incredulously while Ben and Torg stay silent, their faces much more neutral. A glance at Ali has him giving me a thumbs-up, and I finally offer Lana a nod.

Lana looks quite satisfied, smiling like the cat that just got cream. "Now, let's talk about what we're going to do with the town after we're done."

I nod, content to let the lady lead the discussion. Between her experience on the General Council in Whitehorse and the information she's managed to garner here, Lana's got a much better idea than I do of what's going on and what needs to be done.

***

The next few hours passed in a blur. Learning about the town kept Lana and me focused, and Ben and Torg pulled in various other notables to talk to us through the day. Sam wandered off in about fifteen minutes, helping to settle our refugees and spread the good word among the general populace. I also recall him muttering something about finding a suitable workshop, but I ignored that bit. Mikito continued to put the hunters, all but the few extra guards still watching over the farmers in the northeast, through their paces. And Ingrid—well, who knows where she was.

We did it all in the middle of the street, just standing there and talking to people, letting anyone and everyone who was interested listen in. And there were a lot. People streamed in and out of the crowd that gathered around us, listening, chatting, and pointing as they confirmed the news that the Sect had been kicked out. It took me a bit to realize that Lana had chosen the location on purpose, a not-so-subtle hint that things were changing. I admit, I approved, though I hoped no one expected us to do it all the time. Governance by committee made me roll my eyes.

Ben was, unsurprisingly, quite helpful. As the leader of the only independent group in the town, he knew nearly everyone. His presence by our side, talking congenially, probably helped allay a lot of fears. It was nearly as useful as his knowledge of the town's resources.

Torg, on the other hand, contributed in a different, if no less useful, way by providing us examples of the way the Sect and other Galactics did things. Whether it was discussions on farming and gathering to zoning or Credit generation, he had ideas and examples from his time on other worlds. It seemed Torg had been bounced around a lot, always moving from settlement to settlement to help start up their latest farmland. The man had a knack for organizing individuals and problem-solving. It was unfortunate that he never actually got his hands dirty farming, keeping his Levels low.

My understanding of the town grew while I expanded my knowledge of the people around us. Late in the evening, when the others had begun to flag, the sensors pinged. I was a bit surprised, having expected them to come tomorrow. But I guess with the longer daylight hours of late spring, it didn't matter.

"*Incoming, boy-o,*" Ali interrupts, flashing the map in front of Lana and myself. He taps something and text message notifications go out to the rest of the team.

From the map, I can tell that the group from Kelowna is coming in loud and brassy, not even bothering to hide their presence. Arrogant. Five dots, Levels popping up in short order. They're headed straight in on the main road, which means they'll miss the mines but will have to deal with the beam towers. If we let them get that close.

"Time to go," I say, triggering Sabre to roll closer to me. I swing my foot over the bike even as Lana hops up on one of the puppies.

"Not sure I'm going to be much help here," Sam's voice cackles over the radio, and I have to agree. He's better off where he is, fixing the sentries. Not being a frontline fighter, he'd be a liability if he came right now. While he's done stellar work during the fights we've dragged him into, there's no point in risking him when we don't have to.

"Roger," I say while Lana bids the group goodbye. I add my own belated and almost forgotten goodbye, the group splitting apart with worried expressions. Helmet on, I speak into the radio, giving rapid-fire orders. "Mikito, get the fighters up high. We'll take them right outside the shield. Tell them to hold fire till we command it. Or we fall."

I get an acknowledgement from the Samurai before her voice barks commands to others. I tune it out, glancing at Lana, who rides Howard next to me.

"You up for this?" I ask, my eyes roaming her form to assess her state.

Her armor has seen better days, and there's a tightness to her shoulders I don't like. But when she turns to me and flashes me a smile, it's filled with confidence and I recall that this is the same woman who followed me into the Kluane Icefields without a word of complaint. A rush of hormones comes with that memory. That brazen courage even in the face of fear and anxiety was damn sexy. I make a mental note to find some time alone with her at some point. There's always one thing or another in the way.

"I'll be fine. You're going to have to handle at least two of them. Maybe three. Are you up to this?" Lana says, violet eyes crinkling as she stares at me.

"I'll be fine," I say, patting my bike. "I've got Sabre."

"You don't look it," she says, staring at my face. "You've got a weird look on your face."

"Just disappointed, I guess." At her cocked eyebrow, I go on. "I spent a lot of money and time planning out potential avenues of attack. Bought new sensor arrays and a minefield, figuring they'd try something smart. Instead, they walk right up to our front door."

Lana stares at me for a second before snorting in amusement, a smile dancing along her lips. In minutes, Mikito falls in line on her bike, guiding it to flank me. Ingrid's still gone, but that's no surprise. She'll pop up when she's needed, probably with a blade in someone's back.

As we pass the watchtowers, the shield shifts, opening long enough to let us out before we pull to a stop. Mikito doesn't hesitate, transforming her PAV into mecha mode and walking to the side while the puppies spread out, flanking the road and crouching low in the green, uncut grass. Within seconds, Roland has disappeared, its form shifting as it uses an innate Skill to Stealth itself, leaving only Anna beside Lana. The redhead has her shotgun out and a portable shield array set before her feet, ready for trouble.

We don't have to wait long, the Sect group arriving soon after. They disembark and walk toward us, leaving their hover transport behind. No surprise on that. Replacing vehicles is expensive and since few are actually made for extended combat amongst combat Classes, they break easily.

As they walk closer toward us, I scan the group. The first two are melee fighters. A Level 3 Advanced Class Bladesinger in brown fur wields a pair of swords in each hand, strutting forward on all four legs. Next to him, a sleek, green-scaled Advanced Level 27 Blood Warrior wields a rod and shield. Behind is a faceless Level 47 Elemental Mage in blocky armor and a rock-covered, seven-foot-tall Advanced Level 12 Rock Thrower. They're guarding their Level 41 Stitcher.

"You can stop right there," I call out when they're about thirty feet away. Just in case, I check the Soul Shield I've added to Lana and the puppies.

"Nice of you to meet us out here," the Blood Warrior says with a grin, his accent deep East Coast. A part of me tries to pin it down, certain I've heard it on TV somewhere. Idle thoughts. "Saves us the trouble of hunting you down."

"Blah blah blah, random thug posturing." I shake my head at the anger that crosses their body language. Tightened grips and shifts in positioning are universal, no matter what alien society you come from. "You have one chance to get out of this alive. Take your friends and leave BC now and return all the humans you've enslaved."

There's a long pause before a hissing, cackling, and grunting series of laughs erupts from the group.

Since they obviously aren't going to take my generous offer, I follow up with the stick, launching all my high explosive mini-missiles and screaming, "Now!"

The sentry towers open up, lances of red fire striking even before my missiles. A second later, flames erupt from Anna's body, a tightly wrapped beam of fire pulled from the creature's aura. Lana opens fire with her shotgun as Mikito rushes the group, her Hasted body covering the ground within seconds.

The beams reach them first, fracturing ineffectively against an invisible shield. The beam turrets cut off after a second. The mini-missiles land next, creating rippling explosions that throw sand and dirt into the air and a pressure wave of force that hammers into us. A second later, the follow-up shots from the towers and the rest of the attacks land, the shield flickering under the assault.

It holds though, long enough for our enemies to take action themselves. Charging forward, the Bladesinger clashes with Mikito, his greater weight spinning her around as she blocks the strike. The pair blur, flashing across the ground perpendicular to us, their forms barely visible. A spell in the shape of a flaming bird rips through the air and slams into the beam towers, bypassing the settlement's shield, which has dropped to allow the beam towers to fire. The other sentry tower goes down as the Rock Thrower, living up to its name, projects a series of car-sized stone spears.

"Hey. I'm going to have to fix those!" I snap as I open fire with the Inlin mounted on my arm.

The flashing projectiles get cut apart in mid-air by the Blood Warrior. The explosions of the projectiles around him seem to be doing nothing, and even when I shift my target, he's always there, blocking my attacks.

The puppies move forward the moment their shield drops, but they never reach their prey, the shield popping up within seconds. They howl in anger, battering the invisible protection, but there's nothing they can do. Behind the shield, their Elemental Mage waves his hands around, Mana gathering for another spell. The Blood Warrior is outside the shield though, rushing toward us.

"Lana, yours," I shout over the radio, trusting that she can hold the Blood Warrior.

With a slight mental exertion, I trigger Blink Step, teleporting through time and space into the shield. It's a gamble, since there's no guarantee this shield won't bounce me off. I appear next to the Rock Thrower, the Inlin firing into his side even as I summon my sword into my other hand and cut upward. He's fast and trained, throwing himself to the side and backward, my attack only managing to lop off part of his foot. Green blood spurts outward, coating Sabre even as the monster rolls away from me in trained reflex. Spikes erupt from the ground, shattering Sabre's shielding and making it flicker and disappear.

Even as I spin to target the Stitcher, Ingrid makes her appearance finally. Her dagger erupts from his neck, the enchanted weapon, along with her Skills and the surprise attack, cutting through his health and armor. Still, the Stitcher falls to the ground, fingers waggling, and a glow surrounds him. Ingrid's next attack slows down as it enters the white glow, giving the Stitcher time to twist and roll with the damage.

I don't have time to pay any further attention since I've crossed the ground toward the Mage, weathering the sudden Lightning Bolt it throws at me, the arc of electricity jumping through the air and striking Ingrid and the Stitcher as well. I grunt, hair and teeth on edge, but the bleed through is low and nothing Sabre and I can't handle. I butcher the Elemental Mage in seconds, even with his momentary teleport away from me. As I attack, spikes of rock slam into Sabre's armor, but the harassing fire from the Rock Thrower isn't enough to dissuade my attacks. Personally, I think the Rock Thrower made the wrong decision in focusing on me. As I yank my sword out of the Mage's corpse, I'm grateful that Mages are so damn squishy.

A particularly large spike knocks me off my feet, alarms flashing as Sabre reports the increasing amount of damage the monster's attacks are having on me. I roll and bounce back to my feet, ducking to the side as I assess the rest of the battlefield.

Mikito is racing back, the Bladesinger lying still behind her, her PAV scored with damage even through her ghostly armor. A quick review shows she's down nearly half her health, which is surprising. Roland and Shadow are squaring off against the Blood Warrior and a second, blood covered clone. God damn it. I hate Skills, especially ones that we don't have access to.

Anna and Howard are caught in blood tendrils, forced to twist and struggle while Lana hacks away with a machete in her left hand, her right hanging limp beside her. Ali floats next to her, keeping watch on the attackers, a small ball of lightning in his hand. It's a surprising development, one that shows his willingness, if not ability, to do damage.

"Go. I've got these guys!" Ingrid snaps at me over the radio as she pulls her dagger out of the Stitcher's side, which continues to bathe itself in white light.

With a twist of my hand, I toss an insta-cement grenade at the Rock Thrower, holding it in place and buying Ingrid time. Once the grenade has left my hand, I Blink Step toward the Blood Warrior. My attack is anticipated, a pair of tendrils spearing from the blood clone to strike at me the instant I appear. They knock my attack aside, my blades missing the Blood Warrior. With a shiver, the green-skinned humanoid rolls forward, leaving another blood clone to fight me as it engages Roland. I duck and weave as tendrils of blood that acts like acid erupt from the clone and fly through the air as I attempt to cut my way in close to the true body.

Roland howls in pain, the impact of the Blood Warrior's club tossing the tiger away. Even as Roland spins away, its back feet lash out and claws rend wounds along the Blood Warrior's shoulder, displaying grey bones beneath green flesh. Even then, the Blood Warrior twists, another clone appearing as he continues to bleed.

114

"No!" comes a loud, grating shout from behind us.

Then the explosion hits us all, dust and dirt obscuring our vision as we stumble and fall. Even System-enhanced Agility is insufficient to compensate for the force of the explosion. When the cloud finally clears, the Blood Warrior is gone and so is the Rock Thrower and the Stitcher.

"What happened?" I ask, standing and looking around. Sabre's running diagnostics, nano-armor already fixing itself.

Ingrid limps toward us, quaffing healing potions. I watch as her broken fingers pop back into place, bloody wounds disappear, and her body straightens up as pain goes away. "Rocky triggered a Skill. Blew his body apart when I was about to finally kill that damn healer."

Ali floats down. "He's not dead, by the way. Just weakened. His race adds layers of rock and stone as they increase in Level. Blowing up layers of his body destroys his Levels. He must have sacrificed a ton…"

"How did they escape?" I say, frowning. I get the explosion, but we were only knocked down for seconds. Even now, I can't spot them in my minimap, which is disturbing. While I wouldn't say we pulled out all the stops, we certainly weren't holding back. Letting them get away after we've shown them a significant chunk of our abilities is not great.

"Localized teleport," Ali says, grimacing. "Very, very expensive and requires them to have pre-purchased the option in the Shop."

"Do we know where they went?" I say, letting my gaze track over my team. Between a bunch of health potions and the System's healing, we're mostly back to fighting shape, except for the pets. Lana's feeding some of the most damaged pets health potions, though their enhanced healing is already seeing gaping wounds slowly close.

"No idea, boy-o," Ali says with a shrug.

I curse silently, discarding the idea of attacking Kelowna now. There's no way they completely emptied the city of high-level characters just for an assault on us. Add in their local guards and fixed defenses and I'm not looking forward to a direct attack. There's also no guarantee they don't have another of those localized teleports saved up, though I'd be surprised if they did. Unfortunately, even I'm not so irresponsible that I'd gamble with the lives of others.

"We're not going to Kelowna, are we?" Ingrid says, glancing down the road, and I shake my head. "Right then, drinks it is!"

Ingrid flashes me a smile, and I make myself return it. She's right. We might not have wiped them out, but we weathered the first attack. A success is a success.

Chapter 9

Later that evening—or was it technically morning by now?—we're mostly alone, seated around heaping plates of food and beer. Even the curious and interested long ago gave up on overhearing anything interesting. Truth be told, after giving everyone who asked brief assurances, we had little more to say. Thankfully, unlike a "real" town, there was little enough in terms of paperwork that I needed to handle—at least, right away. That allowed me and the team to settle down for a few hours.

"But if I upgrade the Ghost Armor again, I'll add nearly 50% to its hit points," Mikito says to Lana and Ali, waving a fork to punctuate her point.

"And move away from your main advantages," Ali stresses. "You're fast and you hit hard. Better for you to focus on what you're good at. You've got a decent amount of hit points anyway, and can dodge everything else if you pick up Enhanced Reflexes."

"Except if they use an area effect spell. Can't dodge those," Lana points out, shaking her head. "I'm with Mikito. She's plenty fast as it stands. More defense is a good thing. I'm thinking I should get something too."

"Feeling a little vulnerable out there?" Ali says with a glance toward her arm.

"Just a little. The boys are great at keeping most people busy, but if Hondo or someone like Ingrid came along…"

"I wouldn't stab you in the back, Lana. We're friends. I'd look you in the eyes as I did it," Ingrid says with a smile, making all of us roll our eyes.

Sam watches our banter, mostly silent, before he taps the table to get our attention. The seriousness on his face colors his next question. "So what now? Are you going to try to attack Kelowna next?"

"Missed our chance," I say, shaking my head. "If we'd wiped them out, I'd be willing to risk it. Now, there's no guarantee they won't hit us when we leave. Better to stay and consolidate our strength here."

"About that..." Sam says, grimacing and looking around. "You guys. Well, you're tough. But there's a lot of concern about what happens if they send more. If you fall..."

"The city doesn't have much in terms of defense," I finish for him and sigh.

Sam's not wrong. The problem is, I'm not entirely sure what we can do about it. Setting up a training program like we did in Whitehorse will benefit the combat Classers, but it takes time. Bumping up Levels by grinding monsters is easy—there's even a convenient dungeon to run. But real combat experience requires time. Time to make mistakes. Time to repeat those mistakes and learn from them. Until then, we need more than just a couple of easily destroyed sentry towers.

"For that matter, are we staying?" Ingrid says, staring around the table. "I don't recall there being a discussion before we started all this."

"Didn't mind sticking your knife in earlier," Lana says.

"I'm not saying we should leave. But we're discussing sitting still and being a target while our enemies gather their forces. Not smart," Ingrid replies, letting her eyes roam over the group as if she's testing everyone.

"You suggesting we run?" Lana says softly.

"No. I'm making sure we're all in," Ingrid replies.

I cut in, waving in apology. "You're right. We didn't discuss this. I'm sorry, I should have..."

I stop because Mikito is smiling and Lana's laughing softly. Even Ingrid snorts slightly, shaking her head after a moment.

Sam looks between the three before he finally asks, "What?"

"John's being cute. And idiotic again," Lana says with a chuckle.

"Baka." Mikito nods firmly. "We knew you were going to do it."

"I didn't," Ingrid says. "But I should have."

"What?" I exclaim.

"Boy-o, you're a bit predictable," Ali says.

"Oh, come on!"

"You're very predictable, Redeemer of the Dead," Ingrid says, naming one of my titles. I twitch, ducking my head slightly, and she smiles again. "As I said, I should have realized it the moment we saw the Serfs. You weren't ever going to leave this alone. You're just not good at doing the smart thing."

"Welcome to Team John," Lana says, raising her mostly empty pint in mocking salute. "We don't do the smart thing. Or the right thing. Just the necessary."

"You're okay with this?" Ingrid says then shakes her head, chiding herself for wasting words. "Never mind. Of course you are. Mikito, Sam?"

"Where John goes, I go," Mikito says simply.

Sam pauses, his face obviously conflicted before he finally huffs. "My family is in Vancouver. Where the Sect is. I'd rather go there in force than try to beg my way in."

Ingrid stares at the group of us before she throws her hands up dramatically. "Gods! How did I end up with a bunch of heroes?"

"Your asshole team got killed," Ali says bluntly.

Ingrid freezes, all levity drained from her face. For a moment, we can all feel it, the killing intent that rises at Ali's crass words before Ingrid takes control of herself, dampening it. She stands silently and walks out. It's only when she's gone that we dare take our eyes off her.

"Not cool, man," I say, smacking the Spirit. Of course, my hand goes through him, but it's the thought that counts.

"That was very much uncalled for," Lana says. "I'm disappointed in you, Ali."

"Whatever," Ali says, though he hunches his shoulders a bit under our combined disapproval. "She's been bitching about being with us for months now. She was literally telling John to stay a short while ago. It's time for her to choose her Class or let the System do it."

I frown slightly at his non-sequitur then realize it's the Spirit equivalent of shit or get off the pot.

After the silence stretches on for too long, Sam clears his throat, drawing attention back to himself and our original question. "So we're staying. And you're the boss of this town. What do you plan to do?"

"Funny you should ask…" I say, leaning forward and taking the change in topic. Rather than join most of the conversations this evening, I've been thinking. Planning. Time to get to work.

***

The next morning, the team splits up to tackle their respective tasks. Sam's on crafter duty, working with the various crafters to upgrade their talents. His main focus is on the Mechanics in the hope that we can upgrade them enough to build some better defenses and offensive weaponry. Mikito's still on combat duty, continuing her initial work with the combat Classers yesterday. Lana's working with Torg and his crew of resource gatherers to account for and divert what they have to the respective Classes in town and the Shop. For once, everyone's going to get paid.

Lana's job is probably the most important in the group since I've managed to drain the funds for the entire town. Without additional Credits, we can't upgrade the Town—not without physically upgrading the buildings and roads.

At least, I don't think so. But assumptions just make an ass of u and me, so that's why I'm seated in the control room with Ali this morning.

"This is a bit ridiculous. It all came in overnight?" I say, staring at the hundreds of open System windows. The vast majority are messages—requests, demands, complaints, suggestions, and even a few threats. They range from issues about education for children to real estate queries, pleas for help with regard to those taken and even noise complaints. Noise complaints!

"Overnight and they keep coming in. The joy of being the owner of a settlement," Ali says.

"Never knew you could do this. How come I never got Roxley's message box?" I say, staring at the growing number of windows as Ali populates them one behind the other.

"You just walked in when you wanted to talk to him," Ali says.

Oh, right. I guess I never did consider there might be other ways of reporting to him. "This only for the owner? Or can we create a system like this for everyone?"

"Anything's possible. But we don't have the Credits. I do have a recommendation though." Ali's hand twitches.

K'myn Artificial Intelligence Tier III

This specialised AI is designed to take on the administrative processes of new and developing settlements including the legal and bureaucratic processes of the Galactic Council.

Cost: 145,000 Credits

"An AI?" I frown, staring at the information, then tilt my head to the side as I stare at Ali. "Can't you do this?"

"I'm a Spirit. I deal with magic and spells and the System. I don't do bureaucratic paperwork. Not unless you want an audit," Ali says, shaking his head. "Buy it. We can tie it to the town for now so you don't have to use any processing power in your Neurolink if you're that worried."

"What's the difference in Tiers for an AI anyway? I get guns, but AIs?"

"Sophistication, processing power, and restrictions. Higher tiers have fewer restrictions, better coding, and the ability to utilize more resources. Most are restricted to some extent by what you download them into, which is why I recommend tying it to the town," Ali said. "In this case, we're also buying a bunch of knowledge packs so it can hit the ground running."

"Doesn't Lana have one?" I say after a moment, recalling that Ali once recommended she purchase an AI.

"She does, but hers is Tier V and geared toward private businesses. The knowledge base is entirely different. You're going to need her help later if you want this town to run properly, but for now, you need this."

I pause, staring at the Credits cost. Ever since leaving Whitehorse, Credits have been harder to acquire. Not as many high-level monsters to fight and longer gaps between visiting a Shop meant lower revenue. If I bought it, I'd have just over forty thousand Credits left. Not much at all when you consider a single Class Skill could cost sixty plus. But… needs must.

The moment I make the decision, the System flickers. A moment later, the windows before me shrink and disappear, replaced by another, larger window. Text appears on the window in blocky letters.

"GOOD MORNING, SIR. I AM KIM, YOUR SETTLEMENT ADMINISTRATIVE ASSISTANT. I HAVE TAKEN THE LIBERTY OF SORTING ALL INCOMING MAIL. IF YOU WISH, I WILL REPLY TO ALL TRIVIAL AND MINOR ISSUES WITH STOCK RESPONSES. ALL OTHER ISSUES WILL RECEIVE A RESPONSE REQUESTING

PATIENCE UNTIL FURTHER INSTRUCTIONS AND GOALS HAVE BEEN RECEIVED," the text reads.

"Yeah, that'll work. Kim," I say, blinking slightly. An AI named Kim. I can see where he (it?) got its name from, but does that mean every AI purchased from that company calls itself Kim? Or is it just a matter of luck in my case? I shake my head, pushing the thought aside to focus on something more important. "All right, let's get to work. Process the information on the town. We'll discuss the parameters of what we need to set later. Let's talk defenses first though. Those towers went down fast. What can we do?"

"Buy better towers?" Ali says with a shrug.

"They were Tier IV!" I said, frowning.

"Exactly. They'll handle most monsters up to Level 20. Monsters," Ali says, shaking his head. "Sentients fight differently from monsters. You know that."

That was too true. Sentients of the same Level were generally more dangerous than monsters. If that wasn't the case, it would be impossible for a Level 1 sentient to kill a Level 1 monster. The number varied of course, depending on Class, Skill, and skill, but it was generally taken as a force multiplier of between one and a half to two. So a Level 1 sentient could likely fight up to a Level 2 monster on equal terms, not including equipment. Which meant our defense towers could really only handle Level 15 or so fighters.

"Still, they got destroyed so fast," I say, grumbling slightly.

"Did you notice the Rock Thrower and Mage were a lot less active afterward? They used some of their best Skills and Mana to one-shot those towers," Ali says.

"COST OF TIER III BEAM SENTRY TOWERS CURRENTLY GREATER THAN CREDIT RESOURCES."

"No Gremlin poo. Now, be quiet till you're called on," Ali says. "Automated defenses are fine for monsters, but they're all supplementary, boy-o."

I nod and wave the Spirit silent, leaning backward into the chair. I swing it back and forth as I think through what I know. The System pushes people, Classes to higher Levels. External items, equipment, tech is all replaceable, but none of it is anywhere as important as the individual. Mostly. There are exceptions—Linked weapons like Mikito's naginata, my Soulbound sword—can grow. But otherwise, at some point, external equipment has to be discarded. In the end, it's people that matter. That explains why Roxley focused mostly on walls and shields, leaving the security of the city to his guards. Easier to scale, especially with monster swarms constantly popping up. Unfortunately, I don't have his house guards to bolster our low-Leveled forces.

Roxley... I huff out a breath, thinking of the swarthy, tall Dark Elf. Damn but I could use his advice right about now. However, the way we left it, I'm not sure asking him would be the best idea. His decision to join the Duchess, after all we did, did not sit well with me. No. Roxley isn't an option. But that doesn't mean that some of the others I've met might not be of help.

"Ali, let's get some messages out to some friends," I say, looking at the Spirit. "And after that, I guess Kim and you should start briefing me about the city properly. Can't rule it if I don't understand it, and we might be in for the long haul."

***

Hours later, my head's pounding from all the information fed to me. I wasn't a business major or a politician or bureaucrat. But somehow, I was supposed to understand all of these things while running the city.

In some cases, the System simplified what would have been significantly more complicated before its introduction. For example, transactions held by the Shop and transactions done by transferring Credits in the System were all tracked automatically. That made taxation simple, as I could tax individual sales and purchases within the town between Classers with a single adjustment in the core. Of course, then you ended up in the long, long discussion about consumption taxes versus income taxes versus... well, whatever. You get the picture.

Right now, Kamloops is mostly a resource economy. Funds are generated from the farms or Gatherers and Hunters selling their loot. Of course, being a Dungeon World, the sheer amount of Mana in the surroundings speeds up growth and increases monster Levels in comparison to other worlds, so being a resource town isn't a bad thing. However, as most undeveloped countries know, the real money isn't in selling your resources—it's in production and development. Turning those resources into Credits. In our case, that's what Lana and Sam are tasked with jumpstarting. Until then, I have to deal with taking a hit on revenue as we divert sellable material to in-town crafters to Level them up.

Furthermore, that means we have a lot of small transactions happening in the Shop as resource items are sold. The easiest way to generate more revenue would be to charge the tax rate when individuals sell, creating a basic income tax. It might miss a few outliers, but for the vast majority, that'd work.

In Whitehorse, Roxley instituted a flat percentage charge on all transactions in the Shop, which actually impacted production Classes more than anyone else, due to their need to purchase additional products for their needs. That sounds bad at first glance, but it does mean that people are more likely to look into ways of building or developing technologies and secondary resource items in-town rather than purchasing them through the Shop. Which, I'm beginning to understand, is likely what Roxley intended.

The world's complicated, and only the foolish, ignorant, or those with an agenda would ever say otherwise. There are no simple answers to any of these problems, and even when I pop out to the Shop to get myself a quick, downloaded education, it's not enough. Because sometimes, the question isn't what's best but what you're trying to do.

Right now, what we need is income and fast. I can't afford to spend too much time on the long game, which is why I end up keeping a flat five percent tax rate on all transactions in the city. I even extended it to transactions between citizens in the town, ensuring the town gets their fair share. Of course, this was a reduction in the Shop tax rate from the initial twenty percent, so hopefully there aren't too many complaints. Even though we desperately need funds, I have to think long-term as well, and that means helping the city grow.

Next on our agenda was figuring out expenses. This was much simpler, since most items in the city were linked and run by the System. Of course, you could have the System auto-regenerate and fix all registered buildings and facilities, but one thing I'd realized after reading through the more in-depth menu was that this actually took Mana. Or more specifically, Mana regeneration. Across the city, Mana production and regeneration was actually tied to the amount of space a town controlled. So while Kamloops had managed to establish and even develop a higher percentage of System-integrated buildings, it actually produced less Mana than Whitehorse because of its smaller square footage. Not to mention it was situated at a lower level zone.

Interestingly enough, buildings and the town itself seemed to generate less Mana than I'd expected. Compared to the Mana regeneration of an individual, it was paltry. It was only at this level, where I was looking at the Mana generation of a whole town, that it started showing up at all. With Kim's help, I could turn off the default allocation of Mana for individual buildings, letting me store up more. For now though, I left it alone since I had no idea what we needed it for.

Outside of Mana expenses, there were Credit expenses. Since we didn't have to pay for maintenance for the most part—outside of simpler services like cleaning for non-System-upgraded buildings—payroll was the major ongoing expense I could expect. In this case, I actually didn't have any since I hadn't hired anyone and everyone previously hired was either a Serf—now freed and let go—or a Sect member who had fled. On the other hand, that meant I'd have to hire again soon. I mentally sacrifice Lana to this task with a smile before finishing the sparse file.

"What's next?" I say.

"ALLOCATION OF ASSETS."

I grunt, staring at the dire blue words before nodding. Kim flashes up the list of buildings I currently own after kicking out the Sect.

Commercial: 4 (City Center, Armory, 2 x Workshop)

Residential: 178 Individual Residences, 24 Apartment Buildings

Industrial: 7 Farmland, 3 Alchemical Laboratories

Military: 14 Sentry Towers, 1 Shield Generator, External Minefield, Bionetwork Sensor Grid

There used to be one more line here—one for Serfs—but now it's gone. Obviously I'd dismissed all the Serfs and their debts, at least as far as it concerned me. If the Sect caught them within the next month, they'd revert to being Serfs, but after that, they'd be fine. It was, surprisingly, a decent Galactic law and said some interesting things about politics at the Galactic level.

Scanning over the list, I looked to see if any of these buildings had been forcibly taken by the Sect, "purchased," or taken as "collateral" for loans that would eventually force their owners into debt. There were a few, very few, lucky individuals who weren't Serfs but whom I now owned their property because the initial loan was to the Sect. Since the property was registered to the town ownership, I actually owned it, but a few quick swipes transferred ownership back to them. This way, at least they owned the property they'd been paying the mortgage for.

The question now, and it was relatively urgent to answer, was what to do with the buildings that had been taken or had been owned by others before the System. In the second case, I was leaning toward saying "tough." The world had changed—all old property ties were gone, at least in my view. However, memories of a grenade, a shop, and undying anger came to mind. Whatever my personal feelings on the matter, it was also true that we couldn't afford internal strife—especially the violent kind—while the Sect was still a threat.

The smart thing to do is to leave things as they are, perhaps reducing the rent charged. Currently, the rent charged on each of the apartments and buildings is outrageous, specifically geared toward keeping Serfs and other lendees in perpetual poverty. For obvious reasons, I have no desire to do that, but at the same time, the rent is a major revenue source. One alteration I can make is to charge a daily rental fee rather than a monthly one, with the provision that individuals can pay in advance. That would give us more regular income rather than sudden surges. I hope.

Of course, it isn't exactly fair. Or nice. Or right. But…

I sigh, staring at Ali. "This… did they all have to make decisions like this?"

"All?"

"Roxley. The city, the general, council. Rulers."

"Yes. If you think this is bad, wait till you see what bit boy has up next for you."

"Kim?"

"KAMLOOPS REQUIRES SOLIDIFICATION OF ITS RULE OF LAW."

"Shoot me now," I say with resolution.

Having spent enough time with Angela, the ex-RCMP member in Whitehorse, I know how complicated the entire matter is. It isn't as simple as taking our old laws and adding them back to our lives. For one thing, were we willing to set up the full court of laws with judges, juries, and lawyers? Why? A simple purchase from the System could verify the truth of a matter. Never mind the fact that certain Classes have Skills that can divine the truth even without using the System Shop. But if we came to rely on a single individual, did we then create a single point of failure—of corruption?

Property crime was less of an issue, though theft of items continued to be a concern. Of course, it only cost a little additional to "register" items with the System, though few Adventurers bothered. After all, with the increasing Levels, what equipment was useful now might be outdated within a few months. Why bother spending the money then? As such, item theft could be considered a "minor" crime these days, since anything truly expensive would be registered, making it much more difficult to sell the item.

Then you had violent crimes, which needed to be redefined. Since nearly everything outside of actual death was temporary, breaking someone's nose or arm or ribs was a lot less dangerous than before. It was nearly impossible to kill someone by accident these days. Of course, you didn't want to encourage violence either—after all, if you did, combat Classers would trample production Classers. And while that might make certain juvenile individuals revel in their "strength," it did nothing for the community. After all, if all your goods could be exhorted out of you, why would you put in any effort?

I sigh, staring at the information, and get down to it. Luckily, since this is directly related to the town, I can use the town's Credits to purchase information from the System, giving me detailed laws from other settlements that we could base ours off. In the end though, what I want is something simple and easy. I'll leave it to the professionals to develop the complicated bits. My laws basically ran down to—don't be a dick. If you are, don't expect us to back you up.

As for the buildings, I figure I'll lower the rent and leave them in my care for now. Procrastination might not be a good thing, but it does mean I don't have to deal with the problem right this second.

***

Ingrid never makes it back that night. That's okay. What I have planned for her is better said alone. When I finally find her, she's seated in an abandoned office building, nursing a bottle of alcohol in the remnants of a window overlooking the city. I sit next to her, fishing a bottle of whisky from storage to join her in a bout of silent drinking.

"Not going to bitch me out?" Ingrid asks eventually, noting the lack of blunt Spirit next to me.

"No." I shrug and sip on the drink. "Always been your call on what you want to do."

"Is not wanting to play hero that wrong?" Ingrid says testily. "What have these people ever done for me? Or you?"

"Why the change of heart?"

"Amazing, the things you overhear when no one notices," Ingrid says cryptically.

I wait for the teenager to add more. While we sit in silence, I take a moment to regard the First Nation woman and the bitterness that creeps across her face. I wonder what she overheard, what careless words were uttered. God knows, being a lipreader means that I've picked up more than one casual insult spoken when they thought I wouldn't notice. The people here, they're the same ones who were content to live in their own little bubbles and declare that they were "good" or "right" because they never did anything actively wrong pre-System. Just content to let the evils of the world happen because they weren't actively taking part in it. I doubt much of that has changed and so, I understood her feelings.

"But it's not enough," I whisper to myself and smile crookedly when she shoots me a puzzled look. "I don't care what they did or didn't do. Or if it's right or wrong to give them back a little of their own medicine. Because I'm not looking to be them. It's easy to be just about good enough, to be mediocre and normal.

"The world ended, Ingrid. We had a damn apocalypse. If there's ever been a good reason to change, I figure that's it. I won't, I can't go back to just getting by, doing just enough to live. I tried that once, and all I did was mark off the days till I died. Now we're here and I'm still alive and everyone and everything we knew is dead. So yeah, I'll play at being a hero and doing the right thing, because I've tried the other way."

"Not everyone." Ingrid's lips twist slightly, and she tilts her head as she speaks. "You could play at being a villain."

"Meh. Villains are boring." I say mockingly, "Oooh, look at me. I'm bad. I'm evil. Watch me stomp on a baby's head because that's so edgy."

Ingrid snorts at my words and the false face I put on.

"So you in?"

She takes a swig from her bottle, making a face. "Whatever. I don't have anything better right now. But I'm not wearing tights."

"How about some leather?" I waggle my eyebrows and wince as she punches my arm, chuckling slightly. "But seriously, we need your skills. They're going to be sending people at us, and we're going to need as much information as we can get."

"You want me to spy on them?" Ingrid says flatly, and I nod. "Why don't you just buy the information?"

"I have some basics. The rest was too expensive. Spread around North America are four high-level Advanced Classes, fourteen mid-level Advanced Classes, seven low-level Advanced Classes, and just over two hundred Basic Class Sect members. Most of them are locked in combat around Seattle at the moment. The ones in BC are their holding force, the people in charge of keeping things running," I say, explaining things simply to her.

"For all that, the System can't tell the future, so figuring out what they're going to do isn't something it can tell us. Guesses, probabilities, sure. But if you sneak in, look around, maybe ask a few questions…" I shrug. "Maybe you can figure it out. And either way, we're going to have to take those cities later. It'd get pretty expensive if I just kept buying information. That bit of information already cost us two hundred thousand Credits."

"Really? You took one city and now you're looking at more? Getting a bit of a big head, are you?"

"Might as well do it right."

Ingrid laughs softly, tipping her bottle upward and draining it before she nods. "I'll play spy for you. Until I get bored. Or get a better offer." She snags my bottle and leans forward, flipping off the ledge into the darkness below.

"My bottle!" I grumble softly, her dot disappearing from my map. That went better than expected.

Chapter 10

Breakfast. The most important meal of the day. Whether or not it matters for our altered bodies, it certainly helps as a ritualized meeting place for the team. Today, it's Sam's turn to cook, which means we have gruel, gruel, and bacon. At least there's enough.

"Ingrid's not here," Mikito says, dumping some chopped ginger into her gruel.

"I spoke with her last night. She's scouting," I say unconcernedly. No point hiding this information from my team. It isn't even too much a concern about need-to-know issues since anyone who really wants this information can buy it from the Shop. Though I am curious how Ingrid's Skills affect that option. Something to ask Ali about later.

"Huh," Ali says. "Figured she'd have left."

"No thanks to you," Lana says, waving a finger at Ali.

Once the Spirit ducks his head, Lana takes the time to update us on her progress yesterday. The others follow suit, including me. I even take a moment to introduce Kim, who is extremely reluctant to even say hi. Everyone takes the introduction of the AI with aplomb—just another post-System moment.

"Sounds like most of you have things well in hand," I say as we stare at the empty pot. Bland as gruel might be, it was still decent fuel for the day. "Mikito, if you've got teams that are workable, let's get them headed north to the dungeon. Get your best team on clearing it. If it manages to replicate, we'll send another team in till the Mana pool is cleared. We'll also want scouting teams moving to the communities. I know the Sect might have swept the place before, but now that they're out of power, we might be able to convince them to join us. Lana, I've got the basics up and running, but I want you to keep an eye out for talent. Someone's going to have to run the city, preferably someones."

"Benjamin?" Lana says with a raised eyebrow.

I raise my hand horizontally and waggle it. "Let's not rush this."

"I'll look around. But what are you going to do?"

"The city needs money and I need more Levels," I say, grimacing. "If I could hit Level 40…" I shake my head and push aside my regret. "There's a National Park close by, so the zone should be decent. Might even have a dungeon or two."

"Har. So you've got us all working and you're off having fun," Sam says, waving the last stick of crispy bacon.

"Well, yes." I could explain how growing my strength means growing the strength of the city and our team, of how I can hunt, fight, and capture faster than anyone here, bringing in a significant amount of Credits. I could even note that I spent the entire day yesterday stuck doing paperwork, but really, I know he's mostly teasing me.

"Leave your drones, will you?" Sam follows up. "I want to study them."

"And John, can you have Kim stay in the city? She can be useful to me," Lana says. "If you're willing to let me work with her on assigning tasks."

"It's an it," Ali corrects before I can reply.

"THE SENTIENT FORCE IS CORRECT. SURPRISINGLY."

"Enough, you two," I growl softly. "Kim, can you download yourself into the settlement's ummm… core?"

"YES."

"Good. Do that and follow Lana's orders," I say, settling that quickly.

Seeing that no one else has anything else to add, I stand. Time to get rid of some stress and get some experience.

***

Traveling to the national park wasn't hard at all. It was barely fifty kilometers from the town itself. Of course, it's on the other side of the river, which gives the town some protection, but it still isn't much if the monsters decide to go a-roaming. While most monsters don't, finding the higher Mana forests more comfortable, it still isn't a lot of protection. That's part of the reason why I was swinging by, to make my own evaluation of how dangerous it is. If there's an Alpha monster or a dungeon in here, it definitely needs taking care of.

"Is taking over the town's core the only way to win a city?" I ask Ali as I wander through the forest. I don't bother with the trails since I'm looking for monsters, tossing a spell or two when needed and letting the Spirit dump the body in my Altered Space.

"Nope. Easiest way, but there are others. Kill the guy who owns the place, and if they don't have a designated heir, it reverts to the killer or whoever is in the town, depending on circumstances. Only works on places that are individually owned. You can also buy up eighty percent of the land in a town. If that happens, the town automatically reverts control to you because you literally own most of it. Of course, if you drop below the eighty percent and gained it that way, you lose control too. Not common these days of course," Ali says.

"Of course." I sigh, calling for a Blade Strike, and cut down an overly affectionate mutant-pine tree. There's something wrong with the concept of carnivorous trees. Especially ones with pink fuzz rather than leaves. "Any reason they can't just sneak someone in and put their hands on the core to steal the place from us?"

"They could. Been done before, but mostly for places that have better defenses to turn on the original defenders. As it stands, the System notification will alert everyone, so it's not like they'll gain much. Kamloops's defenses would go down in a heartbeat. Doesn't gain them much and loses them some useful people," Ali says. "It's one thing to steal a city, another to keep it. As you're finding out."

"Still..." I frown, glancing backward.

"Not their style, boy-o," Ali reassures me. "And Kim will slow down the changeover long enough for your people to get a-killing. Relax."

I grunt, accepting his words for now. Still, it may be time to set up some additional security when I get back, something Ben could help with. Be a good test for him too, see if he's worth working with.

"You figure they're just going to launch a full-scale attack then?" I say, going back to the original line of questioning. I adjust my saunter through the forest slightly, heading for a few green dots. Better than nothing.

"If you mean a few of their teams, yeah. Might hire some additional help too," Ali says. "The Sect leans toward the quality-over-quantity approach to fights."

"Like the Guard."

"Actually, more like the Dragon Knights. The Erethran armed forces actually leans the other way. Not to say they aren't tough, but they use a lot of tech at the lower levels, which lets them field a larger force than others. More expensive, but makes them nasty to fight," Ali says.

"I've been wondering about that. My Class is only an Advanced one. Seems a bit low for bodyguards of royalty," I say.

"Are you concerned about the rarity or the strength?" Ali says, asking for clarification.

"Uhhh..." I take a few moments to finish off the bounding metallic wolf-like creatures attacking me. They might even be wolves. I don't bother checking. "Both, I guess."

"To get your Class the normal way, you would need to be assigned to the Honor Guard to start and be at Level 50. Obviously, even if you are Level 50 and refusing to progress, you aren't necessarily going to get to join the Honor Guard. A lot of people would rather keep progressing than wait around," Ali explains, dumping the bodies away for me while we head toward the next group of monsters. "As for their strength, I think you're missing the point. They're the Guard, the people you have to fight through to get close to the Erethran royal family. You're not facing one or two or a dozen of them but hundreds. And if you manage to survive all that, well, then you'll be up against their Champions."

"Champions?" I frown, tilting my head to the side. "That the Master Class?"

"One of the possibilities. There's generally only one or two next to the royals—the royals are pretty damn tough themselves. But it's one way to go," Ali says, shrugging. "More independent, better individual fighters. Of course, you need to be granted the title and well…"

"I'm not likely to." I sigh. Right. It's why I'm not as thrilled by the idea of hitting Level 50 as others might be. Whatever options the System might offer me, it's probably not going to be what I want. Not as if there are members of the Erethran Royal Family around to grant me a title of Champion. Lack of opportunity sucks. "Whatever. Future John can deal with that problem."

I grunt, picking up speed as my mind turns once more to the initial question that drove me out here. How do we deal with the Sect? I turn over, again and again, the options offered by Ali.

"We should be drowning them in numbers, shouldn't we?" I finally say, coming to a halt in a clearing and staring at the sunlight that streams in. I touch my helmet, letting it retract, and let the warmth cover my face as I struggle with the knowledge. "We should arm everyone, get them up on the walls for when they hit us. Drown them in fire and numbers, whittle down their best fighters…" Deal with their quality with our quantity.

"That'd be a good idea."

"And kill a lot of people," I whisper, my eyes burning with unshed tears. Anger and pain, mixing on this beautiful day.

"It's their fight too," Ali quietly points out.

"I know."

My mind spins, possibilities opening up. Put the people whose lives are at stake, whose freedom is in play, on the walls to fight. To live and die by their own hand. Help them, sure. But let them sacrifice too.

It's the smart thing to do.

The right thing to do.

I just have to be willing to let others die.

***

Later that evening, Lana finds me seated in the same spot where I found Ingrid. Watching the city, drinking from a bottle, mulling over my options.

"Missed you at dinner," Lana says, plopping down next to me.

In the corner, I'm somewhat startled to note, is Roland, the tiger almost completely hidden except for a pair of glowing eyes. I make a mental note to watch out for the kitty. Its ability to hide is almost as good as Ingrid's.

"Yeah, sorry. Doing some thinking. How'd the day go?" I say, offering her the bottle.

She takes it and swigs from the bottle before handing it back to me. "Pretty good. Kim was helpful in allocating resources and getting people working, including cleaning up some new buildings. Ben is working on reinforcing some of the thoroughfares as well, and adding a few traps. Can't do much fast since he doesn't own the buildings, but his Skills do give us options. He's talking of creating a 'fortress city,' with buildings reinforced and set up to do damage as invaders come in. Kim's also spending the time to reinforce our System security for the settlement, making it more expensive for others to buy information," Lana says. "You?"

"Nothing much. Mostly Level 30s out there, nothing to worry about. I accidentally wiped a lair, some moss monster living inside. Didn't realize it till later, otherwise I might have left it to grow," I say, shaking my head. Pity. We could have used another dungeon to clear and get the XP bonus from. "Might need to range farther out to find a dungeon."

"Not the worst thing in the world. So why are you sulking?" Lana says, prodding me with a booted foot.

I grunt, staring at her. "Not sulking. Thinking." At her raised eyebrow, I find myself elaborating. "Now that we kicked their ass, the next attack is going to be in force. While Ali doesn't expect them to send any Master Classes, even a high Level Advanced Class or two…"

"Will be more than enough to hold us down. And there's more of them than there are us," Lana says, smiling grimly. "That about right?"

"More high Level individuals, yes," I say, looking at her steadily as I finally say what's on my mind. "We could beat them if we used everyone. Draw them in, target and whittle down each of their Advanced Classes and make them bleed as they come in."

"But…"

"But people will die. Probably a lot of them," I say, waving at the window. "And that's if we can get them to agree to do it."

"No guarantee of that," Lana agrees. "Non-combat Classers aren't exactly the bravest bunch in general."

If we had a connection with them, or someone with a very high Charisma score, like Richard, maybe we'd have a better chance of motivating the group. Lana could do it, but she's got her hands full just organizing things. Then again, not being someone's slave is pretty good motivation, I'd think. There's no way to know what they'll choose really, not without trying.

"But you don't want them involved, do you?" Lana says, breaking into my thoughts. "Still trying to save the world?"

"No. Not if I can help it. But I don't see another way."

Lana smiles, leaning forward, her blouse falling open as she does. My eyes stray downward, and while I'm distracted, she flicks my forehead.

"Owww!" I exclaim. "You know, ever since we started sleeping together, you've gotten a lot more violent."

"And you've gotten dumber." Lana smirks. "When have you ever decided to take the options you've been offered?"

"I can't think of anything else!" I snarl. "It's not as if I'm a damn soldier. I'm a failed programmer with violent tendencies."

"You *were* a failed programmer," Lana says, her voice dropping, growing gentler. "Whatever you were, you've changed. Now you're something more. You're our leader."

"Joy," I mutter, suddenly feeling so damn tired. I never wanted this. But somehow I'm here, leading a group of people who trust me and a bunch of people who never asked me to.

"Tell me."

"Huh?"

"Tell me why you don't want the others to fight," Lana says.

I meet her eyes, drawn into those violet whirlpools, the insistence in her voice focusing me. "Because… it's not their job. It's not what they should be doing. Not if they haven't chosen to. Civilization, society, it's been a climb from the bloody muck where everyone fought and killed and died. We built our world with technology and rules and will, so those who weren't suited to a violent world could live in peace. Now, the drums are rolling and we're all part of that thin red line of heroes." Fresh anger bubbles up and leeches into my voice. "And we're forgetting that damn line is there for a reason. The System might have destroyed our world, but the only people who can destroy who we are is us. And I'll be damned if I contribute more to that than I have to."

"Then find another way. And stop complaining."

I nod, clenching that anger tightly again, pushing at the bubbling frustration. Lana watches, her hand on mine until I settle.

Then she edges closer to plant a gentle kiss on my lips. "Sometimes, not thinking about a problem can be the best way to find a solution."

I return the kiss, wrapping my arms around her body and holding her generous warmth to me. I draw a deep breath, smelling that intoxicating mixture of fresh air, ionized air, and something that is just her, and kiss her again, harder this time. Perhaps I do need a distraction.

***

An insistent pinging wakes me from deep slumber, automatic reactions conjuring my sword into my hand as I sit up, startled. I see nothing except for Roland, who stirs slightly at my movements before returning back to watchful stillness, and a still-slumbering redhead. A moment later, a flashing message finally clues me in on what woke me.

"YOU HAVE AN INCOMING COLLECT CALL. WOULD YOU LIKE TO ANSWER IT?"

"Who'd be calling now?" I mutter softly.

Even as quiet as I am, Lana shifts. I freeze, wondering if I woke her, but then I hear the whimpering, the half-filled sobs, and I know. She's having another of her nightmares. I stroke her head, futilely willing calm into her.

"MAJOR LABASHI RUKA."

"*Ah! Yes, answer it,*" I send to Kim mentally.

"CONNECTING."

"Redeemer, you wished to speak with me?" Labashi's voice comes over the air, seeming to resound in my head.

Similar to but different from the way Ali talks to me. It's weird and expensive, since I'm basically paying the System to make the connection, but it does skip past the entire issue of light speed lag and interference. A part of me, the same part that controls my affinity, seems to thrum with familiarity. Unfortunately, I don't have time to explore it.

"*Got a problem. Thought you might be able to help...*" When Labashi doesn't reject my initial proposal, I get right into it, explaining the situation I've dragged the team into. "*Figured with your experience, you might have a few ideas.*"

"Well, my first recommendation would be to augment your forces with external help," Labashi says. "I'll even give you a discount. It won't cost you much since it seems like the Thirteen Moons are already at their limit. There's a stop order on the boards about them."

"*Oh?*" I say, curious.

"Merc boards. We keep a number for information distribution purposes, places for us to talk about things that might affect each other—upcoming wars, new Dungeon Worlds, and the like. The Thirteen Moons have over-extended themselves with their entrance to Earth. They're over-leveraged and their credit rating wasn't that great to start with," Labashi explains. "None of the reputable companies will work with them."

"*Right. So just some companies of ill-repute at best.*" I sigh. Better than I had hoped for. It was one of the reasons I contacted Labashi, the potential of external help on both sides making things even more complicated. But if we can hire and they can't... "*That's good to know.*"

"Figure a platoon or two for your town will provide you the extra muscle you'll need and keep the town safe while you're gone."

"*Gone?*"

"If you're outnumbered, you shouldn't be waiting for them to set the tempo. Hit them and keep hitting them. I wouldn't recommend taking another town though, not unless you're willing to abandon it," Labashi says.

"*Guerilla tactics?*"

"Not exactly. You have a well-known base of operations, among other things. But close enough for your purpose."

"*That can work. Send me the contract. If we can afford it...*"

"If not, we have access to some banks," Labashi says smoothly.

"*Send it all. And thank you,*" I say, my shoulders finally relaxing.

So. Another option. Well, another two options. Help and a plan. Well, a direction, but I can work on it from there.

***

Awake now, I find my mind bouncing from thought to thought like a sugar-rushed fairy. With sleep eluding my grasp, I leave a note for Lana and take to the streets, walking my new domain. That's how I find myself seated in the stands of a baseball field as dawn creeps over the horizon, watching Mikito and a hunter team train together. Facing the tiny Samurai in her Ghost Armor are four individuals: two in melee combat, a spellcaster over thirty feet away, and another fighter who intersperses his body between Mikito and the caster, firing a pair of pistols in staccato rhythm.

A jumping twist sends Mikito spinning through the air in a dodge, her naginata sweeping around her body to force her second assailant to dodge. The moment she lands, she's spinning aside, taking the impact of the explosive rounds on her armor and building speed to sweep the legs off her initial attacker. Freed, Mikito darts toward the spellcaster.

Before she can reach the caster, the ground erupts in front of her, a rolling, attacking wave of greenery that grasps and stabs. A second is wasted as Mikito cuts and dodges, giving the others time to catch up with her.

"Nice use of the spell," Ali says softly to me. "A bit wasteful for Mana but against itty-bitty…"

"Yeah," I agree.

There are three methods of targeting for crowd control spells—manual, area effect, and System-targeted. The first requires you to cast and hit the target—think Spiderman's webbing, grasping ivy, and the like. The second is like my Polar Zone spell—target it at an area and anything inside gets affected. Including allies, which is less useful for group fights. And lastly, System-targeted spells go through the System, so there's no dodging them, only resisting. Of course, in terms of cost, the spells go from low to high in order, so while System-targeted spells might be more effective in theory, they're also significantly more expensive.

I watch the fight, the group surrounding Mikito doing their best to contain and take her down while Mikito takes shots of opportunity at the close-in fighters and attempts to get at the caster. Lowering her body to within inches of the ground and spinning on her feet, Mikito dodges a series of shots that impact against one of the sword-wielders behind her. Surprisingly, the bullets seem to do nothing, glancing off his body.

"What…?"

"Class Skill," Ali says and flicks his finger.

Friendly Fire (Class Skill)

Reduces damage done to designated friendly targets by attacker. Number of designated friendly units and damage reduced is dependent on Class Skill Level. Mana Regeneration reduced by 5 per Skill Level.

"Useful. But expensive," I say.

I can see why it's not a common Skill. Even with their group, he'd need at least two Class Skill points dedicated to it, reducing his Mana regeneration by ten. That's ten attribute points just to stay even, which can be painful, especially when you're starting out. On the other hand, the way he's taking part in the close-combat fight, I can see how they've integrated his ability into the fight. Curious, I pay a little closer attention to the shooter, calling up his information.

Mel Furh (Level 26 Gunslinger)

HP: 187/240

MP: 290/290

Conditions: Eagle-eye, Steady Hand

"Interesting," I say.

The two conditions seem to be exactly what they say—boosts to accuracy and speed of targeting, allowing Mel to run and shoot at Mikito, adding to the sheer volume of attacks she has to deal with. It probably would work better against someone who didn't have the control of the battlefield that the Samurai does, as she exhibits an uncanny understanding of where everyone is. As she's explained before, it's more an understanding of the options available to each individual in relation to the attacks they may use on her than a sixth sense. It's still impressive.

Close to Mikito, the second melee fighter drops low and pushes his hands outward, fire exploding from his form. It's the third time he's done this attack, so it doesn't catch Mikito by surprise, even if it does blow her aside enough into the path of the bullets.

Rhys Hnaris (Level 23 Mage Adept)

HP: 141/280

MP: 284/380

Conditions: Hasted, Flame Armor, Kinetic Absorption

Who would have thought there'd be a Mage who was willing to get in close? Using a combination of martial arts and spells, he's holding his own. Mostly. He's not skilled enough to compete with a dedicated melee fighter, doesn't have enough physical stats to overpower others, and his Mana pool isn't that deep. Kind of like a middle ground of all bad choices, if you looked at it statistically. Of course, none of that matters when you're flexible and prone to pulling out surprises—which the Mage Adept is doing right now. The exploding flame, rather than retreating to his body, flows toward Mikito and wraps around her.

The ranged spellcaster doesn't hesitate, waving and calling forth her moving greenery spell. This time around, instead of wrapping Mikito directly, she uses the spell to dump earth around the Samurai, entombing her. The swordsman and gunslinger pull back, the former guiding the Adept even farther away by hand. I frown, flicking a glance upward to note that Mikito's health isn't dropping too much before I relax.

A slow ten count, the green-brown mound shuddering and jerking with each of those seconds. But while she's fast, smart, and destructive, Mikito isn't that strong. She relies on her weapon and precision to add force multipliers to her attacks, rather than raw power like me. In a situation like this, it's a major disadvantage.

"Impressive," Ali says.

"She wasn't fighting that seriously," I point out. In the few minutes that we've watched, I already saw the holes in their offense that she could have exploited if she had gone all out. Among other things, she wasn't Hasted. "But yes, they're pretty damn coordinated. Might actually be better than us. Reminds me of Capstan and his original group."

"They've put in a lot of time training their coordination. And they've done it in a disciplined manner," Ali agrees.

As the mound slowly falls apart, a bladed polearm leading the way, I hop down to introduce myself. I'm a bit puzzled why a group this skilled and disciplined isn't higher Leveled. The fact that they're willing to be out here in the early hours of the morning speaks to their dedication.

"Hello there," I greet the group, smiling. Not that they haven't noticed me.

I get grunted and verbal greetings. Mikito offers me a single nod before she casts a Cleanse spell on herself to rid herself of soot and dirt.

After a round of greetings, I congratulate and praise them. It's something I know needs to be done—boost their self-confidence, let them know they're doing well. Lead, I guess, if you wanted to think of it that way. Which is why I'm surprised when the Gunslinger snorts.

"No need to pour sunshine up our ass. Mikito was holding back," Mel says, the well-built brunet grinning as he speaks. "She could have taken us at any point if she hadn't limited her abilities and tactics."

His harsh words get a round of nods from his team—and it's clear, it's his team.

"Huh." His bluntness gives me pause for a moment. "How come you guys are so low Leveled?"

"The Sect," Rhys answers, grimacing. "They took on anything that was higher Level, limited our hunting to lower Level zones and limiting the amount of time we could hunt. They wanted us to stay well below their Levels. Made it easier for us to be controlled. Rather than get 'relocated for better opportunities,' we decided to limit our growth ourselves."

"They could stop us from Leveling, but they couldn't stop us from training," Mel says, his hands casually resting on the butts of his pistols. I look at the pistols again and realize I recognize those giant, ugly pistols, but I'm unsure why. Seeing my look, Mel smiles slightly and pulls one out, finger off the trigger and holding it pointed up and away slightly, for me to see it properly. "Desert Eagle. More a toy than a weapon before the change, but with my added strength…"

"You were shooting exploding rounds," I say, frowning. "Didn't realize they had those."

"Class Skill. I'm able to make specialized ammunition that works with my weapons. Upgraded them all myself too, so they work with the System," Mel explains.

"Can they…?"

"Nope. Tried it already," Mel says. "Seems to be locked to me, so I can't provide the rounds or guns to others. Might change at higher Levels, but for now, it's only the craftsmen who can do that."

"Your Class…" I ask, unsure about the etiquette on this matter but curious anyway. We're all still figuring things out after all.

"Gunslinger. You could call me a bit of a gun nut before this. Was in the army for a few years. Infantry. Was in between deployments to Afghanistan when the System hit. That first day, I grabbed at the Class when it came," Mel says. "Wasn't thrilled with the idea of being a Rifleman."

"Ah." I nod in agreement. Yes, the System was known to hand out skill- or hobby-appropriate Classes. Still, surprising that he got what I'm assuming is a somewhat uncommon or even maybe rare Class in a city like this. Then again, luck does have a part to play in all this. "Seems like an interesting Class."

"I think so," Mel says, flashing me a grin. "Mikito tells me you were planning on hitting Kelowna earlier, but stopped?"

"Yup. I figured it'd be good to attack them if we wiped out their Advanced Class team, but..." I shrug, acknowledging our failure. "Didn't work out. Probably a bad idea anyway."

"Why'd you say that?" Mel says, frowning.

"Well, a friend pointed out that we'd be over-stretching ourselves. We wouldn't be able to defend either place adequately," I say, remembering Labashi's advice.

"Only if you intended to defend it. Nothing wrong with wiping out their people then pulling back, draining the place of any resources you can get your hands on," Mel says. "Hell, if you threw up some basic defenses, no guarantee they'd be willing to go after it."

"Oh...?"

"We're right smackdab in their zone of control. Only reason the other team wasn't here was because they were expanding out east. If you knock them out, all the cities around us would be in a precarious position geographically. Nothing to support them—which means they might not risk more people to take a marginal place," Mel says.

"Risky," Mikito says, frowning.

I note that Rhys is nodding as well.

"Of course, but what do you lose out? Might widen their options, but if you don't care about losing the cities…"

"And the people who live in those cities?" I ask softly, my voice cold.

Mel's broad shoulders move in a dismissive gesture. Before I can say anything else, another group wanders into the training grounds. Mikito takes the opportunity to order the groups to train together, gripping my arm to pull me away.

"Bit of a dick, isn't he?" I say, not bothering to lower my voice.

"He's actually got a pretty decent set," Ali says, glancing at me.

Mikito ignores the rude Spirit, speaking to me instead. "He's not wrong. Nor are you. But I don't think you are here to talk to my people?"

"Your people?" I say, then move on before she can answer. "I was, a little. Thought I'd get a firsthand look at them, maybe give a few encouraging words. Also wanted to let you know that we've got some Hakarta coming in to reinforce the city in a few days, once their transport drops them off. Well, and I sign the papers."

"Hakarta?" Mikito frowns then glances at the group before nodding. "You want me to warn the hunters."

"Right. I'll get Lana on it too, but well…"

"They're more likely to do damage," Mikito says, nodding. "Consider it done."

"Thanks." I watch the groups spar. I frown, shifting my feet, considering if I should stick around.

Mikito steps in front of me, blocking my vision. "You should go."

"But…"

"You have better things to do. And your presence is not beneficial," Mikito says, smiling slightly to take the sting out of her words.

"I…"

"Go. I have this," Mikito says, waving.

"Fine," I grumble and head off, kind of upset she's kicking me out.

I'll admit I'm not the most charismatic or nice individual, but I'm not that bad! Still, I do have paperwork to review and others to speak with. Resigning myself to further work, I head off.

Chapter 11

"Again," Mikito says firmly as I come to an end of the form.

I glare at the woman for a moment before sighing and walking back to the center of the room we've taken over to restart the sword form. One of the advantages of owning most of a city, places like a school gymnasium are easy to find and the bonus in training speeds is a plus.

Before I can begin, Mikito says, "Focus on your edge. It's still shifting at the end. And at step three and seven, shift back a half inch."

I grunt, nod, and begin. The form I use, that I train, is the same one I deduced over a year ago from what I saw on recordings of Erethran Honor Guard fights. In particular, there's a certain blue-haired woman whose style I'm attempting to mimic, a way of using the Soulbound weapon more effectively. It requires me to summon and banish my blades as I attack and defend. Together, Mikito and I have further refined it, adding the additional blades from Thousand Blades so that I can form a never-ending ring of swords around my body. In theory—and with some practice—the form allows me to attack and defend at the same time, constraining openings as the floating blades cut off lines of attack.

Sadly, while Mikito might be trained, smart, and dedicated, she was also limited by her past. Human martial arts don't contain much knowledge about floating weapons that move in their own paths, so we're both struggling to figure out the best ways to use this Skill of mine. Since the recordings we have are of the lady in actual combat, replicating them into forms that I can use to train was difficult. If it weren't for the fact that I heal constantly, I'd be littered with wounds.

It's only after I've run through the forms another four times that Mikito calls it a day. At least for the theory portion of our early morning training session. As I stretch and rub at the latest cut, smearing blood over my skin, Mikito is gently stretching.

"Ready?" the young Japanese woman asks me.

"Limits?" I answer.

"No Skills for the first three rounds. Then we'll increase. Choose one Skill or spell to add each round," Mikito suggests.

I nod. "Sounds fun."

I grin, calling forth my sword and getting into my guard. Right foot forward, hand held slightly above waist high and slightly outside my right knee. Left hand close to my angled body, weight distributed evenly.

Once Mikito sees I'm in guard, she moves, leaping forward. My eyes widen slightly, the change of pace and style catching me off guard for a microsecond. Luckily, my reflexes don't stop, shifting my sword to aim toward the fast-moving body, and it clashes with her naginata even as the Japanese woman spins away. I catch a glimpse of laughing eyes, the sheer joy of letting go without concern for safety, before I have to focus. Still, a grin creeps across my face.

An hour plus later, we're both seated on the ground, panting. Stamina might not necessarily be a major concern during fights for either of us—well, me—but training is different. We're purposely attempting to remove all our Stamina, pushing ourselves to the state where we're tired and start making mistakes. The kind of mistakes that only happen when you can barely lift your hand.

As I stare at the ceiling, I can't help but ask, "How are you doing?"

"Recovering. Eight minutes," Mikito says wryly.

Of course it's eight minutes. It's mostly the same for me. That's one of the oddities of the System—it takes the same amount of time for everyone to reach their peak level. Of course, what that peak level is is different, but still. An oddity. Only Class Skills make a difference.

"I meant with the hunting groups," I say, clarifying matters. It's been days since we arrived and Mikito has taken on the role of guide without complaint.

"It is good. They're more hesitant than those in Whitehorse. More jumpy. I'm spending time building up their confidence," Mikito says with a frown. "The Sect has done well to condition these guys to play it safe. Getting them to risk a little has been the hardest thing."

I nod, understanding her point. Still, it wasn't what I was asking. Even if we've only known each other for a bit, she's still a friend. And a year ago, she lost her husband and her family. Now I'm asking her to take care of strangers and train them to put themselves in front of monsters. "And you?"

"I'm fine," Mikito says, offering me a slight smile.

It's a deflection. I know it. She knows it. But I don't push it, because, well, it'd be rude. And talking about our emotions, about how we feel, isn't really something either of us is comfortable doing. Blame our culture, our upbringing, or just our nature. In the end, the results are the same.

"Okay then," I say softly. "So tell me what I did wrong this time."

Mikito smiles slightly, leaning forward to speak. After she's done, I'll give her my own notes. And then, well, we'll do it all again tomorrow.

***

I frown, staring at the converted block of buildings. What used to be squat, utilitarian concrete buildings have transformed, becoming one squat, utilitarian concrete building with weapon emplacements. A concrete extension, seeming to have grown from the corner of the building, joins the apartments to the two-story retail shops next to it. Above the retail stores, sandbags and molded steel sit on the rooftops, providing cover and protection for defenders. Just above, mostly hidden, I see flashes of greenery where the apartment complex's garden thrives. As Lana said, the building is impressive.

As I walk up to the main entrance, Benjamin walks out to greet me with a smile. Behind him, protected by sheets of metal, are guards, each carrying registered rifles. Out of the corner of my eyes, I see security cameras dotting the walls, watching me as I approach.

"Johnathan, thank you for taking me up on my invitation," Benjamin says with a smile, offering his hand.

"It's just John," I say, shaking his hand. Once again, I eye the thin Architect. His invitation was a surprise, though it shouldn't have been. After all, I had "felt out" Roxley myself. There's no reason Benjamin wouldn't want to do the same with me.

"Come on up. Or would you like the tour first?"

"Mmm… dinner first," I say with a smile.

Interestingly enough, Benjamin doesn't live on the top floor but the sixth. His apartment is small, cozy even, with the look of a well-lived building. Children's toys and discarded clothing are scattered on the floor of the living room, around a worn beige couch, and a smiling lady greets me as I step in.

"This is Susan, my wife," Benjamin says, then he's tackle-hugged at the knees. He pats the child's head. "And Julia, my daughter."

"Mr. Lee." A hand is offered to me, which I shake. Ben's wife has long, curly, light brown hair and is wearing a simple summer dress that hugs a thin figure. "Please, sit. Dinner will be served soon."

"Thank you," I say, letting Ben and Susan guide me to the dining room. Surprisingly, I find Mel seated already. "Mel."

"Ms. Sato mentioned that we should have Mel over for dinner too," Benjamin says as we take a seat.

"Not a problem," I say. "Mikito tells me your team was the one who managed to clear the dungeon?"

"Yes. That completion bonus was quite good," Mel says, eyes glinting with humor. "I'm beginning to understand how you guys Leveled so fast, especially if what Mikito said was true about the number of dungeons you had to deal with."

"There were a few," I say, leaning forward. "Tell me about this one."

Mel tilts his head, regarding me for a second before expounding on the dungeon. I lead him on, getting a feel for how they did and what he thought. Mel's interesting—he's dry and clinical and extremely detailed about the dungeon, almost as if he's providing a report. Only when Susan arrives with dinner do we switch topics and speak about lighter matters. The weather, cute new animals, the burgeoning education and daycare system she's involved in. Topics more suited for the ears of the four-year-old joining us.

The meal is delicious and filling—matzah ball soup followed by a roast with pureed carrots and potato pancakes, and after that, mashed potatoes and salad and a stew. Beef stew perhaps, though I wouldn't have bet on that for the meat. Tasty and chewy anyway.

When dinner is over, Julia is taken by Susan to her room, Ben's wife giving him a look I'm unable to read.

"Shall we take a walk?" Ben asks, gesturing toward the door. "I'd love to show you around the apartments."

"Sure," I say readily, curious about the building and his Skills. It doesn't hurt that we'll actually get to the meat of this meeting finally. As nice as a home-cooked meal and the evening was, it's pretty draining playing at this social game.

No surprise, Mel follows us as we walk.

As we head down the corridor to the elevators, Ben speaks. "Sam tells me he's not really from the Yukon. He joined you later?"

"Yes."

"Ah…" Ben pauses, realizing I'm not going to elaborate. "Well, he seems to have gotten along well with you."

"He's got an interesting Class," I reply.

Mel's eyes tighten, but he doesn't say a thing.

"Very true. There's been some interesting synergy between his Class and the Mechanics, Engineers, and other craftsmen in town. Now that they're working together with a wider range of resources, they're managing to develop some interesting inventions," Ben says. "Ah, you might be interested in this."

Ben stops at a door, opening it and pointing at where the original apartment building expanded to join the retail stores. For a time, he explains the various security measures and his Skill, detailing Mana and point cost, the self-improving nature of the building. It's an interesting discussion, but as we speak, I can see Mel getting more and more impatient.

When we're finally out of the join, Mel speaks. "What are your plans for us? For the residents."

"What do you mean?" I say, raising an eyebrow.

"You don't seem intent on leaving. Are you intending to choose people based off their Class and Skills? Off Levels?" Mel says belligerently.

"Choose what?" I ask softly, playing obtuse.

"The people in charge. Don't think we've not noticed that everyone in charge is someone with a high Level or one of you Yukoners."

"Well, we are somewhat more experienced," I say, shrugging. "Thus the higher Levels."

"Bullshit," Mel snaps. "Ben here knows more about city planning than you do. He was on a damn city council, for god's sake. And Mikito might know how to fight, but she's still learning about tactics. At least you've got Sam and Torg dealing with your farming and crafting."

"Figuring we're not competent?"

"Not competence. Lacking a little experience perhaps," Ben interjected.

Mel says, "You kids have—"

"Kids? You might be a decade or two older, but we're not exactly children," I snap, then draw a deeper breath. "And who's the kid? You both are nearly half our Levels. Whether you like it or not, those Levels matter."

"As does pre-System experience!" Mel snaps. "You think your Levels are all important while—"

"While you aren't paying us enough respect for what we've done."

"I'm sure Mel wasn't insulting you on purpose," Ben says quickly, stepping between us. "We're all just looking to help out where we can."

"Maybe. But calling me a kid isn't helping," I say angrily. "We've got the experience of actually building up a city in this new System world. And yeah, we might not have the same skills you had, but we sure as hell have done it before."

"And we understand that," Ben says, shooting a glare at Mel to shut him up. "But we'd also like to know what your plans are for the city."

"Not much to tell. We're going to do our best to get the city into shape, give you all the boost that we've found worked in the Yukon to become a functioning city," I say. "We'll kick the Sect's ass too, while we're at it. In the meantime, if you guys want to help, we need you to continue Leveling up and helping keep things contained. Whether you like it or not, till the Sect is dealt with, we're the city's best hope."

"Fine. We'll continue Leveling up, but you guys better start talking to those of us from Kamloops. We won't take being locked out of our city. Not again, and not by a... by humans," Mel says huffily.

I nod. He's a bit short-tempered and gruff perhaps, but I get it. And I do have plans for them—but it's not time to tell him just yet.

***

The next week passes in a blur. The Hakarta platoons arrived yesterday. They integrate pretty well, mostly because my team and I take the time to ensure everyone is settled with their presence before we head out. I guess when you have a walking, talking, mostly polite humanoid and compare it to the slavering, carnivorous monsters that lie outside the cities, you get a little bit of perspective. Helps when the polite green humanoid looks as though he could rip you apart if you weren't polite.

In the course of the week, Mikito's able to drag the average Level up by one, which is pretty impressive when you consider how few high-Level zones are around here. I'm once more reminded how "lucky" we were in Whitehorse.

"DRONES ONLINE," Kim flashes at me, and my minimap updates.

A second later, another larger map appears in front of me, providing a real-time feed of the surrounding areas. While the bionetwork continues to grow out, the modified sensor drones will help fill in the gap and provide more detailed information. For now, Kim has them on a routine sweep.

"Thanks." I stare at the information, watching data flicker and update before stabilizing. I dismiss the map after a second, and the view of the roadway where we wait reappears. The rest of the team hasn't arrived yet, so it's Sam and me standing in the middle of the road west, sharing the map information that he's fed to the settlement. "Good work there, Sam."

The Technomancer grunts his acknowledgement, head still in the bowels of his modified truck. Now that he has had the time and supplies, he's been upgrading his transportation, adding everything from anti-gravity plates to plate armor. The most eye-catching addition is the anti-tank beam cannon mounted on the roof, a weapon that feeds off its own power supply. It doesn't have a lot of shots, but it'd hurt even me.

"Keep the teams to the north for now," Mikito instructs the group that trails her as she turns the corner. "Remember, the Hakarta are here to help, but you all are still the primary defense force. You need to pull the teams back in time for you to join the convoy. Watch your rotations!"

"We got it," Mel grumbles, shaking his head. "I've done this before you know."

Mikito's lips purse, but she nods shortly, leaving the group.

Coming from around the other corner, Lana's doing much the same with her tiny retinue. Torg, Benjamin, and a few others who make up the new city council listen to the redhead. While they still aren't happy, the short-term solution of using a group of locals to oversee the day-to-day has settled the locals down somewhat. Unlike Mikito, Lana's mostly just saying goodbye and letting them know our general plans. Rather than breaking away, the group follows Lana all the way to me.

"John," Benjamin greets me with a smile, eyes sweeping over our group as we get ready to leave. "We'll keep the city ticking for you."

"Thanks." I smile in gratitude. I'm not stupid—I understand the risk in giving this group of strangers as much access and power as I am, but it's not as if I have that much time. Better to trust that Lana picked them right and that Kim can keep them contained while I get on with the important parts of keeping everyone alive. Not to mention the fact that unless they're really stupid, they'll wait to take over until the current danger has passed. No reason for me to stick around and help them out if they take the city from me.

"Not sure what I'm doing on the council," Torg mutters, shaking his head as he returns to a familiar complaint.

"You know farming. System farming to be exact. The city mostly does farming. Seems like the perfect fit to me," I say.

"I'm just a Serf…" Torg peters off as everyone else looks at him. He sighs, giving up.

Still, I make a mental note to keep an eye on him and look for a replacement. Never know if he'd choose to leave for a more established city.

"Right, you guys keep the city running. Get the convoy up and running. We won't be gone too long, if everything works out well. Kim can contact us if necessary and has an idea of what we want done. Mostly though, keep building, keep growing in Levels, and keep strengthening our defenses," I say.

After that, getting on the road takes no time. Lana joins Sam in his truck while Mikito and I ride ahead. About half an hour later, we exit the sensor envelope around Kamloops and find the last member of the team waiting for us.

"Ingrid." I pull Sabre to a stop, leaning forward as I sweep my gaze over her body. Nothing out of place and she looks, if not relaxed, at least somewhat neutral.

"John. Ladies," Ingrid says, her gaze lingering on Sam's truck before she shakes her head and dismisses whatever thought is bugging her. "You got my message?"

"Yes," I say, tapping my helmet so I can at least speak with her eye-to-eye. Really, a part of me wonders why I bother with a helmet. I'm strong enough that I could fall off the bike onto my head at a hundred miles an hour and only get a tiny ouchie. But years of training seems to hold true, making me feel really uncomfortable on the bike if I don't have the helmet on.

Before Ingrid can answer further, Shadow, who has crept up next to her, assaults her with a giant, slobbery tongue. A few minutes later, after Ingrid has finally pried herself away from Lana's puppy and its shadow—and how a shadow slobbers and licks is somewhat mind-bending—she is more calmly greeted by the girls and Sam, leaving me drumming my fingers in impatience.

"They pulled everyone from Vernon?" I say slowly.

"Yes," Ingrid says.

"And you're certain there isn't anyone in town?" I mutter.

"Certain? No. But I'm pretty sure the Sect grabbed all of their people and their Serfs," Ingrid says. "If they're there, they're so well hidden we can't see them. They might really be gone."

"What do you intend to do?" Lana says, tilting her head toward me, a lock of hair falling across her face to be angrily brushed aside.

"Take the city. Organize those who are willing and have them leave for Kamloops. Then I'm going to sell the city back to the System," I say.

"What?"

"Huh?"

"Maji?"

"Why?"

I turn to Sam, who asks that last question. "We can't hold the city. And with our population so shot, there's no point in keeping a ton of tiny little enclaves. Better to concentrate our people where we can to grow faster. Also, the Credits from selling a town can be—"

"Lucrative," Ali says, flashing a wide, shit-eating grin. "That's how John got Sabre."

I see lots of nods, but of course, it's Ingrid who asks the obvious question. "You going to share?"

***

Organizing Vernon and getting its citizens moving back toward Kamloops is painful. People are stubborn, emotional, and irrational, and even in the face of incontrovertible proof that their town is dying if not dead, many still refuse to leave. It takes all of Lana's significant Charisma to convince most of them to pack. There's no way we can guard them all, no way to keep them safe from the monsters or the Sect if they are out on the limb. And yet, some refuse. Some because they don't believe us. Some because they believe it's another test. But Lana does her thing as do the others to a smaller extent, and we slowly get a stream of others in. Of course, the next problem is transporting people back to Kamloops.

"We ready yet?" Sam asks. "The convoy should be ready by now."

"How long will it take?" I frown, trying to mentally gauge how long it'd take to send a message back to get the convoy moving to us. Then again, until we have at least the majority of people sorted and out of the way, I'm not going to even attempt to enter the City Center. Just because we haven't run into any traps or resistance yet doesn't mean there isn't any.

"Hour or so. Should just be about right for the pickup," Sam says, turning to his truck. He stares at it for a second, and a panel in the back rolls back, a drone floating upward. I can see portions of my drones in it—the dragonfly's base framework has been bulked up and altered. The resulting drone is no longer a surveillance drone but something bigger, nastier, and greyer. A pair of beam rifles stick out from its side, and a smaller dish hangs below the undercarriage. "I'll let Kim know. Shouldn't take more than an hour and it can hone in on me later."

"When did you build it?" I ask, looking over the new drone. Not what I was expecting, since this drone is significantly different from my own and the ones around the city.

"In the last few days, after I modified the others for Kim. Have about a half dozen drones in store, though I can only control three right now. Well, three with any degree of control," Sam says quite proudly. "I got fed up of hiding inside Mikito's PAV."

I smile and send Sam off to send the message while I walk around quietly. As always, Mikito has taken on the role of dealing with the few hunters while Lana's in the midst of organizing the others. I pitch in with Lana where I can, cajoling and answering questions, but it's no surprise that Lana and eventually Sam are the main go-tos. I'm more than content to let them deal with the crowd, and I eventually break off when Ingrid makes her way back.

"So...?" I ask.

"Traps. Lots of them. The entire building's wired to blow. Multiple spells and turrets are set up to deal damage if anyone tries to enter the Core. Probably some mines too," Ingrid says, shaking her head. "Wasn't easy to get close enough to look. The townsfolk cordoned off the place. I hear a few people were injured before they realized the problem."

"Can you disarm it?" I ask.

"What do I look like?" Ingrid says sarcastically.

I wince at her tone and glance at Sam, wondering if he could be of use.

"Don't bother, boy-o," Ali says. "He doesn't have the Skill for this. Or skill. Disarm Traps or its equivalent is a specialized thing. You'd need both to do a proper disarm."

"Great." I frown, considering my options.

"What are you worried for? Toss your Soul Shield on and walk in," Ali says, waving. "Just keep casting your Heal spells and you'll be good."

"Just walk in?" I say, somewhat amused. "One does not just walk in—"

"With your health, Skills, and spells?" Ali says. "Yes. Yes. You do. Unless you want to take a few days slowly whittling down the defenses."

"Then we stick to the plan," I say, gesturing to the group of humans still being slowly moved and guided out.

The second convoy departs as I speak, enough transportation scrounged together to make a group large enough to make sense to send out with our limited number of hunters. I can only hope the rest of the hunter teams arrive from Kamloops. We didn't want too many of our own people in the initial scouting groups, but now that we know what the situation is, it's time to get moving.

***

Hours. It takes hours for transportation to arrive from Kamloops and the refugees to pack themselves in. The hunter groups from Kamloops are finally here, spread out to play guard over the convoy. Lana and Sam are in the midst of it all, organising people and directing them to vehicles, bargaining and explaining why, no, bringing Grandma's armoire isn't going to work. It's stupid, irrational, and emotional and why I'm dodging it all, seated as I am on a nearby office tower and watching the roads, staring at the data Ali feeds me.

It's there that Ingrid finds me. "Nothing?"

"Not yet," I say, my fingers rolling a chocolate bar around and around. "I could have sworn they'd have hit us by now."

"Might be waiting for you to take the city," Ingrid offers, gesturing toward the abandoned building which houses the City Core.

"They can't think I'm that stupid." Maybe I'm being paranoid, but this feels too much like a trap. There's no way I'd go in while the city is still mostly populated, never mind the threat of an attack if I'm stuck making my way to the City Core.

"Stupid is as stupid does," Ingrid says.

"And boy, have you done some stupid things," Ali adds.

"We set?" I say to Ingrid, ignoring Ali, and receive a nod in reply. I relax slightly, grateful that whatever the reason for the delay, we've set up our own little series of surprises.

"Would I be here otherwise?" Ingrid snarks back.

I open my mouth to reply, but something on the horizon catches my eye. I frown, zooming in with the helmet, the dot growing bigger at an astounding rate. A pair of stubby wings, a flattened, cone-shaped body in grey, and stubs of metal pointing out of it is what I see. Behind it, bigger, blockier airships follow at a more sedate pace.

"Shit!" I mentally command the radio on. "We have incoming airships. Get everyone off the streets and hidden. Sam, we're going to need that gun of yours. Ingrid, Mikito, get ready to intercept when their ground-pounders arrive."

Even as I speak, the dot I noticed has expanded significantly, now visible to the naked eye. A moment later, its weapons start tearing up buildings with brilliant blue beams of destruction. I throw myself off the building, crossing the distance to another, my Soul Shield flaring into a brilliant corona of reds and blues as energy bleeds over.

I run and dodge, the attacks seeming to be fixed on me. A few eternal seconds later, my Soul Shield having fallen and my exposed skin blackened, the attack cuts off. The booming echo of too-fast airships and crumbling buildings rings through my ears. My breath comes hurriedly, the filtered air from the helmet stale and sterile. On a partly crumbled building, I swing my hand up and ignore the falling black dots that make up air-inserted Sect members. My team will have to deal with the invaders disembarking from the transport ships. My job is to fix my mistake. I should have known about the damn airships.

My hand rises, my mind fixing on the fast-retreating airship that is already turning, and I make the connection. Lower the potential on one side, increase it on the other. Use Mana to restrict the flow, my Elemental Affinity to reduce the bonds in the channel. Then more Mana to start the process, even as arcane symbols and thoughts flicker through my mind. Lightning explodes from my hand, reaching across the distance in a blink of an eye, and I channel the raw forces of nature. Ali darts forward into the stream, focusing the flow and intensifying it with his ability.

Around the gunships, shields flares to life, taking the damage I dish out as the lightning jumps from ship to ship. Those shields are more than enough to deal with my initial blast, but I have the connection now and I refuse to let them hold the high ground. A part of me rails against my stupidity at forgetting that there is no dragon to rule the skies. That out here, airpower is actually possible. People are dying, people have died, because I made a mistake and all I can do is pay them back in kind.

Beams of fire targeted at my unmoving form, my refreshed Soul Shield glowing as it sheds damage. Seconds before my shield falls, so does the lead gunship's. More power, channeled through Ali, shorts out electronics and melts armor while my flesh cooks. A corner of my mind spots a beam of destruction stab upward from the ground, Sam's truck taking out the second airship. Pain wraps around me like clingfilm, my nerves frying, my body burning. Suddenly, blessed relief from the mounting pain as the beam cuts off, the remaining airship peeling away.

"Enough, boy-o," Ali shouts, and I realize he's been doing so for a couple of seconds.

I kill the lightning, collapsing to my knees as my body struggles to heal. Flesh reknits, my hair slowly regrowing, burnt skin flaking off. A hand scrambles to the side and injects a health potion into my body to speed up the healing process. I know the System reduced some of the damage for me, reducing the actual effect of the damage to simulate my resistances and my health points. Hell, it even reduced how much it hurt. System-weirdness.

"Time to move," Ali says, expanding the map so that I can see the converging red dots.

I made a target of myself, and if it weren't for the hunter teams from Vernon and Kamloops and my friends slowing them down and distracting them, I'd be dealing with the landed Sect members.

John Lee
HP: 487/1700
MP: 729/1310
Conditions: Crispy

I stagger upward, eyeing my condition, and cast a quick Greater Healing and Greater Regeneration in short order. Should have done a second earlier, but I was so damn angry. Still am, but the armor I'm wearing is mostly gone and my health is nearly shot. Sabre first, then combat.

"Status," I say over the party communications, wondering how things are going as I drop to the ground. Sabre's on autopilot as it winds through the broken roads to me.

"Forty-three Sect members are in the city. They're working in groups of five when they can, but we're working on breaking them up. Levels range from around 30 plus to Advanced Classes, I'd guess," Sam says, his voice gruff and hurried, as if he's got something better to do. "Mikito and Lana and her pets are leading the combat teams in direct fights, but that Blood Warrior and Rock Thrower you were talking about are tearing through any group they find. We're avoiding them for now but…"

"Forty-two," Ingrid says, breaking into the conversation. "But we need you out there, John."

"On it. Just getting Sabre." I hurry toward the intersection I know Sabre is rushing into. Instinct and the map make me jerk to a stop before I enter the intersection and expose myself. A large twisting cone of energy and vines rips through the air in front of me. "Might be a bit delayed."

I conjure my sword and a few trailing blades, gather myself, then jump upward and sideways slightly. I land against the building's wall, legs bunching beneath me as they take the impact and release, throwing me at an angle upward and forward. Spinning through the air, I lash out with Blade Strike as I clear the building, sending blade energy streaking toward my attackers.

Small fry, I note quickly, even as I conjure a fireball. I send it toward the group scrambling from my earlier attack. The fireball flies toward the group, a Sect member already raising his hand to conjure a shield of ice. That's when I surprise them by Blink Stepping into their midst, ignoring my own fireball. It's an insane move, stepping right into your own explosion, and that's why none of them expect it.

Cutting right, I slice apart the fast-acting Mage, breaking his incipient spell and ducking behind his bleeding form, using his half-severed body as cover for when the fireball arrives. Everything is moving in slow motion it seems, but it snaps back into place when the fireball erupts, throwing red and gold destruction around like a child given a bag of confetti. Compared to being cooked alive by the gunship's beam weapon, this just hurts.

"Die," I snarl, lunging forward and skewering another Sect member.

A third, struggling up from being thrown aside by the fireball, gets run over by Sabre. I throw myself toward the bike, triggering the change and stomping on the struggling form with one newly metal-covered leg. The others are easy to mop up after that, the added firepower of the mecha adding to the carnage.

Exhaling, I take a couple of seconds to get my breath back. Then it's time to get moving. Minutes of running and dodging, hunting down the glowing red, green, and blue dots of enemies on my minimap ensue.

There's no planning on my part, instead giving control to Sam, who has a better view of the fight with his drones and isn't directly in combat, stuck as he is in his truck. I bounce from group to group, adding an onslaught of sudden death to existing and burgeoning fights, never stopping as I attempt to close with the Blood Warrior. Problem is, he's split himself a couple of times and his blood clones are running around, clogging up my minimap. The two I manage to catch are easy enough to dispatch—one easier than the other—but even watered down, they're too tough for anyone except the core team to deal with. And if any of the team actually runs into the main body, it'll go real bad real fast. Thankfully, Sam reports that Lana and her pets have run into the Rock Thrower, the group and her hunting team ganging up to take him down.

I round the next corner and spot a glowing threesome ready for the picking. Except I'm not the only one with sensors and information and these three hit me with a combined spell. Wind, electricity, and kinetic force cut, fry, and smash into Sabre's shield, their combined spell throwing me through a nearby building and the next one too.

Sabre's shield had taken a beating even before this and doesn't last under the onslaught, meaning that the mecha's armor has to take the brunt of it. Damage bleeds through—it always bleeds through—cracking a rib and searing newly healed skin, the smell of slightly cooked flesh re-assaulting my nose. I keep rolling, getting out of the line of sight, which does little when they fire a series of grenades inside and blow me out the other side of the wall.

This time around, I Blink Step mid-explosion, throwing myself onto the top of a nearby building using Ali's line of sight. Head spinning from the attack, I struggle to orient myself as I stagger to my feet. A glimpse of figures below is all I need to act on instinct and return fire, launching my entire rack of missiles at the group. It's overkill for a trio of Mages, but they pissed me off.

"Sorry about the trap, boy-o. They layered some invisibility spells to hide what they were up to and I didn't manage to pierce them in time," Ali says.

It's a horrible trade, three Sect members for two-thirds of Sabre's armor and even more of my Mana. I snarl, running again as I search for more, the smoking remnants of the town surrounding me. Vernon was never a big city— mostly three-, four-story office buildings in short blocks—which means I end up on the road again in short order. The city is ruined, smoldering hulks of buildings and spreading fires all around me. The Sect cares not a whit about collateral damage as they attack our people.

"Two blocks down, keep going this way," Sam says, his voice urgent. I speed up, refreshing my spells and the shield's, watching my Mana drop again. "The Blood Warrior—or one of his clones—is about to intersect with you."

I grin wolfishly, happy that something is going my way. I raise the automatic rifle strapped to my arm, making sure that the armor piercing and high explosive rounds are cycled and ready. Comparatively low amount of damage, but the Inlin spits out enough projectiles that it makes up for some of it. In my other hand, I have my sword, ready to release a Blade Strike. On top of that, I prep the sonic pulser, pulling out all the stops when the Blood Warrior arrives.

The ear-piercing shriek, set at decibels high enough that it can shatter glass and screw with an individual's inner ear, explodes outward the moment the Blood Warrior crosses the road. The red, fluid figure informs me that I'm not fighting the original, just one of his clones. Still, the sonic pulse is enough to make it shudder to a stop, disturbing ripples flowing along its "flesh" as the pulser assaults it. Time enough for me to drop all of my rounds into it, the projectiles alternately exploding or piercing its form.

"You!" the clone snarls. "You killed my friends."

"Maybe you shouldn't have tried killing us!" I snarl and keep running at it, releasing a wave of energy from my sword and its trailing counterparts.

The clone twists and dodges by jumping over and between the flying crescents of energy, a display of agility that has me slightly envious. Even with my own enhanced stats, I'm not entirely sure I'd be willing to try that, especially not with the amount of time he has to react.

"You attacked us first," the creature says as it lands and thrusts its palm at me. A spike of blood juts outward, slamming directly into my shield.

Momentum shatters the spike and the Soul Shield at the same time, letting me tackle the monster to the ground. I reach upward and slam my sword down to the side of him, trusting the arc of my attack to send the blades that trail alongside to cut into the ground beside the clone, trapping it. Doesn't matter where it goes, it's going to get cut.

"This isn't over!" the clone snarls, stabbed through its chest by one of the trailing blades as it squirms aside.

I channel Freezing Blade, tired of listening to it, when the blood clone ripples then explodes, the explosion throwing me backward.

"Asshole," I say with a groan. Flashing lights in Sabre telling me that the explosion has done even more damage to the poor mecha.

"That's another group gone," Ali says, coming over to where I struggle to my feet.

That makes four. Even if I'm locating and killing the damn Sect members as fast as I can, they've got the initiative here. We have the numbers, but they've got the Levels and the initiative, with our people too spread out across the city as we attempt to save everybody. They're hitting our people piecemeal, taking out teams while we scramble.

"We're losing," I say after a glance at the map. "That's it. Everyone, this is John Lee. Pull back on Sam. Grab whatever civilians you can, but everyone pulls back. Sam, coordinate them to fall back on you." A part of me hopes I'm using the terms right, that everyone understands what I mean. It's what I know from reading a few books and seeing a lot of movies, terminology that probably means what I think it does. "Ali…?"

"Head down this street and take a left. There's a group of hunters pinned down with civilians about four blocks down," Ali says.

Better to rely on my Spirit now; Sam's got his hands full.

I curse inwardly, knowing we're abandoning people, leaving them to be taken or possibly killed. A part of me figures that the Sect won't actually go after the civilians, not when it's clear we won't be coming for them anymore. But another part of me wrenches at the thought of abandoning them, of leaving them to the mercies of the Sect. Still, I have an obligation to the fighters, the warriors, to my men. Sending them out to die is one thing, but doing so for a meaningless gesture? That's the greatest betrayal I can think of.

***

We pull out what feels like hours later, the surviving combat Classers and the civilians we managed to gather in an assorted train of transportation vehicles. We have everything from gravity sleds to a 1940s Ford in the retreating convoy, bloody and shell-shocked civilians in all of them. No open wounds—or not many anyway, since the System is busy healing everyone. No more chance these days of someone dying from lingering injuries. Cold comfort, that thought.

But the Sect is letting us pull back. The fighting since I called for our retreat was brutal, the last fight a brief clash with the Blood Warrior's main body right next to Sam's truck. Dancing with him, containing his attacks while his friends fired at our grouped civilians, was stressful. The Blood Warrior pulled back fast once Mikito arrived, leaving the field of battle to us. Even the ranged attackers ran away after they realized they were steadily losing people to an unseen attacker. We managed to kill nearly two-thirds of their combatants in all the fighting. We bloodied them enough to force them back, but it's a Pyrrhic victory at best.

"They still holding?" I say to Ali, even though I can see the information on the map as clearly as he can.

"Yes," Ali says, fingers dancing. "I don't think they'll be dropping more people, but we should keep moving."

"Sam?" I say, speaking to the Technomancer in the center of the convoy. "Can you talk to whoever is in front to speed up?"

"On it," Sam says. "We need some hunters out ahead though. The civilians aren't willing to walk into a monster attack."

"I'll send Roland and Shadow," Lana chimes in from beside me, cradling a beam rifle. "Mikito…?"

"I'll ask around and find some hunters," Mikito says, something in her voice that I'm unable to read.

I frown slightly, turning to stare at where Mikito stands on the bed of a truck, but I can't read anything behind her mecha's armor.

"Thank you," I mutter, wondering if this is it. Hoping it is.

I don't have the numbers, not yet, but I know we lost quite a few of the hunter groups. We lost—badly, this time—and a part of me rebels at the idea.

At the loss of life for no damn reason, of the pain and suffering. I find myself gritting my teeth, staring at Vernon while the column draws away from me.

I want to get back in, to make them hurt. But if I do that and they attack the column, I'd just be compounding one mistake with another. Better to stay here. And anyway, Ingrid's doing her thing, hunting the stragglers, making them hurt inside that city. No. As much as I want to fight, right now, right here is my place.

But I swear, I'll make them hurt.

Chapter 12

A day later, we're gathered at the city center's central office lounge. We being the entire team, excluding Ingrid, and my "council," including Mel as a representative of the combat Classers. We're scattered in a rough circle on whatever random chairs and other surfaces we can find. A part of me notes we need a real meeting room at some point, but right now, I want to be near the City Core.

"We lost four full teams and another fourteen combatants from those who came from Kamloops. The Vernon fighters lost the most. We barely have eighty of them here, and that's including the ones who came in the earlier convoys," Mikito says, pain in her eyes. "I don't know how many actually died in the city. I wasn't able to get a real count."

"Definitely the same for the civilians. No losses from the earlier groups of course," Benjamin says, shaking his head. "We've got over a thousand new people, some of them still shell-shocked. I doubt many of them will be of use to us in the next few weeks, though anyone who has survived thus far…"

"Are survivors," Mel says, grunting. "They'll get over it."

I grimace but nod, understanding the harsh truth in that statement.

When I look at Torg, he answers the next question easily. "We have enough food for them. Food is tighter, but we've shifted a few of the farms to producing consumables and those should help the overall situation. Our stores are more than sufficient for now."

"For now," I say, repeating the qualified statement. I almost ask how long "for now" means, but I figure if it was a major issue, he'd bring it up. Better to let the experts do what they do best without me jogging their elbow.

"Space isn't an issue. There are still a significant number of abandoned buildings, even System-registered ones," Ben says softly. "I've been upgrading them as I can, but at least they're warm with running water."

Again, I'm struck by the absurdity of me leading anyone. I don't know, don't understand any of this. Even the downloaded knowledge from the System doesn't cover the fact that I just don't have the experience or temperament to do this. As leading a bunch of hunters to their death showed.

"ATTACKERS HAVE BEEN DETECTED AT THE PERIPHERY OF THE SENSING ZONES. SHOULD WE DEPLOY DRONES FOR ADDITIONAL COVERAGE?" Kim says, flashing the notification in front of me and everyone else.

"Yes," I say.

"No," Mel says at the same time then glares at me. He draws a breath before explaining himself to me. "A drone will likely be picked up by them, letting our enemies know the limits of your sensor net."

I nod slightly while Mel queries Kim for further information. I take a more direct route, pulling up the map and scanning the information. Two groups—four and six people respectively. That's literally all the information there is, the biosensor network not particularly good at providing anything else. Well, outside of the fact that they're on foot.

"We'll deal with this," Mel says, standing. I frown at him. "My people need the experience gained from fighting them."

"But—" I protest.

"Lana is lending her pets to us, so we'll have enough muscle power. And we've got trained groups who are stealthier than you and yours," Mel says, cutting me off. "We have plans for this. Let us do our job."

I grimace but nod and let him leave. I hate that he's right and I hate that his people, the combat Classers, are going to do the fighting while I'm seated here, safe and useless. My glowering form keeps the silence until Mel leaves, at which point Ali clears his throat.

"Well, then. I got some good news," Ali says, waving.

A list of information pops up: details of weapons, armor, and assorted magical and technological accessories.

"What's this?" Benjamin asks, frowning.

"Loot," Ali says, grinning and goes on to explain where he kept disappearing to throughout the fight. "I grabbed whatever bodies I could while we were in Vernon, dumping them into storage and John's Altered Space. Gear's decent and definitely an improvement for the city."

We fall silent for a time, scanning through the list. I randomly stop at various pieces of equipment, assessing the information.

Kmino One-Size-Fits-All-Humanoid Battle Armor (Tier IV)

The Kmino Battle Armor provides a Galactic Council approved, Tier IV defense on all covered regions. Note that the Kmino Battle Armor is sized to fit all standard humanoid forms and will restructure (within Galactic Council approved limits) to fit with a high degree of comfort, suitable for even the most rigorous combat conditions.

Durability: 83/125

Inlin Solarburst Beam Rifle v4.8

The Inlin Solarburst is the classic, proven primary rifle for two hundred seventeen governmental armed forces—and one hundred eighty-three rebels.

Base Damage: 48

Mana Battery Charge: 25/25

Ground Elemental Clay

Most commonly used by professional demolition experts and the military, Ground Elemental Clay has been stabilized through an arcane process, ensuring the mixture is non-volatile and stable in most conditions.

Base Damage: 200

I grab the clay, because extra explosives are always nice. Anyway, I've got a skill—sort of—for explosives.

Proxima Earrings of Regeneration

The Proxima brand of luxury jewelry provides the best designs and the highest regeneration. Show your faith to the one you love, buy Proxima.

Health Regeneration: +15

Mana Regeneration: +3

"*Anything else like this?*" I send to Ali, admiring the earrings.

"*Sort of. There's also a penis ring, but considering the Worick we got it from was about as wide as your arm, I don't think you'd want it. The other more traditional stuff is in the low single digits, other than a ring I set aside for you,*" Ali says. "*That means no stealing this for yourself.*"

"*Lana then?*" I say, glancing at the earrings. I haven't actually bought the young lady anything… I consider matters and decide that perhaps I should avoid giving my sort-of girlfriend dead body loot as my first official gift. "*Remind me to go shopping.*"

"*Got it, boy-o. I'll let Mikito know we got this if you don't mind,*" Ali says, and I send my mental agreement before going back to reviewing the list.

Q'mmn Never-ending Flask of Inebretiation

Blessed by Clerics of the God Q'mmn, the never-ending flask provides extremely high proof alcohol. This flask generates Ilmunax, a traditional distilled alcohol drink derived from the crushed bodies of Yuma worms.

"*Is it really never-ending?*" I ask Ali.

"Not really. The blessing runs out of after a decade or so, but it's good enough for most people."

"Huh." I waggle my fingers, removing that particular item from the list.

In the end, I give up scanning the list in its entirety after extracting a promise from Ali that we've already kept all the really good stuff. A bit selfish on my part, but my team is still our best defense and anything that increases our survivability is good for the town. Or you know, that's one way of justifying it. Really, I'm honest enough with myself to know I just don't want to share.

"Share the rest among the combat Classers and anyone who came through Vernon first, then allocate as appropriate," I say finally, giving orders to the group. After a second, I send a note to Kim to keep track of who gets what, a niggling concern about corruption in the back of my mind. After all, I really don't know these people well.

I get more than a few surprised looks, even though Ali had purposely brought all this information out in the council meeting because we were going to share it. I ignore them, instead delving into the next issue that has arisen from dragging so many refugees to town. There're a lot of problems, and housing and food are just the start of them. Even if I'm not the best person to make the decisions, someone still has to rubber stamp what comes through.

***

Hours later, I'm lying on the floor in the Core's room, feet propped up on a chair, and staring at my character sheet. Now that we're out of trouble, I figure it's time for me to catch up on the notifications that have been awaiting my perusal. Most of them are experience notifications, the vast majority of which I've learned to ignore because as Ali once pointed out, knowing doesn't change the reality. I either have the experience or I don't. Better to view the actual character screen and the new Levels.

Status Screen			
Name	John Lee	Class	Erethran Honor Guard
Race	Human (Male)	Level	39
Titles			
Monster's Bane, Redeemer of the Dead			
Health	1780	Stamina	1780
Mana	1370	Mana Regeneration	98 / minute
Attributes			
Strength	98	Agility	169
Constitution	178	Perception	61
Intelligence	137	Willpower	139
Charisma	16	Luck	30
Class Skills			
Mana Imbue	2	Blade Strike	2
Thousand Steps	1	Altered Space	2
Two are One	1	The Body's Resolve	3

Greater Detection	1	A Thousand blades	1
Soul Shield	2	Blink Step	2
Tech Link*	2	Instantaneous Inventory*	1
Cleave*	2	Frenzy*	1
Elemental Strike*	1 (Ice)		
Combat Spells			
Improved Minor Healing (II)		Greater Regeneration	
Greater Healing		Mana Drip	
Improved Mana Dart (IV)		Enhanced Lightning Strike	
Fireball		Polar Zone	
Freezing Blade			

All that death and destruction was useful for something at least. I smile grimly, noticing I've edged ever closer to that elusive Level 40. Just a little more and I'll actually gain access to my Tier III Class Skills. If I'd had those Skills back in Vernon, if I was just a little stronger…

I exhale, pushing aside the anticipation and regret, and remind myself once again that what is, is. Still, I'm human and not a damn monk—the shaven-headed, robe-wearing ones who sit under waterfalls and don't have superpowers of kung fu—so I distract myself by poking at the equipment Ali saved for me. He's even been nice enough to label them as mine.

To start with, I pull out the ring he mentioned. It's a simple circular band of black stone with unknown runes carved onto it. Or it might be a language. In either case, holding the ring up to my eye, I pull up its information.

Kryl Ring of Regeneration

Often used as betrothal bands, Kryl rings are highly sought after and must be ordered months in advance.

Health Regeneration: +30

Stamina Regeneration: +15

Mana Regeneration: +5

"How come the health regeneration is so much better than the Mana regeneration?" I ask. I ignore the Stamina regeneration, since that's never been an issue for me. I just don't have the kind of Skills where it would matter, and my base regeneration is so ridiculously high, it's never been a concern. Mikito, on the other hand, with her Haste spells and other Class Skills actually has to worry about it.

"Mana regeneration's always the worst," Ali says.

"I asked why."

"Just is," Ali says, shrugging, obviously unconcerned with the why.

I grumble, hating how the Spirit can be so blasé about the way the System works sometimes. Then again, I never bothered to learn how indoor plumbing worked, so who am I to talk?

I stare at the ring once more, debating how I feel about the fact that this was someone's engagement ring, before I shrug. Considering it's so good, it must have belonged to a Sect member, and they were all slavers. Stealing from them was the least I could do.

Having resolved my doubts with what is probably a highly questionable moral equivalence, I slip the ring onto my finger, watching as the ring grows to fit. "Hey, this self-adjusted. Would some of the other stuff have done that?"

"No. Kryl rings are actually expensive. Most of that junk was mass-produced," Ali says before he flashes up the next notification.

Monolam Temporal Cloak

This Temporal Cloaks splices the user's timeline, adjusting their physical, emotional, and psychic presence to randomly associated times. This allows the user to evade notice from most sensors and individuals. The Monolam Temporal Cloak has multiple settings for a variety of situations, varying the type and level of dispersal of the signal.

Requirements: 1 Hardpoint, Tier IV Mana Engine

Duration: Varies depending on cloaking level

"English?"

"It makes you invisible by making your actual presence appear either in the past or future. It's not actual invisibility and it can, on occasion, cause more trouble than it's worth, but it's also extremely effective at hiding your presence immediately," Ali says. "You can set it up so that it sends your presence anywhere from a few minutes to a few years down the road. Of course, the more you interact with the world, the higher the cost on drainage."

"Huh," I say, rubbing my chin. This is real weird and scientific. Or maybe it's magical, considering we're talking about time travel of sorts. I'm not entirely sure at this point. "This looks like it needs to be connected to Sabre."

"Got it in one," Ali says. "Doesn't make up for the QSM but..."

"But it could be useful. How long a charge do we have?" I say.

"If we keep it to draining only about twenty percent of Sabre's battery, which I recommend, anything from two seconds to about an hour."

"Nice. Let's get Sam to install this when he can."

I turn next to the notification for a circular brown bracer which also has—if different—runic script on it.

Tier III Bracer of Mana Storage

A custom work by an unknown maker, this bracer acts as a storage battery for personal Mana. A must-have accessory for Mages and other Classes that rely on Mana. Mana storage ratio is 50 to 1.

Mana Capacity: 0/350

"Zero stored?" I blink, staring at the information.

"I drained it of the last amounts it had stored," Ali says. "Can't mix Mana types in enchanted equipment like this. You won't even be able to use it just yet. You'll need to acclimatize the system to you, which means putting in a little bit of your Mana at a time."

"Still, that's pretty decent," I mutter and strap it on my left arm. I push my Mana toward it, careful to control how much, and immediately understand what Ali means. The bracer rejects my Mana immediately, forcing me to repeat the process slower and with significantly more focus. I expend nearly two-thirds of my current Mana pool before even a single point of Mana is stored in the bracer.

"Don't worry, it gets better," Ali says reassuringly. "What you input will disappear in a few hours, so make sure to keep refreshing the storage to assimilate it."

I grunt in acknowledgement and get to the next notification, curious to see what kind of weapon Ali might have picked up. Interestingly enough, it's a simple greenish steel dagger with no runes or other mystical markings, with a blackened steel hilt that fits snugly into my hand. It's incredibly well-balanced, definitely made by someone with actual skill.

Fey-steel Dagger

Fey-steel is not actual steel but an unknown alloy. Normally reserved only for the Sidhe nobility, a small—by Galactic standards—amount of Fey-steel is released for sale each year. Fey-steel takes enchantments extremely well.

Base Damage: 28

Durability: 110/110

Special Abilities: None

"This thing's sharp," I mutter, staring at the base damage.

Of course, sharp isn't the right word—better to say that the System considers it extremely damaging, allowing it to do a higher level of damage—but in either case, it's nasty. I'm also intrigued by the note that it can take enchantments well, though at this moment, I know no one with that ability.

"It is. All Fey-steel is like that. It's why they're so sought-after. The body I pulled it off of was one of the higher Level Classers. Must have been one heck of a story about how they came to own this," Ali says.

"About that…" I frown, tapping the dagger. "How rare is this?"

"How rare were those Teslas?"

I nod, somewhat gratified. Rare but not entirely uncommon. Still, it's not something I need to be showing off, so I dump it into storage. "No guns?"

"Nothing too much of an upgrade." Ali shrugs. "You don't really use rifles much, and while the weapons they had were improvements, it was mostly marginal. Better to stick with what you know than to chase a minor bump in stats."

I have to agree with Ali on that. Changing up equipment might be fun in a game, but it always takes a little while to get used to new equipment. If the other weaponry isn't much better than what I have already, what's the point?

Next up are a series of mines and explosives, some omni-directional, some directed. I pull out a few, just for fun.

Shim Lun Razor Tripwire Mine

Rather than triggering a specific attack, this mine sends its razor-sharp tripwires across its targeted region, laying a trap for unsuspecting targets within its attack zone. Best paired with Shim Lun's Skin Contact Poison Mine Canisters.

Damage: 15 per tripwire

Ollie's High-Explosive Slime Mixture

Don't let its name fool you, this is a high-explosive mine. Made from an unstable chemical mixture and a slime core, Ollie's High-Explosive Slime Mixture is infamous across the Galactic System and banned in six Galactic regions for unusual cruelty to animals.

Damage: 125 Explosive Damage

Ares Burrowing Droid Pressure Mine

The Burrowing Droid Mine releases a series of droids that impact and attempt to burrow into target bodies. Once they are embedded in target bodies, the droids attempt to reach its target's vital organs by burrowing toward the body. Please note that the Burrowing Droid may not work against certain non-standard, non-humanoid races.

Damage: 15 HP per second

"Ali, how much money do I have right now anyway?" I say. I know I got more from the fight, though I hadn't bothered to do the math.

A quick look shows I've got just over thirty-eight thousand Credits—a pitiful amount considering how many I killed. Unlike the equipment Ali looted off dead bodies all around town when we passed by, Credits are only collected when I actually kill the individual in question myself. I personally think that's a bit of a cheat, but then again, it's better than the equipment stored in the System storage, which all disappears.

Fun and interesting as looking at the aftermath of the fight is, it's nothing more than a distraction from the bitter truth that we lost that battle. I might have gained something personally, but we'd lost the battle. Even now, the Sect is probing our defenses, sending groups into the surroundings, seeing if they can sneak people close enough to take pot-shots at our shields.

For now, we're in a stalemate with the Sect, but it can't, won't, last. Grimacing, I wave, pulling up a new book. Rather than an esoteric tome about the System, this one's more pertinent to our current problems as it details one of the many, many conflicts the Erethran Empire has been involved in and their tactics. I'm hoping that somewhere in this book is knowledge that can help us. I've got hundreds of points in Wisdom and Intelligence; I must be able to think of something new. Even if those points don't exactly work that way, I can still hope.

***

"John?" Ingrid calls softly early the next morning.

I dismiss the book and clamber to my feet, walking out of the Core's room to greet the Assassin. "You made it back."

"About an hour ago. I wanted to eat and change first," Ingrid says. "Managed to take out another high Level Basic while I was in the city, but they started clamping down on security after that. Mostly, I just watched them."

"Fair enough," I say, knowing that Ingrid did the best she could have. Frankly, she did better than anyone else could, so I have no complaints.

"They're hunkering down now. I don't think they intend to leave. Probably use Vernon as a staging ground to attack here," Ingrid says. "Any humans left aren't being allowed to leave for their 'protection.'"

"Why don't they just make them Serfs?" I say, frowning.

"Galactic Law. As much as you might call them slavers, the Galactic Council doesn't legally allow slavery. Serfdom—and the entry to Serfdom—is actually very structured. Outside of being legally convicted for breaking laws, you have to voluntarily agree to enter a Serf contract," Ali says. "Of course, the number of loopholes involved in 'convincing' people to enter Serfdom is wide and varied, but they can't just throw your entire people into Serfdom."

"They added another ten or so combat Classers to the city after you left, but that was it. Didn't look like they intended to add any more, but…" Ingrid shrugs, leaving unsaid the fact that she did less than a day's worth of scouting. "One of the new classers was a hunter of some sort. It nearly caught me twice. Weirdest thing ever—six feet, purple-and-pink-furred lizard thing. I don't think I'd be able to sneak back in any time soon."

"They're called Badas," Ali supplies. "Sentient umm… well, sentient."

I stare at Ali, curious as to what could make even Ali pause but discarding the thought. I'm sure there's a story there, but for now, time to focus on Ingrid and our problems. I raise my hand, pulling out a map of the surrounding settlements. British Columbia has a ton of small towns, but outside of Kamloops, Vernon, and Kelowna, most barely have any population.

"Don't think they're going to do any major staging out of Merritt," I mutter, tapping the town icon to the south of Kamloops. "So it's probably a temporary base there." At the *hmmm* from Ingrid, I clarify for her, "They're attacking us from that direction. Probing with a few groups. So far we've counted about five different groups. All low Level though."

"Okay. You want me to kill them tomorrow?" Ingrid asks, straight to the point.

"No. Mel's got the teams doing that, using the Sect as training. Not sure they're getting a lot of Experience, but…" I shrug.

Mel's given me an overview of his plans, intending to let the groups come in and probe our defenses and even letting them succeed at times, saying it's better to hide the full range of our abilities than to win every fight. I'm not entirely convinced, but his logic is sound, so I'm letting him run with it. As it stands, his results so far have been decent—no losses on our side and one death on the Sect's. Unfortunately, unless we're able to achieve a fatality, any injuries are easily healed. It's probably why wars are so vicious in the wider System galaxy. If you don't put them down, they just keep coming.

"Okay then. When you figure out what you want me to do, let me know," Ingrid says, waving. "I'm going to get some rest."

"Of course," I say to Ingrid, waving goodbye. "Thank you again."

I don't get an answer as the woman strides off, leaving me alone again. After a moment, I look upward and stare at Ali.

"Been thinking about that Mana flow. We use it to power the settlement shield and the sentry towers, correct?" I say to the floating Spirit.

"Yes. Though it's mostly from the background flow," Ali says.

"Can we use the built-up reserves in a more active way? Maybe boosting the sentry towers and shields occasionally?" I say.

"Not the traditional way of using Mana overflows…" Ali says.

"And non-traditionally?" I say with a frown.

"Spells. Generally a settlement-wide enchantment of some form," Ali explains.

"IT IS POSSIBLE. UPGRADES WILL BE REQUIRED FOR BOTH THE SENTRY TOWERS AND SHIELD GENERATOR, AS WELL AS THE PURCHASE OF A SETTLEMENT MANA STORAGE BATTERY."

"Where is the Mana stored now?" I ask with a frown. After all, I can see the Mana numbers right in the settlement information.

"MANA ACCESSIBLE BY THE SETTLEMENT IS KEPT IN CIRCULATION THROUGH THE ATMOSPHERE OF THE TOWN."

"What kind of rituals or enchantments are we looking at?" I ask Ali next.

"Anything you want. I've seen weather control rituals, life enhancement, fertility, crafting rituals. You name it, you can get it. Including defensive ones," Ali states.

"So defensive rituals," I say, nodding. "Think this is a conversation I'll need to have with Mel."

"And funds to build it up," Ali points out. "Enchantments—combat enchantments in particular—are expensive."

I groan. Of course they are. Anything good is always expensive. Though I absently make a note to ask Aiden about this. I know he's got some experience with enchantments in Whitehorse. Perhaps we could con him into helping out here. Humming to myself, I start composing the message.

***

Tracking down Lana the next day isn't hard. Even if I didn't have access to the full surveillance apparatus of the city, the buxom redhead is both noticeable and well-known. She's also a bleeding heart, which is why I'm not surprised to find her with the refugees in a makeshift office, making suggestions and offering advice to the crowd that has gathered. Luckily, there's no shortage of jobs to be had, so it's a matter of assignment more than anything else.

I wave to Lana, catching her attention before stepping back and waiting until she's done. I spend the time watching the refugees, curious to see how they're doing. They're a mixed lot, though the group here leans toward the shell-shocked and somewhat disheveled. It's interesting how even when your clothing and self is perfectly clean, you can look utterly wasted. There's a truth in there somewhere, one that I'm too tired to consider.

"John?" Lana says, drawing my attention back to her.

"Oh hey." I lean in to give her a quick kiss. She returns it before raising an eyebrow, querying my presence. "I wanted to give you this."

I hand her my purchase, the small velvet box dwarfed in my hand. Lana takes the box, lips pursed in thought as she pops it open to see the simple silver and gold chain, each link inscribed with runes. Her lips part slightly as she stares at the necklace and the information that displays.

Proxima Necklace of Regeneration

The Proxima brand of luxury jewelry provides award-winning designs and the highest regeneration in its class. Show your faith to the one you love, buy Proxima.

Health Regeneration: +20

Mana Regeneration: +5

"This…"

"Here, let me," I say, taking the necklace and walking around to her back. Lana lifts her long, wavy red hair, letting me clasp the necklace. For a moment, my fingers fumble slightly as I stare at the graceful expanse of white skin. "Done."

Rather than answer me verbally, Lana turns around and leans forward, planting her lips on mine as she wraps her arms around my neck. After a time, she breaks the kiss. "Thank you."

"No worries," I say awkwardly.

"What brought this on?"

"Ummm… nothing. Just thought I should," I answer, deciding against mentioning my initial inspiration.

"Mmhmmm…" Lana says before she smiles one of those radiant smiles. "Thank you again. You know, Richard would be taking you out for a talk if he saw you give me this." There's a brief flicker of sadness, one that she forcibly pushes away.

I nod slightly, understanding her pain. I miss that idiot too.

"Was this it?" Lana says. "Not that I don't value your presence…"

"Yes," I say, rubbing my nose and taking my dismissal graciously. "If you didn't have anything for me, I was thinking about checking out the farms, then talking to Mel and his people."

"No, I've got this," Lana says, waving me off to do my rounds. "I'll see you tonight."

I smile, hearing the unspoken promise in those words, my stride having a slight bounce to it that wasn't there before. The gift for her was well worth the Credits, even if it did drain my funds.

***

"Can we help you?"

Polite or not, the question is obviously meant to dissuade me from wandering into the small strip mall. With its internal walls taken down and a short wall obstructing the parking lot, the strip mall no longer looks as inviting as its original architect envisioned. Which is the point, I'm sure. There are even a pair of guards standing outside the main entrance, mostly looking bored.

"Just wanted to check out how things are going," I say, peering past the woman who stopped me.

The stout raven-haired woman steps sideways, hands on her hips as she blocks my view. Over her head, her Status says she's KC Markowitz, a Level 21 Gunsmith. Absently, I wonder how she ended up with just initials for her name. I've never seen that before.

"I'm sorry. I don't know what they told you, but this area isn't open to the public," the Gunsmith says, glaring at the pair of guards with displeasure.

"My name's John Lee." I flash her a grin. When she doesn't get it, I add, "The guy who kicked out the Sect? Your boss's boss?"

"Oh..." KC gasps. "I'm sorry. I didn't..."

"It's fine, KC," I say, waving toward the building. "Ben's reports mentioned that he set up a gun factory and I was curious."

Having started at the use of her name, KC draws a breath before nodding. "If you'd like, I can show you around?"

"That'd be great." Part of my visit here is curiosity. Part of it is a desire to get more bullets for Sabre, though I'm not entirely sure these guys are up to the task. Which is the point of coming and finding out for myself, obviously.

"Well, we've got the workshop—umm, factory—set up in three parts right now. Outside here"—KC gestures to the group of plastic tables covered by cheap pavilions probably looted from the closest big box store, where a few craftsmen move about—"we work with the high explosives and other, ummm... volatile materials."

"Isn't that dangerous?" I frown, walking over. On closer inspection, I realize that the tables are cordoned off from each other with portable shield generators.

"Well, better than constantly fixing the walls inside," KC says with a shrug. "We all carry multiple healing potions, and we never keep more volatiles out here than we can stand from an explosion. Those of us working with the volatiles have also either invested in our Constitution or have a Class Skill to reduce ummm… self-created mistakes."

"Ah…" I pause at the nearest table to watch while half-listening to KCs explanations.

The individual is working on what looks like tiny missiles—mortar shells, perhaps—alternately pulling various parts apart, screwing parts together, putting the two-thirds complete item upright, and gently filling one of the four vials in the shell with a purple liquid. Once that's done, he switches to filling another vial, this time with a red liquid. He continues doing so, adding different liquids to each vial, before sealing the vials with a glass stopper and screwing the entire assembly together. After that, he holds his hand over it, focusing while the product glows.

"He's using a Skill to complete assembly. It's called ummm… Assembly," KC says. "If Sherman gets simple-to-assemble parts, he just screws and mostly finishes them then uses his Skill. The Skill finishes everything for him, making it a complete product. Like that." She gestures, and I nod.

The glow around the shell is gone. In its place is a single smooth item, rather than the screwed-together contraption that he had before. What he does next surprises me.

Hands glowing again, Sherman waves his hand up and down the table, his movements centered around the mortar. He does that for twenty seconds, the area where his hand moves slowly growing brighter and brighter. Then suddenly, with a slight rumble of displaced air, another ten mortar shells cover the table.

"Wha…?"

"Mass Production," KC says, shrugging. "All of us have it. If we don't get it as part of our Skill tree, we buy it from the Shop. It can only be activated within five seconds after you've completed your most recent work, but it lets the System generate even more copies. There are a few variations, including a channeled version like what Sherman has and a single-use Skill like mine."

"Wow…" I say, blinking. That's amazing. Then again, it's taken Sherman about five minutes to produce eleven shells. And as I watch, Sherman slowly puts together the other piece, his movements slow and careful.

"Check out his Mana level, boy-o. He's nearly out. So each cast takes about ten minutes to finish eleven." Ali grunts. *"Not horrible for a Basic Class, but not great."*

And of course that explains why hand-crafted projectile weaponry is so expensive. Each of his shells does high-explosive, flaming damage over a range of ten feet on impact, but only a base damage of 53. Not great. If he was making bullets, I could see why it would cost multiple Credits to buy even a single bullet. Still, it's better than the single-digit damage levels of non-System generated weaponry.

"So outside, we have the volatiles," KC says, continuing her initial conversation and leading me into the open doorway. "Inside, we've got the basic, solid-shot projectiles. Everything from basic armor-piercing weaponry to just bullets like I make. Then there's the warehouse section, where our runners put the finished product and we take inventory."

I nod, listening to KC as she guides me around, showing me the place. It doesn't take long, even with introductions to those who look interested.

When we finally get to the warehouse and KC finishes her spiel, I turn to her and hold out a single projectile. From the looks of it, KC's probably my best bet. "Are you able to make this?"

"Ummm…" KC frowns, staring at the projectile as she turns it around in her hand.

It looks a bit similar to our own bullets, physics—basic physics, at least— not changing much. She pulls a small pair of plyers from her tool belt and pulls apart the backend with a twist, brows furrowed. After a minute of silence as she continues to tap and play with the projectile in silence, I clear my throat.

"Oh, right. Sorry. No," KC says, shaking her head. "I don't have the blueprints for it. I'd need to get that first or research it. It doesn't look hard…" KC taps one edge before casually tossing a part onto the concrete floor. It explodes with a small puff of smoke, shattering the concrete and making me jump slightly. No one else even flinches. "Nice reagent… I think… yes…"

I cough, bringing her attention back to me.

"No. Can't do it. Don't have the materials. I could cobble something together with what we have in a few weeks once I've researched it, but it wouldn't be as good. This is very nice work."

I sigh, nodding. For all the advantages of owning a settlement, getting free bullets doesn't seem to be one of them. Not yet at least.

"Can I keep this?" KC says, holding up the pieces of the projectile.

"Sure," I say, shaking my head.

KC grins, walking away while muttering to herself as she stares at the projectile, abruptly leaving me alone in a warehouse filled with ammunition.

"Well done, boy-o. A real charmer you are."

I grunt, shaking my head, and walk out. Best get to my next project.

***

I knock on the door of the apartment building gently—mostly because I spotted the pair of high-explosive mines hidden in the wall. Between that, the surveillance cameras, a shield enchantment, and probably a few more toys I haven't seen, this building is probably the most well-defended in the city. Which isn't surprising, considering who lives here right now.

"Redeemer," the Hakarta greets me, his face solemn. I notice he's standing almost at attention. "Is there a problem?"

"No, no problem," I say, frowning. "Why would you think there's one?"

"I did not. Are you here to speak with the lieutenant then?" the Hakarta says.

"Well, I…" I consider my answer and finally nod. It's obvious the private I'm speaking to would prefer I speak with his boss. "Yes. Please."

"Very well. I shall lead you to him," the private says, letting me in before closing the door and resetting their security precautions. After that, he leads me upstairs a couple of floors and to a corner apartment, where he knocks on the door before gesturing for me to stand to the side. "Wait here please. I shall inform the lieutenant."

Once the lieutenant is informed, it takes only a minute to get the formalities out of the way, leaving me with him in the comfortable living room filled with a beige L-designed couch and lounging chairs. I absently note that all the family photos are gone, stacked in a corner, while the Hakarta reside here for now.

"How are you doing, lieutenant?" I say.

"We are well. There are no complaints, sir," Lieutenant Nerigil says. "Major Ruka briefed us on what to expect beforehand. And your… commander is competent and willing to listen to suggestions."

"Good. Very good," I say, nodding. "I understand he's got you guys on guard duty mostly?"

"Yes. Our contract only extends to the direct defense of the town. While it could be argued to include the hunting of your harassers, it was decided that our strength was better used in town, providing guard services and occasional training companions," the lieutenant answers stiffly. "If that is acceptable, Redeemer."

"Oh, I'm not here to meddle," I say, waving away his words. "I'm actually just checking in on you guys. Making sure none of my people have started fights because you... well..."

"We look like your orcs."

I cough, nodding slightly with embarrassment.

"It is understandable. My people's major occupation does place us in an antagonistic position with most settled races. We have fought against, and fought for, most races. It is no surprise that the Mana Leakage you experienced cast us as a warlike race," Lieutenant Nerigil says.

"Ah... I'm glad you understand," I say, smiling. The lieutenant nods and I get up before shaking his hand in farewell. "Well, I won't bother you on your day off anymore. I just wanted to make sure you guys are doing well."

"Our comfort is well within the parameters of the contract," the lieutenant confirms and sees me out.

It's only when I'm out of the building that I realize he never did say if his people had gotten into any fights over our impression of them as orcs. I turn around to knock again, a bit annoyed at being blown off like that.

"Leave it, boy-o. If he didn't want to say, that's his problem. You did your part."

"But..." I feel guilty. For what? The entire human race? For racist or idiotic assholes? Maybe it's the Canadian in me that feels the need to apologize.

"Leave it. You've got your own battles to fight."

I sigh, giving up. Ali's right. I've got a lot more work to do, more people to check up on, more training to conduct. More Levels to gain. A few hurt feelings and broken noses, if there are any, is something I can leave for others.

Chapter 13

It's been eight days since we returned from Vernon. The refugees have settled down, mostly, with many taking part in the development of our city. It helps that there's enough vacant real estate that rent is still incredibly cheap. Even if large swaths of space are owned by me directly, there just aren't enough people to actually populate most of the locations. The small increase in population barely makes a dent.

Eight days and the Sect has not stopped launching probing attacks. Current consensus is that they don't have the manpower to actually take Kamloops— at least not without losing more people than they'd be willing to risk. Between the Hakarta, my team, and the combat Classers from Kamloops and Vernon, we've got a sizeable force in an entrenched position. While we don't have the resources to upgrade the town as much as I'd like, our defenses do give us a bit of an edge, especially since Benjamin is working on the approaches. Some of the things that mind of his has come up with are nasty. And innovative. Still, letting the Sect past our shield is the last thing I want to do.

Mel has been keeping our combat teams sweeping out to the south of the Thompson River to harry our attackers, the group playing hide-and-seek in the lands around. Between Class Skills, technology, and forested areas, the hunting groups are just as likely to stumble across an opponent by chance as find them with Skill. It does mean that we have the north of the river to continue to run hunting and Leveling though, which is nice. It allows some groups to Level in more controlled environments while others gain experience in real combat. Like everyone else, I've been sneaking out to Level too, making use of my greater Constitution to squeeze in grinding sessions late at night and in the early morning. Unfortunately, stuck as I am at Level 39, the monsters available are a drop in the bucket.

My musings, mostly procrastination as I go through the morning mail from Kim / the Settlement is interrupted by a call.

"John."

"Mel. What's wrong?"

"We need you at the gates. There's… something weird. We've got the shield up just in case, but you'll want to see this."

"On my way," I say, dismissing the notification and heading out.

It takes me only a few minutes to arrive on Sabre and I find myself joining Mel and Mikito and another teenager at the edge of the settlement shield, staring through the shimmering force field at the blood-covered sole survivor of a group. As I walk up, the exhausted brunette outside the shield looks up, eyes locking with mine even as she cradles her stomach.

"You're here," she says with relief.

"I am…" I glance at Mikito and Mel. "Why aren't we letting her in?"

"She's got a weird Status effect," Mikito replies.

I actually look at her and her status, noting the woman's injured condition and another that I've not seen before. Blood Vector.

Carla Flowers (Level 28 Wisp of Flame)
HP: 44/490
MP: 210/210
Conditions: Injured, Blood Vector

"Class Skill. She's infected. If we let her in, she'll explode and spread the disease to everyone else. As it is, she's dying," Ali explains. Even as he speaks, I see her health drop a little.

"He let me go," Carla Flowers says softly. "After he killed all of my team. My friends. He took his time, pinned me to the ground while he cut them apart, again and again. Said that he wanted you to know who is killing us."

"Who?" I say.

"Utrashi Wyt," the survivor answers, her voice coming out softer, weaker. "Promise me. Promise me you'll kill him."

I grit my teeth, rage flaring. I walk forward, stopped only by the shield, as I meet her eyes filled with pain, despair, and rage. Her hazel eyes are filled with the knowledge that she's dead already and won't be able to enact her own vengeance.

"I promise. I'll cut his head off."

When she hears my promise, Carla smiles slightly. She raises her hand, calling forth her Mana, and fire comes, so hot and so fast that she probably doesn't feel it. Much. Mikito lurches forwards for a second and then stops, held back by the shield and good sense. Out of the corner of my eye, I see the stranger standing next to Mikito step backward, face pale before turning away and refusing to watch. Mel's lips tighten but he doesn't look away. Neither do I.

I watch her burn until there's nothing left of her or her equipment. We watch in silence, my stomach churning with the acidic knowledge that I can do nothing but witness her death.

Only when it's done do I speak. "What happened?"

"The Blood Warrior—Utrashi—was hiding in the group they attacked. Just waiting for them," Mel says, shaking his head. "My fault. I should have expected something like that. We've been seeding the beasts and Mikito among the hunter groups. Should have realized they might have done the same."

I turn to Mel, my eyes glowing with anger. His fault. Her death, their deaths, was his fault. I open my mouth and Mikito steps between us, the tiny Japanese woman craning her neck upward to meet my eyes. The teenager shifts slightly too, his hand falling to the katana at his side. I glance at Mikito automatically and she stares at me, daring me to speak.

"Not your fault," I grate out, not needing Mikito's reminder. I'm angry, but I understand we make mistakes. For that matter, any of our groups without Mikito in it probably would have died too. Even one with the pets. "Mikito, we should let Lana know. Her pets..."

"Already done. We'll group her pets up more, keep them in tighter groups," Mikito says, understanding my hesitation. Neither of us wants Lana to lose another pet. For all her strength now, she's still somewhat emotionally fragile from losing her brother.

"Who's the kid?" I tilt my head sideways.

Mikito looks uncomfortable for a second before her face turns placid again. "This is Lee-kun. I'm training him as an Aonisaibushi."

Lee turns to me, bowing slightly, and I have to keep my face from twitching. It's weird to see a blond-haired, blue-eyed teenage male bowing while wearing a katana.

"Aoni..." I give up. Mikito said it so fast and fluently, I had no chance of repeating it after her. "That was your Class before, no?"

"Yes." Mikito nods.

"You can give it?"

Mikito glances at Ali, who sighs, looking at me.

"Not exactly. With certain prestige Classes, you can train others in it. Not all Classes, and not all people, but if you managed to achieve a rank higher than the one you'd like to train, it's possible," Ali explains. "It's still no guarantee the kid will be able to get it, but it makes it possible."

"I can only take three apprentices at a time," Mikito says, waving at the kid.

I nod, noting that his Class hasn't changed from Artist yet, which I assume means he's still learning under her. Still, knowing Mikito's Class, I can see how upgrading someone could be useful.

"Drawbacks?" I say. There has to be some.

"Experience. He doesn't lose his old Class. This one just replaces it eventually and he restarts at Level 1. However, his experience requirements to go up to Level 2 are the same as his previous level," Ali explains.

I can see how that'd suck, but with his Level only at nine, the kid isn't likely to be hurt much by this.

"Thanks," I mutter to Mikito for her explanations. Then I turn to Mel, who was patiently listening. "All right, tell me what you plan to do about this."

***

Later that evening, Lana finds me lying down in the old office leading into the core room, staring at the ceiling. Ali's disappeared, driven off by my silence and grumpiness. I never bothered to replace the furniture in here, so lying down is my best option. It's not even dirty—the building modifications keep the floors and ceiling so clean you could eat off them.

"Missed you at dinner," Lana says, taking a seat across from my prone form, sweeping aside a discarded chocolate wrapping paper. The timer before it gets absorbed runs out a few seconds later and the wrapping paper dissolves into nothingness. Such a useful feature, though some people turn it off as they don't want to inadvertently lose something important.

"Didn't feel like the company," I say, continuing to stare at the ceiling.

"Brooding?" Lana says, a half-smile on her face.

"Thinking." A shred of self-honesty forces me to admit, "Maybe brooding a little. Labashi mentioned we should be on the attack. Throwing them on the

207

defensive, rather than stay on it ourselves. We failed, rather spectacularly, at trying that the last time."

"We couldn't just leave the refugees in Vernon," Lana says pointedly.

"Really?" I say, frowning. "I don't think that's right. We could have passed right through the town, hit the Sect in Kelowna like we'd planned, or at least met their planes in the air. But we decided to stop, take the town because it was offered to us, and we fell for their trap. Then we lost people trying to cover the civilians rather than concentrating our forces and hitting them hard. We might have killed that Rock Thrower in Vernon, but we should have finished off that Blood Warrior."

"You're saying you're regretting saving their lives," Lana says warningly.

"I know. But if we had hit them hard, focused on killing their people rather than playing defense, maybe they'd have gone on the defensive too. If we'd pressed the matter, left the civilians to evacuate themselves and pushed against the Sect's forces…"

"You don't think they'd have sent more help?" Lana says.

"I don't know." I exhale roughly, shaking my head. "I'm not a general. No tactician. I just wonder if we could have done something else. And now, we're here. We're back to playing defense when they were meant to be on defense. It can't last. The Sect must be sending people over, or consolidating their people, or something."

"So you want to go attack them again?"

"Yes. But we've got to keep the city covered too. The Hakarta aren't enough, not anymore. Not after the losses we suffered early on. And we can't afford more," I say, shaking my head. "That means keeping the team here. They've moved enough people up that if we left, they might be able to take the town. Maybe do some real damage…"

"Worried they might destroy the town?" Lana says softly, concern in her voice.

"Yes. They've shown they're willing to kill civilians, and while it might be frowned upon, it's not entirely taboo. No UN here to stop them. Not that it did much good in our world…"

Lana sighs, squeezing my hand, and I return the squeeze. The losses during the fight weighs on all of us, even if we've had experience losing people. Too many empty homes and abandoned buildings on our trip down, too many people we couldn't help, no matter what we did. For all that the System has changed us, we're still human.

After a moment, Lana lies down, resting her head on my stomach, and holds out a hand to me. I frown, then pull a chocolate and hand to her. We lie in silence, ruminating on our losses and what we can do. Still, with her silent presence, it doesn't seem as bad.

***

Alarms, deep in the night, wake me from dreams I'm thankfully unable to remember. I jerk awake, staring at shrill noise, as Lana does the same. Without asking, Ali's already displaying a map, showing the attack on the settlement's Shield.

"Who is in charge?" I say, hands flicking as I pull clothing from my storage and dress.

"Not sure. Mel and Mikito are asleep," Ali says, frowning. "Ah… Leopold."

"Who's he?" I say, glancing at Lana.

She's already up and dressed fully. She gives me a nod, moving toward the door and leading the way to the attack.

"One of the residents. Has some prior military experience, which is why he was chosen," Ali says, eyes flicking as he reads his screens. "He's ordered the hunting parties to converge. Should we countermand the order?"

I grunt, staring at the cluster of dots. Just over sixty Sect members with some assault vehicles are opening fire, hammering the settlement Shield. Not enough to take it down immediately, but if we leave them at it, it'll go down in four or five minutes. On the other hand, we've only got two hunting parties—ten people—out there, and who knows how many other hidden attackers are on the Sect's side. For that matter, I'm curious how they got in so close without alerting us. Behind the Shield, the guards are gathering, over thirty of them already there and more streaming in.

"Let them close in but don't engage. They're dead if they do," I say, rubbing my chin. "Can the beam weapons help?"

"A little," Ali says, shrugging. "They're still liable to be destroyed the moment you open the shields."

"Damn it," I growl, running down the streets. We really need to figure out a better option for those guns. "Patch me in to Leopold." Once Ali gives me the thumbs-up, I say, "This is John Lee. What are your plans?"

"This is Mel. I've taken over for Leopold," Mel says. "Once we get a critical mass behind the shield, we'll lower it and hit them hard. Everyone has been given specific targets. Our goal is to kill as many as fast as possible."

Too bad we can't continuously raise and lower the shield. It'd give our people even more of an advantage. The shift costs a lot of Mana, and if we did that, we'd weaken and eventually destroy the Shield ourselves.

"Are we sure it's only this group?" I ask.

"Drones are already sweeping the rest of the field, and we've got guards on all the other entrances. We've got it covered," Mel says.

"Lana and I are nearly there," I inform Mel, only half-seeing the shadowed streets we run through. Without a main generator, each building is left alone to generate its own electricity and lighting, which means the streets themselves are intermittently lit by residual lights.

As we turn the corner, the bang, crackle, and hiss of weapon fire and Class Skills can be heard. Our beam weaponry opens up as well, automatically adding their own damage.

"Hold fire," Mel orders a couple of seconds later.

No surprise that a lot of shots go off even after the command, the order having to be repeated again and again. Mel and a few others growl and curse out the shooters half-heartedly, obviously more concerned about what they can see. As I near, I frown, noting how all the enemy dots have disappeared from my minimap. That doesn't seem right...

Rather than ask a stupid question, I jump onto the short wall that we use to give our people elevation for the attack. The scorched and broken earth is testament to the damage dished out by the group around me, but rather than bodies, there are but a few broken automated weapon turrets.

"Ali...?" I say, unsure of what is happening.

"A FLUCTUATION IN THE DATA PROVIDED BY THE SYSTEM WAS NOTICED ONCE ATTACKS IMPACTED. IT IS LIKELY THAT A CLASS SKILL WAS USED TO PROVIDE FALSE SENSOR INFORMATION," Kim flashes to me. "IT IS CONJECTURED THAT THE SAME INDIVIDUAL HID THE SECT'S APPROACH."

"And the damage to the Shield?" I frowned.

"DELAYED. ON ANALYSIS, ACTUAL DAMAGE WAS DONE A MINUTE BEFORE BUT WAS RELAYED TO OUR SENSORS LATE."

"You can do that?" I say, blinking. What kind of insane Skill is that?

"YES."

"This has got to be the work of an Advanced Class. I'll do some research, see if I can dig up what Class Skills and Classes this might be, but don't hold your breath. There're a million options in the System for anything you can think of."

"Where are they now?" Mel asks, obviously having received the same information. I don't see them on our sensors, which is disturbing to say the least.

"UNCERTAIN."

"Pull the hunting groups back," I order Mel. If those sixty Sect members—which I can't even be certain of anymore—meet ours, they'd wipe out our hunting groups in no time flat. Better to pull back right now.

"What's the point of all this?" Lana growls, her hair a frazzled mess.

"They're attacking our morale," Mel says, waving at the puzzled people around us.

Most look confused, a few looking enlightened as Kim's analysis trickles down. More than a few are annoyed, some thrilled as they boast about driving them off.

"Doesn't look that way," Lana says, and Mel snorts.

"Not right now. But if I'm not wrong, they're going to start doing this every night. Maybe more than once a night. It'll go from annoying to dangerous because we're going to have to keep people on watch all the time." Mel sighs. "The Afghanis used to shoot mortar rounds into our camp randomly. You could never really relax."

"Recommendations?" I ask, looking outward.

"Not much," Mel says. "We can up our hunting groups, hopefully figure out how many they're actually sending. If we can counter them on an attack and actually make them bleed, that'd be best. But…"

"They're likely to be waiting for that," I say, grimacing.

Mel nods. "We're also trying to protect a whole city, so our perimeter is too large. Maybe after a few weeks, if there's a pattern, we can get Ingrid or some of the other teams out. But until then, there's no guarantee we'd be able to find them."

"Will they be back tonight?" I ask, and Mel shrugs. "I'm headed back to the Core. Maybe there's something we can find…" I wave goodbye.

Lana indicates that she'll stick around a bit, which leaves me walking alone even as Mikito and her apprentice come strolling up.

"Kim, this information distortion, can we do something about it? Get better data?" I ask out loud.

"BASED UPON CURRENT FUNDS, THERE IS ONLY A 34% CHANCE FOR US TO UPGRADE SENSORS TO REMOVE INTEFERENCE."

"How much would we need to spend to do even that much?"

"ALL OF CURRENT CREDITS AVAILABLE."

"Bad odds," I say, shaking my head. "Forget that for now. What else can we do?"

"MANY THINGS. WHAT ARE YOUR OBJECTIVES?"

I growl, annoyed at the pissant AI. Luckily, I've got a Spirit who knows how to handle these things.

"Bits-for-brains, we're dealing with the attacks. What can we do to make it less annoying? Or hurt them when they attack us?"

"CURRENT DAMAGE OUTPUT BY ATTACKERS WILL REMOVE SHIELDING IN FIVE MINUTES, TWENTY-THREE SECONDS OF CONTINOUS ATTACKS. WE HAVE SUFFICIENT CREDITS TO INCREASE RECHARGE RATES OF THE SHIELD TO INCREASE TIME REQUIRED FOR SHIELD FAILURE."

"WE MAY ALSO UPGRADE THE SHIELD TO ALLOW SINGLE DIRECTION FIRE, ALLOWING SENTRY TOWERS TO ATTACK IN RELATIVE SAFETY. ADDITIONAL ATTACK METHODS MAY BE PURCHASED, INCLUDING INDIRECT ARTILLERY FIRE, FROM THE CENTER OF THE CITY. LASTLY, WE MAY PURCHASE A SETTLEMENT ENCHANTMENT TO REFRACT A PORTION OF DAMAGE TO THE SHIELD TO ITS ATTACKERS."

I frown, tilting my head upward. Even if I can't see it, I know that the current shield is a dome. Indirect artillery fire would basically make a hole in the dome in the center. Of course, the Sect has shown that they've got airplanes, so that might not be the best idea. On the other hand, airplanes are at least easier to spot.

"Sounds interesting," I say. "Show me."

Tier IV Defense Shield Regeneration Rate Increase
Increases regeneration rate of settlement shield by drawing a higher level of ambient Mana.
HP Regeneration Rate: 250/minute
Credits: 1.98 Million Credits

Tier IV Defense Shield Upgrade—One-Way Fire
By altering the frequency and direction of the shield, one-way fire out of a settlement shield is viable.
Allows intermittent fire from inside to outside the shield. Must be activated.
Duration of activation: 5 Minutes
Credits: 2.5 Million Credits

Automated Tier IV Artillery

By connecting directly to the sensor network in a settlement, these automated artillery pieces can range up to 50 kilometers away (dependent upon sensor range).

Base Damage: N/A (dependent on ammunition)

Capacity: 5

Fire Rate: 1 per 5 second

Reload time: 30 seconds

Credits: 2 Million Credits

Settlement Shield "Bite Back" Runic Enchantment (Tier V)

Named by original creator Rqweervs Hivemate, the Bite Back Runic Enchantment absorbs damage done to a settlement shield and applies damage directly to its attacker. This Runic Enchantment comes in a wide variety of levels of effectiveness.

Base Damage: 2% of Damage

Requirements: 200 Mana + 20 Mana Upkeep

Credits: 5 Million Credits

I scan through the options, wincing at the cost, and pull up the Settlement information once again in short order. One and three-quarters million Credits. You'd think that anything over a million would be enough, but as I go up in Levels and deal with the town, a million has started to feel like pocket change. Unfortunately, with me wiping out the majority of the Credits earlier and the economy only just beginning to pick up, making millions of additional Credits is impossible. Frankly, it's amazing that we've managed to earn as much as we have. Right now, we're making roughly forty-five thousand Credits a day as a settlement, which might seem like a lot, but that includes all the rent, sales of Sect-owned goods like farm produce, and taxes we've levied.

My hand rises as I get ready to wipe out the options we can't afford, then I pause. Not because I can't really activate the purchases till I'm in the Core. Not because we don't have enough money to make the changes matter. No, because I realize, once again, we're reacting. Playing to their game.

My hand falls and I stare at the information, stopped in the middle of the street as my mind whirls with possibilities. A glimmer of an idea approaches me, skirting around my perception. Time. Space. Action. Reaction.

Even if I do take the steps I want to, need to, I'll need to visit Sam and the Shop. But maybe, just maybe, there's an option.

Chapter 14

There are things you do because you have to. There are things you do because it's the right thing to do. And then there are things you do because you're just good at them. However, what you think needs to be done and what others consider to be right are often markedly different. Once again, that thought was reinforced as I told the team about my new plan over our delayed breakfast.

As I sneaked along the ground outside of town, I recalled the arguments, the glares, and the less-than-happy expressions. It was one thing, at least to them, when Ingrid upped and disappeared. She was the Assassin, the scout, the rogue who did all those things. Sending her off from the city, even when we needed her to do some hunting close by, was acceptable. Expected even. She was the free spirit who flitted around. Me? I was supposed to stick around, help settle the refugees, and figure out purchases and defenses and all that crap.

Never mind the fact that I'm really not suited to all that. Or that there are much better people already in place. Even if I feel—I know—my greatest contribution is in the field, most of the others aren't particularly happy about my choice. As I left, there were even some muttered comments about me regressing.

Truth is, they might be right. That's the thing about the human mind—we can find justifications for everything and easily rationalize our decisions. In my mind, decisions like what to buy, when to buy, the optimization of our defenses and upgrading buildings and rents... all of that can be handled by others more inclined than I am to do so. Kim can run the math and guide the others on my overall goals. The council can do the actual work, and Lana can watch over them all. Mikito is better at handling and training each of the hunting groups, while Mel seems to have a handle on our day-to-day strategic fighting decisions. As much as I might dislike the older man, he's doing a decent job so far.

In my mind, there's nothing I can do that can't be done by them. But none of them has my Class, my Skills, or Sabre. Of them all, I have the greatest mobility and punching power. Which leads me to traveling across the relatively open ground around the town, leaning on my stealth skills to find the hunting groups. I've dumped Sabre into my Altered Space, deciding that going unarmored is a better choice for now. Mobile as it may be, stealthy isn't something I'd call Sabre in either mode.

Thankfully, the monsters around me stay away. They can sense the Level difference sufficiently to avoid me when they do pick me up, and I make sure to swing around them otherwise. Thus far, in the last few hours, I've yet to find signs of our potential attackers.

Which isn't too surprising. The ground to the south of Kamloops is pretty flat and bare, more plains than forests for around five kilometers before they get hilly and forested again. In the end, my goal isn't to head into the woods where I know most of the hunting groups stay or to flush out our attackers but to make my way farther south.

South, perhaps swinging by Logan Lake to the southwest a bit, but eventually making my way to Merritt. I might not be able to do as much damage as Sect can with their attacks, but if I can get close enough, when they're not watching, I believe Ali and I can at least gather further information about our attackers.

Hours of sneaking and scouting finally elicit a result—a small group of alien creatures, only two of which are humanoid. It's the weirdest group I've ever seen, including a nightmare fish-like creature in an oval liquid containment unit with tripedal mechanical legs; a flowing mass of yellow-cream tentacles and mouths; and a ram-headed, cat-like creature with an extra pair of hands. At least the two humanoids are mostly human, even if they are weirdly colored and something you'd see in *Farscape* rather than *Star Trek*.

"*What are those things?*" I send to Ali.

"*Don't see them much. The aquatic is a Pismeen, tentacle-goo is a Mohran, and ramses is, well, we'll call them Satyrs. You can't properly pronounce or hear its name, so we'll go with Satyr,*" Ali says easily. "*Must be one of the Sect's mixed hunter groups. It's not uncommon for Galactic organizations to put the minority species together.*"

I grunt. That's something I've noticed, that groups like the Truinnar, Hakarta, or the Yerick tend to be single species groups. I guess when you're the dominant power in your region, it's easier and better to keep to a single species for your groupings. Which makes mixed species groups rarer since they are, by virtue, a minority.

"*We going to bury them?*" Ali asks after he finishes naming the other two species.

I ignore their names for now, already pondering my choices. "*No. We're going to stalk them. I want to see if they meet up with our midnight attackers. Tell me about the weirdos.*"

I make sure to let the group pull away even farther, just inside my ability to track them. Even now, their markers are weirdly shaded in my minimap, Ali's way of indicating that they're there because I can see them and not because he's getting the information from the System.

"*Okay. Well, let's start with the Satyrs. Firstly, don't ever get into a drinking contest with one—alcohol actually doesn't affect their bodies at all...*" Ali begins.

I only half-listen, since I do actually have to make sure I'm not caught. Still, it passes the time and gives me a little bit of information about new species.

***

The next few hours are surreal, watching the enemy group travel across the map, doing their best to hide so they aren't found out while at the same time looking for our hunting groups. Groups which I have full view of in my map. Twice, barring a hill and a particularly dense piece of forestry, the Sect nearly stumbles upon our people—and vice versa. I'm glad it doesn't happen though, since it'd waste all the time I've already invested.

So strange to think of a simple turn left or being five minutes slower and what could have been. Then again, isn't that the truth about our lives? Half an hour one way, a different decision, and our lives would be so different. If I had never gotten a cup of coffee on that Saturday, I might never have met Anne. Trace it back further—if I had gotten up when my alarm first went off that morning, I'd have had time to make coffee for the day. Without meeting Anne, I'd never have traveled to Whitehorse. Never gotten my Class. Never met Lana or Ali.

Small decisions, small changes, and the course of our lives could alter by such a wide margin. Every day, we chide ourselves for past mistakes, past actions, calling forth a myriad of what-ifs of times past. We might never know of the hundred thousand small decisions that might have changed our lives. Still, we reprimand ourselves for the decisions we make as if, somehow, we know the optimal path.

As evening comes, I watch the group peel away, slowly heading south. I wonder if they'll finally bring me to my prey. Of course, it's not that easy. Twenty kilometers from Kamloops, and well out of sight of the settlement, the mixed species group gets on the road and calls forth various instruments of transportation, pulling away at speed. I stare in amazement at the mecha shrimp, shaking my head at the weirdness of the System world. Mecha. Shrimp.

I take my time getting on the road soon after and following, knowing I won't be able to keep up and stay hidden. A failure of some form perhaps. There's something to be said about knocking out their people, again and again, killing even the small fry till they have no one else to send.

But…

Sometimes, you have to wait. Play the long game. Hope to get the whole pot rather than bleeding them for a few chips here and there. So I head down the road, staying to the shadows and waiting. Maybe I'll find something. Maybe I'll fail. But for the first time in days, I feel useful again.

***

The message from Mel later that night was exasperating in its conciseness and the news it provided. Another attack, launched at ten and again at two in the morning. In neither case did the individuals who launched the attack come via the road I was watching. Which meant that my presence watching the road was of little use.

Yet… negative progress was still progress. Or could you call it negative progress? Probably not, now that I was thinking about it. Which tells you the kind of thoughts that occupy one's mind when you're seated in a small depression overlooking a darkened road early in the morning after spending the entire day awake.

I'll admit there's a small chance that the group involved might have sneaked past me. But a Skill that could hide sixty individuals from the System—or at least their data from people drawing information from the System—was powerful. So powerful that it must have been upgraded quite a few times. A Skill that could hide sixty people from the System and from visual and other line-of-sight sensing at the same time was insanely powerful. If my understanding of power levels in Classes is correct, that'd be a Master Class Skill. And if there's a Master Class Sect member out here, they wouldn't be bothering with all this bullshit.

Which leaves me with the question of what to do now. Option one—return to the area around Kamloops and work with the hunter groups to locate the attackers. That's the safe option, the smart one. Take out the attackers, give the settlement some rest. But it's also likely the one they're expecting.

The other option, the one I want to do, is to ignore the attackers. I know the group I stalked left for another area. Probably a staging area in Merritt or somewhere else. Hit those guys, make their lives miserable. But the moment I take out one of their hunting groups outside of their city, I'm also letting them know that we've changed tactics and I'm out here.

Doing so would call down the dogs of war. Which means I need to make sure that when I do act, it does the most amount of damage possible. I sigh, leaning back, and go back to watching the road, turning the thoughts over in my mind.

Hours later, I finally give up on locating any hunter groups on this stretch of road and look at my brown friend. I don't have to speak, but there're no monsters or Sect members and I'd like to actually hear my own voice. "Am I selfish?"

"Yes," Ali says automatically, then pauses as he considers my question. "Yes. What brought that on?"

"Lana," I say, remembering the accusation leveled at me.

"Ah." Ali shrugs. "Don't worry about it. You're sentient. Outside of a few, rather dumb, races, we're all selfish."

"Thanks, I think."

"Oh, come on, don't sulk. What's that thing you're always muttering? What is, is?" Ali says. "This is the same thing. You're selfish for wanting to go out and do this alone, because it gets you out of the city. Lana's selfish for wanting you back in Kamloops, safe and with her. You're both right to be selfish."

"Greed is good?" I mutter, and Ali rolls his eyes.

"In moderation, sure." Ali shrugs. "What, you don't want to Level up?"

I grunt, thinking about that single Level I need to hit 40. All those Skills, all that power. Yes, I can admit it. I want to grow, to Level up. To become more powerful. And that's greedy and selfish, but also practical and sensible and yes, sociable since I'm the bulwark for my group and town. "So... selfish. And greedy, charitable, and angry."

"Or as I like to put it, sentient," Ali says.

"Speaking of sentience..." I frown. "Why didn't you recommend I buy a military AI? Or upgrade Kim to a military AI?"

"Probably because it's a bad idea. You seem to think AIs are like your Skynet. They're closer to the Machine."

"The Machine?" I frown, raising an eyebrow at Ali, and he sighs.

"*Person of Interest*. Great show," Ali says. "AIs are limited, both by the constraints placed upon them by the Galactic Council but also the information they're able to ascertain. They're only as good as the information provided, and you, my boy, are limited on the information you can provide. A good military AI needs a lot of information to function, to make the best guesses possible. It also needs to get trained to function properly."

"Why?" I frown, shaking my head. "Can't it, you know, figure out the optimal choices with what we have now? I thought buying the data stores gave it the training."

"Not that kind of training. Look, let's keep it simple. If I told you that we should kill all the ex-Serfs to remove the Sect's objective for taking back the city, would you?" I glare at Ali, and he nods firmly. "Exactly. But it's a viable, potentially even the easiest, solution. An AI might see that option, decide it's the best option, and tell you that. Now, when you tell it no, you've got to explain why. Teach it."

"Ah…" I tilt my head to look at Ali. "And how long does it take to teach an AI that?"

"How long's the tapeworm?" Ali says. "Varies on the type, tier, resources, and how good you are at teaching and actually knowing what you want. With you? Quite a while."

I sigh and nod. I can see Ali's point and, on further thought, his point about lacking knowledge for the AI to actually make better decisions. It's not as if we're tapped into the Internet or anything, so the AI would be stuck with limited knowledge of the world. Unless we wanted to spend a ton of money purchasing information from the System, I can see how it'd be limited. It's only because Ali is a linked Companion that he has access to as much information as he does. Even Kim is forced to rely on tapping into general System information channels and the information provided by the settlement.

For all his assurances, I am concerned about the AIs used by larger organizations. But since I can't do anything about them right about now, I decide not to ask about it. I've had enough nightmares to last me for a while, and a galactic-wide, networked AI is one I don't need.

***

After that, it's a simple matter to continue my journey to Merritt. When dawn finally breaks, I'm situated on an appropriately far away and vertically dominant position to watch the tiny town. The hill I'm on is between the 5 and 97C highways, letting me keep an eye out for movement on either road—mostly via my map rather than visually—and also actually stare at the town itself. At this distance, and with my new Out of Class Skill I bought from the Shop and with Ali's help, I should be safe. Once again, I read the Class Skill description, more for comfort than anything else.

Shrunken Footprints (Out of Class Skill Level 1)

Reduces System presence of user, increasing the chance of the user evading detection of System-assisted sensing Skills and equipment. Also increases cost of information purchased about user. Reduces Mana Regeneration by 5 permanently.

After the attack, I'd done further research into the ways they could have evaded our sensors. This, among many other Class Skills, was present. Some, like the Skills Ingrid uses, hide the user entirely—pure Stealth Skills—but are expensive to purchase as they're normally restricted to their Classes. Many of them are active Skills, draining Mana from the pool immediately. While theoretically, with my Mana regeneration, I should be able to use some of those Skills, I'm also a direct combatant. Keeping up such a Skill seemed a bad idea, especially as constant use of an active Skill has deleterious side effects.

Others Skills, like the Shrunken Footprints, are less powerful overall but much more focused in their effects. And, obviously, cheaper. In this case, since I can rely on my real-world stealth skills, I just needed to reduce my System footprint. As it stands, so long as I don't actively push matters, I should be pretty well hidden from casual scanning. Along with Ali's help, we can even doctor some of the information given out.

Smiling at that knowledge, I turn back to the town spread out below me. Known more for a country music festival than anything else, the once-populous town is a ghost of itself. Not that I ever made it to the festival. Don't get me wrong, I'm not against country music, but the thought of the press of humanity at such an event is enough to make me shudder.

225

Still, the city shouldn't be as much of a ghost town as I see. For the last hour, I've seen maybe a dozen different individuals, most of them alien-looking creatures. Yet not a single human can be seen. This could be because everyone died, which, while unlikely, is possible. However, I'm leaning toward a forced evacuation or a group of citizens so terrorized they aren't willing to show their faces.

Once more, I cycle through all the visual processing options available on my helmet. Infrared, UV, X-ray, magnification, none of it helps. The distance is too great, the buildings too sturdy to leak any details. I can't even tell if the city is a Village or Town, a safe zone, or just a series of unclaimed buildings, divorced by our System overlord.

Frustrating. But I spend the time watching anyway, quietly building up a count of who resides in the city and how many. Scouting, because when and if I attack them, I want, nay, I need it to count for something.

***

Days. Watching, counting, planning. Days, while a trickle of information sent by Kim through the System keeps me updated. As expected, morale is dropping, the constant harrying attacks and the occasional fight and death doing nothing to help. Sure, we occasionally come out better, but without an idea of how many we're facing, it just seems like a constant, never-ending fight. Even our Leveling parties to the north have reported being attacked, making progress ever slower. The Sect is wearing us down, containing our people until they are ready. It's a siege, even if there are no catapults or entrenched lines.

Days of watching has seen some progress though. I know now how many Sect members are in Merritt—twenty-three—and I've even managed to figure out their groupings. By now, I have a firm grasp of the group's schedule. I've seen how they always keep at least two groups at home, rotating who's on hunt each day. On two occasions, a full group came back less an individual or two. In one case, I'd even seen them return somewhat cockily and, on that same day, learned that they had nearly wiped out an entire hunter group on our side. That was a bad day and I had to contain myself from rushing in.

Truth be told, I had all the information I needed at least a day ago, but I'd hesitated from attacking because I wanted to verify if this was a trap. The fact that they stayed apart, sleeping and leaving at different times, made it seem just too easy. After all, an empty town with only Sect members in it is somewhat suspicious. But however closely I looked, I just couldn't see the trap. In the end, sometimes all you can do is set the trap off and hope to get out.

Resolved to doing something mildly stupid, I make my way stealthily into town after the second group finally left for the day. If they followed their rough schedule, a third group would leave at some point within the next hour, leaving two groups behind to rest for the day. That was the time I had chosen to act.

Hunkered behind a convenient house, I pulled Sabre from my storage and transformed it. I waited for a second, listening and watching to see if I had been found out yet. Seeing nothing, I started up the Temporal Cloak, beginning the process of sneaking in deeper. My forehead creased as I received no notification that this was a claimed city or town.

"Ali?"

"John. I love you too."

"What's going on with the town?"

"They sold the town key a few weeks ago. Probably at the same time they started moving people out. Data on the town activities dropped off around the same time in the System, so I'm assuming that's the case," Ali says, eyes flicking over notification windows.

"Well, that at least removes the town's sensors from the equation," I say, looking for a bright spot.

I kind of wanted Merritt. It's a decent midway point, but with the key sold, we'll either have to pick up each of the buildings individually or repurchase the town settlement key ourselves. Though that does bring up the question of why the populace hasn't purchased enough land to keep it as their own. After all, as Ali pointed out, you could just purchase enough property to force the System to create a settlement for you.

Idle thoughts as I continue to carefully make my way in. I grunt, bringing my attention back to the rather important point of not being found out. While the Sect seems to cluster in the city center, that doesn't mean that they won't or can't explore.

For all my caution, I run into little trouble until I'm a half-block into the historical downtown district. Historical like North American historical—so within the last hundred years—not European or Asian historical, which is within the last few hundred or thousand years. Stubby little commercial buildings from around the turn of last century make up the city center. The Sect members have taken over the Coldwater Hotel, each of them probably lounging in the equivalent of a suite or something. Not a bad idea really, since one of the upgrades in a designated hotel includes laundry and other cleaning options. Assuming someone purchased it, which I'd have done.

"That is purchased, right? Any idea about the upgrades?" I ask Ali since, well, I might as well.

"It's registered. That's about all that's relevant available. Climate control, Mana engine and battery, sonic showers and plumbing, I could go on…" Ali says with a shrug as he floats beside me.

I'm not surprised. It's not as if I'd make the security upgrades I'd bought available for people to learn. Unfortunately, that does mean I'm not entirely sure how strong those walls are.

As I ponder my next steps, I watch a humanoid reptile-like creature walk out. The sleek emerald-green Sect member strolls down the street without a care in the world, the morning sunlight glinting off the purple highlights of her body.

???? (Level 29 Warrior (?))
HP:
MP:
Conditions: Oblivious

"What's with the question marks?"
"Don't want to probe too deeply right now."

Pulling backward, I make sure to stay hidden while checking the timer of the Cloak. I'm going to need to make a move soon...

Still, I let the Sect member leave on whatever business she has. If I were Ingrid, this would be the perfect time to kill her. Sneak up, backstab and mute the attack, murdering her in silence before anyone knows. But I'm not Ingrid and I have no Skills to mute the attacks or her call for help. It's not like I could walk up and slit her throat like in the movies—the System's interference makes it hard to kill another with a single hit. Not impossible perhaps, but hard. Better to let her go than risk losing the element of surprise against everyone else.

Once she's gone, I proceed with my initial plan. All around the building, I quietly add a series of explosives. Since I don't have any real skill in demolitions, I go with the tried-and-true method of using more rather than less. After all, I need to destroy both the building and the people inside. And if you think about it, I'm just returning the looted explosives. See, I can be generous.

Only when I'm done and on the building across the street, crouched low and under cover, do I relax. Thankfully, the Sect isn't a military organization. Rather than having scouts, watchers, and a fixed timetable, the members lounge about and relax, obviously content to take their time off. It reminds me a lot of the Adventuring Guild in Carcross and their members, rather than Capstan and the Truinnar or the Hakarta.

Rather than pursue that thought, I trigger the explosives. Interesting thing to note about explosions—you never hear them until after the explosive wave front hits you, the air moving faster than the noise. In addition, once the explosion has finished expanding, there's a secondary "pull," as nature abhors the vacuum. Even with the explosives directed to send the majority of their blast inward and upward, what does escape is enough to batter poor Sabre's shield and my meager cover. Look, as I said, I'm not exactly trained in demolitions.

"One down," Ali announces even as I pop up, waiting.

The building across the street is gone, now a mass of System-enhanced wood, steel, and concrete. Fires burn around the building and against a few others that were caught in the explosion, small and not-so-small craters in the ground where the explosives were laid. If not for the System's enhancements, the explosions would likely have done more damage to the Sect members resting within.

Even as I think that, the rubble moves. A strong, multi-armed, orange creature with a topknot shoves a column away, a pair of short humanoids following it. In a corner, red smoke pours out of the broken concrete, swirling in a circle. A few seconds later, a cone of ice erupts from the ground a short distance away from the smoke, a figure encased in it like a human tootsie roll center.

Before the group can fully recover their senses, the covers over my mini-missile launchers open and let loose. A fraction of a second later, my left hand rises and a fireball forms, flying outward. I don't stop, repeatedly casting the spell as fast as I can. While I have a personal preference for Lightning Bolt, the group below is too spread out for that spell. At least, right now.

The multi-armed topknotted creature snarls, grabs a piece of intact rubble twice its size, and holds it up in front of its body as the missiles streak toward it. The twin humanoids duck behind the monster, curling slightly to shield their bodies against the explosions. All around, the Sect members defend themselves—all but an unlucky bastard who manages to dig himself out just in time for the explosion to hit.

High-explosive missiles send waves of flame and compressed air through the surroundings, throwing up debris and turning it into shrapnel. Moments later, my first fireball explodes as well, flames moving in an aborted globe that envelops those below. The second and third explode soon after, the Sect members doing their best to protect themselves.

"Three more down," Ali tells me even as I unload another fireball.

But my sneak attack is over and the group is firing back. Spells, beam weapons, an acidic fluid, and more target me, hammering Sabre's shield and then mine in short order. Rather than duke it out at range, I focus and Blink Step forward, hiding myself from the incoming fireball behind the mostly melted spike of ice.

"Owwww! Those spells hurt," Ali sends to me as he zips forward, still invisible. *"You could have warned me you're leaving."*

Raising my foot, I pivot, my blade sinking into the Mage's body. It exits through his shoulder, the severed arm flopping to the ground, accompanied by a scream of pain. Arming and dropping a grenade by my feet, I Blink Step away to Topknot, ignoring the continued complaints from my Spirit. Even as

231

the grenade explodes, finishing the job of killing the Mage, I'm attacking Topknot.

Topknot is good. The knife that might as well be a sword in his hand moves with impressive speed, blocking my surprise attack and the follow-ups. We dance, trading blows, while next to him, the last humanoid struggles to its feet, body thoroughly cooked. No time to finish it though. Just enough time to take a cut to my leg as I plunge my sword into Topknot's chest and end that fight.

"The third group is on its way. Twenty seconds," Ali tells me, his short form swooping down to clock the cooked humanoid in the head with his tiny fist. Tiny or not, between momentum and the creature's injuries, the monster falls.

"Good job!" I grin at the now-visible Spirit. Just in time to see him get smashed aside by what looks like a giant crossbow bolt.

Turning, I see the female reptile monster turning the corner down the block, running away with the crossbow held up toward her body. I snarl, thinking of chasing her before recalling Ali's earlier message. Rather than wasting time, I jump away from the wreckage, my hands moving as I deposit mines all across the street. Some land on the ground, tripwires exploding outward and almost disappearing from view before my helmet highlights them for me. Others burrow away, covering their casings in the dirt as they await their chance.

"Three seconds," Ali says, once more invisible and intangible. Still, as he floats beside me, his hand clutches his side where he leaks blue light.

"Thanks," I grunt.

I stop dropping mines and spin around, pulling my beam rifle from storage and snugging it to my shoulder. The first Sect member to turn the corner takes a beam to his waist, the sight of melted armor and burnt flesh making an appearance as he gets cut up. He throws himself to the side, attempting to dodge the shots, but I follow him, firing again and again.

Bolts of red and green land around me. A massive metallic spike shatters against Sabre's shield, and wind blades crack the shield apart. I take another shot, injuring the sucker before I skip backward, eyes dancing over the group as I take in their Levels. No names, just Classes and Levels. A mixture of combat Classes, most simplified to "Warrior," "Gunner," "Healer," or "Mage" for right now, while their Levels sit in the high 20s to mid-30s.

I snap off shots from the Inlin and launch missiles in a more controlled fashion, backing off slowly as I weave through their attacks. Even with my higher Agility, the sheer volume of fire means that I get hit constantly, my Soul Shield crumbling every second. Still, I persist, luring them closer.

The first pair of warriors reaches the mines, explosions and gloop flying. One is thrown into the air, a chunk of flesh sliced off his foot from a razorwire. Another is caught in insta-concrete as he struggles to free himself and pull at his own flesh as worms burrow into his body. The Healer slows down before it can reach them, the mechanical-biological body pulling to a stop as it waves four-fingered tentacles, magic wrapping around its friends. The others, ranged attackers, keep firing, chipping away at my defenses.

Polar zone. I raise my hand, casting the spell, and the temperature around the group drops immediately. The next second, I trigger the sonic pulser, the teeth-clenching shriek throwing off their aim and making my attackers stumble. Ali darts into their midst, his invisible body glowing as he activates his Elemental Affinity, tapping into the vibrations and molecules around. I can vaguely sense what he's doing, the way he's enhancing—or perhaps more accurately, breaking down—the stability of molecules around us. A neat trick, something I'll need to work on later.

Disoriented and under attack or not, the group refuses to run through the minefield. The pair caught in it are attempting to extract themselves, the Healer too disrupted to finish its spells at the moment. Rather than letting them take

233

the time to recover, I call forth Enhanced Lightning Strike, my Mana already down to a third. Too much. While electricity arcs through the air and dances between bodies and the ground, I have Sabre inject me with the Mana potions it has stored. The tightness around my temples from an incipient Mana headache disappears even as my body feels refreshed, since the Mana Regeneration potions adds to my natural regeneration rate.

Natural. Har!

I cut the Lightning Strike spell off before it drains me too far, knowing I can't afford to let it go on much longer. Instead, I dash forward into the mine field, continuing to target the Healer with the majority of my attacks. Ducking around the mines and making sure I don't trigger the ones that don't have a friend-foe sensor eats up time. My sonic pulser shuts down, no longer able to sustain the caterwaul, allowing the group to recover.

"Oh man, I was just getting into the groove," Ali moans, his invisible Spirit body stopping its waggling.

The group is experienced, I have to admit. Hurt and damaged as they are, the Healer is drinking its own healing potions while the Mage slams his hands together, earth erupting from the ground to hide the Healer. As the Mage does so, the ranged attacker lobs a canister over the emerging wall, the cannister exploding in a brief cloud of dust. A second later, I get a new notification.

Nano Machine Pollution detected.

Mana Regeneration decreased in surroundings for 5 minutes by 31.4%

I growl, my prey out of sight, even as one of the melee fighters throws out his hand. A single silver needle multiplies until thousands of them fill the air, glowing with a malevolent dark red light. Without stopping, they bypass my Soul Shield and stab through Sabre's armor into my fleshy body.

You are poisoned!

-13 HP per second (after resistances)

Duration: 00:0:33

Pain erupts from the needles, as if acid is spreading from the needles throughout my body. I snarl, noting the duration, and change directions. In passing, I throw a grenade at the twitching form of the stuck melee fighter, focusing instead on the one that poisoned me.

You'd think a poisoner would look, I don't know, devious and evil. Slimy perhaps. What I see though is a flamboyant, thin creature dressed more like a swashbuckler with a colorful, patched half-cloak. Very humanoid-looking too, other than the single eye that dominates his whiskered face. Running forward, I throw a Blade Strike, forcing d'Artagnan to duck even as he throws a pair of spikes at me underhand. Those, at least, don't pierce my Soul Shield, though the shield suddenly shifts to a sickly-green color.

Soul Shield Corrupted

-15 HP per second

"Boy-o, they're retreating. And teams one and two are on their way back. I've got team one on my screen already. They're making damn good time," Ali updates me.

I snarl slightly, covering the last few feet as my damaged and worn shield finally gives way. I lunge forward, my sword caught and pushed aside by d'Artagnan using one of his spikes. What he doesn't expect is for the sword to disappear, throwing his balance off just long enough for me to step forward and cut up, bisecting his abdomen and chest. Even as he screams, I conjure a sword into my other hand to finish the job, lopping off his head. As he dies, I swipe my hand through his body and dump it into my storage space, glancing back at the burnt and twitching body of his compatriot, the worms making a mess of my attacker.

"Remind me to buy a cure for those mines," I send to Ali even as I run to put the poor man out of his misery.

The Spirit pops out of the earthen wall a moment later, flying toward me as he flicks a small screen up in front of me. The remnants of the group I recently engaged slow down as they link up with the second group even as the first group to leave town appears on the edges of my map. It's clear that they aren't coming at me piecemeal anymore, gathering together for safety.

"Can I reach them?" I send to Ali, wondering if maybe I can pick off a couple more from the consolidated group.

"The running group? Sure. But they're likely to play for time, bog you down," Ali says.

A quick glance at my Mana level and its hampered regeneration shows that I'm running dangerously low again. That's why I chose not to use Blink Step earlier, knowing that the Skill is expensive. Better to save a little just in case I need to run.

"Recommend you get out of the nano cloud at the least, boy-o," Ali sends as I dither.

Nodding, I jump onto the roof of the nearest building, using Sabre's jump jets to help cover the distance. Not that I couldn't do it just using my stats, but the jump jets and anti-gravity plates make it a lot easier. As I fly through the air, I refresh the Soul Shield, wincing as my Mana drops again.

"Time to go," I say and suit words to action.

Better to get out of here before they gather and try to track me down. I might be able to win, but getting encircled by a group of Advanced Level fighters worries me. No guarantee they don't have a plan to get some real players in. Without the QSM – my Quantum State Manipulator which lets me phase partly into another dimension - my options for running away have decreased, so better to draw this out and keep hitting them one after the other.

Anyway, I've struck my blow. Now for the next part of my plan.

Chapter 15

A day and night later, I finally relax. Sons of bitches had someone with tracking Skills on their side, so I'd been forced to run and fight against the consolidated groups, reinforced by another hunting group that didn't originate from the city. While I had no idea which one of three I managed to kill in our last encounter had the tracking Skill, I was finally confident that I had lost them. Either that, or they're laughing their asses off while I hide at the bottom of this lake.

Once again, I go over the gains in my mind. There's something to be said about fighting multiple sentients—the experience gain is definitely better than what you'd get killing monsters. I'm now three quarters to my next Level and I earned another seventy thousand Credits. Sadly, most of the equipment I looted is less than useful—some mediocre personal weapons, some damaged armor, and the usual slew of Mana and Healing potions. However, there are a few interesting things.

Triffgits Leeches of Poison Neutralisation

Guaranteed to remove most Tier V and IV poisons if applied within two minutes of infection. Do not store in System inventory.

I stare at the tiny bottle of writhing leeches, my face twitching in disgust as I stare at the black-and-green creatures. They really do look similar to Earth leeches, though I'm promised they feed on poisons rather than blood. Still, I'd have to be pretty desperate before using these.

Q'saex Nano Swarm Grenade

This specially designed nano-swarm will not directly damage your opponents but will instead constantly reproduce, using the ambient Mana in its surroundings to multiply the swarm. This will reduce all Mana regeneration in the affected regions during this period.

Affect: -40% Mana Regeneration

Duration: 20 Minutes

"That's dangerous," I mutter, staring at the pair of grenades in my hand. I slip them back into the external storage locations for Sabre.

"Worried about your grey goo scenario? Don't be. The nanites are programmed to shut down after twenty minutes. And even if they weren't, the System would shut them down soon after," Ali reassures me as he darts around the lake, chasing a few barracuda-looking fish. At Level 3, those things aren't dangerous to me and supposedly make good eating.

"How sure are you?"

"Very. It's pretty well-recorded that the System has defenses against nanite encroachment. In fact, a lot of studies show that the System hampers nano-machines and reproduction, along with out-of-control AIs," Ali says.

"So I noticed it says forty percent here," I say. Of course, it might be that the group all just had different toys, but this seems like something the team might have pooled money together to purchase as a group.

"Forty percent based off Galactic Standard, remember? We're in a Mana-rich environment in a Dungeon World, so the effect is less," Ali sends back.

"Right," I say, listening to the echo of my voice in my helmet.

I draw another breath of recycled air and I swear, I can taste my own unbrushed breath. I know it's psychological, that the helmet and Sabre's environmental filters have removed it all, but I've been here for hours. Still, I force patience on myself again. Two more hours, that's what I promised myself. Two hours and I'll be out.

***

We forget how big Canada is, when the roads are perfect and the weather is great. While the weather today is nice—a warm summer day with a light breeze blowing—the roads themselves are a mess. There's an entire stretch on the 5 between Merritt and Hope where the ground is a swamp, the road buried under murky waters where *things* reach out to grab at Sabre. I'm grateful I picked up the anti-gravity plates for the PAV, allowing me to traverse the sudden change in environment with ease.

When the roads are great, we forget the size of our country thinking that a three-hour drive is a reasonable thing to do on the weekend. It's something more than one overseas acquaintance has pointed out, that the same amount of time would put you into a new country in many parts of the world.

But without roads, with monsters and enemies all around, what should have been a few hours' drive takes me days. Alternately, driving alongside the road, or in some cases, diverting entirely away, I find myself finally nearing the Lower Mainland. Not Vancouver itself, but Mission as I switch to the 7.

A part of me wonders if I'm entirely insane, going directly into the lion's den. Of course, it is insane, but I'm banking on Ali and Shrunken Footprints to make it less so. Ingrid could do this better, sneak right in and stab someone to death, but she's got her own job to do. Between my stealth Skills, the Class Skill, and my ability to run away really fast, I'm the best choice for entering Vancouver. Or at least, that's what I keep trying to convince myself on.

Once I near Mission, I get off the road. Traveling takes longer off-road, since I have Sabre stored away and am on foot. I weigh the pros and cons of keeping on my skintight, high-tech armor and eventually go with on. While I'm not sure how many humans in this area might have it—certainly, everyone in Whitehorse took to wearing a variation of it as a matter of course—it's black, doesn't make much noise, and offers some additional passive protection. Rather than take that away, I just opt to take more time sneaking in.

Alleyways and side roads do well for me, leaving me with few encounters and none of note. Ali's ability to sense others means that we can swing wide around potential problems long before they see us, leaving only a few low-Leveled monsters that we can safely ignore. Not that we see many sentients anyway, other than the occasional scavenger party breaking into abandoned buildings, looking for necessities.

Curious, and nearer to downtown Vancouver itself, I make my way into an abandoned office building, this one once hosting individuals that used to sell million-dollar shacks. There's an irony in watching the very people that the realtors used to prey upon ransack those same structures. I watch the scavenger group through the windows, curious to see what they take. Food sometimes, jewelry of course, but more mundane items are common too. Toilet paper, menstrual pads, books, LPs, and DVDs are more common.

It takes me a while to puzzle that out. Consumables and jewelry sure, but the LPs and DVDs only make sense after I realize it's culture. Music. Things we can't get or produce anymore, that comfort in times of stress and uncertainty. A wave of sadness washes over me with the realization that we might never get another ZZ Ward, Meatloaf, or Whedon creation. All that we have, all that is made, that's all we'll ever have.

After a time, I push down the grief and focus again on their scavenged goods. In a nuclear war, we might be scrounging for oil and food, but here, food is all around us. Oil is useless since most of our machines are dead and Mana engines are so much more efficient. Guns—non-System registered guns—are laughable toys that barely affect anything other than the lowest Level vermin.

No, in this apocalypse, the most important resource is Levels. People create Levels, so people are important, but a single high-Level individual is still more important than a series of low-Levels.

"You know, the System is a bit of an elitist," I whisper to Ali, rubbing my nose as I hunker down, watching the group on my map as they move to another building. This time, they've decided to leave someone on watch. When Ali sends me a mental *huh*, I explain my earlier thoughts.

"Talk in your head. And of course it is," Ali says. *"That's the System for you. But don't tell me you thought your society was fair either. At least with the System, you've got a chance to Level up."*

Rather than argue with Ali about the merits or demerits of democracy, I ask him another question that has been bothering me. *"Whatever. Can't change it, can we? Tell me something else. What's to stop a really rich or powerful group from loading up on Shop-bought Skills, making them invincible?"*

"Mmm… nothing? Or well, practicality, I guess. Obviously Mana regeneration limits the passives," Ali sends, waggling his fingers. *"And since you can't really stack most Mana regeneration-boosting Skills, there's no way to get around that. For the active Skills, you've got the problem of Mana pool to worry about. Easy enough to get a ton of different Skills, but if you can't afford to use them, they aren't much use. But yes, there are people who pack a lot more punch for their Level than they should have because they've bought a bunch of Skills."*

I slowly nod. In the end, those with money and influence have a head start, whether in the System or our old world. Add in the fact that we're working a knowledge deficit compared to the rest of the galaxy, and us humans are at a severe disadvantage. But that's okay. As my dad once said, even if you have to work twice as hard to be half as good, most people aren't willing to put in the work to start.

What I see before me, from my map and the occasional glance out the window, tells the truth of that too. The Sect members I've fought are decent, smart and experienced. But compared to the human teams at the same Level, especially those from Whitehorse, they're missing something. An edge, a drive, that we have. I can even see it in these kids, the way they move and scavenge. Come to think of it, the Yerick have it to a slightly lesser extent too.

If we survive, if we manage to make our way through the colonization of our world and not fall into despair, we might just do okay. To do that though, we have to have our own areas of control, our own cities. And that means beating the hell out of the Thirteen Moon Sect. Settling comfortably again, I wait for the group to get moving so that I can get back on task.

***

My first big hurdle is the Pitt River. Rather than cross it along the actual bridge, I swing north for a bit, running in the dead of the night through empty streets till I hit an abandoned golf course. From there, I swim across the river in the early morning light and hide out in someone's expensive and torn-up home. Whoever built the house was a fan of the typical West Coast design with lots of windows, which meant that when the monsters came, there was nothing sturdy to hold them out. I ignore the months-old signs of struggle, grateful that the scavengers have removed the bodies.

After that, I scavenge some old clothes. Blue jeans and a T-shirt with a goth girl with an ankh design on it replaces my combat gear. I keep the sidearm and a beam rifle though, wearing both out in the open, along with the combat boots. While the weapons might be a tad more expensive than normal, everyone's packing these days. A quick discussion with Ali has him shifting some information on my Status. He can't do much about the Level, but I now read as a Level 39 Guard. High enough to raise more than a few eyebrows, but at least to all casual scans, I'm just a Basic Class.

Working my way towards downtown Vancouver the next evening is easy. Making sure to come in with the scavenger groups means I'm just another dot on the Sect's sensors as I walk in through the streets of Coquitlam. That's the thing about the Lower Mainland and Canada. While we might have lost ninety percent of our population, Canada's population has always been concentrated in a few major cities. Even ten percent of a million is a lot of people, and with all the towns around the city abandoned, the survivors have concentrated significantly. All those people need to hunt, farm, build, and otherwise improve themselves. Which means hunting parties, scavenger parties, farming groups, and more. The Sect might own and run the place, but they don't have the numbers to check out everyone.

That's the next thing I notice. Roxley had his guards in his livery to make themselves easy to notice. Policemen normally are noticeable; after all, it helps keep the rabble in line. The Sect members do the same here, mostly by just being *different* than us humans. It takes only a short while for Ali to point out that not every single alien is a Sect member though. After that and a bit of grumbling, he adjusts the aliens' descriptions. Now, every Sect member who publicly displays his allegiance—which is likely all of them—is marked above their heads via their Status bars as well. That's good, because I really don't want to kill an innocent.

It's interesting to watch the reactions of the other humans to the other species. Few humans talk to them. Even fewer seem friendly with any of the aliens. Oh, some are worming their way into the Sect's good graces by toadying up, but whether it's because they suck at that or are just exaggerating for the

245

aliens, picking out their motives is easy. But for the majority, the silent edge of resentment and anger is there in the sidelong glances and twisted lips when the Sect members aren't looking.

Not that the Sect members are helping matters. Most act like the small-time bullies they are, giving a shove here, a shakedown there. Lording it over the humans wherever they can.

"They're making this too damn easy," I send to Ali, glancing at a pair of beast-like creatures shaking down a scavenger party. It also explains why most of the humans use normal bags rather than their storage. Though I'm curious how the Sect is stopping people from sneaking things in via storage.

"Auditors. They've got the ability to look into your storage, with your consent or without if they've got enough strength," Ali says, answering the implied question. *"Go right here. There's a group of Sect members coming down the street who are looking bored. Better to skip around them."*

"Got it," I say, sighing. I'm not the only one who does that, though most who duck out are ahead of me, I notice. Pissing off the humans they guard is definitely helping me blend in, since no one wants to meet the Sect members if they can help it. *"Not many Serfs here."*

"We're still on the edges. They'll keep the Serfs close on hand. Don't want them running away," Ali says.

I nod, rubbing my chin absently as I assess the areas. Truth be told, so far, the city looks much like the towns I've seen. Windows and doors broken, abandoned cars rusting on the streets, occasional monsters popping up then hiding as they sense the Level difference. On occasion, a few utterly insane monsters attack and are put down. More cars of course, a lot more cars on the major roads, abandoned and useless, but I don't stay on those byways much.

But in time, I spot the differences. The Mana flows in a big city are more concentrated and grow greater as I head deeper into the Lower Mainland.

While Coquitlam might be a "Village," it could easily be considered a Level 10-20 zone, with a few of the wooded parks and neighborhoods jumping up another zone level again. Monsters grow and populate around here, seeming to thrive on the unregulated flow of the city.

The blooming dots of monsters at certain buildings—the hospital, the campus, a weird strip mall—all speak to monster hives that haven't been dealt with. Maybe even dungeons in the making. And then there are the occasionally destroyed neighborhoods, entire buildings wrecked in what must have been periods of intense fighting.

But no humans—at least none who have made it their goal to live out here. Which is surprising. I expected holdouts, groups settled into defensible regions, creating their own tiny communities. Instead, I see none of that. A few groups here and there stay alone, but no large settlements.

"Is this normal?" I say to Ali.

"Nothing's normal. But if I were the Sect, I wouldn't want an independent group all the way out here. Be really easy to put pressure, draw them in where you can keep a better eye on them," Ali says. *"And those who don't... well, there are monsters out here."*

"Convenient excuse," I say, grunting. Anger flares for a moment before I push it down. Not the right time. Still, a part of me burns at the thought of people being forced to give up the little stability and protection they've built for themselves, all to make the Sect members' lives easier.

"It's kind of what you guys did too," Ali says, sending a chiding thought to me. *"How many towns and people did you drag back to Whitehorse or to the next safe zone?"*

"I always gave them a choice," I say, pointing out the major difference.

As much as I wanted to, I never, ever forced my choices on others. Even if it meant their deaths. God knows I wanted to. Especially for those idiot families who decided it was still safer to hang out in the middle of a monster-infested zone than to proceed to a safe zone because humans are evil.

Idiots.

They were so fixed on their beliefs that humanity is evil, that we devolve to our basest instincts the moment the lights go off, they refused to accept the evidence before their eyes. And doomed their children and themselves to struggling and fighting in the wilderness alone. Some days, I wonder if I should have just taken the children.

There's no good answer here. Pull the kids away and I'd probably have had to kill their parents in front of them. I somehow doubt that would help them become well-adjusted, stable individuals. Even if I didn't, who would take care of them? Do I drop them off at the nearest town and hope that there's some kind soul willing to take in a group of traumatized children? It's one thing for a government that, technically, has a series of methods to take care of such children. It's another for my team and me to kidnap children because we don't think their parents are doing a good job.

Yet... I can't help but think about them sometimes.

"Getting late out here. You might want to get a move on it." The voice, low and rich, breaks me out of my morose thoughts.

I blink, staring around, and find myself grinding my teeth, hands clenched while standing in the middle of the street. I blink, shaking my head. "Sorry."

"Don't worry about it. We've all been there," the guy says, smiling at me kindly. He's in his late thirties, a hint of wariness in his eyes as he offers me his hand to shake. Six feet tall, thin, with brown hair, he's got a guitar slung across his shoulders and a bag by his feet. A quick check shows his Class and Level— a Level 21 Appraiser. "Damian."

"John," I say, shaking his hand. I'm glad he doesn't ask why I was frozen in the middle of the street, but the way he looks at me sympathetically, I can guess what he's thinking. All of us have our own nightmares.

"That's Analyn and Jonah." Damian indicates a short Filipino woman armed with a beam rifle the size of her body and an older, almost grandfatherly, man who seems to be their pack mule, carrying four bags on his shoulders. "You a hunter?"

"How'd you know?" I ask.

"No bags, so you're not a scavenger," Damian explains, pointing at my guns. "And those look like they've seen some use. Like you."

"Pretty smart," I say, smiling at Damian. I don't move away, since I'm curious to see where he's going with this.

"Get anything good?" Damian waves down the street, indicating we should continue walking.

I fall into step with him. "A little." I shrug, thinking of the various random animal bits I've picked up from the monsters that have refused to leave me alone. It's more habit than anything else that has me grabbing the loot, since the amount of Credits I'd get is pitiful. "I was mostly scouting this time."

"Outside the Mainland? You're either brave or stupid," Analyn says then smiles slightly.

"Going alone lets me hide better," I say, shrugging. "I have a few skills in that area."

"Ah…" Analyn says, nodding.

"If you made a map, I know a few people who might buy it," Damian says. "Good information about the land outside is hard to find. Everyone's focused on the dungeon the Sect made in UBC and the new dungeon formed in SFU."

"The UBC dungeon must be Town-formed. Expensive, but it's a great way of focusing the Mana flow in the region. The dungeon northwest of here that they're talking is natural," Ali sends to me. *"The places around here are all villages, except Vancouver itself, which is a full Town."*

I grunt in acknowledgement of both, letting my eyes roam over the area. We're making good time, even burdened down with gear. The higher-than-human stats means a normal walking speed is nearly a jog pre-System, without any concern about running out of stamina.

Since Damian seems talkative, I probe him for information, just basic things. He's more than happy to discuss the Sect, giving me a spotty overview of the city. I do my best to hide my ignorance, asking leading questions while letting Ali fill in the blanks.

As Ali mentioned, the initial period was bloody. Monsters, both mutated and portalled, showed up all over the city. A lot of people died, but things held together surprisingly well after the initial death toll as people learned to run, hide, or fight. Unlike Whitehorse, a number of really high-Level monsters had appeared, including a land drake that had taken the entirety of Stanley Park as its home. Even then, things had settled down, the local army and police managing to deal with the evolving monsters.

Unfortunately, the System—or maybe the Council—decided that wasn't good enough and portalled in more high-level monsters in a single night. The devastation was amazing. The entire False Creek area, including the brewery and armory, had been destroyed, the Sky Giant finally dying under the continuous assault of hundreds. The land drake actually took out one of the portalled monsters when a multi-headed chimera was forced into the park.

The sacrifice of the fighters didn't stop thousands from dying that night. That same tragedy repeated over and over again all across the city. Any major staging area had to deal with an attack by a high-level monster. At that point, resistance had been shattered and groups broke up into much smaller sections.

"*Suspicious, no?*" I send to Ali.

"Would you be interested to know that it isn't a singular experience? In the same period, there's constant sudden drops in your population—from such attacks, I assume. I'd need to buy the information to be certain but…"

I keep my face neutral, continuing to listen to Damian, but a part of me growls. There's a story there, and one I need to dig into at some point.

A week later, the Sect appeared and claimed all the cities of the Lower Mainland. According to Ali, they actually purchased the village keys nearly the same day they were released. Rather than improving the rest of the cities, the Sect focused their attention on Vancouver only, turning it into a Town in four months. Pretty much the entirety of the downtown is their exclusive property—outside of the Downtown Eastside, where some humans gather.

Unlike our smaller towns, quite a few Shops are clustered in the Lower Mainland. Each city has their own, with Vancouver having two—one in the art gallery downtown and another in the middle of Queen Elizabeth Park. Burnaby's Shop is in the Metrotown which has a significant human presence living in the giant shopping mall and thus outside the Sect's direct sphere of influence. Unlike the downtown of Vancouver, where most of the Serfs live, the mall in Burnaby is actually owned and run by free humans according to Damian. Well, technically rented mostly, but it's close enough.

When I hear that news, I change my mind of where I intend to go tonight, deciding against a direct trip to downtown Vancouver. If I'm going to find out what I want, and potentially locate a safe place to rest, the mall seems to be a better choice. As we get closer to Burnaby, I notice more and more humans. Some of them are rather interesting too…

George Pierre (Level 19 Breacher—Sect Member)

HP: 380/380

MP: 170/170

Conditions: None

"Fucking traitors," Analyn swears under her breath when she spots the group of five Sect members, each of them with a simple grey cloth with the Sect's symbol on their arms.

My eyes flicker over them while Damian glares at the lady before he glances at me, concern on his face. I flash him a little smile but make sure to swing around the group. That action makes him relax slightly.

"Seems to be more of them," I say to Damian softly.

"The Sect pays well, gives discounts on goods in the Shop, and if you join them, you're immune to becoming a Serf," Damian says, his tone neutral. "After they crushed the resistance, can you blame them?"

"Yes," Analyn hisses while Jonah nods firmly.

"Dangerous words," I say, my tone light. I'd love to ask about the resistance, but it seems a bit too obvious to duck into that question right now.

"Eh, everyone's said it," Damian says with a careless shrug. "No one likes them, but…"

But it's a way of surviving, and we all have a certain degree of empathy for each other over things like this. We might not like it or agree, but we can empathize. There's been so much going on that a period of safety or comfort is attractive. Even if you have to sell out.

Having skirted around the human Sect-members, we head south. Surprisingly, the group follows me to Metrotown. Or perhaps not, considering the views they've expressed to me, a nominal stranger. Once we get past the rather foreboding warehouses and industrial complexes—many of which are breeding grounds for groups of monsters—we hit the residential zones. Those, as usual, are depressing lots, which is why we continue south at a jog. Conversations grow sparser and less useful, turning to the usual jokes and ribbing, which I eventually tune out.

Before I know it, we're down at Kingsway, which runs at a diagonal to most streets with its multi-story retail stores, and only a stone's throw away from the Metrotown mall itself. Surprisingly, none of the retail stores are owned—most shuttered, others vandalized and looted. I stare at the buildings for a second, shaking my head as happier memories clash with reality before I hurry up to follow the group.

If you've been to one shopping mall, you've been to them all, it seems. Or maybe if you've been to one mid-class, sprawling giant mall, you've been to them all. They're all filled with brand-name shops, each segregated into their own little niches, with bright, artificial lighting and a food court or two with "food" that is, at best, barely edible. In other words, soulless and vapid.

Not much has changed, it seems. With the Shop located in what used to be a giant bookstore, the rest of the mall has been partitioned to make buying and selling goods easier. Rather than ask questions that might expose me for the stranger I am, I follow the group, playing as if I'm happy to continue chatting with them. Occasionally, I pull things from my storage to sell too.

Each portion of the mall seems to be taken over by different groups. We spend most of our time in the scavenger area, where "normal" human goods are bought and sold. While Spells are nice, dishwashing liquid, hair gel, toilet paper, and replacement sets of clothing are all still desirable. Sure, you could scavenge it yourself, but convenience trumps cost for most people. I don't get a lot of Credits and the group spends some time haggling as prices fluctuate depending on what other groups drag in, but eventually everything is sold.

After that, it's off to another part of the mall to sell monster parts. Interestingly enough, there are two sections, one for food and one for non-consumables. We hit the non-consumables first, haggling with various merchants who are only willing to buy a portion of what we have. This time around, I take a more active role, as my cover as a hunter means I should have more loot.

"You know, he ripped you off there," Jonah says, shaking his head. "Five Credits for Creller teeth? You should have gotten at least eight each!"

I shrug, not wishing to comment. Ali looks unhappy as well, floating invisibly next to me, obviously itching to get involved. While it might be a break from my role, I just don't have the patience to waste time haggling over a few Credits. A single good kill could easily replace all the funds I lose. That's why I never bothered with it all in Whitehorse, leaving the money matters to Ali.

From glancing around, it's obvious that many of the individuals buying in this portion of the mall are just middlemen picking up small numbers of lootable components for others. The way the various merchants perk up as the direct buyers wander along is an obvious tell, since direct buyers generally don't haggle as hard. It also helps that I can see their Classes, which range from the mundane Toolmaker to the specialized Weaponsmith or Alchemist. Some are truly weird, like the Augurer and the Binder.

After I'm done, we make our way to sell the meat, which makes up the majority of what everyone has to sell. While monster components do form when we Loot monster corpses, the vast majority of the time, at the lower Levels, it's just meat. Unsurprisingly, the food section is made up of the food court and a portion of the shops around it. There's almost no haggling at the food stalls. Large cardboard signs hung above each stall state both what they're selling and buying with the respective prices.

"Mrs. Cho's selling her burgers again!" Damian says excitedly, eyes glowing slightly. "I'll line up. You guys sell my share."

"Done!" Analyn answers excitedly, taking his bag while shooting me a look. "You don't want to miss her burgers."

"Ummm…" I glance at the long line then finally nod to Damian. "Get me a half dozen then."

In short order, we've sold the last of our gains—or at least, what I'm declaring as my gains—and retreated from the stalls respectfully.

"This place is crowded," Analyn says, glancing around pointedly. "We've got a place in one of the apartment complexes here. Let's go eat at home."

The invitation is obvious. So too is the potential trap, but after a moment, I nod. Realistically, even if they triple the number of individuals involved in the trap, there isn't any concern for me. Between Ali's ability to sense things and my Level, running away is simple.

Once I agreed, the three of us quickly left the building to head to their apartment complex. I definitely had no intention of visiting the Shop here— for one thing, anything I bought would likely get taxed and the Credits added to the Sect's coffers. Why the heck would I do that?

The pair of condo buildings is interesting, surrounded by stern steel walls that are obviously not part of the original architectural plans. On top of those, a series of small orbs sit, ready to unleash magical hell. Once inside, the building itself doesn't seem very different, keeping most of its original design and furnishings, including the cream tile floor.

"Are you guys just renting the place?" I ask.

"No, parceled ownership. We own the apartment but have to pay into the general security fund. Votes on changes to our maintenance fees and major upgrades are all handled via the System, though there are a few administrators," Jonah answers, obviously enthused by this. "Much better than a damn condo board. Anyone can propose a change with votes monthly. Of course, the administrators can block the proposals, but only three times in a row. Keeps the silly requests from appearing mostly."

"Ah," I answer, my curiosity more than assuaged.

However, my non-committal answer does little to slow down Jonah's enthusiasm, and I get a whole lecture about the way the System works in terms of managing a multi-property location, the various options available, and the pros and cons of it all. I keep a mostly attentive expression to stay polite, but I can't help but sigh in relief when Damian returns, hands filled with bags of food.

Toward the end of the meal—which, I have to admit, is superb—Damian's demeanor changes and he looks unexpectedly serious. He puts down his burger, motioning toward Jonah, who pulls out a small device and taps it before nodding to his team lead.

"Where are you from? Really?" Damian asks, his face stern.

I stare at the group and absently note that Analyn's hand is on her gun, which is pointed in my general direction. Not directly at me yet, but close enough. Jonah's backed off too, his fingers rolling a small metal disc over his fingers.

"Whitehorse originally," I answer truthfully. I'm curious to see where this is going. "But more recently, Kamloops."

"We've heard about Kamloops. Even heard that you managed to fight off one of their invasion groups when they came to take it back," Damian says, shaking his head. "You need to work on your blending in. You're way too confident and assured of yourself for a local. No one walks like you do out here."

"Except the delvers," Analyn points out.

"Oh yeah, but we know who they are," Damian answers.

"Delvers?"

"Dungeon delvers. The high Level, independent combat Classers. They're forced to pay a high daily tax rate, so they have to do the Dungeons again and again to keep up," Damian answers easily. "None of those guys waste time walking. They're all about the luxury vehicles."

"Doesn't sound practical to me," I say, shaking my head.

"Who's talking practical? It's not as if it's expensive to get them fixed up," Damian points out and shrugs. "It's all about indulging in past fantasies. Who doesn't want to drive a Jaguar?"

"Thanks for the information," I finally say, considering what Damian said. Since I can't alter my Status any further, sneaking in might be an even bigger task than I thought.

"Ask them why there are so few high-Level combat Classers that he thinks he'd know them all," Ali sends urgently.

After a moment, I realize the Spirit's point and pass the question on.

"Ah… that's the other thing we need to talk to you about. Are you here to cause trouble for the Sect?" Damian says.

"I asked you first."

"Are you a child?" Damian mutters, rolling his eyes. When I refuse to answer, Damian sighs. "We lost a lot of people a few months ago when the Sect put down the rebellion. Grabbed everyone involved, after they beat them, and shipped them all off-world."

"What?" I say, my voice rising as I lean forward. I note Analyn shifting slightly at my sudden movement before she calms down.

"That's why I'm asking your intentions. We can't—we won't—start a new fight with the Sect. We've learned our lesson—numbers don't matter when they've got enough Advanced Class people to kick our asses. And every time someone gets close to reaching an Advanced Class, they disappear," Damian says with a grimace.

"Technically not legal to kidnap people, if that's what you're thinking. But laws without people to enforce them are just bits in the electronic stream."

"I do intend to do something about the Sect," I say. I'm curious to see what they do. If they intended to sell the information about me, they could have done so already. And if this makes them decide to do it now, well, so be it. I could kill them, but they've treated me fairly well so far. "They've been attacking Kamloops non-stop for the last few weeks. If we continue to let them do that, they'll eventually win."

"What do you intend to do?" Damian asks, his eyes glinting.

I sigh. "Truthfully, I'm not entirely sure. I planned on sneaking in and figuring out what is going on before I acted. It'll probably end up in blood and tears though. It always does."

"Did you not hear the part about their Advanced Classers? They've got seven of them in this city," Damian says sternly.

"How do you know that?" I say. Obviously, from the way they've been speaking, these guys can't tell my Level.

"They told us. A friend of mine who's an Auditor confirmed it. Seven Advanced Classes, six of which are combat Classes with Levels ranging from 14 to 39, and one non-combat Advanced Class Level 38 Administrator," Damian says. "You can forget about stirring up trouble in Vancouver. The moment you do, they'll kill you and then make it more difficult for the rest of us."

"I'm not that easy to kill," I say, both as a warning to them and a statement of confidence. I get a few eye rolls. They've obviously run into overconfident people before. "But thank you for the information."

"You're not going to change your mind, are you?"

"Not one bit," I say, smiling slightly. Even if I look relaxed, internally, I tense up as I wait to see what they're going to do next.

"No new figures around us. If they've called for help, it hasn't arrived yet," Ali reassures me.

"I assumed that." Damian exhales, slumping. He rubs his face, fatigue and grief showing on it as he speaks. "They left those of us with lower Levels alone after the revolt. Just left us, even though they must know who we are. There might be hundreds of us, but we're all in the twenties. That's how useless we are.

"Anyone with a higher Level, they're being kept at the Olympic Village at False Creek. Easy enough to control them. And even then, there's only, like, fifty of them. They keep a couple of the Advanced Class combatants around them all the time, including a Summoner with his demonic dogs and a Warden."

"Not a lot of you guys left," I say neutrally.

"Not a lot. After the revolt, that's when we found out how different things were. The entire downtown is theirs, remade into their world. They've got security cameras everywhere, and anyone who wants to go in has to wear a bracelet marking their identity. Their Serfs are all incentivized to tattle on anyone not authorized to enter the downtown, so we couldn't sneak most of our people in. Even when we did, they'd upgraded the main library to have its own shield to keep the City Core safe."

I open my mouth then close it, frowning slightly at what Damian says. And how he says it. I tilt my head, looking at Analyn, whose face is blank, and Jonah, whose face holds a trace of anger and resentment.

"For a guy who is complaining a lot, he's giving me a lot of useful information," I send to Ali.

"General deniability. If they know who he is, this way, he can still say he's learned his lesson," Ali says, looking at Damian and the group with a tinge of respect.

"That sounds tough," I say, rubbing my chin.

"Har! Tough. Tough were the damn Advanced Classers. They had an invasion team during the revolt, including that Blood Warrior, though he's out of town right now. His clones really messed with our groups. Then there's the Psychic. Not much for area effect, but its spells one-shotted everyone it hit. Brain-blasted them till they all fell unconscious," Jonah snaps, shaking his head.

"At least you didn't have to fight that Bone Monster. It didn't matter what we shot it with, we couldn't punch through its armor. I'd upgraded my Penetrating Strike Skill four times by then and it still didn't hurt it!" Analyn says, shaking her head. "And that Sect Enforcer was nothing to sneeze at. He switched between his rifles and other Skills easily, filling in the gaps whenever they needed him."

"If they hadn't been holding back to keep our people alive, we'd have had a lot more losses," Damian says quietly, his eyes fixed on me. "You should give up and go back. Don't bring more trouble for us."

I sigh and nod, looking at the group for a moment more. "Thank you. For the food. But since we aren't coming to an agreement on this, I'm going to take my leave."

"You won't last a day out there," Damian says, his tone foreboding. "Just get out of the city."

Rather than answer Damian, I smile and shake my head, walking out. None of the three move to block me, leaving me with my thoughts.

"Figure they're going to sell me out?" I ask Ali while waiting for the elevator.

"They'll probably give you a little head start, but I'm sure they will. You sure you don't want to head back? We've picked up a bunch of information. And out of town, we've got a lot more advantages," Ali says quietly, concern in his voice.

"We're not done yet. I still want to take a look at the downtown. If they give me even an hour, I can get in."

"And then what? They said it already—they've got surveillance everywhere."

"Then we dance," I say with a savage grin.

Chapter 16

No matter what people say, I'm not entirely insane. Foolhardy, short-tempered, and overly confident sometimes, sure. But not entirely insane. I don't say completely sane, since well, I doubt any of us are entirely sane compared to pre-System standards. Though that does raise the question of if the standard of sanity has changed, with the "norm" shifting as we fight and kill for our survival.

Having been, quite literally, warned to leave, I was of course going to stay. I'd come to Vancouver for a few reasons, and I wasn't satisfied with getting a partial complete on a couple of them. Firstly, scouting out the city was important. Sure, I could have bought the information, but there's something to be said about actually seeing the changes. Never mind the fact that to buy the information, I'd have to know what kind of questions to ask and then pay for it. Cheaper and easier to visit and see it with my own eyes. Thus far, I'd only managed to make it to Burnaby which, at best, is a suburb. No, I need to visit Vancouver itself.

Secondly, splitting their forces is important. If they start fearing an attack in Vancouver, it means they'll have fewer forces to devote to Kamloops. Us staying purely on the defensive would just allow them to concentrate whatever leftover forces they had. While my fight in Merritt had helped reduce and alert them, it wasn't enough. I needed to make sure they stayed on the defensive.

Right now, I was very much like a chess queen let loose behind the lines. While I wouldn't say I could knock out any single other piece without fail, given the right conditions, I was definitely a danger. That meant they could either let me roam and knock down their pieces or take active steps to go after me. But that only worked so long as I wasn't cornered. Which meant I had to be unpredictable—and that meant going right into the lion's den.

Thirdly, I needed to kill more to get my next Level. While hunting monsters was doable, at the level I was, I needed tens of thousands of experience points to advance. Bullying monsters wasn't going to get me there any time soon and finding a higher Level zone, while possible, meant that I wasn't being a threat to the Sect. Whether it was right or not, the Sect members were giant bags of experience and Credits.

Lastly, taking over Vancouver was necessary to ending this. To do that, we needed to understand how tough these guys were going to be and see if we could get some help from the residents. That meant poking at the forces they'd left behind to safeguard the city and opening channels of communication. The Sect might have beaten the initial resistance, but they'd left enough people around that, if they believed we could win, would be of great use to us. No matter what the kids thought, numbers do have an important quality—even if it's not as much as pre-System.

Of course, talk is cheap. The fact that we're putting up a fight in Kamloops might be heartening, but it isn't convincing enough in and of itself to get them to risk their lives or their freedom. And it shouldn't be. We've all struggled so hard to survive, throwing it away at the smallest hope is a bad idea.

Which means I need to prove that we can do more than hurt the Sect. We can beat them. And the best way to do that is to prove it right here, right now. In the middle of their stronghold. Of course, I'm gambling with my life. But as I trot down Kingsway at a speed that a cheetah would find fast, I'm grinning beneath my helmet.

Because this? This is the kind of shit I live for these days.

***

I hit Broadway in twenty minutes at a pace that is slow only because I had to skim around a couple of Sect groups while traveling down Kingsway. From here, it'd be simple enough to cross over to the downtown from the Cambie St. Bridge or swing around and go through the downtown eastside. Either would get me into downtown Vancouver. Problem is, even if I can't see the bridge itself from here, I can see the numerous dots clustered in a line at regular intervals on my minimap that indicate people are lining up to get in. Trying to get in might kick things off immediately.

Which is why I move out of the way of the flow of people all around me while I consider my next steps. There's no way for me to get downtown without making a fuss, which means it's got to be at the bottom of my list of things to do. From here, it'd be a simple matter to visit the former Olympic Village and check out the buildings and the delvers who live there. Of course, there's no guarantee anyone's home and I'm not entirely sure what I'd say to them either. But…

A solid projectile impacts my stomach, bending me slightly. A second later, beams of energy cook my flesh, tearing my clothing into pieces and throwing me through the café windows, its internal walls, and out the other side even as magical arrows chase my body.

"Stupid." The word reaches me after the attacks fall, the group smart enough to hold back on taunting me until after they struck.

By the time I hit the ground and start rolling, I've got my Soul Shield in place to catch the next wave of attacks. All around me, the bleed-off from the attacks flares up, reducing my vision significantly. Which is weird, but probably a purposeful side effect.

"You really dared to come into our city," the same voice taunts. "When we bought your location from the System, we couldn't believe you were here."

I kick backward, hopping out of the immediate attacks, and then again, finally able to see who I'm fighting. For a second. A rolling green cloud covers the area, paint and plastic peeling and melting on contact with the cloud. I see my Soul Shield weakening under the effects of the corrosive poisonous cloud, even as the screams of innocent passersby reach my ears.

"Assholes," I snarl, borrowing Ali's eyes as he hovers overhead to Blink Step out of the area of effect.

I appear directly above one of my attackers, allowing me to drop straight down and slice the son of a bitch open, twisting the blade while its inside his body. I'm not even sure who I'm killing, the attack too sudden and unexpected for Ali to populate System information for me.

Kicking off the Sect member's body, I bounce backward before more shots arrive, and I blink in surprise as the body pulls itself together, what I thought was a soon-to-be corpse healing before my eyes. The pale-skinned creature turns toward me, a mouthful of fangs and too-big eyes facing me as blood flows backward into its body.

"Yuck! Genetrolls. They're genetically modified creatures who have troll regeneration added to them. They stopped being produced a few hundred years ago after repeated failures. About ninety percent of their test subjects just went insane. The survivors creep around the edges of society," Ali sends to me, his fingers flying as he populates data all around me.

"Not. Now," I snap, a fireball flying outward to impact next to the genetroll as Ali speaks, my focus on surviving the next few minutes.

Flames explode, coating the creature, which screams in pain and catches some of his friends in the blast as well. Within seconds, I'm sprinting away, trying to put some distance between my attackers and me. Smoke grenades are pulled and tossed from my inventory as I focus on running and dodging. My Soul Shield falls, another shot ripping it apart, and the laser beam splashes on my skin, burning it away and leaving muscle and tendon exposed. I jerk reflexively, moving away from the path of the beam before I Blink Step away, furious at myself.

I should have known they'd buy my location from the System. Once they realized there was only me out here, the first step would be to figure out where I am. Not track me, just buy my information. Even if it was expensive, they could do it once or twice to narrow down my location, then send their teams at me. The only good thing is they shot their bolt too early. Rather than consolidating their forces and hammering me all at once, they sent their closest groups to attack me.

Ahead of me, blocking my way to the river, is a group of nine Sect members. Half of them are human, the other half aliens. A couple of reptile folk, a wolf-like creature, and a Hakarta open fire the moment they see me. My hands twitch, and I pull the remains of a Level 38 hard-shelled beetle the size of a car from my Altered Space. Holding it in front of me, I let the corpse soak up the damage as Ali darts ahead.

Seconds to cover the ground, to give me the distance I need. I Blink Step again into the sky above the group and release a Blade Strike downward, the wave of blue and red light cutting my attackers below me. I could have added more blades, more Blade Strikes, but I need to conserve my Mana. A part of me regrets the deaths of the humans, wishing they'd stayed away. But we all make choices, and theirs was to attempt to kill me. Idiots weren't even Level 30.

"Above us!"

The scream cuts off abruptly as I land directly on the gnoll's body, my knee and shin crushing its collarbone a microsecond after my blade enters its body.

I rip sideways, tearing the head off the creature, then dance among my attackers, blood flying. Basic Sect members, all in the mid 20s to low 30s. Nothing exceptional, some having as little as a few hundred health points, none above five hundred. Seconds to cut and injure, to kill. Soulbound, my sword does nearly a hundred points of damage without enhancement and targeting. With their pitiful armor and defenses, my attackers fall all around us, their screams of despair resounding. Experience flows into me as more Sect members die. Each second, I inch toward my next Level.

A giant bone hand swings, catching in my hastily brought up guard. A hand reinforces my blade, the force of the blow sending me skipping through numerous buildings as physics and a Skill knock me away. My arm cracks under the force of the blow, nearly a quarter of my hit points disappearing under that single attack. As I struggle to my feet in the rubble of a building, the Bone Monster is rushing toward me.

I plunge a needle into the exposed flesh of my thigh, the healing potion injected directly into my body. Flesh knits and my arm pops back into place with enough force that I drop my sword. Staring into the glowing freight train of a monster, I grin and Blink Step away.

"Gotcha," I chortle as I get away from the Advanced Class.

I'm between my initial pursuers now, the group having spread out a bit as their running speeds pull them apart. Next to me is a Mage or support Classer of some form. Truthfully, I don't have time to tell, only noticing that his health pool is tiny.

I spin, sword recalled into my hand, to lop off his foot above the knee then plunge the blade into his body. As another Sect member raises a gun, I grab the Mage by his face, pulling him in front of the attack to take it before I cast Mana Dart, forming the spell right on my hand. As I shove the Mage at his teammate, I release the spell, the Mana Darts ending the Mage's life and giving me time to cover the distance to his friend. Something slams into my side, breaking a pair of ribs and dragging out a whimper.

"*Mana,*" Ali sends to me as I cut apart my latest target, grinning savagely in pain.

More dots, ever more dots converge on us and I take off running again, each step shooting pain through my body. A hand flickers, stabbing a Mana Regeneration potion into my body as I run and form another Soul Shield.

"*Hopscotch,*" I send to Ali.

Too many Sect members are boiling out of downtown now, some flying across the water, others screaming across the bridge and up Main St. No way for me to cross, and I've got less than half of my health points left. Still more than most of the Basic Sect members, but each time I stop to kill, they target me and chip away at my regeneration. And scarily enough, I've only seen one of their big guns.

"*On it. Stay alive!*" Ali sends to me.

I nod, taking a second to duck behind a house that nearly instantly gets obliterated by a pair of spells and what looks like a mortar shell. The explosion kicks wind and debris around me, hammering my Soul Shield as it drains down again.

Twisting in the air, I call forth Sabre and start the transformation process. I haven't done it before because I didn't have enough space and cover, the transformation process being the most vulnerable time. Even as I think that, another spell hits me, wind blades combined with a freezing spell cutting into the mecha and my shield.

We land, Sabre already blinking yellow as readouts tell of damaged circuits caught during the change. Immediately, I layer the mecha's shield on top of the Soul Shield and take off running, picking up speed.

A laser beam fires, this one coming from the Wall Center, and cuts through both shields before losing its effectiveness against Sabre's armor. A single shot did over a thousand points of damage! At a guess, that'd be the Sect Enforcer in play. I shudder and start dodging, glad that whatever Skill and weapon he's using, it must take some time to charge.

"Ali…"

"Almost there, boy-o," Ali sends.

Walls erupt ahead of me. I grin behind my helmet, jumping upward and hitting the jets to get me higher. That's when tentacles come bursting out of the wall, reaching for my body. Even as one grabs my torso and another my head, I reach through Ali's senses and trigger Blink Step. Surprisingly, I see my Mana drop even further than normal.

A microsecond to recover my footing, another to grab and smash my fist into the Sect member. This time, it's a gilled purple creature, its eyes widening comically as my blow catches it. Surprisingly, the Sect member folds over, bones crunching under my attack. I don't stop, can't stop, as I spin around it and plunge my sword through its back. A quick twist, a strangled scream, and I'm off. Experience flows again and another notification flickers in the corner of my vision.

"That was too easy!" I send to Ali.

"Non-combatant Sect member," Ali sends to me as he flies away.

A part of me winces—a small part, since I'm too busy running away. We're behind the main converging line now, the group turning to follow us. Ahead of us, even more Sect members are hurrying forward. I pick a group to fight, watching my health creep up as my regeneration kicks in and pulls ribs back into place. Just over nine hundred hit points, but only three hundred Mana. This is going well. For getting caught in an ambush.

"Aaaarrrgghhhhhhhhhhh!" Ali's mental scream catches me by surprise.

I look back and see the Spirit twist in the air, clutching his head. A second later, he disappears in a burst of light, banished. Through our connection, I can feel the burning pain from the psychic attack he was under.

Swearing quietly, I trigger the Temporal Shift module and a Mana potion from within Sabre. It floods my body, giving me a few hundred more Mana to play with. That's enough of a leeway for me to Blink Step to a nearby power pole. A second to orient myself, then I trigger it again. And then once more, crossing nearly a kilometer and a half in seconds. No time to rest, so I port straight to an abandoned alleyway and transform Sabre so that I can take advantage of the greater speed and mobility the bike provides.

Without Ali, I can't skip away as far as I want to. Can't even sneak out, not with everyone looking for me. The only advantage I have is that I'm in Burnaby now, outside of Vancouver itself, which means the main sensors they've installed are probably reduced in effectiveness and I broke out of their initial encirclement. Speed is my only advantage right now.

This might have been a bad idea.

***

Once my breathing calms down, I assess options as I eye my much-reduced minimap. Without Ali's greater sensing ability, it's shrunk to only what my Greater Detection Skill can provide. Less detail, lower range. It's still better than what most others have, I know, many having to rely on technology or enhanced senses. Still, without Ali, I feel half-blind.

A small blinking notification in the corner of my eyes attracts my attention, pulling me from my worries as I gun down side streets. A moment's thought is all I need, the notification making me grin. Finally!

Level Up!

You have reached Level 40 as an Erethran Honor Guard. Stat Points automatically distributed. You have 9 Free Attributes and 3 Class Skill Points to distribute.
Tier III Class Skills Unlocked

Now we're talking. I slam the first free Class Skill point into Portal, my long-range teleportation ability. It flashes, the details coming up within seconds. I crouch down further behind my bike, watching attacks splash harmlessly against Sabre's recovered shield as I zoom past another group of attackers.

Portal (Level 1)

Effect: Creates a 2-meter by 2-meter tall portal that can connect to a previously traveled location by user. May be used by others. Maximum distance range of portals is 100 kilometers.
Cost: 250 Mana + 100 Mana per minute

Damn. I'm slightly disappointed with the range. Nowhere near as far as I wanted it to go. After all, once you're bending the laws of space and time, why should distance matter? I push the thought aside, knowing that bitching about distance isn't the point right now. Still, I take a turn down a side street and onto a main thoroughfare, catching the next group of Sect members by surprise.

The sonic pulser gives me enough time to use my blade as an impromptu spear as I lean dangerously away from the bike. I leave my sword speared in the Sect member's chest where his heart should be. If its physiology is human-like. The fireball I launch afterward finishes the job, a blip in the corner of my eyes telling me I probably got experience for that kill. No time or desire to check it.

I leave the other two points unused for now. While I have plans for them, those plans rely on me surviving the next few hours. Tapping into those points for a sudden power boost might be all that I need to make it out of here.

By reflex, I turn my head, scanning around me. Something high above, a flicker of light, catches my attention. Looking up, I see not one but a half-dozen drones spreading out along my lines of retreat. With a crunch, a flicker, Sabre's shield goes down again. Something pink and fluttery, meaty and garishly blue flies past me as I turn forward again and pay attention to where I'm going. No experience notification this time, so I probably didn't kill whoever—whatever—I just ran over with my bike. I mentally shift the power drain by the shield recharger higher, drawing more from the Mana battery and overheating the poor shield.

A bare couple hundred Mana left in my personal pool. Barely enough for a pair of Blink Steps, then I'm in Mana withdrawal and nearly useless. The few Sect members who get close get shot at, more to keep their heads down than in hopes of hurting them. But their attacks hurt, chipping away at Sabre's shield. After that, its armor and my health. I'm reminded once again that Skills don't matter if you don't have the Mana to back them up.

I keep swerving, hoping to give whoever's out there a harder time of shooting me. Instinct makes me change direction earlier than usual. A second later, the ground where I'd have been evaporates, asphalt gone and the sewer system exposed as the Sect Enforcer fires again. Even the near-miss is enough to melt my nanite armor and scorch my bare flesh, sweat evaporating in an explosion of steam.

Damn it! I can't risk it any longer. A second later, I trigger another Mana potion, the second one within an hour. My Mana goes up immediately and I open the Portal, driving straight into its sinister void seconds before the potion feedback hits, sending me screaming into darkness.

Chapter 17

"Well, that was stupid," Ali says, floating beside me in the inky blackness of the lake.

We're back at the same lake bottom, the location of my Portal, surrounded by fish and the damaged portions of my mecha. Thankfully, the Portal could be set to be one-way, which meant no one had any clue I was at the bottom of a lake. And I know that because if they knew I was here, I'd probably have eaten another laser beam of death. As it stood, after porting in, I'd pretty much fainted from the potion backlash, the lack of Mana, and the damage done to me. I'd barely managed to trigger the mecha's transformation to encase me in the suit and keep me alive under the water.

"Damian didn't tell me about the laser beam of death," I grumble to Ali. Sabre's down to a barebones output of Mana, just the Temporal Shift module, life support, and the nanite factory. By the time I awoke, I'd fully healed and even the Mana headache had mostly subsided.

"He probably didn't use it," Ali says. *"Remember, they were trying to keep the humans alive. Can't get good prison labor out of corpses."*

"That reminds me. Necromancy...?" I ask.

"Works. You can get zombies and skeletons and the like, but it's no more effective than any other summoner. The undead aren't particularly smart, so an undead workforce isn't useful outside of the most rudimentary tasks."

"Good to know." I sigh, taking the time to allocate the last two Skill points I have. Once I'm done, I pull out my new status, curious to see where I am.

Status Screen			
Name	John Lee	Class	Erethran Honor Guard
Race	Human (Male)	Level	40
Titles			
Monster's Bane, Redeemer of the Dead			
Health	1850	Stamina	1850
Mana	1400	Mana Regeneration	102 / minute
Attributes			
Strength	100	Agility	175
Constitution	185	Perception	61
Intelligence	142	Willpower	142
Charisma	16	Luck	32
Class Skills			
Mana Imbue	2	Blade Strike	2
Thousand Steps	1	Altered Space	2
Two are One	1	The Body's Resolve	3
Greater Detection	1	A Thousand Blades	1
Soul Shield	2	Blink Step	2
Portal	3	Instantaneous Inventory*	1

Cleave*	2	Frenzy*	1
Elemental Strike*	1 (Ice)	Shrunken Footprints*	1
Tech Link*	2		

Combat Spells	
Improved Minor Healing (II)	Greater Regeneration
Greater Healing	Mana Drip
Improved Mana Dart (IV)	Enhanced Lightning Strike
Fireball	Polar Zone
Freezing Blade	

"You nearly died out there, boy-o," Ali says softly.

I have to agree with the Spirit. While I had meant to take the risk, and planned for it, I hadn't expected it to be quite that risky. If it hadn't been for the Body's Resolve and my ridiculously high health, along with judicious use of Soul Shield, I would have died quite a few times. Thankfully, I can take a lot of damage, and Blink Step means it's really hard to pin me down in a fight. Even the Erethran Honor Guard's resistances help in small doses, mostly from side effects of damage, like fire and cold resistances.

That's why I had to be the one to do this. Mikito is tough and fast and frankly, fast becoming deadlier than I am in a straight-out fight. Her weapon can dish out more damage than mine, has better reach, and she's both more skilled and Skilled for straight-on duels. Lana would have died fast because she's just too squishy, and Ingrid… well, okay, Ingrid probably wouldn't have been caught even if they knew where she was.

"So how long are we staying here?" Ali asks, waving his hand around the water.

"Not sure. Debating if they'd spend more funds to locate me. If they don't, this is a great place to hide. If they do, I need to be on the move," I say, reaching up to rub my chin and finding my helmet in the way. I frown, itching to eat something but not having the option to do so. Well, outside of the damn food paste the nanites can produce. But we don't consider that food.

"Recommend you portal out of here anyway," Ali says.

I sigh. This time around, with more points stuck into Portal—all my remaining ones, in fact—my range had significantly increased. Even so, wielding Mana in any form hurts right now. Even summoning Ali had been painful, but I felt safer with his presence.

Still, the damn Spirit has a point. A few minutes later, I'm stretching and savoring the experience of being free of both Sabre and my armor while standing in Kamloops's City Center. Painful as it might be, a Cleanse spell a second later makes me feel so much better, though I promise myself a hot shower too. But first...

"Guys. I'm back," I say over the radio, sending a notice to the group.

Lana and Sam answer immediately, and I make promises to see them soon. Food first though, as my stomach's rumbling again.

"Ingrid's left a few messages," Ali says, waving at the city center orb.

I grunt, walk over to place my hand on it, and pull up the messages.

In Seattle safe. City is weird—multiple Shops situated throughout the city with each Shop creating its own "city," unlike in Whitehorse. The Sect has control of most of the minor towns north of Seattle and about a quarter of the Shops in northern Seattle itself. :(They have lost major ground recently as the humans have been pushing back hard. Will update later when I know more.

I frown, reading the message quickly. Good to know she managed to make it down safely, even if the message itself was weeks old by now.

No messages for me? You suck. :P

Met some friendly—too friendly in some cases—humans. Quite a few groups of survivors down here, each of them competing and centering their bases around the Shops. Some are going all Mad Max while others are trying to be nice. Nicer groups include a bunch of geeks who nearly all Classed as Mages of some sort centered around Microsoft's headquarters and another group of hipster coffee makers who make the best coffee ever. We got to get some of this going—their coffee tastes like heaven and bumps up Mana regeneration without affecting other potions. I'm writing this right now on it. So good.

You were right. The humans down here are really keeping the Sect on their toes. They're fighting back and stubborn and the Sect has to keep most of their troops down here. I've spotted quite a few scouts watching the Sect. Any time they shift forces one way or the other, someone attacks the weakened group. If they didn't have so many Advanced Classers, they'd be wiped out already.

There are other groups that Liam—the coffee brewer boss—promises to introduce me to. He's real nice and says he's interested but figures everyone is too tightly wound to actually help. Best we can hope for is a bit more of a push. But I'll see what I can do. Might have to kill a few Sect members to prove things.

P.S: Forgot. Almost everyone who leads a group has an Advanced Class, though no one's above Level 15. Highest is a 13 so far, but I think they've been funneling kills to him because everyone else on his group is in the 30s. Mage group is nearly ready to break into their Advanced Class—give them a few months and their elites will be there. They're scarily good but very cautious.

Interesting. It seems like at least one group has learned how to cheat the System's experience a bit. Or I might be over-thinking things. There could be a dozen different reasons for why the leader has much higher experience points. Still, something I'd love to look into later…

Still no messages? What, do I smell bad? Making a girl feel a little abandoned here.

Remember how I pointed out I wasn't real good at this talk nice to people thing and you should send Lana? Well, don't say I didn't warn you. I might have had to kill a few Americans. In my defense, they were racist, sexist, misogynistic, torturing pigs. Also, they were trying to kill some new friends of mine and had good loot. So yeah, keep an eye out for the Sons of Odin when you come down.

I'll keep talking to people here, but I don't think we're going to get that much help. They're a bit too fractured. If they weren't, they'd probably have kicked the Sect's ass by themselves anyway. I'll keep trying though. It's been fun.

I rub my face as I read the last message. Just what we needed. Another group of enemies. Then again, considering their name, I could guess the kind of idiots they are anyway. Any group that decides the Vikings are people they want to emulate will never be high on my friend list. Seriously, study some history, people.

I consider what to write before I jot down a quick message thanking Ingrid for her help and letting her know that my part of the plan had some progress. After that, sending out a few more letters, simple messages to old friends, makes sense.

Once that's done, I do a quick check and wince. Nearly two hundred million to set up an anti-teleport formation. As useful as that might be, I decide against it. Not that I can afford it, but it's the thought that counts. After all, a long-range teleport Skill that includes more than one individual is pretty rare.

Stepping away from the orb, I assess my surroundings again. Sabre's lying on the ground, its Mana battery slowly recharging, nanites crawling over the frame to fix gouges and burnt-out components. Traces of dried blood lie all across the exterior and interior, somehow not washed away by the water. I raise my arm, ready to cast Cleanse on it and pause, staring at the trembling digits.

Strange. I stare at my hand, puzzled, unable to grasp what I'm seeing. Then the shakes hit my legs, a wave of weakness taking me to my knees as my breath shortens. I struggle to draw a breath, my chest tight as my hands tremble uncontrollably. The shudders reach my body, my teeth chattering as memories of the battle erupt, taking me back. The laser beam, a sword that cuts through armor, a bone fist. Moments of crisis, of imminent danger. One after the other.

Aftershocks. I know what this is, understand the effects. How could I not? The reliving of memories, the shakes, it's all natural. Now that I'm safe, my mind is finally releasing the clamps that have kept me from unraveling. It's good for me even as my mind processes the violent encounters, reorganizes, and resets my nerves and body.

Natural perhaps, but tears drip from my eyes nonetheless. A woman thrown aside by an explosive, brown eyes filled with shock and betrayal. An innocent caught in the midst of my grandstanding. A green-eyed, slit-pupiled alien staring at me from inches away as his life drains. Screams of pain, a still-kicking leg against a grey concrete sidewalk. Memories.

The shudders slowly stop, the memories subsiding as my breathing evens out. I scrub my face, wiping away the tear tracks, and spit to clear the blood from the lip I bit through. Perhaps I could, I should, be able to handle this better with the System's help. Certainly I don't fall to pieces like this all the time. Perhaps I could wipe away all of this with an application of will and Skill.

But I'm glad I don't and can't. So little of me that I can unilaterally point to as being human is left. So little of the quiet programmer I was pre-System.

Better to have a breakdown once in a while, to hate and regret the lives I take and the violence that has happened, than to remove it all. Because if I did, I'm not sure I'd like the person left.

By that point, my stomach's growling and occasional bars of chocolate eaten while working is no longer sufficient. Thankfully there's a restaurant—the Loose Goose—nearby, which I visit at Ali's insistence. Truth be told, I don't have much energy to gainsay him. I have to admit, I nearly choke when I see the sheer amount of Credits they're asking for—until I realize they're offering an all-you-can-eat buffet. Still, I'm amused that they changed the name but not the red-and-steel décor of the previous chain.

Food paired with blessed peace and silence all slowly pull the shards of my calm together. By the time Sam finds me, I'm mostly myself once again, my mental and emotional equilibrium restored. Just another "gift" from the System. Or perhaps too much experience.

"You know, as the titular owner of the city, you shouldn't be trying to eat your people out of house and home," Sam says, grabbing a seat next to me.

"Nice to see you too," I greet the Technomancer, nodding at the silver-haired gentleman.

"You do what you planned to do?" Sam says.

"Pretty much. Attacks still coming?"

Sam nods, his face grim.

On seeing that, I add, "What?"

"We nearly lost Mikito two days ago. The Blood Warrior and his team hit her group while they were hunting in the park. Focused their entire attack on her, and since she refused to run away..." Sam shakes his head.

"How'd she survive?" I say, concern tingeing my voice. Only a little bit, since he said nearly. Anything that doesn't kill us in this world quite literally makes us stronger.

"Her trainee stuck by her side long enough for the team to get far away enough and sneak back to counter-ambush the group. The team managed to kill a couple of their people and let Mikito injure the Blood Warrior. Her trainee didn't survive though."

Shit. I wonder how the Japanese woman is handling that. Losing a trainee, an apprentice can't be good for her.

"*Where is she?*" I ask.

"*Out.*"

Of course she's out, hunting and dragging the groups around to Level them up. Whether it's because she's got an over-developed sense of responsibility or just a need to bury her grief, she's out with her people.

"Lana says she needs some time," Sam says softly at seeing the worry on my face.

I nod, accepting his words. Still, I make a note to see if I can have a word with my friend.

"The night attacks?" I ask.

Sam makes a face, telling me all I need to know. Of course, he does explain it anyway, listing all the different ways Mel has tried to catch the group before they run away. Even having the entire town up and watching with groups ranging around at night has done little to stop the annoyances of the midnight attacks.

"We could have used Ali for the night attacks," Lana says, dropping into a chair next to me as I finish picking my latest plate clean.

Stomach finally satisfied, I push the plates away and stare at my some-time girlfriend. From her unhappy expression, I can tell she's still not gotten over my abrupt departure.

"Hi, Lana. Ali couldn't find them the last time. Don't think he'd be of much help even now," I say with a shrug. "And I needed him."

"And how many times did he almost get killed?" Lana asks Ali sweetly, violet eyes glinting with the promise of violence if Ali doesn't tell the truth.

"Ummm… we talking total or number of battles? Just two major fights. About… a dozen times? Something like that," Ali says with a shrug. "I kind of lost count."

"Only a dozen. I take it that happened in Vancouver," Lana says, still ignoring me.

"Mostly. Running away in Merritt was tougher than we thought—they had a tracker," Ali says as way of explanation.

"Ah. And of course, buying a Stealth Class Skill would not have helped," Lana says again, her voice dripping with sarcasm.

I twitch, recalling her asking me to take her Credits to buy myself that Skill and my subsequent refusal. Pride—for using only my own Credits—and idiotic stubbornness stopped me from doing so. Even if she doesn't say it directly, I can hear the "I told you."

"Well, a single point probably wouldn't have helped boy-o against the tracker," Ali says, coming to my defense.

"Maybe not a lot. But what is it you guys keep saying? That everything's on a razor edge?" Sam says, getting into the conversation. "Me, I like having lots of Skills. Even if I can't use all of them very well, having more options seems like a good idea."

"Yes, but you can also integrate those Skills into your machines," Ali says pointedly to Sam.

I blink, since I didn't even realize that that was an option for Sam. Someday, I really need to explore Sam's full Skill list and what he can actually do. I have a feeling I'll be pleasantly surprised.

"If we're done talking about how stupid I was…" I glare at Ali, who opens his mouth to retort, before I continue. "I did Level. How are we doing on the rest of the plan?"

There're a few quick smiles at that one, but Lana looks around at the obviously unsecured area. I nod to her to go on.

After a moment, she does. "We're getting there. We've managed to double our revenue, so we should be able to pick up some decent upgrades for the city. The hunting groups have picked up a few more Levels as well. However, morale continues to be down and we've lost a full group since you've been gone."

"Good," I say, considering her words. "There's a lot I need to talk to you all about."

"Tonight?" Lana asks, glancing out the window to the sky outside.

It's only a few hours left till dusk —time enough for me to wash and rest and Mikito to get back. Still, I hesitate, judging my mental and emotional balance.

"No. Tomorrow," I say.

Lana frowns, seeing something in my face because she just nods and kisses me on the cheek. "I'll see you tonight then."

I open my mouth then close it, shutting down the automatic rejection. Mentally cursing myself, I keep quiet. Why would I reject her presence tonight?

"*At a guess, because you're stupid and don't want to look vulnerable to your girl,*" Ali says then chuckles softly as I shoot him a startled glance. "*Oh please. I've lived with you for over a year. Reading you is easy.*"

I grunt, watching the redhead walk away before glancing toward Sam and realizing the older man has already left. A moment of scanning shows he's working his way through the buffet tables with a giant pile of meat. I'm in worse shape than I thought if I missed his movements that easily. On that note,

I decide to take the rest of the day off. Tomorrow and all that it will entail will still come.

Chapter 18

Surprisingly, at least to me, the evening with Lana progressed pleasantly. Annoyed or not, the woman seemed to understand that I needed a bit of time to decompress, and so we spent the evening mostly in companionable silence. With a very pleasant massage that did not lead to anything too strenuous afterward. Perhaps it was because of that that I found myself waking up late the next day, alerted by Lana shifting on my arm to stand up.

"Morning, beautiful," I greet Lana with a smile. Once again, I admire the redhead, her pale skin and lightly freckled body combined with a subtle level of athletic muscles that enhanced her femininity.

"Morning," Lana says, turning to smile at me as she dresses. "Feeling better?"

"Yes," I say, tilting my head. "Was it that obvious?"

"To those of us who know you? Definitely," Lana says.

"You seem better…" I say slowly, cautiously. She does seem less agitated, less angry, than the day before.

"I just needed a night off. Time to understand, to know, that you're back. Alive." Lana sits back down next to me, clad only in her shirt, and puts a hand on my arm. "I know you are who you are. I even… well, it's what attracts me to you. But it's not easy, knowing you'll always throw yourself into the fire."

I blink, stopping to consider her words. After a moment, I squeeze her hand and smile at her wryly. "Sorry. I didn't really think about it that way."

"No, of course you didn't. You idiot," Lana says affectionately before kissing my forehead. "Now go brush your teeth. The rest are waiting for us."

I nod, watching as Lana finishes getting dressed before I move, a strange feeling in my stomach. It's been so many years since I had someone who actually cared about what I did or where I was that it was strange. It was a feeling that I had been missing with Luthien, an aspect of our relationship that

I probably should have taken as a sign. Shaking my head, I promise to try to be better.

***

Pushing aside the remnants of my breakfast, I stare at the group around me. This time, it includes everyone on my team and the erstwhile council, including a very tired-looking Mel. Curiously, no attacks were made last night, though it didn't stop the Gunslinger from staying up all night.

"Right," I say, cutting through the conversations. "Let's begin."

For the next hour or so, my team and the council gives me a more thorough briefing about the city's status. It can all be boiled down to not much change but mostly for the better. More Levels, a growing economy, a more settled populace are all the positives. The negatives all concern the Sect and their continued presence.

"Thank you," I say after everyone finally runs down. "Ingrid's reported in, as many of you know. We aren't going to get much help from the US, but it's unlikely the Sect is willing to risk pulling out more forces to hit us. Not until they can stabilize their situation down south. That means we only need to concern ourselves with the players in BC.

"Vancouver's doing worse than we hoped for. The Sect's a lot stronger there than what we've seen here." I quickly fill them in on the revolution, the deportation, and the Advanced Class members I fought. More than a few of my audience suck in a breath or show their uncertainty as I describe the fight. "That's pretty much where we stand now."

After I'm done, there's a bit of conversation, whispered words between the council members and Mel, between Sam and Lana and the others. Mostly, my team holds off on talking to each other, knowing me as well as they do.

After the initial conversation trails off, I break in. "The way I see it, we have the same two choices we started with weeks ago. Hunker down, keep growing our people, and hope we can Level everyone faster than the Sect can shift resources to the planet. All while they have free rein to attack us and whittle our people down. Of course, they've got to divert their people to bothering us but…" I shrug, figuring they understand the point. The Sect doesn't need to Level their attackers, not the way we do.

"Or…?" Torg says.

"Or we take a little risk. It's why I left." I pause before committing to telling these guys what I planned. The team knows, of course; it's why we argued. "We take the fight back to them. Hit Vernon again, then Kelowna in short order. Except instead of just my team, this time we take a large portion of our fighting force and do it properly. At the same time, we attack the group that's been hounding us at night."

"We don't even know where they are!" Mel says bitterly.

"We can buy their location from the Shop," I say. "It'd be expensive and probably take most of our savings, but we can do it."

"You'd be leaving the city undefended! It's only a few hours' drive from Vancouver. If those Advanced Class members or a few groups come, we'll lose everything," Benjamin says, shaking his head. "I can't agree to a risk like that."

"And you're talking about hitting at least two, if not three, groups. We don't have the people," Mel adds.

"We've still got the Hakarta here. And that's the other reason I left. You see, I've got this Skill now," I say with a smile.

It doesn't take long to fill them in on Portal. Mel grasps the advantages first, the others requiring a little more prodding before they understand. I don't mind. It took me a bit to really grasp what Portal can do. In the end, it comes down to a simple thing—mobility.

"I'll admit, you'll be able to reinforce us quickly, especially if we use Skills and technology to keep you informed but…" Ben says, doubt in his tone. "It's still a risk. The Sect has a lot of Advanced Classers out there."

"That's why we asked some friends to visit," Lana says with a smile. "They can't leave their homes for long, but for a quick strike, they'd be happy to help."

"Friends?" Mel says, something glimmering in his eyes as his gaze sweeps over my team. "I take it they're tough."

"Some of the toughest we know," I say, smiling.

"When were you thinking of doing this?" Ben says, worry on his face.

"Well, today," I say, looking up as Ali signals me that we've gotten a reply.

***

As the council streams out unhappily after being railroaded, I find Lana standing beside me, waiting. It's only when they've left that she speaks.

"Why did you bother?" she says, her tone filled with curiosity.

"Bother?" I repeat.

"Giving them an option. You knew you were doing this anyway," Lana says.

"Ah… I was told that as a leader, you should at least try to explain your reasoning to others."

Lana stares at me, her eyes widening incredulously before she giggles. I frown, a bit annoyed by the giggling. Fine. I'm not exactly used to leading. At least not like this. Hell, even pre-System, I mostly just did my own thing in the jobs I worked.

When the giggling comes to an end, Lana says, "I'm sorry. But next time, maybe you can work on giving people more time to get used to the idea before insisting on your way."

I consider what I've seen of her skillsets then nod. A glance at the time shows I've still got a bit of time before I should open the Portal.

"John?" Lana draws my attention back to her. "Why are you still the owner of the town?"

"Hmmm?" I say, tilting my head.

"Why haven't you just given it back to the townspeople?" Lana says. "Set up some democratic elections or something? Keeping it isn't really your style."

"Tired of me giving you all the hard work?" I say, teasing her.

"Actually, yes," Lana says huffily before she relents slightly. "People do like to know what the hell is happening. You keep things too close to your chest sometimes."

I pause before nodding. "Sorry. And you're right. I've gotten a little more paranoid since the System. It's just that since everything said can be purchased..."

"You're worried someone might learn what you're doing?" Lana says.

I nod. "It's stupid really. All-encompassing surveillance might be great in theory, but it doesn't help if you don't look. And we're so insignificant..." We really are, in the greater scheme of things. "But I can't shake the feeling that I shouldn't talk about my future plans."

Lana stays silent while I grapple with the practical and the emotional considerations. At times, I open my mouth then shut it, finally giving in to the practical.

"Do you know much about how the Galactic Council operates?" At her denial, I continue. "Think of it like the UN. Each world gets a representative on the general Galactic Council. Within the Council itself, there's an inner circle, a smaller group that makes all the decisions, like the UN Security Council. Except these guys actually have a lot of power and get things done. They're the ones who made Earth a Dungeon World, for example.

"To get a seat on the general council, you've got to be in control of your world—or at least the majority of it. Sort of like the way you can get a city, you've got to do the same thing with your world. Of course, owning that much of a world can be impossible, so in those cases, you'd have to enact voting of some sort," I say, looking at Lana to see if she gets it. "It's worth noting that no Dungeon World has ever had a seat on the Galactic Council. Too many interests fighting for control, so no one gets a seat."

"And you want to change that," Lana says quietly, staring at me. I nod slowly, and she grimaces. "That's ambitious."

"Just a little. But you've seen the Yerick. They lost their world. I don't want us to be like them. But to get involved in the voting process, to start the ball rolling even, we need—I need—a stake in it." I wave my hand around us, encompassing the city.

"You don't ever think small, do you?" Lana says, giving me a hug.

"No. But it's what we need. As a race," I say softly.

I won't let us become like the poor Yerick, just another race forcefully added to the System. Now they don't even control their own home planet, forced to drift through the Galactic System as adventurers and transients. They do well—for third-class citizens—but it's not what I want for humanity. Maybe it's insane to think that I can make a difference, but it's better than sitting around adding Levels for the hell of it.

"Speaking of the Yerick…" Ali says leadingly, tapping his wrist.

Nodding at the Spirit, I detach myself from Lana. Time to get back to work.

***

For the first time, I get a chance to marvel at the Portal I can conjure. It's the third Portal I've cast, but it's the first time I've done so when I'm not being shot at or hiding in a lake. Neither of which is particularly conducive to admiring your work. The Portal itself is a gaping hole in space bordered with shimmering golden light. The center is nothing but a stygian blackness, one that neither reflects light nor provides any clue of what lies behind. If I wasn't the one who had summoned it, I probably would have found it difficult to transit through. Luckily, my friends are more trusting and less paranoid than I am.

The first to exit is a giant Yerick. Just under ten feet tall, the leader of the Yerick in Whitehorse is broad-shouldered, ripped, and bull-headed. Literally. The Yerick are what we knew as minotaurs, creatures of great strength and an infallible sense of direction. Of course, the reality is that they're just Adventurers who hit dungeons a lot, but that's Mana Bleed for you. Behind him, a shorter female Minotaur in a simple armored jumpsuit follows, her eyes dancing with amusement as she looks around.

"First Fist. Nelia!" I greet both of my friends/ex-teammates with a smile and a handshake.

Capstan takes my hand with care, not crushing it, as does Nelia.

"It is good to see you, Redeemer. I see you have Leveled again," Capstan rumbles, his voice low and gravelly.

"And you. Thank you for coming," I say.

"No thanks needed. Just payment." Capstan flashes me a smile.

I know he's mostly joking. Even knowing that he's a friend, I find the smile intimidating. Leaving Lana to continue greeting the pair, I turn to the next individual to enter. "Mike?"

"No need to sound so surprised." Mike Gadsby, the Level 8 Regional Guardian, smiles at me. I return his smile, taking in his new Advanced Class and the gunmetal-and-chrome arm. "And yes, I upgraded it." Mike flexes his left arm, grinning at me, his mustache waggling as he does so.

"Sorry, just surprised. I figured—"

"Jason would come? Not a chance. Rachel isn't letting him out of her sight, not with her so close to giving birth," Mike says with a smile. Before I can ask about their health, Mike grows serious. "Anyway, protecting the citizens of Canada is my job. Gave my oath long before the System."

"We both did," Amelia, the stocky ex-RCMP officer, says as she exits the Portal. She is once again dressed in her old uniform, this one adjusted slightly to cover her armored jumpsuit. After she clears the entryway, she shudders as she stares at the Portal. "That thing is so creepy."

"Hmmm?" I'm curious to hear what she has to say. Transportation is instantaneous and doesn't even feel like anything, at least to me.

"Just the entire teleportation thing. So weird..."

I nod in understanding. Amelia's not gotten her Advanced Class yet, though she's only a couple of Levels away. No surprise there. Since Jason has been on guard duty, Mike has been forced to take on more active roles in Carcross, resulting in his Level jumping up. Amelia, on the other hand, has been in town, dealing with the day-to-day policing issues.

I blink as Vir, Amelia's Truinnar partner, steps out behind her, hands clasped behind his back, wearing his silver-grey uniform. Among other things, Vir is Lord Roxley's right hand and what I believe to be his spymaster as well as Amelia's on-off partner while she works the streets of Whitehorse. Of course, considering how high Vir's Level is, I'm not likely to turn him down. Still, I can't say I'm happy to see him or what he represents.

The black-skinned, pointy-eared humanoid greets me with a tight-lipped smile. "Mr. Lee."

"Why are you here?" I frown.

"John…" Lana chides me, walking forward to greet Vir.

"Mr. Lee's reaction is expected, Ms. Pearson." Vir kisses Lana's hand as he bows over it. "He is, as always, predictable. My lord has requested I provide what I am able to in your most recent endeavor."

"And of course, report what is going on," I say with a bite.

"Of course," Vir says, refusing to be ashamed of his secondary goals.

"Well, you're here." I close the Portal after I ascertain no one else is coming. "Let's get started."

***

Hours later. First, greeting and introducing everyone, then explaining the roles I had planned for them. Then, there're all the questions I have to answer about potential problems, all the contingencies I've made or all the ones that we need to make.

In the end, the plan boils down to what we've discussed already. By shifting a few of my people and the Hakarta platoon in-house, we'll be able to send my team, the Yukoners, and the hunting groups to hit the other areas. Of course, there was quite a bit of discussion on whether to split or attack sequentially. In the end, the fact that we feel we have enough people to launch simultaneous attacks tipped the balance in that direction.

It's mid-afternoon by the time we're done, and between lunch and needing to brief everyone involved, there's no way to get going until tomorrow. As it stands, the unlucky few who have to stay behind have to familiarize themselves with the city.

"Tomorrow then," I say, looking around the group.

"Still don't see why I have to guard the city," Amelia says grumpily to Mike and Lana.

"Well, Guardian, your Skills fare better on the defense. Buying time is the entire point of those left behind," Lana explains patiently.

"Mike gets to go!" Amelia protests.

"My Skills let me boost those around me, along with dishing out the pain. You're geared toward individual fighting and wide-range defense. I'm the better choice for an attack, especially if that Bone Monster or Sect Enforcer is out there," Mike says patiently.

Amelia makes a face but falls silent.

Capstan finds me at that point, looming over me. "I am uncomfortable with leaving Nelia behind."

Nelia snorts quietly by his side.

"Sorry. We need a Healer back here to help drag things out. The hunter groups out here are a lot more healing intensive than Whitehorse, so the attacking teams should be fine," I say.

"Aye. Still, I have a suggestion…" Capstan is cut off by the blaring of alarms and the flashing notification that appears in front of us.

"What…?" I exclaim before staring at the newly populated map.

Red and green dots everywhere. Even as I'm reacting in surprise, another notification shows up, indicating a sudden drain on the settlement's shield.

DECLARATION OF WAR

AS THE OWNER OF KAMLOOPS, YOU ARE HEREBY NOTIFIED THAT A STATE OF WAR NOW EXISTS BETWEEN THE THIRTEEN MOON SECT AND THE VILLAGE OF KAMLOOPS (OWNER JOHN LEE).

ALL WAR PROVISIONS ARE ENACTED AND WILL BE ENFORCED UNTIL A MUTUAL STATE OF PEACE HAS BEEN ADOPTED, THE DESTRUCTION OF ONE PARTY, OR A PERIOD OF ONE GALACTIC YEAR HAS PASSED.

The System notification window—this time a giant blue screen, all in block letters—appears. I blink, reading through it quickly before dismissing the note. Ali announces, "We're under attack."

Chapter 19

Everyone in the meeting is a veteran. Whether we chose it or not, we understand that speed at certain times is essential. The only order I give is to hold my team back as a reserve, allowing everyone else to rush to the walls where we have been attacked. Even as the Yukoners run, Mel's barking out orders to slot them into his plans.

"Whoever was hiding the attackers is still masking their Classes and Levels," Ali sends to everyone via the city's notification system. It'll be confusing for those not involved in the defense, but it's also the fastest way for us to get out essential information.

"Got it," Mel says, his voice cackling over the radio. "I'm briefing the newcomers on the communication protocols. We'll be able to talk properly soon. Hold all non-essential communication till then."

"I've started the online process for the sentinels," Sam says, his eyes half unfocused. "We've done a few upgrades to them since you've been here last, John. Got my drones in the air too. Give me a couple of minutes and I can feed us more detailed information."

"Shields are holding, but they won't hold for more than another two minutes," Lana says.

Out of nowhere, Roland pops into existence next to me, nearly making me jump. Would have, if Ingrid didn't do it all the time and made me slightly inured to friendly creatures trying to make me soil my pants.

My mind's spinning. If they're taking down the settlement shield this fast, it's got to be because more than their original attack group is here. In fact, there's got to be quite a few people. A glance at the icons on the map is enough to tell me that there's at least one hundred twenty. Probably including a bunch of Advanced Class players. The question, of course, is what they're doing here.

Actually, that isn't the question. The question is what I intend to do about it. Without a word, I'm heading for the City Core.

"No point in keeping funds for figuring out where they are," I mutter as I sprint down the corridor, closely followed by Lana riding her tiger. A part of me is curious if that's a Skill or a skill.

"Hold your fire till I tell you to. Yes, you too!" Mel's voice snaps over the radio, ordering the teams that gather.

"And that confirms that Sect Enforcer is here," Ali says.

I note the drop of nearly a third of our shield's rating from a single hit, the effects of the Enforcer's attack.

"Kuso," Mikito curses.

"Can we locate him?" I snap at Ali. We need him taken down. If we get into a fight and he's out sniping, it will not go well.

"Nothing," Ali says, shaking his head. "The System's giving me nothing on these guys."

"A pair of my drones got a good look on that shot. I'm trying to triangulate his position now. I'll send some over in that direction," Sam says, speaking over the team's radio channel.

Finally at the orb, I slap my hand on it while calling out, "Recommendations!"

"Three options. Mana field—it'll increase Mana collection in the surroundings and up Mana regeneration for everyone in town. Get the upgrade and it can exclude the Sect members. It can be tied into an enchantment later that can boost its effectiveness, but I don't think we can afford that right now. Tier IV Sentinels would be a nice addition. Can't get many of them, but it'll give us something that can potentially handle the lower Level Sect members. Last option, upgrade the Shield. Buy us more time," Lana says, her eyes gleaming.

"I CONCUR WITH MS. PEARSON," Kim says.

No surprise there, as Lana and Kim have been working together to keep the city secure. On that note...

"Kim, you've got control of the beam turrets. Target low-Level Sect members when you can, concentrate fire, and take them out. Switch to air suppression once you need to do so," I order the AI. It's only after I've done that that I realize I might be contradicting orders from Mel. Ah hell...

"UNDERSTOOD."

I nod, thinking quickly. The last option is discarded immediately—might have been viable if the Sect Enforcer wasn't around, but even with an upgraded shield, he'd cut through it eventually. Not worth the cost. I can also guess that's why we weren't going for things like artillery and even the beam weaponry— too likely to hit our own people when the fighting really started. That left either the Mana Regeneration module, which could give us a slight edge if things dragged on, or the Sentinels. Unsure, I pull up both stats.

Mana Collection Field

Using a mixture of symbols of enchantment and upgraded nanites, the Mana Collection Field increases total Mana flow within the settlement. Higher-grade fields increase regeneration rates by a higher amount. Note: in non-stable regions, this can lead to an increased spawning rate of monsters.

Effect: 5% Increase in Mana Regeneration Rates

Cost: 2.3 Million Credits

Upgrade: Mana Collection Field may be targeted (+1.5 Million Credits)

Monolam Tier IV Sentinels

A staple of cities throughout the Galaxy, Monolam Sentinels are equipped with sonic, beam, and kinetic weaponry to deal with a wide variety of monster threats.

Cost: 500 Thousand Credits each

When Lana said we couldn't get many of the Sentinels, she wasn't kidding. I wince at the cost. And I know, I just know, that if I buy them, they'll be destroyed within minutes of the fight actually starting. A part of me rails against the waste, refusing to throw hard-earned Credits away so simply. Hoping that cheaping out won't get anyone killed, I buy the Mana Collection Field.

"MANA COLLECTION FIELD PURCHASED AND INITIATION BEGUN," Kim flashes a note before me. "MANA REGENERATION RATES WILL INCREASE TO 5% IN INTERVALS AS INTEGRATION PROCESS PROCEEDS."

I swear softly, realizing that the process won't be instantaneous and thoroughly regretting my choice. Still, better than nothing.

"Shield is down," Lana says.

"Now!" Mel's voice roars at the same time.

The ensuing explosions and wave of Skills briefly overload my display, the dots that indicate the Sect members disappearing for a second. Unfortunately, we're not the only ones who can plan for an expected attack, and it doesn't seem like anyone was injured.

A moment later, I watch as our people and the existing Sentinels roll forward to meet the attacking Sect members outside the defunct Shield and the city itself, and the battle truly begins.

***

Dots. From here, all we can see are dots. I'm dressed now, Sabre's still-repairing form wrapped around my body. Structural and armor integrity is in the low 30s, significantly worse than what I'd like, but it is what it is. Mikito's PAV has finally reached her and she's armed and ready, standing beside me patiently. Sam's outside, driving ever so slowly in his modified truck to the fight while he commands his drones, providing us a real-time display while he hunts down the Sect Warrior. And around us, all of Lana's pets crowd the control room. From here, all we see are dots that blip and move, shifting as they engage one another.

Each dot a life. Each point that vanishes is one more death to lay at my feet. I could see the actual images, the actual fight, if I wished. Easy enough to train cameras to watch the blood flow, hear the screams of pain. But I don't. Callous and cold as I might be, watching their deaths is more than I can do. Because we have to wait. To hold…

"Guardians, pin that Psychic down. We can't let him hit anyone else. Healers, get that Minotaur up now! We need him back on that Bone Warrior; the elf can't hold him alone. Sam, can you do anything about the cyborg? Who's got eyes on that Assassin? Teams two to six, you need to swing around to deal with those Mages. The rest of you, hold that Blood Warrior…" Mel's voice, snapping orders constantly on the radio, details things for me.

The Hakarta are engaged with the Blood Warrior and his clones, along with the majority of the Sect's forces, in a wide-ranging skirmish constrained only by the mine fields. In some cases, not even that—I note more than one dot moving quickly across the map to land in the fields. Someone—or someones— out on the field seems to enjoy tossing Sect members around.

In each fight, the Advanced Fighters, or those close to it, are separated by a large area around them, no one willing to get between those titans. Even as they fight, the colors and markings on my map shift as Ali adds information. Soon, each enemy Advanced Fighter gets his own special purplish-red color to mark his position, with me wincing at how many of them there are.

"Looks like they pulled all the Advanced Classes they could get their hands on to hit you guys first," Ali says as his fingers dance in the air. *"Being forced to use Portal to run away probably tipped our hand."*

I can only nod, holding my emotions close and tight. Can't, won't, let them out. This is neither the time nor place. Regret worms through my guts anyway, escaped from the tight control I have on everything else. Just once, I'd love for a plan to work out...

"Who's that... arrgh. We've got a damn Assassin out here. We've got to find him." Mel's voice again, even as a dot flickers and disappears.

No mention of us yet. I'm not sure if that's confidence that we'll do the right thing at the right time or he's forgotten that we're out here.

Clusters of blue appear around the walls again and on the buildings that lead into the city. I realize after a moment what those dots are—non-combatant reserves coming to pitch in. A flicker as a pair of dots disappears. A simple straight line that we could draw, if we wanted to. A signal.

"I have him." Sam's voice is cold.

A new dot nearly a kilometer away. I know that place, know there's a building there, though I've never been to it.

"I can't drop us off right there," I say, already reaching out with my Skill. I can only create Portals where I've been, or within a few tens of meters of where I've been. That location is too far. "Mikito, Lana, hit them from behind. The Sect Enforcer is mine."

Acknowledgements come even as the Portal opens. The other side of the Portal exits behind the Sect's lines, between the Sect Enforcer and our attackers. A chance for us to split their forces, make use of our ability to move around the battlefield. Of course, the spell itself drained nearly a quarter of my Mana and I still need to finish this fight.

I don't look behind me as I run toward the Sect Enforcer's location, trusting my friends to hit them as hard as they can. I'd considered dropping us off closer to the fight, allowing the girls to hit them faster, but that Sect Enforcer is a greater danger. It's not even the sudden death that he can drop on others— it's the fear that he engenders. And it's no surprise people are afraid. Even with my shields up, I can't take more than a single shot from him.

A glint, a flash of light as the Enforcer shifts his gun. A moment, and then I'm gone, Blink Stepping to beneath the grey office building he lies on. Too far by just a bit, but the flash of light across my peripheral vision tells me that delaying would have been disastrous. I launch myself through the air at the edge of the building. A moment later, concrete shatters around me as my body hurtles through the flimsy building.

A hand on the building edge, I pull and twist, flipping up even as I ready a Blade Strike. The Enforcer is gone though, having left his sniper rifle alone. I stare down the extra-large, tri-barrelled sniper rifle, my fingers tapping it gently to sweep it into my Altered Space. Too long. I spent too long, and I pay for it. My world becomes fire as the silver-clad, six-limbed creature drops its reflective invisibility cloak and opens fire with a large, shoulder-mounted weapon.

The explosion throws me backward, Sabre's shield failing first and my Soul Shield nearly half gone. I can do nothing to stop my body from being blasted off the building, the explosion throwing me straight into the air. Still, I trigger the mini-missiles, each tiny warhead roaring through the sky to impact around and on the Enforcer. Even as I fall, the roof collapses, dropping the Enforcer into the building as it crumbles beneath our onslaught.

Recovering from the fall, I stare at the building, rotating through the various vision options available through my helmet. Strangely enough, I see nothing but the shadows of the collapsing building. Nothing until a gleaming spear flies through the air, forcing me to jerk aside in a hasty dodge.

"The Enforcer's shielded by his—its? hir's?—armor. I'll do my best to boost your Greater Detection abilities to outline hir," Ali says.

A flicker of surprise and curiosity, but I don't have time to deal with weird alien gender issues and English language limitations.

My sonic pulser opens up in a wave of sound that sets my teeth on edge and disrupts the Enforcer's equilibrium. Not much, just a second before hir's helmet shuts down the majority of the noise, but long enough for Ali to tag hir. After that, I let loose a blast from the Inlin, unloading everything in another round of explosions and kinetic death. A small, portable shield flares to life around the Enforcer, deflecting explosives that shatter even more of the building. It groans as supports buckle, dust kicking up everywhere, obstructing my vision even further.

He's good. Hir's good. Very good. Even between the shots, hir's moving, grenades fired from another weapon exploding around me. The next few moments are a running, jumping, shooting, and dodging series of attacks, each of us trying to land a hit. All the while, I attempt to close on hir and the Enforcer attempts to keep the range and evade.

Now.

At the thought, I Blink Step to where I expect hir to be, spinning to cut with my sword and meeting nothing but air. An explosive roars, hitting not me but the air around me as insta-concrete spreads, covering my shield in goop. I shove against the ground, attempting to break free, but it doesn't help. The gears in Sabre strain, as do my muscles, all of it futilely.

"Move, boy-o. He's dropping mines all around you!" Ali snaps.

Crouching as much as I can, I shove with both feet. The insta-concrete holds for a microsecond longer, then shatters. Not a second too soon, as the mines explode, throwing me farther into the air. The remnants of concrete and my shield explode at the same time, destroyed as I spin through the air.

"Son of a bitch," I snarl even as a laser beam cuts into my body.

I twist in space as the beam tracks my movement, melting armor. A Blade Strike tears apart the smoke and dust, clearing my vision as the attack shatters the remote-controlled laser rifle.

"Behind you!" Ali says, sending me an image of the Sect Member setting up a shot with another single-barreled rifle. My Spirit can see him, and that's all I need.

I'm a second too late, the shot ripping into my back and through my chest, tearing off a third of my hit points before I Blink Step away. Fingers already leaving the trigger, the Sect Enforcer is rolling and moving aside, but hir's too late for once. A Thousand Blades Blade Strike sends numerous waves of blue and red force through the area beneath me even as I land. Caught in the projected energy strike, the Enforcer can only block and absorb, pink blood flying from injured limbs.

On the ground, too close for hir to run away, we clash. A pair of short swords are in hir's top hands, one glowing with a sickly green light, the other shimmering at its edge—a clear indicator of a monofilament weapon. Well, as close to monofilament as you can get. A weird glowing stick and a small oval shield are in hir's bottom hands.

The Enforcer is good. Fast and smart, discarding weapons that get entangled or damaged, switching to new attacks at the drop of a hat. A taser, a whiplike baton that wraps around my sword, a blade that explodes, all of it comes into play as it uses Instantaneous Inventory as I do my soulblade. Too bad for hir, I cheat too. The Freezing Blade I hit hir with initially slows the Enforcer down a bit, and the other strikes I keep piling up slows hir further. Any time hir tries to take my sword from me, I dismiss it and call it back.

The Enforcer's good, but Mikito and Roxley are better. And I've trained with them long enough that my edge in Skill and speed shows up. As Mikito has pointed out, Skills are nice, but skill is just as important. That, and a willingness to die.

A thrust with the monofilament blade targeted at my heart. Hir's over-extended, expecting me to fall back and away. Instead, I twist just enough to ensure I'm not speared directly by it, but I refuse to miss the chance hir's given me.

I cut sideways, using the momentum of my dodge to disembowel the Enforcer. First the left hand, tearing apart and shattering the shield and destroying the last of its armored suit. Then my right hand, holding a second blade, follows close enough that there's nowhere to dodge. After that, I take its top arms and head in short order, pinkish blood flowing down around me.

Cradling my side, I realize that Sabre's wrecked. I pull it back into my Altered Space, discarding what little protection the mecha can provide for now as I force myself to breathe and inject myself with a healing potion. After that, I layer my Healing spells and turn toward where the main fight is happening. Gods, I hope they're winning.

***

A plane lies shattered and smoking to the right of me. Tracking a second airborne attacker, the beam weapons of the city swivel, firing again and again.

I wonder how I missed the plane exploding, but dismiss it for the moment as I run toward the fight. Scooting around above are Sam's drones, each with weapons that he controls to snipe at fighters below. Few people care to attack those drones, most too busy with other, larger problems.

Near the plane, the Bone Warrior swings its fist, only to be met with bone-shaking force by Capstan's axe. Bone is shattered all across the Warrior's body, showing the yellow flesh beneath as Capstan pushes his attack. Both fighters began with huge amounts of health and defense, but only Capstan has a dedicated high-Level healer, and the difference is telling.

In the center, where the fighting is fiercest, the Sect's forces are split between guarding forward and dealing with Lana and Mikito and the pets behind. The puppies lunge and bite, tearing into Sect members as Roland pounces and ends anyone who threaten Lana. Anna's flames keep control of their side of the battlefield, blinding and injuring waves of reinforcements. Fighting by herself, Mikito weaves between a pair of Blood Warrior clones while dealing damaging blows to both and any Sect member unlucky enough to close in on her. She's a blurred ghost, moving so fast that none can keep up.

In front of Lana and Mikito lie the bulk of our forces. In Amelia's case, literally. Over her body, another woman crouches, glowing white light coming from her hands held above the fallen Guardian. A glowing bubble explodes from Mike, shimmering forward for a second before collapsing down a bit and repeating, even as the Regional Guardian beats aside a Sect member with his trusty baton. I can see him struggling forward, attempting to close on the Psychic who just stands there, staring at Mike.

"*Psychic attacks aren't really visible,*" Ali says, as if I needed an explanation.

Even as Ali speaks, the Psychic flinches as lights spark on a shield around him. Mel bounces off the shield, still firing at the Psychic as other Sect members target him. Fighters on both sides clash, spells exploding in a riot of colors, smoke, and dust twisting in a cyclone of superheated air above the battlefield. A moving ice elemental smacks around a pair of hunters, half-engulfing them, while a musician strums an electric guitar whose music forms famous figures in front of him, literally assaulting his attackers with the power of song.

On my left, Vir stands over the smoking remnants of a twelve-foot-tall metallic creature that bleeds and smokes. Blood drips down Vir's hand, miraculously not staining his clothing, as he surveys the surroundings before dashing into the middle of the fight. Among the torn remnants of our sentinels, a giant crocodile-like creature swarms forward to intercept Vir.

All of that and more flashes across my vision as I run, mind weighing and balancing where my help will make the most difference. But whatever I do, the answer seems to be quite clear. We're winning.

Chapter 20

My sprint allows me, roaring, to slam into a Blood Clone. Closer, I can see the differences, the sheer red visage that looks up at me in surprise before it splatters into a waterfall of blood. Mikito uses the distraction to spear her Clone as well and split it apart.

"Punch through the center," I snap at Mikito. "I'll get the Psychic."

"*At last,*" a voice comes, reverberating through my mind the same way it feels when I speak with Ali. Except this voice feels like a thousand nails going down a chalkboard.

"*Oh shit. Boy-o…*"

Ali never completes his sentence. Thankfully, he doesn't have to. The information pops up above the Psychic's head as I stare at him.

Patrag Yn Drnak (Master Psychic Level 1)
HP: 570/570
MP: 1483/2120
Conditions: Mana Enhanced, Psychic Storm, Telekinetic Shield

One second we're winning. The next, a psychic bomb goes off in all our minds. It's not super-damaging, at least not to me—the Erethran Honor Guard training helps to allay half of the attack. But it's powerful and distracting enough that all our people are thrown for a loop. And in a battle of life and death, a single second's distraction is enough.

A missed dodge. A misfired Skill. A moment of distraction, multiplied dozens of times across the battlefield, is enough to turn the tide of battle. Capstan is slammed in the chest, his body flopping through the air as the Bone Warrior rushes Nelia. Vir's Skill misfires, his attack failing to form, allowing the crocodile creature to rush him. Roland snarls, missing a Sect member that slips past him to stab Lana in the stomach.

"I must thank you for your attack. If you hadn't taken action, I could never have convinced the Elders to allow me to sacrifice more Serfs," the Psychic says directly into my mind. His voice is taunting, glee-filled. Seeing I'm still on my feet, he turns to face me directly.

Forward. I rush forward, Soul Shield back in place. The area around him is packed too tight for me to Blink Step over. At least not on the ground. A second to look, then I reach out for my Skill to Step into the sky.

Too late. A spike of psychic force slams into my mind, shocking me still. I can't move, forced to freeze in place as an Assassin appears at my side to slam a spear of force into my shield.

A moment, then a naginata strikes, tearing into the hamstring of the Assassin. The Sect member falls even as I stagger forward, bulling aside another attacker with my momentum. My Soul Shield has barely a third left. An explosive projectile hits the shield, the explosion spreading around me to collapse another attacker's shield and giving me a momentary gap to move through. Before I can move though, another psychic spike slams into my brain. This one brings pain rather than paralysis.

"This isn't something I can help with," Ali says as I fall to my knees, an outstretched hand all that stops me from falling on my face.

Liquid warmth drips down my nose, the salty taste of iron on my lips. My free hand rises, Lightning Strike on my lips, when another attack erupts. This time, the pain is so bad, it feels as though I'm crying, warm tears running from my eyes as my brain feels as though it's being pulled apart. The pain is so great, I can't even scream.

"I'm impressed. You still live. I wonder what kind of resistances you have to survive this long?" the psychic sends, taunting me. *"Oh wait, your friends seem to be doing well. One moment..."*

Pain again as the psychic bomb goes off. Instead of a spike, it's a wave that ripples through my mind and jars the cells of my body, making me stagger. While not as powerful as the individual attack, it still hurts.

"That Guardian of yours is very annoying. One moment, I need to kill him."

"Noooo..." I stagger upward to look around me.

Chaos reigns, our people forced back after their brief resurgence. Amelia is still down, Mel and the healer flanking her prone body. Mike's bubble is a quarter of the size now, only a small portion of our people covered by it. Those who are protected look steadier, their hit points significantly better. As I step forward, my brain too fried to call forth a Skill, I see the Psychic raising his hand toward Mike.

I can deal with pain. Pain's a companion, a friend. It's an artifact of the mind, a brake to stop you from hurting yourself. It's powerful and strong, but in the end, it's illusory. Don't believe me? Then tell me what the hell heartbreak is.

Pain is a mirage, as is anger. A simple thing then. Open up the floodgates and allow that churning sea of rage to push back the pain.

"Ali. FRENZY," I roar, warning him and my friends.

Then I snap, triggering the Skill. If the Psychic wants to shut down my brain, then I'll help him. The Psychic's eyes narrow at my scream. Long hair flows behind him as he flicks his hand, the next Skill effect targeting me instead of Mike.

The psychic spike drills into me, but the pain is secondary. Remote. It means nothing to me, not anymore. Just a number in my display, a little blood on my lips. Swords in hand, I dash forward, cutting and stabbing. A remote part of me notes that all my people are pulling back, clearing the way and getting far away from me.

My Soul Shield fails around this time, another blow crushing my outer protection. Not good enough, not by far, as I grab my attacker by the neck. Small neck, smaller torso, a simple squeeze chokes my attacker to death while I acquire a new, fleshy shield.

Another spike of pain, this one carrying a hint of fear. Fear he should, as my eyes glow with undiminished rage as I near the Psychic. Sect members throw themselves at me, trying to slow me down. Some are intercepted by our hunters while the Sect pours on attacks.

I run forward, the Sect member's body held before me, twitching as each attack pours into his body and tears apart skin and exposes bone. Cruel. Unworthy. I don't care, not right now. A Lightning Strike forms around my other fist, channeled to the point of my sword. I raise it, releasing the spell to wreak carnage across the muddy, bloody field. Sect members scream as the spell dances, draining my Mana and their lives.

A growing headache as Mana disappears, but it matters not. What matters is that I'm near the Psychic, the long-haired punk scrambling back as he attempts to put some space between us. Too slow, too slow by far. Lightning dances against the edges of his shield, stopped from crossing over even as bolts of elemental fury split away to strike others. His face tightens and the Psychic makes a shoving motion. I skid backward, an invisible force pushing me away.

Twisting at my hips, I throw the smoking corpse at the shield and watch it bounce off, leaving a streak of green blood across the invisible barrier. Three steps carry me closer to strike the shield directly, the glowing arc of my sword crashing against the invisible bubble. The Psychic steps backward, the shield slowly retracting with each blow. A hand comes up, swiping at blood that flows from his nose.

"You Soonak Worm!" he snarls at me, anger lacing his words.

A spike of pain at his words. I don't care. My focus is on attacking, again and again, smashing my sword into the shield. Occasionally I feel the impact of another attack, another strike that digs into my legs, my chest, my arm. But it's secondary, utterly secondary to the importance of ending this, of ensuring that the Psychic hurts no one else. My arm feels heavy, the ground slick with muddy blood. Bloody mud?

"Heal him!" Mel on the radio. I wonder which him he is.

"ENACTING PROTOCOL 148.2.8. SECONDARY ASSISTANCE PROVIDED TO OWNER. TARGETING ALL ATTACKERS."

A soothing warmth rushes over me and my body moves a little better. Ali swoops down, brows furrowed for a second, then he shifts, coming into this world fully. A second later, he glows as beams of light stab at my closest attackers.

An explosion tears at me, flesh burning, nerves screaming. I pick up a giant black marble creature that attempts to wrestle me away and toss it at the Psychic's shield, throwing my sword a moment later to pin the monster to it. A quick step and I plunge a second blade into the body, punching a hole through the shield.

"Control, boy-o. Control! The Skill should leave you a little more control than this," Ali screams into my mind, concern in his voice.

I don't have time to deal with his concerns. After all, the Psychic is still alive and retreating. A hop and skip away, just a little more. But that damn Blood Warrior is there now, blocking my way with his pair of clones.

We dance, me ducking and cutting, attacking with each motion. Sacrificing skill and my body for the opportunities they offer me to hurt, to kill him. In the corner of my eyes, I see Mikito caught in her own dance, fighting that Assassin who nearly speared me while Lana and her pets corral the remaining

Sect members, containing those trying to come near me. Sam's drones are floating above, providing a minor distraction as they hammer at the Psychic's shield while it continually attempts to reform.

"You will fall!"

A psychic bomb, lashing out at everyone, hits us again. People stagger, pain overwhelming their senses as their minds are assaulted once more. I spin away from a cut and watch as the Sect Assassin slams a blade directly into Mikito's thigh, impaling it entirely. My sword blocks another cut, disappearing from my hand a second later as I convert my momentum into a lunge. The clone gurgles and explodes, its blood stinging like acid as it coats me. Another wave of soothing light washes over me even as I recover my backfoot, catching a cut high before I drive the blade to the ground and open up my attacker's defense.

I swing, a Blade Strike hissing from my hands to cut the Blood Warrior while his fingers dance. A moment later, the blood that leaks from me floats, connecting to the Blood Warrior before me. It's not only my blood though, but the blood all around us is attaching itself in floating red tendrils.

"Regeneration Skill. The more blood there is, the more he'll heal. You can't let him keep that up too long," Ali says, no longer glowing but floating beside me, immaterial once more and looking exhausted.

Laughter bubbles up within me. The Blood Warrior's fingers freeze for a second, the strands of blood freezing with him as he hears me. A brief hesitation before he continues while I wade forward, my blade seeking his life. If he wants to block me, I'll take his life too. Another psychic spike attacks me even as the last remaining blood clone blocks my way.

A few slashes and a Blade Strike that makes my head pound later, my Mana dips precariously low as my regeneration is nerfed by the Frenzy. But it doesn't matter, because the clone is dead and I'm pushing through to the Warrior. A flicker of fingers and the blood around him drops as swords appear in his hands.

"You will not survive this. So I vow on the blood and hearts of my friends," the Warrior says, sliding back and blocking each of my cuts.

I don't waste my breath, the Warrior but a speedbump to the Psychic. After so many attacks, the Psychic's Mana must be drained, much like mine. But still, he was dangerous. Smart usage of the psychic bomb had done a ton of damage to our troops.

No more Mana means no more spells. All I have left to rely on is a little bit of technology and the skills drilled into me by Mikito and Roxley. That, and the rage within my chest. A cut aimed to take out my feet. I take it, letting the blade sink into my calf, which gives way. But it means I have a brief opening. I grab the Blood Warrior's arm and yank him forward onto my weapon. My sword plunges upward, cutting into his body as I wiggle it around, searching for his heart. A moment's struggle, the blade in my leg jerked out, but strong as he is, I'm stronger. We jerk and twist, repeated spells of healing landing on me and him, but finally, finally he stops.

Then I'm there, the Blood Warrior's corpse discarded as I barrel into the Telekinetic Shield. It flashes, seeming to compress like a bubble under my assault before snapping back. In that moment, bullets strike the Psychic, piercing the shield and bloodying him as Sam's drones target the man.

"*Probably a Mana-linked Shield. Impossible to break fully until he runs out of Mana,*" Ali says, eyeing the shield that continues to flicker.

A wordless snarl is all I have as an answer for Ali as I pull backward and lunge with both hands on the blade now. It pushes against the soap bubble of a shield, bowing it.

No more bravado, no more taunting. All I see in the Psychic's eyes is fear as he attempts to back away.

"Why won't you die?" the Psychic screams.

His hands move, pulling out Mana potions, smoke bombs, and grenades, even a pair of drones and a summoned flying sword. None of those matter, not to me. They're just distractions that burn and shoot and cut my body while I push forward in a frenzy of rage and pain. Occasional washes of blue and white light hit my body, regenerating and fixing the damage, while Sam's drones attack the summoned items for me.

It doesn't matter, because in the end, it's a battle between my health regeneration and stamina against his Mana regeneration. And unlike him, I have help. The shield pops and my sword driven by enhanced attributes plunges forward, spearing the Psychic in the chest. He coughs up blood, eyes wide with disbelief before he slumps over. Damn glass cannons. I extract my sword the hard way, ripping it out of his prone body, before glaring around me.

His death was satisfying, correct even. But I'm not done, not at all. They dared to attack my city, to hurt my friends. If they want to die, I'll be happy to fulfill their wishes. A savage grin spreads across my face before I dart forward into battle.

Chapter 21

The only thing sadder than a battle won is a battle lost. Staring at the blood-soaked fields, the corpses of allies and enemies all around me, I find those words ringing through my mind, a minor sense of gratitude that we won floating through me. The smell of burnt flesh mixes with the sharp, acrid sting of melted plastic and corroded metal. Low voices—some filled with pain, others with loss—wash over me, accompanied by a low ringing as my abused hearing recovers. Blood drips from my wounds, skin and muscle restitching themselves, and bones shift and grate within my body, finding their true positions.

Control and clarity returned in dribs and drabs as my enemies fell. Standing alone on a hilltop, my body slowly healing, I wonder for a moment if that's a good thing. Brief, because for all the usefulness of the Frenzy Skill, losing myself to it like I had was frightening.

Except... could you say I had lost myself to the Skill? Would it not be more correct to say that it had made me more myself? Is a person in a rage no less that person? If they are, then is someone in love considered different? Or are we just sliders on a scale, who we are and what we are changing from breath to breath? In the distance, the sun is briefly occluded by a cloud, darkening the scene before me.

"That Skill, you said it doesn't do that normally?" I send to Ali as I search for something concrete, something real.

"Exactly. Anger yes, but not that much. It's probably because you didn't buy it or gain it from a Class but actually earned it yourself," Ali says, rubbing his chin as he floats cross-legged beside me. *"Add on your usual... hmmm... emotional state, and voila."*

"Voila indeed." I sigh, rubbing my face. At least I had been more in control, more present than the last time I had triggered that state. Back then, I'd

basically had a breakdown. Here, I just didn't give a damn if I was going to die. All that mattered was their death.

"John…?" Lana says, limping toward me. I look over, staring at the torn and bloodied redhead blankly before I smile tiredly. She returns it, her eyes searching my face before relief comes. "Better. Much better."

"You don't like crazy, enraged John?" I say, trying for a light tone that I don't feel.

"I'm not Betty Ross," Lana says. At my puzzled look, she sighs. "Bruce Banner's girlfriend. The Hulk?"

"Oh. Right." I nod firmly. I was a programmer; of course I knew who Bruce Banner was. The question was, why did Lana?

"I like Liv Tyler and Edward Norton," Lana says as way of explanation.

"How many did we lose?" I say, breaking the strained lightness as my need-to-know pushes its way to the front.

"Too many," Lana says, giving me a hug. She winces, pushing away as she wrinkles her nose after catching a whiff of me. "Amelia is badly hurt. Vir promises that Roxley can fix her with the Shop, but she's in a coma right now. We also lost half of the hunters in Kamloops and a quarter of the Hakarta. And Mel."

I wince slightly, considering her words. "No one else?"

"No," Lana says softly, shaking her head. "We were lucky. I doubt they expected our reinforcements. If you hadn't kept the Psychic busy, it would have been a lot worse."

"I remember Mikito…" I say softly, recalling the stab.

"The Assassin got away," Lana says softly, shaking her head. "Ran off when they realized things weren't going their way. Only reason she's still alive, I think."

Exhaling in relief, I let my eyes roam the battlefield again. A corner of my mind, the part that pokes and prods at wounds, notes that Lana failed to mention the actual numbers. Or any civilian casualties. Though I'm hoping, considering we kept the fighting to the outskirts, that there are none. A part of me knows that the details of our fight, the long list of losses still waits for me. But for a moment, for this period of time, I can at least revel in the fact that none of my close friends are dead.

Just for a second.

"What's our move?" Mike asks, stomping up to me. He's injured, but like most of us, his body is already healing. Between Spells and Skills and the System's healing, injuries never last long. At least, not the physical ones.

Among the hunters, Mikito moves quietly, casting her Minor Healing spell while helping others up or, in some cases, aiding in the looting of the corpses.

"They must have pulled everyone they could to hit us before we hit them. My Portal Skill must have frightened them," I say, mind already having traveled down the likely paths of reasoning. It wouldn't have taken a military genius to realize how we could concentrate our forces and hit them harder with more safety than they could. And so, they hit us first.

"You want to take over their cities," Lana says softly, worry evident on her face. "I don't think our people…"

"I'm in," Mike says, nodding firmly.

"We will accompany you. Our fee was dependent upon the number of cities conquered, after all," Capstan says as he walks over with Nelia, enhanced hearing obviously useful for more than picking up enemies on the battlefield.

"Our defenses…" Lana objects.

"SHIELD IS AT 38% CHARGE. ALL SENTINELS ARE CURRENTLY DESTROYED. ELEVEN BEAM TURRETS ARE

CURRENTLY ACTIVE. PERSONNEL HAVE BEEN DISPATCHED TO BEGIN REPAIRS OF SALVAGEABLE TURRETS," Kim flashes for us all.

"We won't bring everyone. Once my Mana is back, just a few of us. We'll pop in to Merritt, verify it's clear, then drive to Kelowna. If we're right, it's just a bunch of Basic Classes left. If that's true, we'll pop open a Portal here and wipe them," I say.

"A solid plan," Capstan agrees softly as he unstraps his axe and places it on the ground, head first. Hands on the shaft, he nods at Mike and Nelia.

Pursing her lips, Lana stares at us before speaking. "Fine. But take Roland. He can keep up with your bikes…" At the look on my face, she stops. "What?"

"Sabre doesn't work," I say. "She'll be weeks before she's useable again. So I was hoping…"

"To use the puppies?" Lana says, her eyes narrowing with disapproval.

"Well…"

"If they don't come back, you better not either," Lana says threateningly. Some might consider that an idle threat, but I know it's not.

"Of course."

"We would not dream of it. Beast Tamer."

"I'll prioritize their healing."

***

A short hop later, we found ourselves in Vernon. This time around, it took us only a few minutes to confirm that the city was really abandoned, without a single soul—hidden or not. Once we confirm that there's no enemy to fight in Vernon, we head to Kelowna. Not before taking the city of course.

Holding Howard's body as the puppy runs, his movements eating up ground with ease, I have nothing to do but wonder and worry. Rather than

Kelowna, we could have gone straight to Vancouver, but a part of me wants to ensure we take care of the much closer location first. Cover our flanks before we take on the real challenge.

Kelowna is, strangely enough, empty of Sect members. Not of humans though, many of whom are standing around discussing matters in extremely puzzled tones. The group scatters slightly as we approach, concern and tension ratcheting up as they spot our disparate, partly alien team. As the crowd pulls back, I find myself staring at an older gentleman who stands his ground confidently.

"Afternoon, son," the old-timer greets me, grey eyes flicking over me with casual ease as he leans on the cane in his hand. A Cleanse spell and a new set of clothing ensured that most of us look presentable. At least, on casual inspection. I check his Status bar, amused to see he's a Level 18 Vintner. "Name's Kyle Reimer."

"John Lee," I say, hopping off Howard and strolling over to shake his hand. Kyle returns the handshake before my gaze returns to the cane.

"An old habit. Bad hip before the change," Kyle says easily. "Mind telling me what your intentions are? Seems like you've got a beef with the Sect."

"*War notification that you were invading went off when you crossed the boundary,*" Ali sends to me as an explanation.

"The Sect wasn't particularly pleased with us taking Kamloops. I'm intending to do the same with Kelowna. Where are they?" I say, eyeing the curiously empty minimap in the corner of my eyes. Not that it's empty empty, just empty of any hostiles.

"Left in a real hurry about an hour ago." There's a low drawl to Kyle's voice, a wheezy sound that older people have, but there's still a lot of strength left in there. "Other than grabbing a few of their favored Serfs, they didn't stop for much. Last we saw, they were headed east."

"Ah…" I run a map of the province through my mind. East really doesn't bring them to Vancouver, but considering they have shown the ability to use airplanes, it might just be the most convenient location to gather. "Great. Want a job?"

"Pardon?" Kyle says, startled for the first time since we have started talking.

"I'm about to take the city, but we're going to be moving soon after. Going to need an overseer of sorts. So, interested?" I say with an encouraging smile.

"And what makes you think you can trust me?" Kyle says, his eyes narrowed. I note that he isn't actually declining the offer.

"A few things. First, you didn't jump at the job, so you've got some brains. Second, you're willing to talk so you've got some b—courage," I change what I say, feeling somewhat uncomfortable swearing in front of the older man. "And thirdly, if you do screw around, I'll just come back and kick your ass." The last sentence is, of course, chosen with purpose.

"You probably could," Kyle says, but there's no hint of fear at his words. "And I'll let you know that I won't stand for this Serf nonsense. Or any of these new System laws. We're still in Canada here, and we'll still follow our principles. Peace. Order. Good government. And if not, you can send me on to meet my Maker."

I smile slightly at the older man. Got to admire his balls. Then I turn sideways to point at Mike. "That man's a friend. He's also an ex-constable. If I was going to do something other than that, he'd be more than willing to put a stop to it."

"That true, boy?" Kyle calls to Mike, who nods, his face serious. After a moment of consideration, Kyle nods and offers me his hand. "Then you have a deal."

"Good. Be back in a sec," I say before turning to get back on Howard to go to the city center. On the way, I can't help but ask, *"Why hasn't the Sect sold the city and their buildings?"*

"No point. When they declared War on you, it limited their options for sale. Stops either side from selling off all their assets if they think they're about to lose and forcing the other to purchase it from the System. If you were to do that now, the other side would get it for free and all the Credits would be taken directly out," Ali says.

"Wait. I can't sell the town now?" I say, frowning.

"Oh, you can, but if the Sect were to take over the place before peace was declared, they'd just get it free," Ali replies. I open my mouth, about to protest that doesn't make sense, before I sense a long sigh. *"I'm simplifying the legal process for you. Just trust me, it'd make no sense wasting time selling off assets. And no one smart is going to buy it."*

I could dig into this and I probably will, but right now is not the time. Placing my hand on the floating sphere that makes up this city's core, I flick through the notifications with practiced ease. Yes, I want to take control. Yes, I'll hold and wait while you inform the Sect that I'm attempting to grab their property. Yes, I'll be on tenterhooks while awaiting a potential attack. And finally, yes, I'll assign rights to someone.

After that, porting to just outside of the Lower Mainland is a simple matter. The Sect abandoning Kelowna wasn't completely unexpected, but I was caught off guard when all the small towns we passed as we journeyed toward Vancouver itself were devoid of the Sect. Even the normal population was mostly hiding, the constant System notifications and the grapevine alerting all but the most desperate to stay off the streets.

"This is concerning," Capstan says as we leave the New Westminster city center. Only two major centers left before we reach Vancouver itself. For the most part, we're just moving, intent on finding the Sect first before we stop to deal with the rest of the administration, especially since no one is stopping us.

"Thinking they're concentrating their forces in Vancouver?" I say softly.

"Yes." Capstan looks around and sighs. "It is possible that they have, for the moment, decided that their losses have reached significant enough levels that it is no longer viable to hold position in this Dungeon World."

"You make that sound worse than a straight-out fight," Mike chimes in. "I know you guys like fighting, but I'm ready for some peace."

"At what cost?" Capstan asks, shaking his head. "If they wished peace, they would have sent an envoy. Without one, and with the Redeemer confined to this world, it is unlikely that peace will be achieved."

"What he's saying, for those who are a little slow"—Ali stares pointedly at me and Mike—"is that they're pulling back to bring their people to another of their many, many fronts. Once they've won there, they'll come back to finish this. And they won't take you guys so lightly the next time."

With that morbid thought, the group travels through the remaining cities. Not once do we see a Sect member, and the only real resistance we find is automated weaponry. Realizing that it's quite likely we would have to pay for repairs, we do our best to limit the damage we do. We stay on guard, previous traps clear in our mind.

Things only change when we finally make it to downtown Vancouver.

When I arrive at the outside of the stone-and-glass coliseum-inspired building that makes up the public library, I find an interesting crowd of individuals. There are three distinct groups, each forming a wedge of the small pie-shaped cluster, arguing with one another. Even without Ali's prompting, I can tell they're mostly made up of combat Classers. Or at least individuals like Damian who have risked their lives regularly. It's the way their eyes keep moving, the relaxed stances with just a hint of tension, their weight distribution and spacing between them. Small things that add up to a bigger conclusion.

"Evening, folks," I say with a smile, hopping off Howard.

More than a few tense at the sight of Capstan and the puppies, but no one becomes overtly hostile. Still, there's definitely an unfriendly vibe to it all. Damian's eyes are a little wide when he sees me and obviously pieces things together.

"And you are?" The question comes from a tall East Indian lady in a simple cream blouse, blue vest, and jeans combo, obviously the leader of one pie wedge of people. Interestingly enough, the late-thirty-year-old has no visible weapons. Even if she is a Mage—and her Mana pool indicates as much—it's still strange not to have even a single weapon on hand.

"Evening," greets an older Caucasian gentleman at the same time. He looks to be in his mid-40s, broad-shouldered, with a rifle and sword at his side and his smile is all kinds of welcoming. Except if you looked into his brown eyes, which are devoid of any real warmth.

Seeing that they spoke to me at the same time, the pair glares at each other.

I'm almost tempted to let them continue, but I decide against it and answer both. "Evening. I'm John Lee, and these are my friends." I quickly introduce each of those behind me, not forgetting to include the puppies and Roland. Of course, I leave out their Classes and Levels, though I can see more than a few people whispering that information to others.

"What are you doing here?" the East Indian lady snaps at me, hands on her hips.

"I'm going to take control of the city, of course, Anika," I say with a smile while pointedly using her name. Anika Kapoor, Level 39 Summoner.

"Christian Hecker," the older man announces softly as I turn to him. Level 38 Infantry Soldier. First one I've seen actually. "It seems that you have some knowledge about what is going on. Perhaps you'd care to inform us."

"Well, I'd be happy to chat. After I've removed the Sect's control," I say, stepping forward.

The group actually contracts slightly, obviously intent on stopping me. My eyes sweep over the fifty or so combat Classers, none of them above Level 40. These must be the "elites" Damian spoke of. Or at least a portion of them. Interestingly enough, the third part of the wedge, which includes Damian, doesn't move.

"I'm sorry, but we can't let you do that just yet," Christian says, regret tingeing his voice. However, there's none of it in his body. Politeness for politeness' sake it seems.

"What makes you think we're going to let you take our city? If the Sect is gone, we sure ain't going to just let you take it," Anika says as she glares at me.

"Well…" I try to figure a diplomatic way of saying this.

"Look, kids, you couldn't stop my boy-o if you wanted to. Not him alone, and certainly not with his pals," Ali says as he makes himself visible to everyone. I see more than a few hands and weapons rise up before stopping.

"Just a little confident for a Level 40, aren't you?" Anika says with a smirk.

"This is going to be a thing, isn't it?" I say exasperatedly.

The flat looks Anika and Christian provide me are more than answer enough. Beside me, I see Mike moving forward to say something while Capstan and Nelia stand next to the pets, watching the surroundings. While the library square is wide open and clear, there are buildings around us, some of which could easily contain snipers. In fact, they probably do contain snipers.

If Lana was here, perhaps we would have sat down and talked to them. But the lady is back in Kamloops, taking care of our people. And I've just finished a very long day, one filled with blood and death. And these people just want to keep arguing, talking about who is the top dog. All these thoughts and the bubbling frustration over the day's events filter through my mind in seconds. By the time Mike reaches me, I've made up my mind.

Blink Step doesn't require me to be moving to activate; it just requires sight. I'm next to Anika in a second, a foot sweeping out and dropping her, a sword pressed against her neck as I crouch over her. Another hand lights up, Lightning Strike forming in the palm I point toward Christian. I don't let it loose, since right now, all I'm doing is posturing. Unfortunately, before I can open my mouth to speak, I'm cut off.

"Blink Step. Enhanced Lightning Strike. Mana Imbue and a Soulbound sword." Damian's voice carries quietly, his eyes raking over my body. "His Soul Shield will also deflect most attacks. At least, long enough for him to finish this." I raise an eyebrow at Damian, who shrugs. "What? You want them to fight you?"

"Well, I was hoping to…" I frown as I'm interrupted by a punch to my body. It doesn't actually penetrate the Soul Shield, but the flaring of the shield and the sense of pressure catch my attention.

Still held down, with a trickle of blood from where she cut herself as she shifted, Anika snarls at me, her hand still glowing. "Get. Off. Me."

I pause, making sure she knows that I'm doing this on purpose before I slowly stand. As it is, I'm already surrounded by the wedges. "As my friend said, I can take you. All of you." Okay, that's probably a bit of an exaggeration, but I'm not going to tell them that. "But the point of this is if you can't even stop me, what makes you think you can hold up against the Sect? Or anyone else?"

"You would have us give control of our city to you? To rule at your whims?" Christian says, some of the politeness slipping from his tone.

"I'm not very whimsical," I reply, looking around the group. "But right now, arguing about who's going to own the city forgets one thing. The Sect still does. So I'm going in and taking it away from them. Then we can talk about what happens afterward."

"And if we don't like what you have to say? You going to beat us all up? Might makes right?" Anika says, her voice tinged with contempt.

"Not right perhaps, but certainly effective. Until you can defend the city from me, or anyone else interested in it, you really don't have the qualifications to argue," I say, eyes sweeping over the group. "Or have you forgotten what happened the last time you had a little revolution?"

The moment I say that, I realize I might have pushed things too far. The way many bristle, growl, and even hunch down means I've hit a sore spot.

Thankfully, Damian breaks the silence and holds up his hands, stepping backward. His movements sparks movement in his group, who backs off too. "We'll let you take it. For now. But we will have a longer discussion."

"If you swear to hold a meeting to discuss both the Sect's actions and yours, I will, reluctantly and temporarily, agree to you taking control of the city," Christian says. "Understand that we will be watching you."

"Of course," I say, though I really just want to say "yeah, yeah, yeah." But I'm no child, and while I hate playing these political games, it's better than an all-out fight. Using my Skills was to show my strength. But too much and I'll push them into a corner and we will end up swinging. And that's the last thing I want.

Anika growls at me, her eyes moving to my friends and the puppies then me before she touches the already closed wound at her neck. Rather than speaking, she steps back reluctantly, since the other two sides have given way.

With the path clear, I give a command to the rest of my team to keep watch, then I walk onward. I'm not surprised, though somewhat annoyed, that once again, the group in play is mostly combat Classers. Well, outside of the scavenger group of Damian's, which even then is made up mostly of combat Classers. It's a pattern we've noticed again and again. For all their talk of

330

equality, it's always the combat Classers who take the lead, swinging around their oversized swords.

Thoughts like that take me to the top floor of the library and the city center orb. Thoughts like that keep me busy until I take over the city, send a note to Lana and co., and another note to Ingrid before replacing the security measures I damaged on my way in. Luckily, repairing things is cheaper than buying them outright. For the most part.

"So, boy-o, they did bring up a good point," Ali says.

"Hmmm?" I say to the Spirit as I turn around to head downstairs. I glance at the restored metal door, stationary gun turrets, and traps as I walk out. "What point?"

"You really should consider creating your own group. Right now, if you die, everything reverts to the System. Without an organization of sorts, you're just... well, you."

"They didn't..." I sigh, shaking my head. Whatever. Ali can jump to whatever conclusion he wants. He still is right. But for this second, I'd rather not consider it. For all the blood and tears, for all those lost, we've managed to succeed. Vancouver is ours. The Sect, as best we can tell, has withdrawn from BC. It might be a short-term ceasefire, a moment's respite, but it is real. We have won the fight, if not the war.

And for that, I'm grateful. In this blasted world, small moments of peace and gratitude are all we can hope for. So I'll take it and the Portal back to Kamloops and leave the worries about what to do next for another day.

The End

John and company will be back in

Coast on Fire (Book 5 of the System Apocalypse)

with more problems!

Author's Note

Thank you for reading Book 4 and I hope you enjoyed it. This book was a real struggle to write, with some aspects of the System and the larger Galactic System requiring backend fleshing out before I could go ahead. In addition, I struggled a lot with how much to include in the settlement building, between my own desire to explore the concepts involved and John's reluctance to actually get his hands dirty.

I'd like to reiterate that I am grateful for the support all of you have provided. While I'd still be telling myself John's story, I certainly wouldn't be spending time writing it. ☺

If you enjoyed reading the book, please do leave a review and rating!

Make sure to follow John's continuing quest in Book 5 – Coast on Fire: https://readerlinks.com/l/729167

In addition, please check out my other series, Adventures on Brad (a more traditional LitRPG fantasy), Hidden Wishes (an urban fantasy GameLit series), and A Thousand Li (a cultivation series inspired by Chinese wuxia and xianxia novels). Book one of each series follow:

- A Healer's Gift (Book 1 of the Adventures on Brad)
  https://readerlinks.com/l/729327
- A Gamer's Wish (Book 1 of the Hidden Wishes series)
  https://readerlinks.com/l/729151

To support me directly, please go to my Patreon account:

- https://www.patreon.com/taowong

For more great information about LitRPG series, check out the Facebook groups:

- LitRPG Society

   https://www.facebook.com/groups/LitRPGsociety/

- LitRPG Books

   https://www.facebook.com/groups/LitRPG.books/

About the Author

Tao Wong is an avid fantasy and sci-fi reader who spends his time working and writing in the North of Canada. He's spent way too many years doing martial arts of many forms, and having broken himself too often, he now spends his time writing about fantasy worlds.

For updates on the series and other books written by Tao Wong (and special one-shot stories), please visit the author's website:

http://www.mylifemytao.com

Subscribers to Tao's mailing list will receive exclusive access to short stories in the Thousand Li and System Apocalypse universes:

https://www.subscribepage.com/taowong

Or visit his Facebook Page: https://www.facebook.com/taowongauthor/

About the Publisher

Starlit Publishing is wholly owned and operated by Tao Wong. It is a science fiction and fantasy publisher focused on the LitRPG & cultivation genres. Their focus is on promoting new, upcoming authors in the genre whose writing challenges the existing stereotypes while giving a rip-roaring good read.

For more information on Starlit Publishing, visit their website: https://www.starlitpublishing.com/

You can also join Starlit Publishing's mailing list to learn of new, exciting authors and book releases.

https://starlitpublishing.com/newsletter-signup/

Glossary

Erethran Honor Guard Skill Tree

John's Skills

Mana Imbue (Level 2)

Soulbound weapon now permanently imbued with mana to deal more damage on each hit. +15 Base Damage (Mana). Will ignore armor and resistances. Mana regeneration reduced by 5 Mana per minute permanently.

Blade Strike (Level 2)

By projecting additional mana and stamina into a strike, the Erethran Honor Guard's Soulbound weapon may project a strike up to 20 feet away. Cost: 35 Stamina + 35 Mana

Thousand Steps (Level 1)

Movement speed for the Honor Guard and allies are increased by 5% while skill is active. This ability is stackable with other movement-related skills.

Cost: 20 Stamina + 20 Mana per minute

Altered Space (Level 2)

The Honor Guard now has access to an extra-dimensional storage location of 30 cubic feet. Items stored must be touched to be willed in and may not include living creatures or items currently affected by auras that are not the Honor Guard's. Mana regeneration reduced by 10 Mana per minute permanently.

Two are One (Level 1)

Effect: Transfer 10% of all damage from Target to Self

Cost: 5 Mana per second

The Body's Resolve (Level 3)

Effect: Increase natural health regeneration by 35%. On-going health status effects reduced by 33%. Honor Guard may now regenerate lost limbs. Mana regeneration reduced by 15 Mana per minute permanently.

Greater Detection (Level 1)

Effect: User may now detect System creatures up to 1 kilometer away. General information about strength level is provided on detection. Stealth skills, Class skills, and ambient mana density will influence the effectiveness of this skill. Mana regeneration reduced by 5 Mana per minute permanently.

A Thousand Blades (Level 1)

Creates two duplicate copies of the user's designated weapon. Duplicate copies deal base damage of copied items. May be combined with Mana Imbue and Shield Transference. Mana Cost: 3 Mana per second

Soul Shield (Level 2)

Effect: Creates a manipulable shield to cover the caster's or target's body. Shield has 1,000 Hit Points.

Cost: 250 Mana

Blink Step (Level 2)

Effect: Instantaneous teleportation via line-of-sight. May include Spirit's line of sight. Maximum range—500 meters.

Cost: 100 Mana

Frenzy (Level 1)

Effect: When activated, pain is reduced by 80%, damage increased by 30%, stamina regeneration rate increased by 20%. Mana regeneration rate decreased by 10%

Frenzy will not deactivate until all enemies have been slain. User may not retreat while Frenzy is active.

Cleave (Level 2)

Effect: Physical attacks deal 60% more base damage. Effect may be combined with other Class Skills.

Cost: 25 Mana

Elemental Strike (Level 1 - Ice)

Effect: Used to imbue a weapon with freezing damage. Adds +5 Base Damage to attacks and a 10% chance of reducing speed by 5% upon contact. Lasts for 30 seconds.

Cost: 50 Mana

Instantaneous Inventory (Maxed)

Allows user to place or remove any System-recognized item from Inventory if space allows. Includes the automatic arrangement of space in the inventory. User must be touching item.

Cost: 5 Mana per item

Portal (Level 3)

Effect: Creates a 2-meter by 2-meter portal which can connect to a previously traveled location by user. May be used by others. Maximum distance range of portals is 1,000 kilometers.

Cost: 250 Mana + 100 Mana per minute (minimum cost 350 Mana)

Shrunken Footprints (Level 1)

Reduces System presence of user, increasing the chance of the user evading detection of System-assisted sensing Skills and equipment. Also increases cost of information purchased about user. Reduces Mana Regeneration by 5 permanently.

Tech Link (Level 2)

Effect: Tech Link allows user to increase their skill level in using a technological item, increasing input and versatility in usage of said items. Effects vary depending on item. General increase in efficiency of 10%. Mana regeneration rate decreased by 10%

Designated Technological Items: Neural Link, Sabre

Spells

Improved Minor Healing (III)

Effect: Heals 35 Health per casting. Target must be in contact during healing. Cooldown 60 seconds.

Cost: 20 Mana

Improved Mana Dart (IV)

Effect: Creates four darts out of pure Mana, which can be directed to damage a target. Each dart does 15 damage. Cooldown 10 seconds

Cost: 25 Mana

Enhanced Lightning Strike

Effect: Call forth the power of the gods, casting lightning. Lightning strike may affect additional targets depending on proximity, charge and other conductive materials on-hand. Does 100 points of electrical damage.

Lightning Strike may be continuously channeled to increase damage for 10 additional damage per second.

Cost: 75 Mana.

Continuous cast cost: 5 Mana / second

Lightning Strike may be enhanced by using the Elemental Affinity of Electromagnetic Force. Damage increased by20% per level of affinity

Greater Regeneration

Effect: Increases natural health regeneration of target by 5%. Only single use of spell effective on a target at a time.

Duration: 10 minutes

Cost: 100 Mana

Fireball

Effect: Create an exploding sphere of fire. Deals 150 points of fire damage to those caught within. Sphere of fire expands to 3 meters radius (on average). Cooldown 60 seconds.

Cost: 100 Mana

Polar Zone

Effect: Create a thirty meter diameter blizzard that freezes all targets within one. Does 10 points of freezing damage per minute plus reduces affected individuals speed by 5%. Cooldown 60 seconds.

Cost: 200 Mana

Greater Healing

Effect: Heals 75 Health per casting. Target does not require contact during healing. Cooldown 60 seconds per target.

Cost: 50 Mana

Mana Drip

Effect: Increases natural health regeneration of target by 5%. Only single use of spell effective on a target at a time.

Duration: 10 minutes

Cost: 100 Mana

Freezing Blade

Effect: Enchants weapon with a slowing effect. A 5% slowing effect is applied on a successful strike. This effect is cumulative and lasts for 1 minute. Cooldown 3 minutes

Spell Duration: 1 minute.

Cost: 150 Mana

Sabre's Load-Out

Omnitron III Class II Personal Assault Vehicle (Sabre)

Core: Class II Omnitron Mana Engine

CPU: Class D Xylik Core CPU

Armor Rating: Tier IV (Modified with Adaptive Resistance)

Hard Points: 5 (5 Used)

Soft Points: 3 (2 Used)

Requires: Neural Link for Advanced Configuration

Battery Capacity: 120/120

Attribute Bonuses: +35 Strength, +18 Agility, +10 Perception

Inlin Type II Projectile Rifle

Base Damage: N/A (Dependent Upon Ammunition)

Ammo Capacity: 45/45

Available Ammunition: 250 Standard, 150 Armor Piercing, 200 High Explosive, 25 Luminescent

Ares Type II Shield Generator

Base Shielding: 2,000 HP

Regeneration Rate: 50/second unlinked, 200/second linked

Mkylin Type IV Mini-Missile Launchers

Base Damage: N/A (dependent on missiles purchased)

Battery Capacity: 6/6

Reload rate from internal batteries: 10 seconds

Available Ammunition: 12 Standard, 12 High Explosive, 12 Armor Piercing, 4 Napalm

Monolam Temporal Cloak

This Temporal Cloaks splices the user's timeline, adjusting their physical, emotional, and psychic presence to randomly associated times. This allows the user to evade notice from most sensors and individuals. The Monolam Temporal Cloak has multiple settings for a variety of situations, varying the type and level of dispersal of the signal.

Requirements: 1 Hardpoint, Tier IV Mana Engine

Duration: Varies depending on cloaking level

Type II Webbing Mini-Missile

Base Damage: N/A

Effect: Disperses insta-webbing upon impact or on activation. Dispersal covers 3 cubic feet.

Cost: 500 Credits

Shinowa Type II Sonic Pulser

Base Damage: 25 per second

Additional Effect: Disrupts auditory sense of balance on opponent during use. Effects have a small chance of continuing after use.

Cost: 25,000 Credits

Other Equipment

Silversmith Mark II Beam Pistol (Upgradeable)

Base Damage: 18

Battery Capacity: 24/24

Recharge Rate: 2 per hour per GMU

Cost: 1,400 Credits

Tier IV Neural Link

Neural link may support up to 5 connections.

Current connections: Omnitron III Class II Personal Assault Vehicle

Software Installed: Rich'lki Firewall Class IV, Omnitron III Class IV Controller

Ferlix Type II Twinned-Beam Rifle (Modified)

Base Damage: 57

Battery Capacity: 17/17

Recharge rate: 1 per hour per GMU (currently 12)

Tier II Sword (Soulbound Personal Weapon of an Erethran Honor Guard)

Base Damage: 98

Durability: N/A (Personal Weapon)

Special Abilities: +10 Mana Damage, Blade Strike

Kryl Ring of Regeneration

Often used as betrothal bands, Kryl rings are highly sought after and must be ordered months in advance.

Health Regeneration: +30

Stamina Regeneration: +15

Mana Regeneration: +5

Tier III Bracer of Mana Storage

A custom work by an unknown maker, this bracer acts a storage battery for personal Mana. Useful for Mages and other Classes that rely on Mana. Mana storage ratio is 50 to 1.

Mana Capacity: 0/350

Fey-steel Dagger

Fey-steel is not actual steel but an unknown alloy. Normally reserved only for the Sidhe nobility, a small—by Galactic standards—amount of Fey-steel is released for sale each year. Fey-steel takes enchantments extremely well.

Base Damage: 28

Durability: 110/100

Special Abilities: None

Made in the USA
Middletown, DE
27 July 2021